PHOEBE

PHOEBE: A STORY

(with notes)

Pauline Creativity
in Narrative Form

Paula Schroder

HODDER &
STOUGHTON

PHOEBE: A STORY

(with notes)

Pauline Christianity
in Narrative Form

Paula Gooder

HODDER &
STOUGHTON

First published in Great Britain in 2018 by Hodder & Stoughton
An Hachette UK company

1

Copyright © Paula Gooder, 2018

The right of Paula Gooder to be identified as the Author of the Work has been
asserted by her in accordance with the Copyright, Designs and Patents Act 1988.

Scripture quotations are taken from the New Revised Standard
Version of the Bible, copyright 1989 by the Division of Christian
Education of the National Council of the Churches of Christ
in the USA. Used by permission. All rights reserved.

A CIP catalogue record for this title is available from the British Library

ISBN 978 1 473 66972 7
eBook ISBN 978 1 444 79175 4

Typeset in Sabon MT by Hewer Text UK Ltd, Edinburgh
Printed and bound in the UK by CPI Group (UK) Ltd, Croydon CR0 4YY

Hodder & Stoughton policy is to use papers that are natural, renewable
and recyclable products and made from wood grown in sustainable
forests. The logging and manufacturing processes are expected to
conform to the environmental regulations of the country of origin.

Hodder & Stoughton Ltd
Carmelite House
50 Victoria Embankment
London EC4Y 0DZ

www.hodderfaith.com

For Susie Babington.
You are my sunshine!

Contents

PART ONE

Phoebe's Story

PART ONE

Phoebe: A Story

Chapter 1

'. . . to the only wise God, through Jesus Christ, to whom be the glory forever! Amen.'

The resonant, almost melodic, voice of the reader had at last fallen silent. The final syllables of the letter seemed to hang for a few moments and then waft out into the humid air of the Roman summer evening. All around the garden a silence settled; a silence so profound that Phoebe heard, or at least thought she heard, a solitary leaf part company from the plant next to her and flutter slowly to the ground. Only then did she realise that she was holding her breath, and the odd tingling at the end of her nose suggested that it was some time since she had last remembered to breathe.

The reader hadn't so much read the letter as performed it – his voice thundering in the opening paragraphs, thoughtful and careful in the middle, before dropping to a gentle, cheerful greeting at the end. As she awaited the Romans' response, Phoebe's anxiety grew and grew. In Corinth, Paul's letters did not – to put it mildly – meet with universal acclaim. The receipt of a letter from Paul usually led to what the generous and gentle Gaius euphemistically termed a time of 'vibrant discussion'; a 'discussion' that often ended when one group or another walked out and refused to return. So Phoebe had, unconsciously, held her breath as she waited to discover what form the reaction would take. She had prepared herself for almost anything, except for this: a deep silence. The quiet was such that the chirping of the cicadas felt stridently intrusive.

Phoebe exhaled. Her breath came out as a harsh sigh, and in the stillness, the sound echoed loudly, causing the people in front of her to flinch and look around in surprise. She felt her neck redden in that all too familiar blush that would soon turn her whole face into a beacon of embarrassment. In a well-used defensive movement, she tried to shrink – withdrawing into herself like the snails she used to prod in the garden as a child.

It wasn't long before Phoebe realised the flaw in her plan. What she had never quite acknowledged, until now, was that hunching down meant spreading out; taking up less vertical space required more horizontal space. And there was none. This garden, where she was standing, was crammed with people. And not only the garden. The whole house was full of people. Every conceivable space was full. People were even hanging out of the windows that surrounded the garden, suggesting that the private family rooms inside were similarly full. Granted the house was not very big – it was much smaller, in fact, than her beautiful villa in the sea port of Cenchreae, overlooking the ever-shifting Aegean. It was exquisitely elegant, but not big, and what space it did have was currently full to bursting with human bodies.

During the reading of the letter, this press of humanity had taken on a life of its own. Ripples of irritation or agreement, of assent or outrage, had run through the crowd. As the letter neared its end, and Paul had begun to send greetings to beloved friends, passing acquaintances, and even total strangers, the ripples around the crowd had announced more clearly than words could have done where each person was to be found. The house was so full it almost felt as though the assembled company had to breathe together, just as they appeared to react together to what Paul had written.

As a result, rather than deflecting attention, Phoebe's attempt to appear smaller was attracting it. As she shrank from what she took to be annoyed faces, she took up more room; shoving an elbow in one direction and a shoulder in another, and sending up a flurry of *tut*s as those around her expressed their discomfort into her burning ears. She gave up, then, and let the full heat of her embarrassment flood over her.

Up until now she had done so well in keeping her anxieties in check, though, if she was honest, since she had landed at Ostia, there had been no need for her many concerns. During the long and tedious hours aboard ship from Corinth, she had played in her mind the many possibilities of what could go wrong: being unable to work out how to get to Aristobulus' house, getting lost, losing the precious letter, finding herself in the middle of a riot, having all her money stolen, being captured and sold as a slave in a far-flung part of the empire. No scenario – no matter how unlikely – had remained unimagined. It was only when a performing bear broke free from its chains, consumed Paul's letter in one saliva-laden gulp before squashing the breath out of her body by sitting down on her suddenly, that she allowed herself to consider that maybe . . . just maybe . . . her imagination had run away with her.

It had come as a relief – if also a slight anticlimax – to discover that Paul's network of messages and messengers had ensured, not only that she was expected, but that a small slave boy, with eyes as bright as a bird, had been in the port at Ostia waiting for her, and had proceeded to organise her journey to Rome with an endearing, if slightly comical, assurance far beyond his years.

A low-throated chuckle distracted her for a moment from the heat of her embarrassment. She turned and looked into a pair of sparkling eyes, brimming with life and energy. They belonged to a diminutive woman whose body seemed far too small to contain the life within. Her face was lined with age, but in such a way that hinted at adventures undertaken and challenges faced. Her clothes were well made but also well worn. It was her hands that gave the most away. These were hands of hard labour, gnarled and misshapen from years of plying a trade.

'You'd think we'd be used to it by now.'

'To what?' Phoebe's bemusement showed on her face.

'This,' she gestured to the crush. 'We Romans are always crammed together no matter where we are. And you'd think we'd get used to it. But we don't. A crowd like this makes us grumpy, and we never have time to recover our good humour before we plunge into another horde. I loved Corinth for that. It might have quite a reputation for certain things, but it felt so spacious after Rome. Aquila loved living there – and would have stayed if we hadn't had to travel on to Ephesus with Paul – but, perversely, I pined away for the very thing I hate most when I'm here. The people, the noise, the hustle and bustle, the grumpiness . . .'

As she chattered on, it slowly dawned on Phoebe who this was. Prisca had been well known in Corinth and Phoebe had heard many stories about her. Prisca's chatter had had two effects. One was that she had broken the deep silence in a much more natural way than Phoebe's noisy sigh had done, causing the gentle murmur of conversation to begin rippling through the crowd. The other was that it had turned Phoebe's attention outwards, so that her embarrassment had fallen away.

She looked up and was now able to take in the crowd of people in the house more fully than she had before. On one level, the crowd of faces was comfortingly familiar. As in Corinth, the people gathered together in this place had skin tones of various shades of brown, from the paler bronze of those who originated in Greece and Italy, through the darker shades of those from Galilee, Judea, and Egypt, to a very few faces the deep rich brown of those from Nubia. As she looked around her, she calculated that there weren't quite as many people here as she had first assumed. There couldn't be many more than a hundred. It was the small size of the house that made it feel as though there were more. Before a question had even half formed in her mind, Phoebe found Prisca answering it.

'We don't always gather like this. Have I mentioned how we hate crowds? We only come together for special occasions – like you do in Corinth. We just couldn't agree who would get Paul's letter first, so in the end it was fairest for us all to hear it at the same time. Not everyone could come, of course, as it's the third day of the week and none of us Christians has a house quite big enough for everyone – not like Gaius's beautiful home in Corinth – so we "borrowed" Aristobulus's house for the evening.'

Phoebe's sense of shock must have been quite evident.

Prisca chuckled. 'No need to look quite so surprised. Blaesus, his steward . . . there,' she pointed to a well-dressed and distinguished-looking person standing by the entrance to the garden, 'is his favourite slave. Can't be long now until he is due to get his freedom, though I suspect he'll be as sad to be freed as Aristobulus will be to let him go. He has full use of the house while his master is away – and Aristobulus is away a lot. So, when we all need to come together, we often meet here, though even this isn't big enough for everyone. We decided that the best thing to do was to hear the letter all together, then Stachys – who you heard reading the letter out – will make copies, and before you know it all the gatherings will have a copy. Then the fun will begin.'

Phoebe frowned, her confusion revealing itself in the wrinkling of her forehead.

'I suppose it does depend on what you count as fun,' Prisca conceded, 'but you have to agree that Paul provokes the best conversations. Agree with him or not, it's hard not to have an opinion on what he has to say. Once we have a copy, we can read it again, talk about it, argue if we like. Then start all over again. I've heard lots of Paul's letters in my time, but never one quite like this. I wouldn't be surprised if people are still trying to work out what it means in a few months' time. You can't help wondering whether even Paul knows what he means some of the time. When he's in the flow, there's no stopping him.'

'Not much stopping you either,' said a man from the other side of Prisca. 'The real reason we parted company with Paul was so that some of the rest of us could get a word in edgeways. The two of you together left precious little time for anyone else to speak. You haven't even introduced yourself, woman.'

Despite her embarrassment of a few moments before, suddenly, and to her great surprise, Phoebe found herself laughing. She'd heard of Prisca and Aquila from her friends in Corinth: of Prisca's determination and Aquila's laconic humour; of Prisca's passion and Aquila's compassion. Aquila was universally loved and admired. Prisca, as is the lot of strong women, evoked a more mixed response. Still, loved or not, everyone remembered her.

Prisca, so it was rumoured, had married 'beneath her'. Aquila, originally from Pontus in Asia Minor, was a tent-maker like Paul; Prisca was from a more genteel family. That was why, they said, she was always mentioned before Aquila. Now, however, Phoebe pondered whether there might be other reasons too. Prisca's vitality seared her powerfully into the memory. She could well imagine that when you thought of this couple, Prisca would simply come to mind first. She wondered what it might have felt like to have the twin dynamos of Paul and Prisca in Corinth at the same time.

Phoebe hadn't been part of the community when they had been in Corinth – come to that, she hadn't even been a Christian then either. That was a year she would never forget – the year Gallio was proconsul – and the year when her carefully constructed new life had begun to unravel. But no, she couldn't think about that now, her emotions were unreliable enough as it was. She re-emerged into the present to hear Aquila, with a formality as gently humorous as it was sincere, declaring:

'Phoebe, honoured deacon of the church and revered patron of many, we welcome you to Rome. May you never know loneliness here. We, your brothers and sisters in Christ, stand ready to help you in whatever you require.'

The applause that broke out all around her made Phoebe realise that Aquila's authority, quiet though it be, was strong, and that their conversation was no longer private – if it had ever been. She looked up to see two hundred or so inquisitive eyes trained on her face. For the second time that evening, Phoebe felt her neck flush, but having learnt her lesson moments before, this time she did not try to hide.

'What we want to know,' a voice called out, 'is what *is* the help that you need?'

'When Phoebe is ready, she'll tell us,' Prisca said tartly, 'but now we need to go home.' And, amidst the ensuing outcry, Phoebe found herself guided skilfully through the press of people and deposited outside in the gathering gloom.

Chapter 2

Phoebe woke slowly the next morning, conscious of limbs so heavy they felt pressed into the thin mattress beneath her. The quality of the light in the room suggested that it was many hours since dawn. For an instant, caught in that delicious moment between sleep and wakefulness, she thought herself back in Cenchreae with little more to do than oversee the activity of her household slaves, and, perhaps, a few of the clients who would be lined up outside her house ready to do anything she required. With a lurch, she remembered that she was not at home, but adrift in a strange city with a task ahead of her that she could barely bring herself to acknowledge.

She remembered little of what happened after she left Aristobulus's house. She recalled being conducted quickly and efficiently by Prisca through the dark streets until they arrived at a tenement block (which looked to Phoebe's untrained eye very like all the other blocks they had passed on their way). Once inside, Phoebe took in a vague impression of a large room in which there was an overpowering smell of something that she couldn't quite place. At the back of the room a simple staircase led up to another room above, separated into sections with hangings. Prisca had deposited Phoebe into one of these, and disappeared. That was the last Phoebe remembered until now.

As she emerged slowly into consciousness, she was aware both of the smell again and of a hum of conversation wafting up through the floorboards beneath her. A higher voice talking swiftly and with animation, that was Prisca; then a gentle but authoritative lower voice, clearly Aquila; but there was also a third voice, male, harsh in tone, often speaking over the other two voices and drowning them out. He seemed to be pacing around, as his voice grew fainter, then louder again as he passed under the spot where Phoebe lay.

For a while Phoebe lay still, listening more to the rhythms of what was clearly an argument than to its actual words. The words that did float upwards communicated more about the level of outrage felt by the owner of the third voice than about its cause. After a while, Phoebe could stay still no longer, and she got up swiftly and with purpose. It was only at that moment that she realised, with a gut-wrenching horror, that all her possessions – including the heavy bag of money she had brought with her to see her through her time in Rome – had been left behind at Aristobulus's house.

When she had arrived from Ostia the house was so full of people that she had been utterly confused. She tried to remember what had happened. It was that bright-eyed slave boy who had skilfully relieved her of her travelling chest, at the same time pushing her into the press of people. As she had stumbled forward, the press of people had opened before her, just like the sea before Moses in one of those stories from Scripture that was read when they gathered together on the first day of the week. She'd placed Paul's letter into their eager hands, and filled with enthusiasm a scribe – Stachys they had called him – had read it then and there, his mellow tones lifting the words off the parchment and breathing life into them. He was clearly an expert. So much so that with simple gestures – the raising of an eyebrow here, the sweep of a hand there – he inhabited the words. He did it so well that it wasn't long before his fine Roman features had faded in Phoebe's mind to be replaced with the far less elegant visage of Paul.

Phoebe would never forget the first time she had seen Paul. He had been visiting Gaius in Corinth. With his usual generosity, Gaius had invited the many different followers of Christ to meet Paul in his house. Phoebe wasn't looking forward to it. At that point, she had never met Paul, but she had heard about him. In fact, she had heard a lot about him. His arrogance. His unreliability. The cheek of him thinking he could tell people how to behave. His disgraceful letters sent to impose his view on those he disagreed with. His rudeness. His arrogance (again). She had certainly heard about Paul. So, she went to Corinth reluctantly, as much to please the gentle Gaius as anything else.

When she had arrived at Gaius's house, there had been pandemonium. The normally smooth-running machine of hospitality had broken down. Slaves were running here and there, half completing an errand before running back in the opposite direction. Objects were scattered everywhere. Gaius's usually placid steward looked on the brink of collapse. Even the gentle, gracious Gaius could be heard at the rear of the house, his voice raised in irritation. There had been a lot riding on this visit by Paul.

So, Phoebe had slotted back into remembered ways of being. A command here; a joke there; scooping up a pile of misplaced objects in one hand, while gently nudging an item of furniture back into its proper place, she had walked through the house smoothing as she went. The years she had spent running a household invisibly but efficiently, dealing with existing crises and anticipating new ones, came back to her as though she had never left them behind. Before long the panic was over, order was restored, and Gaius was smiling at her gratefully for all she had done. She had missed Paul's arrival because she had popped out to Corinth's busy market to supplement the food that would be needed for all the extra guests, brushing aside with amusement the steward's horror that she, a grand lady, should do something so menial.

When she had returned a few hours later, she heard a voice. It was, Phoebe recalled, mesmerising. It wasn't the tone of the voice – unlike Stachys' voice the previous evening in Rome, Paul's was harsh and slightly grating. It wasn't the elegance of the rhetoric – Paul was certainly persuasive, but even in Corinth there were many better orators than him. It wasn't even what he was saying – though later she was as captivated by that as others around her. It was his passion that gripped Phoebe. She remembered standing at the entrance to the house, parcels dropping to the floor, while she acknowledged that this was someone who really knew. This was someone who had encountered the risen Lord, and whose life, like hers, would never be the same again. This was someone to be trusted. She couldn't put her finger on why she felt this way; she just knew that she did.

So it had come as something of a shock, as her feet took her from the entrance, through the atrium, and onwards into the garden at the rear of the house, when she had actually seen Paul. She had almost recoiled in horror. Corinth was a good-looking city. After all, it had a lot to prove. It was a new city, having been rebuilt by the great Julius Caesar less than a hundred years before, and many of its population – a vast mix of Romans, Greeks, and Jews – were, just like Phoebe, freed slaves. It was the place you came to reinvent yourself, to live a new life, to begin again. And so the populace, just like the city itself, went out of their way to look the part. Without an ancient family to rely on, money and beauty bought influence. It went without saying that you made the best of what you had. But Paul was different. He was small, very small. Phoebe had later realised that he barely even reached her shoulder. His head was bald, and, as he stood to address the crowd gathered in Gaius's garden, Phoebe could see that his legs were crooked. His nose was huge, topped with deep black eyebrows that met in the middle. Paul was grotesque. There was no other word for it.

But no sooner had Phoebe reached her damning judgement than she began to question it. As she stood there, jaw hanging open in surprise, her eyes met his, and, as they did, something happened. When she tried to find the words to explain it later, she had said somewhat whimsically that it was as though a window had opened into heaven and she could see angels dancing. Even she felt embarrassed at her flight of fancy, but no other words would come. Whatever that something was, it changed her view of him for ever. Then she had blinked, shaken her head slightly, and she had been back in the garden listening to an ugly, entrancing man.

His was the image that had entered Phoebe's mind as Stachys had read the night before. A man full of contradictions. Hideous, but enchanting; with a harsh but mesmerising voice; an average orator whose words struck home time and time again. Stachys had made Paul's words sound so much more polished than they ever were when Paul said them but still the words were Paul's. Phoebe found she couldn't hear them without seeing Paul: brim full of passion, waving his arms around his head, pacing to and fro, spittle flying from his mouth as he tried to articulate all that was in his mind.

Phoebe returned from her reverie with a jolt. There was something that she had been anxious about. What had it been? The memory hit her with even more force than it had done the first time. She had lost everything – her money, her clothes, the other letters of introduction. Everything was gone, and she was quite alone in a large and terrifying city. That thought was enough to propel her into her smelly, crumpled travelling clothes and down the stairs into the midst of the argument that had woken her a few moments before.

As she stumbled down the stairs, inelegant – again – in her terror, she looked up and stopped stock still. The voices she had heard had suggested just three people: Prisca, Aquila, and the unknown third. As she looked up she realised she had tumbled into the middle of a large meeting. There were people everywhere, transforming what last night had seemed a large room into a small, cramped space. People were standing and sitting all around the room. Every chair, table, and window ledge was filled with human bodies. Some were even sitting on a large pile of skins in the corner. Phoebe found herself identifying the pelts as the source of that odd smell, even as that inevitable flush of embarrassment began to work its way from her neck to her face.

'I told you that you'd disturb her,' Prisca's voice cut into the startled silence. 'We're sorry, my dear, we wanted you to sleep as long as you could, but Herodion here couldn't help himself.' Prisca pointed to a slight, dark-haired man, whose long tunic with tassels at the corners indicated that he was Jewish. He looked as though he was about to start talking again, as though the words that Phoebe's sudden arrival had brought to an abrupt halt would spill out again at any moment. Prisca clearly thought the same, as she continued speaking with barely a pause for breath. 'You've missed breakfast, and this great horde consumed every last scrap of our barley bread when they arrived shortly after dawn. I declare it time for an early prandium.' She clapped her hands together, and various people around the room moved quickly to rummage on shelves and in bags at their feet. In almost no time at all, the table in the centre of the room was spread with bread, olives, cheese, and wine.

But Phoebe was entirely oblivious to all of this. As the people moved, they revealed the diminutive figure of the slave boy. The one who had met her at Ostia. The one who had relieved her of her possessions at Aristobulus's house. There he sat, as determinedly and forcefully as his small frame would allow, on what Phoebe recognised with a flood of relief was her travelling chest.

'You can get up now, Felix,' Aquila's soft voice sounded above the melee of food preparation. 'I think he might have been sitting on your chest all night, Phoebe. Absolutely no one could get him to leave it.'

'Felix said he would look after it, and Felix,' he indicated himself with a comically dramatic flourish, 'is always true to his word.' Felix glared at Phoebe fiercely, apparently challenging her to disagree.

Phoebe, feeling herself almost giddy with relief, rummaged among her belongings to find a coin with which to reward him. The first coin that came to hand was a denarius; it was far too much, but so great was her relief that she offered it to him with a smile. No sooner had she held it out than she realised what a great mistake she had made. Felix's face became cold, disgust flowing from every pore.

'Felix was asked to help,' he said with a flinty expression. 'Felix was glad to help. Felix does not take money for his generosity.'

Phoebe stammered her apology for affronting him so badly, and as she did she found herself looking straight into his eyes. At that moment, something changed between them, and Phoebe knew that this small person would become an important part of her life. Felix seemed to know this too since he went to Phoebe's side and stood there, as though he were her personal guard and protector, trying to look as tall as his tiny form could manage.

'I think you have made a friend for life there,' Aquila observed.

'Now we eat,' Prisca declared, and the assembled company turned to the groaning table.

Chapter 3

It was a cramped but joyful meal. There was no reclining, no discreet service, no formality or sedate conversation. None of the things that Phoebe had grown accustomed to in the few years since she had moved to Corinth. This meal was chaotic. Platters of cheese, bowls of olives, and loaves of coarse barley bread, as well as various kinds of vegetables, meandered their way around the room, passed backwards and forwards, high overhead or low between legs. No one – no matter what unorthodox sitting place they had found for themselves – was left out. From time to time, when platters were nearly empty, the passing would pause while someone rummaged in a bag or basket at their feet, pulling out a previously unrevealed treasure.

A happy silence fell as people crammed their mouths too full for speaking. After a while, once the urgency of eating had waned, conversation turned to memories of Jesus and his many impromptu feasts. How he could make almost any meal into what felt like a banquet. How he would surprise his hosts with a ragbag assortment of additional guests, and insist that they be treated with honour. How he would have such feasts with the most unlikely of people.

'If Peter were here, we could ask him to tell us again about how Jesus fed those five thousand people,' Felix said, a hint of wistfulness in his voice.

'You know full well that we've heard it so often, we can tell it ourselves,' his neighbour retorted.

'Go on, Felix, you do it,' people around the room raised their voices in encouragement.

And Felix, still sitting on top of Phoebe's baggage, swelled with joyful self-importance as he took a deep breath and began.

'Jesus went away to a quiet place with his disciples. They were tired and needed time alone. So they got in a boat and crossed over to a quiet part of the shore. But people saw them go and followed. Or should I say they ran ahead of them?' Nods around the room confirmed that he was quite right – he should say that. As Phoebe looked around at her companions she realised that, on one level, there really was no need to tell the story. Everyone knew it already – every beat of the story, every character, every detail – but this didn't seem to matter at all. Everyone gathered there was taking as much pleasure in the hearing of this story as Felix did in the telling of it. As it unfolded, people offered the details they felt were missing: the grass was green; the people numbered five thousand; there were two fish as well as bread. Felix wasn't so much telling the story as conducting it.

The more she listened, the more Phoebe realised that in Corinth they just didn't tell tales about Jesus like this. Of course, she'd heard this, and many other accounts about what Jesus did, and what he had said. Passing visitors, from Jerusalem and Antioch, would share their stories with them, doling out their treasures to the eager Corinthians. But Paul did not. He was far more interested in how Jesus' life, death, and resurrection would give every aspect of their own lives new meaning. Maybe his love of ideas led him to be shy of stories? Until now, it had never occurred to Phoebe to ask why. Was it because he didn't know them, or because they didn't interest him? In Corinth, they had always just followed Paul's example, and given preference to ideas over stories without questioning this. When they gathered together there, they talked, argued, and wrestled over the details of how they should now behave, and what the advent of the Messiah truly meant for the future.

In Corinth, stories like this one told with such gusto by Felix, were heard, enjoyed, but then left behind. Here they were savoured over and over again.

She had not known what was lost until now. She sat back and allowed the joy of the story to enfold and lift her. She felt drawn into it like never before: she saw the crowd, felt the pangs of hunger, tasted the bread (though in fairness it might have been the bread she held in her hand that she could taste). She abandoned herself to the experience in all its fullness.

'And at the end there were twelve baskets over, twelve!' Felix brought his narrative to an end with a delighted flourish, and sat back looking around the room for assurance that, together, they had done the story justice. They had. Having established this, the conversation around the room began to ripple and flow again, as once more the food and drink resumed its winding journey around the room.

A few times Phoebe saw Herodion draw his eyebrows together sternly and open his mouth as though to speak, and Prisca place a quietening hand on his arm so that he subsided. The fourth time this happened, Aquila, who was sitting next to Phoebe, leaned over to explain.

'We are all desperate to talk to you about the letter, none more so than Herodion. Everyone here came early, before breakfast even, but Prisca made them wait, said you had to sleep and they shouldn't disturb you. We started talking quietly, as quietly as we could, but Herodion was too angry. He couldn't help himself. That's probably what woke you?' He looked at Phoebe questioningly. Phoebe shrugged – she wasn't sure; she might have been ready to wake anyway. 'Now Prisca is refusing to let him start again until she's sure you are properly fed and rested.'

Phoebe was confused. 'Why do I need to be rested? You're surely not going to ask *me* what it means? You do know I didn't write it?'

'No – but you brought it.'

With a sinking heart, Phoebe suddenly pulled together a number of details that had lain uncomfortably at the back of her mind, and understood something that had previously escaped her. Before she had left for Rome, Paul had been more than usually keen to meet with her. She'd assumed this was because of The Task – what she'd come to Rome for, or at least what Paul thought she'd come to Rome to do. But now she thought about it, she realised he had also talked about the letter that she was to carry: what he was trying to say in it; why he said it in the way he did.

At the time, she had thought that he was just talking to himself, making sure it made proper sense before sending it off to the city that, though he'd never been to it, occupied such a large part of his heart. She knew that he normally wrote his letters with other people. That earlier letter to Corinth, the one that had come before she had joined the community and that had caused so many problems, had been written with Sosthenes; the more recent one, the one that had laid the foundations for the healing of the rift between Paul and the Corinthians, had been written with Timothy. Phoebe had always wondered precisely how much the co-writers had been allowed to contribute to the letters. The last time Timothy had stayed with her on his way to Ephesus she had summoned up the courage to ask, but he'd just smiled enigmatically and changed the subject.

This letter to the Romans, though, was different. Paul had written it entirely by himself. Over at Gaius's house, Paul had locked himself away for day after day with just Tertius, the scribe, for company. Poor man. Paul would summon him early, shortly after dawn, and had insisted that food be brought throughout the day so that nothing was seen of them until they emerged late each evening. When, at last, they did appear, Tertius looked stunned, his hands covered in ink and his hair standing on end. It was only after it was finished that Paul started talking to her about it, and now, a little too late, Phoebe understood why. He wasn't trying out his ideas on her at all. By then he had written them all down and knew exactly what he had said. Paul had known, as she had not, that she would be asked to explain, to unpack and clarify what he wanted to say, and he wanted to make sure she understood it properly first. The problem was she didn't, or at least not all of the time. Occasionally she did. The ideas kept moving in her mind – shifting like a murmuration of starlings – until from time to time they'd swirl into a particular pattern, a pattern she recognised. Then for a moment she felt she understood, but the next moment they would move again, and all would be lost. The knowledge of this made her feel quite sick. How could she explain to others what, at best, she herself only grasped partially?

'Don't worry, we'll help where we can,' Aquila said.

'Wait!' Phoebe really wasn't ready to begin yet, and desperation improved her desire for small talk no end. 'What I don't understand is why you are all here together again. Paul told me, before I came, to expect you all to be very different from each other. That I shouldn't expect you to meet up like we often did at Gaius's house. That Herodion was the head of a synagogue, and met just with Jewish Christians. That you and Prisca met with both Jews and Gentiles, and that Patrobas, Asyncritus, and the other Gentiles met separately too. I've only been here two days, and yesterday you were all together in Aristobulus's house, and today, here you are together again.' Phoebe's nervousness made her recite the remembered information in a stilted and uneven fashion.

Aquila generously overlooked her clumsiness and chuckled a little. 'Firstly, don't believe everything Paul tells you. He knows a lot, but he hasn't been here, after all. In some ways we are more separate than you Corinthian Christians. We don't have someone like Gaius, whose house is large enough to fit us all in. And in any case, it strikes me that when you all get together you mostly argue?'

Phoebe had to admit that this was often true.

'But,' Aquila continued, 'not meeting all together regularly doesn't mean our lives are separate from each other. Far from it, we know each other well. We care for each other. We make sure that no one goes without, even if they don't worship with us in our own community. Our workshop,' here Aquila gestured around the room they were sitting in, 'acts as something of a hub. Prisca and I are here every day working on the tents – some days more effectively than others – so people know they can drop round. If we need to talk about something that affects us all, or if there is a problem that needs to be solved, people come here.

'Today you can see a collection of people from all our different gatherings. The people who are free and able to come have come; those who aren't haven't. And today this is because of you and Paul's letter. We know Paul has been wanting to come to Rome for a long time. Some of us are keen that he does; others not so much. Some are excited to hear what he wanted to tell us; others have come to have their prejudices about him confirmed. Some want to know how soon he'll come; others to be reassured he's not on the next boat. This letter is important for us, as you know, and you have brought it to us – so now you are important to us too. Now, don't think I don't know what you are doing. You can't put it off for another moment.'

With that he nodded at Prisca, who patted Herodion's arm in a business-like manner and stepped back. Phoebe was reminded fleetingly of the trainers in the amphitheatre who made a similar movement just after they'd freed an animal from its cage. Herodion rose to his feet immediately, and started pacing back and forth – at least he would have paced if the room hadn't been so full of people. As it was, he was forced to pick his way delicately between supine bodies, lending an absurdly dainty air to his pent-up energy.

He flung out his arms in a dramatic gesture. 'That insufferable man has gone too far this time.'

Chapter 4

The force of Herodion's rage broke over the room with the power of a mighty wave on the beach in the midst of a storm. At one point, in his fury he forgot the need for caution while he paced, and brought his full weight down on the leg of Patrobas, a Gentile, causing him to cry out in pain.

'Careful now, Herodion,' Aquila said mildly. 'Unless your powers of healing are as good as those of Jesus.'

Herodion flushed at that, and murmured an apology before continuing.

'He is preposterous. He just doesn't stop. We have stretched and stretched, but apparently it is never enough. First, he insisted that Gentiles didn't have to become Jewish to follow our *Jewish* Messiah,' his voice rose with indignation in both tone and volume, 'then, he made us eat with them.' He spat out the word 'them' with venom.

'Us you mean?' said Patrobas, upon whose leg Herodion had unwittingly just stamped.

Herodion had the grace to look a little ashamed. In his anger, he seemed to have forgotten that the very people he was talking about sat all around him. But it didn't trip him up for long; soon he was back in the swing of his tirade.

'As though that didn't render us unclean. As though it didn't mean that we couldn't go back to eat with our family, unless we had the time for proper cleansing. He just doesn't get it. We've told him and told him that he's being unreasonable, but does he listen? Of course not. Why would he listen to us? He's so in love with being right he doesn't care what damage it does. No, he just decrees and makes the rest of us live with the consequences, while he sits at ease.'

At that, Phoebe, completely forgetting her earlier horror at the thought of having to speak on behalf of Paul, opened her mouth. Surely he wasn't serious? He must know that Paul suffered more consequences than almost anyone else as a result of his views, mustn't he? Not being able to eat with his Jewish compatriots without taking time for intricate cleansing rituals was the least of his worries. Being beaten, stoned, imprisoned, shipwrecked, and ambushed were the kinds of consequences that Paul had to worry about daily. But just as the words were about to burst from her mouth, Phoebe saw Aquila raise his eyebrows and gently shake his head. With great difficulty, she closed her mouth on her outrage.

'Tell Phoebe about your brother,' Aquila said. 'It will help her understand.'

Herodion turned towards Phoebe, and she noticed that his eyes were swimming with tears. 'Like Prisca and Aquila, I used to live here before.'

Phoebe took 'before' to mean during the reign of Claudius before he'd expelled the Jews from Rome nearly ten years ago. At that point, the community had scattered across Greece and Asia Minor, some even returning to Galilee and Judea. After Claudius had died and his adopted son Nero had become emperor, many Jews had started to return, full of optimism that under him life would get better and better. This optimism remained strong even now, despite Nero's reputation for cruelty and for cruising the streets looking for sexual partners, willing or not. Herodion, Phoebe surmised, had been part of both the exodus from Rome as well as the subsequent return.

'When we were forced to leave, my brother Valerius and I thought we'd take our parents back to Jerusalem. Years ago, they had come here with the Herod family. When Herod the

Great had brought some of his household to Rome, they had come too. When he returned as so-called King of the Jews, he left a few of his household behind to oversee his interests. My parents, somewhat reluctantly, stayed. It took a long time, but eventually they settled down and got used to this God-forsaken place. But they never forgot home. They missed Judea so much, but most of all they missed the temple. Every day of my childhood our mother sang out her sorrow: "How can we sing the Lord's song in a strange land"; she got used to the strange land, but never to the loss of worshipping God in the temple as the law commanded.

'So, when the time came to leave, there was only one place to go. We took all we had and travelled home. But my parents were too old and the journey was too long. My mother had never travelled well by sea. She was so sick on the way and one day her heart just stopped. She died with a light in her eyes and "to Jerusalem" on her lips. Her body never got there, but her heart did. This was no comfort to my father. He was heartbroken. I'd heard of broken hearts before, but never seen it myself. He just lay down and gave up. We got him to Jerusalem in the end, but he no longer cared. Without my mother, it meant nothing to him. A month later he died too. We grieved them, Valerius and I. My mother's body is buried somewhere at sea, her bones forever lost beneath the ocean. But we buried my father with all the honours two sons could give him, and as we grieved we grew as close as two brothers could be.'

Herodion paused, his throat working as he sought to control his emotions. 'Then, one day, I was passing through the temple courts and saw a huge crowd. A man was standing there, his face alight with joy, and he was talking to them. He told of a man called Jesus. How he'd been the chosen one, the Messiah. How he'd died and risen again. How in him all God's prophecies had come true. How now, through him, God's people had finally come home, the Exile had ended. How he had shown us all how to be the Israel we were always meant to be, a light to the nations. In that moment, something clicked into place. I had never been a very devout person – not like those Pharisees – but I had tried to love God as best I could. Keeping the law properly was a full-time job, but I did what I could, when I could.

'This was different. What he said made sense. It felt as though what was lost had been found; what was missing had been supplied; a hole had been filled. I was complete and at peace. My life, for the first time in a long time, had meaning. Valerius thought I was mad – and told me so often – but he let me alone. I joined a community of believers. We met together. We ate together. We told stories about Jesus, and, for a while, all was well. But then Peter passed through Jerusalem, on one of his many trips.

'Years before there had been a great row about eating. That troublemaker Paul had argued that Jewish followers of Jesus should eat with Gentiles. Peter had been bamboozled by him into agreeing – especially after a vision he'd had before he went to see a Roman called Cornelius, when God had – so he said – declared everything clean. James simply had to do something; it couldn't go on like that. He sent Peter a message and explained: for the good of our community, for the sake of fellowship and harmony, he had to stop eating with Gentiles. And Peter saw reason. James was pleased. The problem was solved. But then along came Paul, spoiling it all as usual, telling Peter he had done the wrong thing, swaying him back again. We had hoped that he would change his mind again, but he didn't. So when Peter came to Jerusalem that time, he made it clear that we had to eat with Gentiles.

'It was annoying, but didn't really make much difference then. We didn't see many Gentiles anyway, and those that did want to share table fellowship normally ate with the Greek speakers. Growing up in Rome I spoke Aramaic at home and

Latin elsewhere. My Greek was not good, so I preferred the company of people like James.

'The problem began when Valerius and I came back to Rome. What Peter said made a difference here. Now I have to eat with th—' he caught himself just in time, 'you, all the time. When Valerius found out that I ate with Gentiles every week, he moved out. Said he couldn't risk being made unclean. My madness had gone too far, he said; beyond what he could bear. And now my last family member is gone, and I am all alone. And then! After everything, Paul has the temerity to say that we Jews have no superiority. Apparently, now even our circumcision isn't enough. If we don't keep the law, he says, we are as good as uncircumcised scum.'

At this Patrobas cleared his throat loudly and pointedly. Herodion's diplomacy had not lasted long.

'I just don't see why he expects us to give it all up. I am a Jew: the child of Abraham, Isaac, and Jacob; a descendant of Moses and of David. I am a child of the covenant, a member of God's people. How could he,' Herodion's voice suddenly trembled, 'tell us that our proud and glorious history counts for nothing? How could he?' With that, large, sorrowful tears began to flow down Herodion's face, spreading over his cheeks only to bury themselves deep in his beard.

Phoebe silently paid homage to Aquila's wisdom. Herodion's anger was indeed like a storm, and like all storms it had needed to blow itself out. Now was the moment for her to say something . . . but what? Phoebe brought Paul to mind again, and suddenly knew the answer.

'I'm not sure you've quite understood what Paul was saying,' she began, casting around for words, fully aware that only the right words would do in this context. 'You must know how proud Paul is of his Jewish heritage. He goes on and on about it.'

'Never met the man,' said Herodion. 'I just have to live in the devastation he leaves behind.'

'Well, in that case, you do need to know that I have never met anyone more confident in their Jewishness than Paul. He has the best Jewish pedigree of anyone I have ever met.'

Herodion's sceptical sniff suggested that he thought Phoebe – a Corinthian Gentile – might have a limited pool of people for comparison.

'Paul never could resist a pedigree contest,' she continued, 'and in fairness he does normally win. What with his fine family and strong sense of competition, he loves to prove himself to be the best Jew he knows.'

'Not to mention the most humble,' interjected Aquila.

Phoebe thought wryly of Paul's more recent letter to the church in Corinth in which he had taken some of his opponents to task. They'd clearly touched a nerve, and he couldn't help but bite back. He had, with dripping irony, called these opponents 'super-apostles' – Phoebe was quite confident that he didn't think they were particularly 'super', nor was he sure of their apostolic status. But they had thrown down the gauntlet to him, claiming their superiority over him in everything – including Jewishness. To give him his due, Paul had tried to resist the challenge, but he'd failed. You could tell that he knew he shouldn't, but a boasting competition brought out the worst in him. Was he Hebrew? Was he an Israelite? A descendant of Abraham? You bet he was. As good as the rest of them? Better (he hadn't actually said that bit out loud, but it could be heard echoing in the background nevertheless). Then, with a characteristically quicksilver move, he had turned right around, toppling the argument onto its head, boasting of shipwrecks, beatings, and stonings – the very things the 'super-apostles' had used as reasons to despise him in the first place.

'Paul has his faults,' she went on.

'That we know,' said Herodion.

'But you don't do him justice if you think he undermines the heritage you both share. Does he want to undermine Judaism? By no means!'

Aquila let out a loud guffaw. 'We want you to explain what Paul means. You don't need to talk like him too.'

As was her unwitting custom, Phoebe flushed scarlet with embarrassment, but was intrigued to observe that for once it came with no accompanying emotions. The blush came and went; she cared too much about what needed to be said. 'It's catching, you know,' she shot back at Aquila with a smile. 'After a day in Paul's company I start talking in really long sentences too.' Aquila twinkled at her, and she felt a swell of gratitude towards him for lightening the mood.

She turned back to Herodion.

'Excuse me for saying so, but I think you're looking at it from the wrong end. You are hurt, I understand that, and Paul, for all his brilliance, doesn't deal well with feelings – if anyone should know that it's us Corinthians. He trampled all over us in his anger, and then was surprised when we were annoyed. But where he doesn't understand feelings, he does get ideas, and he chases them down to their logical end – even if occasionally he ends up in a blind alley and has to reverse. If you say that it is faith in Jesus that makes someone one of us, part of the covenant, then it makes no sense at all to say that those of you who are Jewish are superior and can keep yourself separate from the rest of us. If we Gentiles aren't fully "in Christ", we might as well give up and go back to how we used to be. Either we're in it together or we aren't, and if we are in it together, don't we *have* to eat together? What kind of Last Supper will we be commemorating if we can't eat together? I think his point is that we've all fallen short of God's glory. We are all in need of his love and grace. I know I am.'

At that a general murmuring broke out around the room, nods and smiles greeted her as she glanced around. She sagged with relief that what she had said appeared to make sense. Her glance eventually made its way back to Herodion. He was look-ing at her, no longer with anger, but with a deep, gut-wrenching sadness. He shrugged his reluctant acceptance of what she had said.

'It does make sense,' he said, 'but things that make sense aren't always easy to accept. It takes time. I can't change how I feel just because Paul has made a good logical case. After all, I've still lost my brother, and am quite alone.'

Prisca suddenly appeared at his side, after quietly working her way around the room. 'Not quite alone, dear brother Herodion. You have a new family now. You may not have chosen us, but we do love you – all of us.' Prisca looked around the room with determination, catching and holding the eye of Patrobas, the man whose leg Herodion had stamped on, and who had objected from time to time to what Herodion had said, so that even he shrugged and nodded his assent. She opened her mouth to continue, but at that moment the door crashed open and a woman burst into the room.

'Is she here? Tell me I haven't missed her.'

Chapter 5

The woman was out of breath. She seemed to have been running for a while, so much so that she had to hold on to the door for a moment or two until her breath returned. She was, to put it mildly, tousled – her clothes were grubby, her face streaked with dirt, and there appeared to be a bruise beginning to show on her temple. She was clearly well known by the people in the room, and if their expressions of delight were anything to go by, well loved too.

'Junia!' Herodion exclaimed, his damp face now suffused with tears once again, though this time they appeared to be tears of joy, not of anguish. 'Where were you? We were starting to worry. You missed hearing that insufferable man's letter.'

'Not so worried that you forgot to be angry though,' said Aquila.

Herodion accepted the teasing with good grace. 'I was distracting myself with well-founded outrage.'

Phoebe found herself marvelling at Herodion's range of emotions – from fury to sorrow to gentle self-deprecation in a matter of minutes. She also realised that the rest of the people in the room were quite used to his emotional displays, since no one seemed particularly ruffled. They continued loving him as he raged . . . then wept . . . then laughed. With a sudden flash of insight, Phoebe realised that this had happened in Corinth too – the only problem there was that there were too many people raging with emotion, and not enough providing the communal ballast for stability and support. Phoebe shuddered slightly as she remembered some of the more extreme outbursts in Corinth

– many of them in reaction to Paul either in person or to his letters.

She had always thought that there seemed to be something deep within Paul that sought out contention. Maybe his time with the Pharisees had taught him a love of argument, or maybe he had been drawn to the Pharisees through his innate love of dispute. But there could be no doubt that the heat of argument lit his inner fires, bringing him to life like nothing else. When he was with the Corinthians, there was no one more passionate, more vociferous, and more obdurate than he. Wherever the loudest, most high-spirited quarrels were to be found, there was Paul at their centre, his voice raised in debate, his eyes sparkling. There were times when Phoebe suspected that he deliberately stirred up the embers of the Corinthian fires so that sparks would fly upwards again. The problem was that Paul loved to argue so much that he couldn't understand those who didn't; those who were in some way undermined or damaged in the process. That was where it had all started to go wrong between the Corinthians and Paul. The fires of argument had blazed too brightly, and many people, including Paul himself, had got burnt.

As Phoebe emerged once more from her thoughts to hear someone asking Junia what had happened to her, she realised she was starting to reminisce like the elderly sailors who sat out day after day at the harbour in Cenchreae more wrapped up in times past than in the present that lay before them. There was certainly something about being far away from everything and everyone she loved that ensured they remained uppermost in her heart.

'She was arrested and imprisoned – again,' came a new voice from the doorway.

'Junia!' Herodion said. 'You have to be more careful. One day you will go too far.'

Various nods around the room indicated that Herodion was not alone in this view.

'Andronicus,' Herodion turned to the newcomer in the doorway, 'you have to stop her.'

Andronicus, who it must be said was as unkempt as Junia, if not a little more so – he certainly had more bruises – laughed at that. 'Shortly after I've captured and harnessed the wind, I promise you I'll turn my attention to my beloved wife; besides, it would be rather hard to prevent her from doing exactly what I do myself.'

'But she is a woman,' Herodion pleaded. 'It is all very well her taking a full part in talking about the Gospel in the privacy of our own houses,' he sniffed at that, his mobile face indicating that he wasn't sure that was a good idea either, 'but out on the streets or in the marketplaces, it is just asking for trouble. Keep her at home. You know you should.'

'I know nothing of the kind,' said Andronicus, 'and even if I did, wanting to and succeeding would be two entirely different things.'

'When you two have quite finished discussing me,' Junia said tartly, 'I ran all the way here the moment they let me out of prison to find Phoebe, not to discuss whether I'm allowed to be who I am.' She scanned the room, looking piercingly at person after person until, at last, her gaze fell on Phoebe. 'There you are, dear; now come and sit down with me: we have lots to talk about.'

At that there was a general outcry. From some because they had questions that they had been burning to ask, but which, because all attention had been focused on Herodion's rage, remained unspoken; from some because they still wanted to know what had happened to Andronicus and Junia; and from some . . . well, who knows what they thought, their voices couldn't be heard in the general hubbub.

Andronicus raised his voice and called for quiet. He was clearly expert at speaking above the noise of crowds because his voice cut through the racket, stilling the storm of protest almost immediately.

'Phoebe will be here for quite some time, yes?' he asked

confidently of Phoebe. Phoebe was aware that Andronicus's authoritative air was such that she would have agreed even if her plan had been a ludicrously short two-day visit. As it was, she had no idea how long she would stay – there was the commission for Paul, as well as the other thing, the thing she had told no one about – so her visit was certainly open-ended. She nodded her assent to Andronicus.

'This then is the plan: I will tell you all about our most recent adventure; then you will go. Phoebe will be here, and you can come to talk to her on another day, yes?'

The people around the room grumbled their assent to Andronicus's statement. They had clearly envisaged staying for many more hours yet. Phoebe marvelled at their acquiescence, but was, at the same time, relieved: her encounter with Herodion – no matter how successfully resolved – had worn her out.

'Now, I promised you the tale of our most recent adventure, if you are ready?' He glanced around the room commandingly one more time. 'Three days ago Junia and I began to proclaim the Good News of Jesus outside a temple, as we have done many times before—'

'No editing the truth, Andronicus,' Junia said. 'Our choice of temple was provocative, as you well know.'

Andronicus grinned. 'When I got married, people warned me of many ways my life would change. They forgot to tell me that my storytelling would be ruined for ever. Have you never heard of a dramatic reveal?'

Junia snorted. This was clearly a well-worn argument between them, though an argument clearly underpinned with deep love and affection. Phoebe also got the feeling that this exchange might even be part of the story itself, allowing them to build drama even while bickering.

'It was the Temple of the Deified Caesar,' Andronicus admitted. 'We wanted to talk about Jesus being Lord, and it seemed the most appropriate place to do it.'

The look of shock on the faces around the room told Phoebe that this was, to put it mildly, a bold move.

'Let me get this straight,' said Patrobas. 'You went to the very place that symbolises the lordship of the emperors, and declared that Jesus is Lord, not them? Are you mad? Do you have a death wish?'

'Not at all, Patrobas,' said Andronicus. 'People will only understand – truly understand – if they hear who Jesus really was and is. There are too many voices claiming truth in this city. If we want them to hear real truth, we have to speak loud and clear. And you don't get a place to declare Jesus' lordship more loudly than at the Temple of the Deified Caesar. It was going well too. People were really listening, but then some of the Praetorian guard came past and took exception to what we were saying. They flung us in one of the upper rooms of the prison. All through the night we could hear the cries of those awaiting execution from the room in the sewers below us. At one point I tried calling out to them, but they were so wrapped up in their own despair I don't think they heard us.

'We weren't sure how it would all end, but, fortunately for us, a huge riot broke out yesterday, so the prison became full to bursting. They decided not to try us after all, and let us go instead. And here we are, hale and hearty. Don't look like that, Patrobas. What we did was important.'

Patrobas clearly did not agree. '*You* weren't here during the troubles under Claudius. You didn't have to live through it all. But we did.' He gestured to a few people around the room. 'We had to live through the fear, and the raids by soldiers to make sure the Jews had all gone. Roman soldiers aren't very good at telling the difference between Jewish and Gentile Christians, so some of our friends met their deaths being beaten by the soldiers for claiming that they weren't Jewish. And when you were gone, we got along nicely without you. We met together quietly. Worshipped and prayed together. We rocked no boats.

We made no storms, and here we are, alive to tell the tale. But then Claudius died, and you Jews came back, triumphant, as though we had missed you, which we hadn't; as though we are better off with you, which we're not. And now you go out stirring up trouble. Courting danger at the very heart of Rome. What we need to do is keep our heads down. Follow the rules. Hope they don't notice us. And that includes you women.' He jabbed a finger in the direction of Junia and Prisca. 'You know full well that in proper Roman society women stay quietly at home; they do not go running around in public drawing attention to themselves.'

'No, they do not,' said Herodion. People around the room exchanged amused glances at this. Patrobas and Herodion had, at long last, found a subject upon which they both agreed.

Aquila, Prisca, Andronicus, and Junia all started speaking at once. Then stopped. Then started again, and stopped again. This carried on until Prisca said, 'Let me,' and the others subsided so she could speak and be heard. 'Patrobas, why are you a Christian?'

'Because I heard Peter telling his stories of someone called Jesus day after day near one of the temples. I couldn't stay away. This Jesus' teaching just made sense, but you know that.'

'We do,' Prisca said, 'but we were wondering whether you had forgotten. If Peter had not made a spectacle of himself outside the temple that day, you would not have heard about Jesus. If you didn't hear, you wouldn't be here now. The very reason you follow Christ at all is because Peter did what Junia and Andronicus did the other day. You may not have missed us while we were away, but . . .' Prisca looked at him meaningfully.

'I didn't mean you, Prisca,' Patrobas interrupted.

'Who did you mean then?'

'No one, especially. What I meant was I didn't miss the trouble you all cause,' Patrobas said.

'Ah! That is another thing altogether. As I was saying . . . You may not have missed *us*, but we would miss you and all the others who have been joined to our number because people like Peter, Andronicus, Junia, and Paul have not kept quiet. Yes, it is risky, but you must see it is worth it? Though,' she turned back to Junia and Andronicus, 'I do wonder whether going to the temple you went to was wise? Couldn't you have talked it through with some of us first?'

'Maybe,' Andronicus conceded. 'It was a spur of the moment decision. We didn't think it through, but it had great impact, and no harm has come to anyone. Besides – Paul would have done it.'

'There's a long list of things that Paul has done that I wouldn't recommend to other people,' said Prisca acerbically.

'Enough!' Junia cut in. 'I ran here all the way to talk to Phoebe, not to discuss whether something we have already done is a good idea or not. Haven't you all got work to do?'

'We have,' said Aquila, 'and if we could have our workshop back, we could get on with it.'

'You did agree to go after I told you the story of our adventure,' said Andronicus pointedly.

And with that, the people began to disperse, one by one, through the door of the workshop, some with better grace than others.

'Now then.' Junia settled into a corner, pulling Phoebe down next to her. 'I hear you have a fascinating story to tell yourself. Where would you like to begin?'

Chapter 6

Phoebe, though delighted to have the chance to be speaking to Junia, whose reputation as an apostle was well known even in Corinth, was aware of an intense gaze dragging her attention away from the woman sitting beside her. She turned her head to see Felix, the boy who had guided her from Ostia and who kept such a dogged and careful watch over her luggage, looking at her reproachfully. She felt a pang of guilt. He was right to reproach her. In their brief, largely silent, exchange over her luggage only a short while before, they had, Phoebe acknowledged, formed a bond. He had offered undying service, and she, in accepting the offer, had bound herself to care for and protect him in whatever way she could. In that moment, each had seen and recognised the other, and, in that recognition, something was offered and received.

Now, in her excitement at meeting Junia and Andronicus, he had slipped clean out of her mind. Just as well she had never been a mother, she thought, in a flash of painful self-recrimination. Phoebe's shame at so quickly forgetting this unspoken pact expressed itself, as always, in the blush that crept its way up from her neck to her cheeks. As it spread upwards, Felix nodded his acceptance of her unspoken apology, and replaced his reproachful gaze with a smile of such delight that Phoebe felt as though a wave had broken over her, warming the very depths of her being. If the previous exchange had formed a bond, this one sealed it, and Phoebe knew that she and Felix would, in some way or other, be bound together for life. As soon as she admitted this, Phoebe realised that there was an obvious but unasked question that needed to be raised. Everything about Felix – from his name to his undernourished, diminutive form – suggested that he was a slave, though not a well-loved one.

'Felix, who owns you? I can't take you away from them.'

The look of astonishment on the faces of the few people remaining in the workshop – Junia, Andronicus, Prisca, Aquila, and two others who clearly worked with Prisca and Aquila because, even as the last people were filing through the door, they had begun pulling skins off the large pile in the corner and into the middle of the room – reminded Phoebe that deep as she may feel it, the bond with Felix had been made almost entirely without words.

Felix drew himself to his full, if tiny, height, and declared with comic solemnity, 'Felix has no master, no mistress. Felix is his own man. Felix does whatever he chooses.'

'Felix was a slave,' Prisca gently interjected, 'but his old master died, and the heir, an adopted son from out of town, no longer wanted him. He is so small that the heir thought he had no great value, so didn't even bother to sell him. He just turned him into the streets. Herodion found him and brought him here. After his outburst today you may not have formed a very good impression of Herodion, but that would be wrong. He is kind and generous to a fault. He pays for whatever Felix needs, and Felix has become indispensable to us all.'

'And now,' Felix said, 'Felix cares for Phoebe. The great apostle Paul asked us to help her with whatever she requires. Felix heard, and Felix will do.'

'I don't think he meant you to do it all by yourself,' said Prisca laughing.

'But Felix would if he needed to,' he said, his chin jutting out with obstinacy.

'How old are you, Felix?' Phoebe asked

'As old as you need him to be,' came the reply.

Charmed as she was by his peculiar turn of speech, Phoebe wondered why it was that Felix only referred to himself in the third person. She feared it revealed a suffering so great that Felix had distanced himself from everything – even himself – out of protection.

'Herodion brought Felix to us two years ago. We think he was about eight then, but it is hard to tell. He doesn't know. No one ever thought him important enough to remember how long he had been alive,' said Prisca.

'Felix,' Phoebe turned to him, 'could you oversee taking my belongings up to my room?' Felix again swelled with pride, and Phoebe felt the tug on her heartstrings that so little attention could bring such joy. 'You don't have to do it by yourself,' she exclaimed with horror, as he began to manoeuvre the chest almost as big as himself up the stairs, but Felix jutted his chin again and continued, until Prisca and Aquila's employees strode over to help out. Phoebe grasped that she would need to be very careful what she asked him to do. He seemed unable to judge for himself what he could and could not manage.

'Poor soul,' murmured Junia, but Felix was not quite out of range, and he shot her a ferocious glance. Phoebe made yet another mental note about how to relate to him. Felix had clearly survived thus far with a tough outer shell; it would take a long time (if ever) for that shell to soften. His fierce loyalty was part of that armour, and it protected him. Sympathy was not something Felix either wanted or invited. She could see that he needed attention, but not sympathy; the connections he formed were strictly on his own terms. Over-familiarity might drive him away completely.

As Felix disappeared up the stairs with the two employees, pulling Phoebe's heavy travelling chest between them, the activity in the workshop increased. Skins were pulled into the centre of the floor and painstakingly stitched together by both Prisca and Aquila. They worked together seemingly effortlessly.

Phoebe, who had never occupied a tent, let alone seen one made, watched mesmerised as they appeared to dance around each other, holding pieces here, placing stitches there; an invisible pattern hanging between them guiding their every move.

'You were about to tell us ALL about yourself,' Junia's voice broke into Phoebe's reverie.

'I don't think she was,' said Prisca. 'You simply declared that she would, while at the same time evicting all our other unsuspecting guests.' A smile softened her words, but Phoebe sensed between them an old feud fuelled by two contrasting but equally dominant personalities.

'Don't worry,' Phoebe quickly said, 'I'd love to tell you everything you want to know.' Even as the words left her mouth she was forced to admit that this was untrue. She fully intended to hide her most shameful secret from them, just as she had from Paul. A clenching of her gut made her realise that it might be harder to conceal in the present company than it had been with Paul, whose mind was more taken up with the weaving of complex ideas than with whatever might be being hidden from him.

'I've come to begin arrangements for the visit to Spain,' she said. 'Paul mentioned it in the letter?' She looked at them to make sure they had heard what Paul had said. Prisca and Aquila nodded their assent. 'I have the necessary funds. I know what Paul wants. I just need to find translators and buy supplies, and we'll be ready.'

'I don't quite understand,' Andronicus said. 'Why make the plans now? Why not wait until Paul comes himself?'

'He's right behind me; he'll be a few weeks – a couple of months at most,' Phoebe said with a confidence she suddenly wasn't so sure she still possessed. 'He has been collecting money for the church in Jerusalem.' Again, four heads nodded their agreement. Paul had said that in the letter too. For the past years, ever since he had promised Peter he would remember the poor, Paul had been collecting money from all the churches he visited in Greece. Now he felt he had finished his work in the east. He had proclaimed the Gospel in all the key cities. The next phase of his journey meant going west, to Spain, and starting all over again. Before he did, he had decided to go back to Jerusalem to deliver the money himself, and then to travel on to Spain via Rome. He had persuaded Phoebe to go ahead of him and make arrangements so that when Paul did arrive in Rome he could set off straight away.

Phoebe had arrived with bags of money – some of it her own, the rest also collected from the churches around Greece and Asia Minor – and a few instructions from Paul. He needed translators. He was equally fluent in Hebrew and Greek, but Latin defeated him; he'd spent too long in the east, where Greek could be used for almost anything. He knew enough Latin to ask for bread or declare his citizenship in dire need, but his usually eloquent tongue stumbled and stuttered when it came to long sentences of Latin, let alone whatever other Barbarian languages they spoke in that alien land. So, Phoebe had come to find translators, people who knew the land and could guide Paul around it, supplies for the journey, and passages on ships. When all that was ready, she would wave Paul off on his next adventure and return with relief to her beautiful villa and uneventful life in Cenchreae.

'After he has visited Jerusalem and delivered the money to the church there, he will follow me here,' Phoebe said.

'That makes sense,' said Andronicus, 'provided he doesn't hit any problems along the way.'

'No need for worry there then.' Prisca paused her needle high in the air between stitches, her eyebrows proclaiming her scepticism. 'Paul never gets into trouble.'

'He won't this time,' said Phoebe. 'This trip to Spain is far too important to him. He's been preparing for it for months. It's far too important for him to allow anything to go wrong . . .

isn't it?' Aware that she had begun repeating herself, she looked again for reassurance and support into the faces of the four people who knew Paul far better than she did, and saw reflected back at her the uncertainty and anxiety that she had only just begun to notice in herself. There was something about the Spanish mission that she couldn't quite put her finger on: an undercurrent of anxiety. If Phoebe hadn't known better, she would have said that Paul wondered whether he would live long enough to get there. It felt as though he were making sure that someone else knew the plan from the inside, so that they could find a way for it to continue if he were no longer able to do it himself. But that was ridiculous. Although his various imprisonments and beatings had taken a toll on his body, there did not seem to be any reason why he wouldn't get there and fulfil his dream. Why then did she have this sinking feeling that he wouldn't?

She shook herself. She must really get a grip. To have all these nostalgic reveries and premonitions about the future was not like her. She was someone who lived for the present, seizing the day, and enjoying whatever it brought. She led an active, busy life with little time for the introspection into which she seemed to have fallen since arriving in Rome. Could it have something to do with her secret? She had locked it away for so long, buried it deep beneath layers and layers of determined denial and constant activity. And it had worked – mostly. But now she was back in Rome, she feared that her carefully constructed edifice of control might crack and crumble. She didn't even know why she'd come back. It was almost as though her heart had taken control and driven her back. She knew it was reckless to return to where it had all happened, but here she was. She had no plan at all, but had come anyway.

Phoebe became aware that the conversation around her had fallen silent; that four pairs of eyes were trained on her with a quiet but sympathetic gaze. She had feared that it would be either Junia or Prisca who pried her secret from her, but when it came to it, it was the gentle, courteous Aquila who asked the question that smashed the fatal hole in the wall so carefully built around her heart – a hole so vast that she had no choice but to let her secret come tumbling out.

'Why have you really come to Rome, Phoebe?'

Chapter 7

When she looked back on it later, Phoebe realised that, deep down, she had desperately wanted them to ask and that her inner determination not to reveal her past connection with Rome had been nothing but a final self-deluding attempt to hide from the truth. Only this could explain her sudden shift from a decision to tell nothing to a yearning to tell everything. Later, and only later, she could admit that Aquila's question, though sending panic coursing through her veins, also made her weak with relief. But now her emotions were very different. When he asked why she had really come, Phoebe froze: her mouth dry; her eyes wide; her heart pounding in her ears. She hardly knew these people, but what she did know she admired. How could she tell them? It would ruin everything. The plans for Paul's Spanish mission would fall into disarray; she would be cast out of this warm and loving community (even if she had only felt its warmth for less than a day). She couldn't tell them. She just couldn't. She sat still, looking at them, simply not knowing where to begin.

'I've come . . . I've come . . .' she trailed off.

The reality was that even she didn't *really* know why she'd come. She had allowed herself to be caught up in Paul's enthusiasm about her taking the letter to Rome – she really was the obvious person to do it – and had fallen in with his plans. She had even persuaded herself that this was exactly why she had come, but in the short time she had been here, the sights and sounds of Rome had awoken in her a whole host of ghostly memories: memories that were crowding in so strongly now that she felt overwhelmed by them. She had thought she had come because Paul wanted her to, but now she wasn't so sure. Now she was forced to admit that she had felt a tug so deep and so strong that she had simply had to obey it. She was here for a reason she hadn't even acknowledged to herself yet, so how could she possibly explain it to these strangers?

'Is this your first visit to Rome, Phoebe?' Aquila asked gently, blatantly throwing her a lifeline; a way into her own story.

'No, I grew up here. In the house of Titus Cloelius Cordus.'

The significant look exchanged between the four people present – Junia, Andronicus, Prisca, and Aquila – told Phoebe that, at the very least, they had recognised the distinguished family name. They might even have heard of Titus himself. He had, after all, come from one of the oldest Roman families; a family that could trace their ancestry back to the foundation of Rome itself.

'But last night, when I brought you here, it was as though you had never been to Rome before,' Prisca said, puzzled.

Phoebe opened her mouth to respond, but before she had the chance to say anything, Aquila interjected. 'I dare say a member of a noble household like that never ventured as far as Transtiberium.'

Phoebe smiled at him gratefully. 'No, I never came this far. This area feels like a completely different city, and besides, I left Rome nearly twenty years ago now; so long ago that much of it feels like a dream.'

'I just don't understand,' said Prisca, wrinkling her forehead in bemusement. 'What connection you had with Titus. I know you are a lady,' she gestured appreciatively at Phoebe's fine, if travel-stained, clothes, 'but surely Titus was way out of even your league. His family is as noble as you get.'

Junia laughed. 'I would never have taken you for someone awestruck by the aristocrats, Prisca.'

Prisca bristled. A brief tension in the air that went almost as soon as it had arrived hinted that Junia and Prisca might, occasionally, rub each other up the wrong way. 'I am not awestruck by aristocrats or anyone else. I was merely interested.' The emphasis Prisca placed on each word of the sentence certainly underlined her outrage, but whether it supported the truth of what she was saying, Phoebe was unsure.

She mumbled an answer, a fiery flush once more spreading upwards to her hair roots. The quizzical look on the faces around her made her realise that she had no option but to get it over with and tell them.

'I was a slave. He was my master.'

If she had taken off all her clothes and danced naked around the room, Phoebe doubted that her audience would have been more surprised than they were now. Prisca and Aquila ceased their sewing, their thick needles held motionless, mid-stitch. Andronicus and Junia leaned forward, their mouths open in surprise. When, after a few moments of silence, her audience regained the use of their tongues, a babble of noise rose around her, peppering her with questions.

Eventually Aquila's quiet authority took hold once more as he shushed the others, all the while chuckling, 'You certainly know how to hook your audience. We are as clay in your hands. Tell on, Phoebe, tell on. I assume you were born into the household?'

'No, not at all. Titus brought me back from his travels as a legate. I was a gift for his wife Aelia. I don't remember much about the time before. Just a few confused images that swirl around me in my nightmares.' Phoebe paused, suddenly overwhelmed by long ignored emotions.

Prisca seemed to sense her confusion. 'This stage of making a tent is tricky,' she declared stiltedly. 'Junia, Andronicus, as our employees are upstairs helping Felix with Phoebe's luggage, can we ask you to help?'

It was a badly concealed attempt to turn attention away from Phoebe's emotion, but, clumsy as it was, Phoebe was grateful. It gave her time to collect her thoughts, to tease out the threads and lay them down end to end.

'What do you remember?' Prisca asked gently from the other side of the skin that moment by moment was being transformed into a large tent.

Almost without her noticing, a memory came rising through the mists of time. The memory that even now haunted her night-time dreams.

'I was sitting on someone's lap. She was warm, her arms tight around me. Her hair tickling my nose. Smoke from the fire got in my eyes. We sat around that fire for many hours, telling stories, singing songs of ancient heroes. I was loved. I belonged.'

The vision swirled away and was replaced by another far more terrifying memory. The tang of blood was in the air – the taste of it in her mouth. The arms, though still around her, were no longer warm. They hung slackly. The weight of a body lying heavily on her was suffocating.

'Then the Romans came as we feared they would. They were burning our village to the ground. It was all a whirl of shouting, running, and fighting. My mother picked me up and ran, but she stumbled and fell, her arms around me. I lay beneath her, waiting for her to get up again, but nothing happened. Her eyes were wide, staring past me, unseeing. I called and called her, but there was no answer. I was sticky with blood and I couldn't breathe. So I wriggled out from underneath her and started to run.' The terror of the memory was causing Phoebe's breath to come in short, staccato bursts. 'I needed to get away. I ran and ran. But then, all of a sudden, the ground fell away. It felt as though I was flying. I was hanging mid-air, held tight between two strong hands. I opened my eyes a fraction and there were two large brown eyes gazing at me. A soldier streaked with blood, mud, and soot. He seemed to be making a decision.

Then I flew again, landing hard and painfully in a cart already piled high with possessions. We travelled for weeks and weeks. I don't know where or why. I remember being held high on a horse by those strong, strange arms, or buried in the cart against the sharp edges of someone else's possessions. Sometimes asleep, sometimes awake, always travelling.

'I don't remember much else until I was at the house.'

'What was it like?'

'Lovely – spacious and elegant. The atrium alone was twice as big as your workshop.' Phoebe felt herself sinking back into memories, long shut away. The phrase she would use to describe it now was 'intentionally exquisite'; then she just thought it pretty. Nothing was placed anywhere by accident. It was beautiful; carefully, thoughtfully beautiful. Every nook and cranny was tastefully decorated with artefacts. To begin with she had started with horror when she found something she had last seen in her village or piled high in the cart next to her on the long journey to Rome, but with a child's adaptability the shock faded. And before long she could remember things only in their new, lovely surroundings rather than in the smoky, well-loved locations of home.

'At the start, I remember wandering through the high-ceilinged rooms marvelling at everything I saw, but it wasn't long before their splendour became normal, and I no longer noticed. By then there was much more to take in. When I first arrived, I understood very little. Their language was odd, and it was weeks before I knew what they were saying. Then, slowly, their words began to make sense; gradually the talk of the other slaves, to each other as much as to me, began to explain what had happened. They said I was a slave. Apparently, the Romans had come and captured my village, killing nearly everyone in it. One of the soldiers, he of the large brown eyes, had taken a liking to me and decided to bring me home as a gift to his wife. It was, the other slaves said, because of my hair – they stroked it as they talked, marvelling at its rich auburn colour that (so they said) shimmered different colours as it waved down my back. This, they said, was why he – Titus – had named me Phoebe: the shining one.

'In those early days, they told me over and over again that I was lucky: I was lucky to have survived. They didn't normally save the smallest children – they were too hard to transport, and were too much of a nuisance on the way. A quick slit across the neck with a knife was the best way to deal with children. But Titus had saved me and brought me home – I was lucky. The slaves who were dragged from their homes to service the vast and unwieldy Roman empire were normally taken to a slave market and sold on from there. Titus had refused to let me go, he wanted me as a gift for his wife, and so had brought me all the way home himself – I was lucky. On arrival at the house I was treated as a treasured plaything. Titus had been right; his wife was delighted with her small auburn-haired present – I was lucky.

'The problem was, no matter how often I was told that I was lucky, I didn't feel lucky. By day I felt numb; at night I would wake up terrified, as night after night in my dreams the warm arms of love that encircled me became heavier and heavier until I was pinned beneath their suffocating weight, unable to breathe.

'Over time I learnt to live a half-life, the outer part of me reacting as someone who knew themselves to be lucky would; while in the shrivelled inside, darkness lurked, terrifying me every time I had the courage to glance its way. It wasn't long before I stopped glancing. It was easier, and far more fun, to live the life of a lucky, pampered child. And I *was* pampered. Titus and his wife Aelia called me their sunshine. That was my role: to live up to my name and shine, brightening up the room with my presence. They would dress me in the prettiest of clothes, command the other slaves to make garlands of flowers for me to wear, and I would play, sing, and dance for them – and the many guests that came to the house.

'It was a charmed existence. It never occurred to me it would come to an end . . . but it did. A few years after I had arrived something changed, almost overnight. I first noticed the change in the other slaves. I had always been set apart from them, superior, able to command them with childish imperialism, and they had joined in with the pampering and indulgence. Then one day, suddenly, it stopped. Without any explanation, I was given jobs to do: floors to sweep; items to carry; errands to run. A subtle change had come over the household. All of a sudden, I was no longer special. I saw less of Aelia. She rarely appeared in the house in the morning, and, if she did, she often had to run away, her face an odd shade of green. No one said anything to me, but I knew something was different. After a few months, I noticed Aelia getting fatter and fatter.

'I mentioned it one day to one of the older slaves, Anna. Her first response was to slap me, hard – that was one of the many things that had changed – I was slapped regularly these days. Then she scolded me for being rude about the mistress. Finally, she relented and shared the news. Titus and Aelia had been married for ten years, but no baby had come. That was why, when Titus returned from his last campaign, he had brought me with him, thinking that I would distract them both from the gaping void of their yearning for a child. It had seemed to work, or maybe they, like me, had learnt to pretend well. But now Aelia found herself swelling with her first pregnancy. Even as she told me this, Anna's lined face wrinkled with anxiety. She seemed to think something was wrong, but further questioning made her tight-lipped.

'At the time, I was too young even to know what Titus and Aelia's change of attitude towards me made me feel; let alone to find words that gave shape and weight to that feeling. But as I look back on it, the sensation that I had simply disappeared from view dealt a blow to my young heart. At the time, I accepted it without a murmur, but I realise now that it sowed within me a need to be seen, to be noticed and, ideally, admired. Back then the need was minute and had only the smallest of impacts, but over the years it grew and grew until it was a desire so strong it drove me headlong into the path of destruction.

'But I'm jumping ahead. I knew nothing of that then. The advantage of disappearing from view was that I was, for all intents and purposes, invisible. Hardly anyone noticed me or, more importantly, what I was doing. Over the next few weeks I crept around the house with my ears wide open, intent on finding out what had made Anna's face so anxious. It didn't take me long to find out. There is nothing so effective as being thought unimportant if you want to find answers to secrets: people forget that you are there and speak anyway. The problem I discovered was that Aelia was frail. She always had been. Anna feared that Aelia's tiny form would simply not survive the brutal strain of pregnancy and birth. The moment Anna had feared was upon them, and all she could do was watch and worry. The shadow of this anxiety fell, unspoken, over the whole household. Even Aelia seemed mindful of the lurking danger. As her stomach swelled, her face grew gaunt, her eyes darting anxiously, often unseeingly, around the elegant villa.

'Only Titus appeared unaware of the gathering gloom, striding off to Senate meetings with hearty good cheer, praising the goddess Fortuna as he went. As the weeks went on, I shrank back into the shadows; seeking to be as invisible as possible, where before I would have made an entrance; trying to avoid notice, where before I courted attention. The shadow that lay over the household grew darker and darker, until it came almost as a relief when the cries of the female slaves rose around me, declaring Aelia to have reached her time, even though it had come too early.

'If the gloom of the previous months had been difficult, it was as nothing compared to the next three days: slaves scurried backwards and forwards with dirty linen, some of it streaked with blood; Aelia's agonised shrieks reverberated around the high ceilings. Even Titus abandoned his cheery confidence, joining the rest of us in slinking as silently as possible around the house.

'In the end, it finished as we all feared it would but prayed it wouldn't. The baby had come too soon; Aelia's frail body had been broken by its own attempt to bring new life into the world. No matter how hard the wise and well-practised midwives had battled, the odds were too slim, and death claimed both Aelia and the tiny baby she eventually squeezed into the world. They emerged from her bedchamber weary and defeated to announce the news to the household gathered around the door.

'One of the most dreadful sights I have ever seen was the moment that Titus's ebullient optimism met reality and was defeated by it. In the moment that it happened he collapsed before our eyes, just like one of the cheap tenement buildings built by uncaring landlords that overnight would crumble into a pile of dust. He simply disappeared inside himself to a place far, far away where no one and nothing could touch him.'

The room fell silent. The half-made tent held in still, unmoving hands. The tragedy of over twenty years before summoned into the atmosphere by the story that Phoebe was recounting.

Chapter 8

'Do you need a break, dear?' Prisca asked.

'No, I think I'd rather carry on now I've started,' Phoebe said, aware that she was now unable to stop the memories that were tugging her on. 'The next few years were long, dreary, and silent. The household continued onwards, but the heart had gone out of it. On the surface, everything was as it had been. We washed, we cleaned, we shopped and cooked, but it was all aimless and pointless. If Titus ate anything, it was in his room. Gone were the days of laughter, playing, singing, and dancing. A stultifying fog hung over us all, with no signs of lifting.

'In an odd way, I was the most content I had ever been there. My insincere exterior that knew how lucky I was and shone with brilliance and fun was no longer needed. My shrivelled inside fitted well in that grieving, silent house. I had no need to pretend. What was needed was what I had to offer.

'Then, one day, Quintus, a cousin of Titus, arrived at the house and so began a new chapter in our lives. Quintus, like Titus, had been a legate in the army, and he had just arrived home with all his newly acquired wealth. He took a house, if anything even more beautiful than ours, a short walk away, and was clearly determined to celebrate this wealth as often as he could. Quintus and Titus looked similar – they both had the Cloelius noble features – but where Titus was attractive in a kind, homely way, Quintus was devastatingly handsome, with chiselled good looks that made the female slaves shiver as he passed by. When I first saw him, it struck me that the difference between the two of them lay in their character. Titus was gentle;

Quintus was ruthless. Titus cared for those around him; Quintus only for himself. Quintus's magnetism lay both in his absolute confidence in his own appeal, and in his determination to find pleasure wherever he went. This ruthless, pleasure-seeking self-assurance was seductive. It was also dangerous. Later I wished I had remembered this youthful insight, but by then it was too late.

'What Quintus did do, though, was return Titus to the land of the living – or at least to Quintus's version of it. Quintus's way of life involved grand feasts, with endless exotic courses, wine flowing as abundantly as water in the River Tiber after a storm, dancing girls, music, and the most beautiful courtesans. To my childish eye the courtesans had a life I could only dream of. Their clothes were elegant; their faces beautiful. They received lavish gifts, and were the centre of admiration and attention. I could imagine nothing more delightful than the lives they lived. If their glamour was hard-edged and brittle, obscuring a hollowness below, I didn't see it then; all I saw was how they were yearned for and admired.

'In their company, Titus and Quintus stumbled their way from day to day in a haze of stale wine. It was living, if only of a sort. From time to time the old kind and optimistic Titus would reappear, gently asking if we – the household – were all right, whether we needed anything. One day he even softly pinched my cheek as he had done in the past when I played, danced, and sang with Aelia, but even as he did so, a look of bleakness came over his face and he turned again to Quintus, who swung him off to yet another night of feasting and all it entailed.

'The reality was that the household was not all right. In the past, it had run smoothly, held firm between Titus and Aelia. The steward had been their willing deputy, but, in the vacuum left by Aelia's death and Titus's withdrawal, he struggled to keep order between the slaves' factions and the servants' demands. We all ended up going our own way, doing whatever

55

we chose – and soon the once elegant house began to reveal our neglect. Artefacts disappeared from the more obscure corners of the house, never to reappear; dust began to build up around the objects that remained; even a few weeds could be seen poking their way through the mosaic floors.

'We staggered on like this for a few years more, until one day, as I was carrying a basket of fruit through the atrium with my head down, my thoughts far away, I ran straight into Quintus. The fruit spilled all over the floor, and, blushing scarlet, I scurried around to pick them up.'

Phoebe looked up from her storytelling reverie to see, from the look on the faces of those present, that her tendency to blush, bright and often, had not gone unnoticed. She blushed at the recognition, but continued nevertheless, refusing to be cowed by the self-loathing that came in its wake.

'Quintus reached out and held my face in a firm grip and gave me a long appraising look. His intense, almost voracious, look at one and the same time satisfied my yearning to be seen and made me desperate for more. No one had ever looked at me like that before. I felt, somehow, both excited and demeaned. "Titus," he called out, "where have you been hiding this creature of beauty?"

'Titus looked over at me and laughed. "That isn't one of your beauties, Quintus. That's my little Phoebe." He looked at me again. "Though I have to admit she has grown up since I last looked at her. She used to sing and dance with Aelia . . ." He trailed off.

' "Excellent," Quintus said. "She can sing and dance for us tonight."

' "No, not Phoebe," Titus said, turning pale. "I'll find you some new beauties."

'But Quintus was not to be dissuaded, and I, scenting a return to the pampered glory of my childhood, did everything in my power to encourage him.

'So began a new rhythm in my life. Back came the beautiful clothes, back came the pampering and indulgence. This time, however, they came with an added thrill that felt deliciously dangerous. At the back of my mind I was aware I was provoking a powerful beast, but my youthful confidence assured me that I was more than able to best it. As I sang and danced before Titus, Quintus, and their guests I felt their eyes taking in my body in a way that felt both exciting and hazardous. The feeling was intoxicating, and I became more and more eager to show off what I could do. My showing off was rewarded with many, many gifts: clothes, jewellery, fine food. Every day something new would arrive at the house for me from Quintus or one of his friends.

'The greater my enthusiasm, the more cautious Titus became. Indeed, the whole household noted, with approval, that he seemed to be losing his taste for Quintus's carousing, only turning up to feasts when I was there, his eyes never leaving me while I was in the room.

'From time to time he drew me aside and begged me to stop. I know now that as my master he could have simply commanded me to stop, but that was not in his gentle nature, and Quintus's ruthlessness and my love of a new and exciting life combined to make an unstoppable force. Somewhat predictably I fell deeply and uncontrollably in love with Quintus, quivering whenever his arrogant gaze turned in my direction. Quintus, I now know, knew this. Indeed, he intended it, and slowly drew me into his power until there was nothing I wouldn't do for or with him.'

'How old were you?' The terseness of Aquila's question revealed that everyone knew how this story had to play out.

'I don't really know,' Phoebe said, 'but probably about thirteen. Now I look back, I see that Titus did everything he could to protect me, but he was too gentle, Quintus too forceful, and I too in love for him to have any real hope of success. It wasn't long before I was to be found in Quintus's bed every night and not long after that, Quintus persuaded Titus to sell me to him as his slave. I knew that I was still a slave, but – perhaps it was my unusual status as a child or maybe simply the dreams of youth – I began to believe that Quintus would free me, marry me, and make me a grand lady of high status. I spent hours imagining my glorious future, draped in the most elegant of clothes and admired by all of Quintus's wealthy friends. Of course, that didn't happen. That kind of thing never happened. It was just possible that I could have become a treasured mistress, but never a wife. But I was young and dreamed big. Eventually my dreams fell to the ground, one after another, until all I had left was the knowledge of my own hubris.

'One of the best memories of this time was my friendship with Chrestus, a slave in the neighbouring house. His name means "useful", and he made sure he was. His elderly master relied on him for everything, and, even though he was only a few years older than me, he ran the whole household with skill. We became friends, and would stop and talk whenever we met. I must have bored him stupid with my indulgent tales of Quintus and his feasts, but I was in love, and I rattled on and on to anyone who would listen. And Chrestus did listen. From time to time he looked as though he might be about to say something, but, every time, he changed his mind, closed his mouth, and listened some more.

'As so often happens, the collapse of my dreams crept up on me, masquerading as good news. I became pregnant. When I first realised it, I hugged my secret to myself gleefully. This was the moment. Surely Quintus would be so delighted at the prospect of an heir that my longed-for future would be within my grasp at last. But even my love-filled, fantasy-fuelled heart couldn't prevent the seeds of doubt from being sown. I woke one morning feeling more nauseous than ever, and, with very little warning, threw up beside the bed I had so recently shared with Quintus. He looked at me, narrowed his eyes, and tersely instructed me to clear it up. I made sure that never happened again, even if it meant running out of the room at speed, but from that moment on Quintus became more and more distant. I couldn't tell him my glorious news because I barely had time to speak to him at all.

'In the end, my body announced what my lips could not. My swelling waist made quite clear what was going on. Nevertheless, despite Quintus's distance and hauteur, I clung on to my dream that he would marry me, and that my future would be bright and joyful. This dream, the first of many, was brutally eradicated one night when one of Quintus's guests looked at me and said, "Quintus, have you been spreading your seed around again?" Quintus smirked his assent as the guest continued. "Surely you aren't going to make us suffer a procession of your conquests? We come here for titillation and beauty, not heifers." Quintus looked at me appraisingly – making me realise it had been a long time since I had felt his full and undivided attention.

' "You!" He clicked his fingers, my name had apparently been wiped out alongside any affection he might have felt. "Out." I left the room burning with shame. Those were the last two words he ever spoke to me. I spent the rest of my pregnancy labouring in his kitchen, running errands and trying to avoid being noticed. This turned out to be easy, since the rest of the slaves, resenting my former glamorous status, took no notice of me at all, save to bark out commands from time to time. During those long, difficult months, the only person who paid any attention to me at all was Chrestus. He would sneak over titbits from his master's kitchen, or flowers from the garden, his only goal – or so he said – to coax a smile onto my face.

'My memories of Aelia stirred in me a deep dread of the moment of birth, though my despair at that point was so great that the thought of the oblivion of death was a salve to my broken (if over-dramatic) heart. I might have been dismissed from Quintus's mind with an imperious click of his fingers, but I struggled to drive him out of mine. My young and eager heart had opened at his touch; the withdrawal of that touch had left a suppurating wound that failed to heal. My already shrivelled inner world shrivelled even further. The only thing that kept me going was the life steadily kicking away in my womb. I had lost everything, except this new life. And I clung with grim determination to the hope it suggested. From time to time I thought about Titus, but quickly dismissed him from my mind. He had begged me not to go, and I, in my youthful confidence, had ignored him. I had made my choice. Now I had to find the strength to live with it.

'Chrestus was with me when the pains began. I had stolen a few minutes in the passageway between our houses to meet him. He was the only person who paid me any attention, and his kindness was a balm to my battered heart. He had brought me some boar and some guinea fowl from the previous night's feast at his master's house. He had remembered me saying how much I liked them in the days when feasts were a part of my life, and had brought me some to remind me of happier times. Before I had time to eat, however, a gush of liquid rushing down my legs, followed a few minutes later by gripping pains, signalled that the baby was well and truly on its way.'

Chapter 9

As she paused for a breath before unveiling the most difficult part of her tale, Phoebe noticed that very little progress had been made on the tent for a while.

'I'm sorry,' she said. 'Shall I stop now so you can actually finish the tent?'

A ripple of 'No', 'Don't you dare', 'Please don't', and 'Who cares about tents?' greeted her question, the last comment from Junia earning a withering glance from Prisca.

'Really, you can't stop now,' said Aquila. 'You have us all hooked.'

Phoebe smiled at them all gratefully, and picked up her story once more.

'It gets worse, I should warn you. Another of my dreams bit the dust when I discovered that bearing a child as an unloved and unwanted slave is very different to doing so as a wealthy and much-loved wife. For me there were no midwives, no anxious waiting of the household for news. In fact there was no help at all; I was banished to our communal sleeping area with the stern command not to disturb them with any yelling. By then I had learnt too well the virtue of silence, and managed all my screaming on the inside. I was young and fit, and the birthing process proved to be swift. It wasn't long before I lifted my daughter onto my stomach, still covered in blood and a thick white substance. I was speechless with the wonder of her deep blue eyes, her shock of red hair, and her perfectly formed but minuscule hands. I felt a lurch of love so overwhelming that I knew my life would never be the same again. She opened her eyes, and it seemed as though she looked deep into my soul; at the same time, she opened her mouth and a thin but persistent wail rose into the air.

'It turned out that I wasn't quite as ignored as I had imagined. Barely had she taken a breath in preparation for a second round of cries than an elderly slave bustled into the room: knife at the ready to cut the cord, and strips of cloth poised to swaddle the squalling child. Her calm efficiency soothed me so much that my emotions, when she swept out of the room taking the baby "for the master to see", once more slipped into the realm of the fanciful. I slid into an exhausted sleep with images of Quintus rushing to see me, joy in his eyes at the birth of so beautiful a child. I was kicked awake sometime later, not to see Quintus's joyful face, but the impassive visage of the elderly slave who had taken my baby. "You are wanted," was all she said before striding off in the direction of the atrium. I stumbled out in a sleep-filled daze, conscious of liquid leaking from various parts of my body. Standing in the atrium was not Quintus, as I had hoped, but his hard-faced steward.

' "You are going next door on loan until they send you back," he said, contempt for my unkempt state written all over his face – a contempt that escalated swiftly when he saw that I was dripping blood all over the mosaic floor. "Get her out of here," he said, shivering with disgust, "and for Jupiter's sake stop her dripping on my floor."

' "My baby?" I stuttered.

' "Dealt with," he said, turning his back and walking away.

'The elderly slave guided me back to my room, nudged me to change my clothing, gave me wads of material to soak up the blood that was still seeping out of me, and listened silently to my impassioned pleas. She was impassive: neither sympathetic nor unsympathetic – more, it seemed, so tired and worn down by years of her own suffering that she had nothing left to offer.

'Eventually she responded, "Has no one told you? Surely you know?"

' "Know what?"

' "About the father's power?"

'The truth presented itself to my gut, but my mind refused to catch up. Fearing the answer, I knew I had to ask anyway.

' "Tell me," the griping fear made me terse.

' "The father – Quintus – can decide what happens to any of his babies. It's the law. It wouldn't matter whether you were a slave or not. The head of the household has the power to choose what to do. He didn't want your baby, so he got someone to deal with it. They took it right away." This was all said in such a monotone, matter-of-fact manner that I wanted to shriek, "*her* – they took *her*," and "she *was* wanted, by me at least," but even as the words formed in my mind I knew there was little point in uttering them so I let them wither and fall, unspoken.

' "How did they 'deal' with her?" I could barely squeeze the words out.

' "No idea," the slave shrugged her disinterest. "Maybe they drowned it? Or took it to be exposed?"

'My mind was numb, my eyes dry. This final onslaught on my dreams – the worst yet – dealt what felt like the death blow to my already battered heart. I was hollow, dried up, and emptied of all emotion. It was at that point that my breasts began to seep, as though my body was determined to weep even if my eyes could not.

' "Come now." The elderly slave – I realised that I had never learnt her name, but now no longer cared – took me by my arm and guided me to the house next door.

'There, waiting for me, was Chrestus, his eyes shining with what I could have sworn were tears. In my despair, I barely registered him. "We have need of a wet-nurse," he said, "and have rented you from Quintus for the time being." He led me to a room at the back of the house where a woman sat up in bed, a babe in her arms. "This is the master's distant cousin, Julia. She has no other family, no money. So she lives with us now," Chrestus declared. "Take care of her, she is precious to him." The declaration of her cherished status made me weak with envy. There was no one – or so it felt – in the whole world who was even aware of my existence. I felt Chrestus's gaze on me and noticed, with surprise, a look of intense compassion on his face. Was I perhaps wrong? Was there someone to whom I mattered? But my misery was too strong, and no sooner had the question crossed my mind than I was sucked back into its bitter embrace.

'The next two years passed in deadened grief. As I suckled Julia's baby, I was assaulted by such bitter-sweet emotions that, in order to survive, I had to turn away from them and reach instead for the strangely comforting, dull numbness. I did everything that was asked of me, and more. In that gentle household, I learnt from Chrestus the skills of management, of running a house so quietly and efficiently that no one noticed. No one would see the washing and polishing that made it gleam with well-kept elegance. No need went unanticipated or unful-filled. I learnt the comfort of competence.

'Then, one day, as I was returning from the street vendors with the melons I had anticipated the master might want later that day, I met Quintus. His initially blank look was immedi-ately replaced with an avaricious glimmer that I remembered all too well.

' "You're mine," he said, with a quiet menace that breached the boundaries of even my numb, unfeeling heart. I couldn't help remembering the time when those words made my heart leap with joy. Now all I felt was the cold chill of dread. Words failed me. I dropped my eyes and hurried into the house, sincerely hoping that his flitting, magpie brain would see and desire some-thing or someone else and so leave me in peace. It was not to be. The next morning, early, as the clients were lining up ready to bring their requests to the master, Quintus barged in, his voice loud and slurred with drink, demanding the return of his property. The look on the face of Chrestus's master indicated that he had forgotten – or never registered – that I was rented not bought, but he was a man of honour, and it was barely five minutes later that, with Quintus's hand bruisingly clasped around my wrist, I was dragged out of my temporary refuge and back to the life that had already stripped me of so much.

'I won't sicken you with details, but the next few months were the worst of my already miserable life. Something had twisted inside Quintus – maybe it had always been twisted, and I had never noticed – but now there was no doubt that his ruthlessness had become full blown brutality. Causing pain excited him; as did humiliating people. A grim realisation settled on me that I might not survive my return to his keeping; swift on the heels of this awareness came a sense of relief and release. There was no way out. All I could do was surrender to the inevitable. One particularly awful night in the company of Quintus and his more debased friends had left me so battered and bloodied that I thought my end really had come. At that moment, I remembered the kindness of Chrestus and the sense that to him, if to no one else, I mattered. All of a sudden, I was overwhelmed with the need to breathe my last near someone kind, not someone twisted by brutality and greed. I dragged myself to the house next door, falling insensible on the doorstep as soon as I arrived.

'I awoke sometime later with my wounds bound, in a bed I did not recognise, to a sense of profound disappointment that my miserable life had not after all ended. As I stirred, Julia, who had been keeping vigil at my side, took my hand and squeezed it, saying, "You're safe now."

'"No," I said, my voice wavering, "I will never be safe. It won't be long until he goes too far. He has before. I thought he had this time – it's why I came." The memory of various women who had suddenly disappeared from the household came to mind. In the past, and in my arrogance, I had assumed that their disappearance was their fault – if they had been as beautiful and charming as me they would have survived and thrived. Now I was one of them. One of those "unlovely, uncharming women" whose fate, in the company of Quintus, hung in the balance, and whose disposal was accepted with barely a shrug – they were no longer either beautiful or useful.

' "No," Julia gently insisted, "you are safe, free."

'As my deadened mind tried to process what Julia was saying to me, I recalled how very caring she had always been. Time and time again, while I was wet-nurse to her child, she had reached out to me with gentle kind-heartedness, but my withered heart had had nothing left to give. Now even the smallest glimmer of hope made it flicker for the briefest of moments, and I was able to accept her kindness for what it was.

'I later discovered that Chrestus had taken all of his savings – the entirety of what he had saved to buy his own freedom – and begged his master to go and buy my freedom from Quintus. And he had. No one would say how much it had cost. I suspected that Quintus had driven a hard bargain – even for a slave whom he now loathed so much that he would take out his disgust on me in ever more creative ways – and that the master, out of his love for Chrestus, had paid even beyond what had been saved up. But eventually the deal had been struck and . . . I was free. I was free!

'The first long months of my freedom passed by in a blur of pain. Slowly mending bones, wounds that wept pus; my battered body took a long time, but eventually it began to heal, and I had to admit that I would have a future. To begin with, freedom meant nothing to me. Quintus had broken more than my bones. I might have been free, but my mind was not. The door to my cage may have been opened, but all I could do was quiver in the corner, too cowed to venture out.

'Eventually and very slowly my mind began to accept my freedom, and that with this freedom came a bundle of other gifts. There was no need to be afraid. I was no longer owned. No longer bound to the capricious will of another. It wasn't long, however, before I realised that there was more to freedom than a lack of being owned. There was no point in being freed from my old life if my new life was an empty, pointless shell. Constantly looking backwards at what I had been freed from, in its own way, kept me in chains. What I needed was to discover what I had been freed for. I only really discovered an answer to that question years later in Corinth.

'Then, in Rome, I learnt that the best road to freedom was one step at a time. I got up – one step; I ate – one step; I spoke – one step; step by step I began to live again. It wasn't that I forgot. You never forget. Nor would I want to. Forgetting would have meant letting go of that one beautiful memory – of my perfect daughter – along with all the rest. Forgetting wasn't an option. So instead I learnt to live one tiny step at a time. I also learnt that life is like a bubbling stream. It does just carry on, whether you want it to or not. Sometimes the best thing to do, even amid the greatest blackness and despair, is to surrender to its movement, to let it carry you along with it . . . and so I did.

'From time to time I remembered Titus, and wondered what had happened to him. I knew it was too late by then. He would never want me back, not after what had happened with Quintus. I was soiled goods. No master wants a ruined slave. Many months later my curiosity got the better of me, and I went back to Titus's house, but when I got there the house was deserted, locked up, and desolate. It had clearly not been lived in for many months. There was no way of telling where he had gone. That part of my life was over, gone, never to return.'

Chapter 10

'Tell me you married Chrestus,' said Junia. Phoebe looked at her in surprise, noting that Junia's cheeks shone with unmopped tears.

'You do know how to ruin a story,' Andronicus turned on his wife. 'Let her tell it in her own time.' A fraction later, he continued, 'You did though, didn't you?' He looked beseechingly at Phoebe as though she had control over how her own story ended. She tipped her head on one side, still marvelling over twenty years later at the knowledge that, thanks to Chrestus, she did have control over her own story. Of course, she couldn't change the past – whether she'd married Chrestus or not – but she could now change the future. Chrestus, sacrificially and generously, had given her control over her own life – and at the same time given up his own long-held dream of freedom. It was that act that had made her realise what love really looked like. Not the grasping, pleasure-seeking, self-centred version she had encountered in Quintus, but real love. A love that gives and seeks nothing in return.

'Of course I did,' she smiled 'I would have been mad not to.' She paused. 'Actually I couldn't to begin with – he was still a slave, and I was in no fit state to offer him anything. Chrestus arranged for me to be a servant in the house. The two years I'd spent in that house as a wet-nurse had taught me many skills, and, in no time, I had remembered them all again. I slipped into the familiar routine almost overnight, and its comforting rhythm contributed to the slow healing of my heart – that, and the knowledge of Chrestus's patient, gentle love.

'It took me some time to be able to respond with the love he deserved. The love I had learnt from Quintus was a raging fire that eventually consumed me. Chrestus's love was like a long refreshing drink on a hot day. I had to learn how to love like this, but Chrestus was patient, and before long I loved him just like I thought he had always loved me. After a few years his master granted us permission to cohabit and later, when Chrestus finally got his freedom, we married. Those were the happiest years of my life, and the years slipped away in contentment and ease.'

'Wait, wait, wait!' Andronicus, who up to this moment had said very little in response to her story, raised his hand, dropping his part of the tent and causing Prisca to tut with frustration. 'I simply don't know how you do this all day,' he said to Aquila, clearly nervous of Prisca's irritation. 'My arms have gone numb.'

'Let's all take a break,' said Aquila. 'I'm used to tent-making, and even my arms are aching.'

They all settled down around Phoebe again, and she noticed that though none of them had touched her at all, she felt held in a warm embrace.

'That's better,' said Andronicus as he stretched his arms, neck and shoulders. 'Now, I know you are hurrying on to the good part of the story, but we're fascinated now and before you do, we need to know how Chrestus got his freedom.'

Phoebe chuckled. Andronicus was quite right. She'd lived so long with the misery of her story that the emotions it evoked made her impatient to rush on to the happier part of her tale, but, in doing so, she had nearly forgotten a crucial piece of information. She gave a slight bow in Andronicus's direction. 'You are quite right; the rest won't make sense unless you know that. Chrestus's master was old, and over the next few years he grew more and more frail, and more and more dependent on Chrestus. In the end, he died, and we all mourned his passing with the sorrow he deserved.'

'He'd freed Chrestus in his will!' Junia declared, with the air of someone who had just solved a difficult and challenging puzzle.

'Perhaps you'd like to tell Phoebe's story yourself?' The acidity of Andronicus's tone indicated that Junia's habit of jumping into a story was a source of ongoing irritation.

'As Junia rightly guessed, that was exactly what had happened.' Phoebe smiled at Junia, hoping she would know from this that she didn't mind. 'But she didn't guess it all. More than just freeing him, Chrestus's master adopted him and made him his heir. In one fell swoop he changed Chrestus's life for ever, and with it mine too. Not only were we free, we were rich beyond our wildest dreams.

'It didn't take us long to decide to leave Rome. It held such terrible memories for me, and Chrestus felt deeply the stigma of having lived there as a slave. We had heard that Corinth was full of former, now freed, slaves. There you could reinvent yourself, shake off the old and put on the new. This was something we were desperate to do. We sold the house, freed all the rest of the slaves (it was an act of foolish generosity, but we couldn't quite bring ourselves to sell them on to an unknown fate and didn't want to take them with us to remind us that we, like them, had been slaves), and set sail for Corinth and a new life. Only Julia and her daughter came with us.

'It took us a while to settle in Cenchreae, but after so many years in the city, we both felt the call of the sea. One day we travelled out of Corinth to see the ships being rolled into the sea from the *diolkos*, and were so mesmerised by its sights and sounds that we knew we had come home. We found a villa three times the size of the master's in Rome, and revelled in our good fortune. We had arrived. We had come home. There was nothing more we wanted or needed. We had our happy ending.'

Phoebe paused dramatically, and Junia sighed with irritation. 'I'd hoped for a more satisfying ending than that.'

Andronicus chuckled with seeming glee. 'Perhaps this will teach you to let others unfold their stories at their own pace? Forgive me if I am wrong,' he said, winking at Phoebe, 'but I think that was a pause, not an ending? Phoebe, like the very best of storytellers, is tantalising you; leaving you hanging, desperate for more. And you, with your love of rushing ahead and knowing the ending before it comes, have walked right into her trap.'

Junia pulled a most undignified face at her husband, but the twinkle in her eye implied that she had accepted his reprimand with relatively good grace.

Phoebe joined Andronicus in a chuckle. 'Andronicus is, of course, right. The story can't end there – I still haven't told you why I came back to Rome. Bear with me, I'm nearly there.'

Her audience of four nodded their happy agreement at this and settled down for more. Phoebe, looking at them, suddenly realised that she was relishing the telling of her story. For so many years she had dreaded the thought of even looking back at what had happened so much that she had locked everything about it – good and bad – away in her mind, but, rather than withering away due to lack of attention, its power over her had grown and grown into a monster so large it had begun to occupy every quiet moment that presented itself. As a result, Phoebe had begun to fear such moments, had shied away from them, and instead, had filled them with endless wearying activity and conversation. Now, the act of turning to face her secret head on had cast the clear light of day on it, and, just as throwing open the shutters on a room of terrifying shadows reveals the prosaic ordinariness of what is really there, so too the shadowy monster that had haunted her all these years was revealed to be little more than a shabby, slightly soiled rag. The more she told her story, the more she revelled in doing so, and, yes, she had been guilty of a dramatic flourish designed to throw the inquisitive, fast-thinking Junia off the scent.

'What no one ever tells you,' she continued, 'is what you lose when your dreams come true. Everyone focuses on what is gained and forgets to mention the rest. Perhaps it is because it feels churlish to mention it, when you have everything you said you ever wanted, but I do wish someone had warned me. You see, it never occurred to me that becoming a fine lady meant I would lose the solidarity and friendship of the slaves and servants. Of course, their company had not always been pleasant – sometimes it was downright unpleasant – but, kind or not, noticed or not, I had a place. Somewhere I belonged. Somewhere to plant my feet and feel as though I fitted. Overnight this disappeared. In our new villa in Corinth, when I found myself with little to do, I would drift to the company of the servants and slaves, but every time I arrived, they would fall silent and shift uneasily around me until I gave up and left. Every time I tried to go to the market, to straighten the furniture, or to remove a hanging cobweb, a member of the household would arrive, gently chiding me that this was not what a great lady should do, and taking the task away from me. I loved my new house, but was not easy in it. After years of yearning to live a glamorous, pampered lifestyle in my own right and free from the ever-changing whim of a master, I couldn't settle to it. I didn't know how to belong in this new life, and the old familiar life – the one I knew as a slave and then servant – gently but firmly closed its doors on me, telling me I no longer belonged; I couldn't go back.

'I became restless and edgy, caught between the life I had wanted and the life I had left behind; and I did not fit easily into "fine" society. Chrestus seemed to have much less difficulty adjusting, and, with time, this began to drive a deadening wedge between us – he frustrated by my seeming ingratitude; I jealous of his ability to reinvent himself into his new life.

'As time went on, I found ways to cope. I had learnt the skills of pretence well as a child, and I discovered that I had not forgotten them so many years later. As an adult, my ability to dissemble and charm slowly carved out a life for me as a successful and much sought-after hostess, but all the time I was gripped by the gnawing fear that someone – anyone—might find me out to be the fraud I knew myself to be.

'Now I'm going to skip forward ten years or so,' Phoebe declared, 'lest you all die of old age before I finish my story. In my defence, you did tell me to begin at the beginning,' she shot at Prisca.

'And excellent advice it was too,' Prisca replied.

'The next ten years were good years – if you take good to mean unremarkable, and after such a difficult life unremarkable was much to be welcomed. Chrestus and I lived a good life. Even I settled into its rhythm after a while. We wanted for nothing – or at least nothing money could buy. I had no further children, and after a while I stopped even hoping that I might. During that time, Chrestus and I drifted further and further apart. Every now and then it felt as though there was an impenetrable barrier between us. I couldn't work out what that could be, and Chrestus shied away from any conversation that might reveal what it was. He remained good and kind and loving, but there was something, something I couldn't quite put my finger on, which meant I felt distant from him. In the end, I found out what it was. What had come between us was a secret. A secret that he had sworn to keep, and which, loyal, generous soul that he was, he had kept through all those long years. It was only on his deathbed that he told me what it was. It was a secret that shook my new life to its foundations.'

Chapter 11

J unia opened her mouth as if to speak, and looked startled
when not only Andronicus, but Prisca and Aquila too,
rounded on her, exhorting her to stay quiet and not to try to
guess what the secret was.

'I was going to ask if Phoebe needed some wine to wet her
throat,' Junia said, with as much dignity as she could muster.

'Thank you, that would be very welcome,' said Phoebe, feeling a little sorry for Junia, but also conscious that her mouth
was dry after talking for so long. She took a sip, placed the cup
down carefully, and continued.

'Chrestus died suddenly and swiftly, and his death turned my
life upside down in more ways than one. It was while Gallio was
proconsul. I'll never forget it. Chrestus and I had been honoured
with an invitation to a dinner at the house of Gallio the day
before. It was, I suppose, a sign that we had at last been accepted
socially. An invitation to dine with the proconsul was a great
honour. The dinner was a small one, with just enough guests to
fill his dining room, and conversation around the table that
evening ranged over many different subjects, from the exploits
of Gallio's brother, Seneca; to the number of traders who had
passed through Corinth that year (and whether they were being
taxed enough; Gallio thought not); to the inhospitable climate
of Corinth (this mostly from Gallio, who, it seemed, hated our
new home); to the troublesome Jew – was his name Paulinus or
maybe Paulus – who had so stirred up his Jewish compatriots
that they had wanted Gallio to condemn him. Gallio had been
particularly vociferous about this episode, enquiring why he

should care how any of them worshipped their funny, invisible God.

'On our return home from Corinth to Cenchreae, Chrestus began to feel unwell. Before long he was burning a high fever, his eyes glassy and unfocused. By the morning it was clear that he had not long to live. He had been stricken by one of those terrifyingly swift and deadly illnesses. The physician who had been called out during the night made it clear that he thought nothing could be done. All we could do was to watch and wait. Some time towards the end of the following day, Chrestus struggled up onto his elbow, his eyes frantic. He grabbed hold of my hand and looked into my eyes. "I can't die without telling you," he said. "You have to know." He waved his hand vaguely, in what the doctor, servants, and slaves took correctly to be a signal of dismissal, and waited for them all to leave. Exhausted, he flopped back onto the bed as he turned his desperate face to me once more.

' "Know what?" I asked.

' "Your baby – she isn't dead."

'My jaw fell open. "What do you mean not dead? Quintus had her 'dealt with'."

' "He sent her to be exposed, but that is a notoriously unreliable method of killing a child. I followed the slave he'd sent to do the job. He was, fortunately for me, lazy. He didn't take her very far before just putting her down on the banks of the Tiber and hurrying back to the house. I simply picked her up and took her somewhere safe."

' "Why did you never tell me?" I was aware my words were coming out as a wail, but could do nothing about it.

' "Because Titus begged me not to."

' "Titus Cloelius Cordus? My Titus?" My brain could barely take any of this in.

' "Yes, your Titus. He felt so guilty about what had happened to you that he paid me to watch over you. He tried time and time again to get Quintus to let you go, but that was the worst thing he could have done. If Quintus had thought no one cared, he might have got bored and let you go sooner, but the more Titus begged, the tighter he held on. So I just watched and waited and told Titus what I saw."

'I remember feeling sick as I howled, "I thought you cared about me. I thought I mattered to you."

' "You did – you do. Not at first of course. At first I watched over you because Titus paid me to. But it wasn't long before I knew exactly why Titus cared so much for you. Soon I loved you with my whole heart, and would have watched over you whether Titus had paid me or not.

' "When I told him you were pregnant, he paid me a lot of money to make sure I saved the baby. He knew Quintus, and knew he'd want to dispose of your child. My task was to make sure this didn't happen. When I saved her, I took her to Titus. He made me swear that I would never tell anyone – especially you – what I'd done. And I didn't. I never have until today. Soon after I took your baby to him I received a note from him telling me he was closing up the house. He feared that if Quintus ever saw your child he would change his mind and claim ownership. So he was going far away. He reminded me of my promise to tell no one. I never heard from him again."

'Chrestus fell back on the bed exhausted, his lips beginning to turn an alarming shade of blue, his breathing laboured, all the time looking at me pleadingly, as though I was meant to say I understood. The problem was I didn't.

'I stumbled to my feet, and then out of the door. I had to get away. I needed to think, to take in everything he'd just said.

'I never saw him again.

'The slaves told me that when they went into the room a few moments later, he had died.

'The next year passed in a blur of misery. I had thought, in Rome, that I had reached the lowest point of my life. I was wrong.

There was a point even lower. The pit went down further than I could ever have imagined. Apparently, the foundation upon which I had built my new life had, in fact, been shifting sand. As the reality of Chrestus's death – and what he had revealed with his dying breath – crashed over me, all those carefully laid foundations crumbled away: Chrestus had not loved me, he cared because he had been paid to care; my child was not dead, she was alive somewhere bringing joy into another's life; Titus had cared for me, as a father, but I would never see him again. To begin with my rage was so great that, at times, I could barely breathe. How could Chrestus have done this to me? How could I have trusted him? Why could I not have seen that he didn't really care? How could he have betrayed me by saving my daughter?

'Kind patient Julia listened to me while I raged. For hour after hour I paced and shouted, shouted and paced. And while I did, she sat and listened. From time to time she tried to speak, but I could hear nothing over the rushing fury that filled my mind and my heart. Eventually one of her gentle questions pierced the armour of my anger. "Can you not remember how much Chrestus loved you?"

'It was that last question that rang in the echo chamber of my grieving mind, and I slowly came to myself. Whereas before his death I had taken his actions and seen in them only love, now I saw in them only betrayal. Perhaps neither was completely true. What felt like a betrayal might have come from love, however misguided I might see that to be. He *had* tried to help. He had *tried* his best to do what was right, but this was one of those occasions in life where there wasn't a right thing to do, only a mixture of wrongs. Maybe, in his shoes, I would have done the same. After all, I knew he had loved me – even if at the start his kindness was motivated by financial reward. After all, he had saved my daughter – even if he had never soothed my battered heart by telling me so. I might wish he had acted differently, but he had done what he thought was best.

'The moment I accepted this was when I was assailed by a fresh wave of rage, this time directed inwards. All this was not Chrestus's fault. It was my fault. *I* had yearned for the glamorous lifestyle. *I* had fallen in love with Quintus. *I* had turned my back on Titus and never bothered to try to return. *I* had allowed my fantasies to present me with a future I could never grasp. *I* had believed my baby dead and had never tried to search for her. And, worst of all, *I* had walked away from Chrestus's deathbed and had never seen him again. My life was in tatters, and it was all *my* fault.'

Prisca broke in at this point, reaching out and grasping Phoebe's arm. 'You do know that isn't true? Maybe some of it was your fault, but not all of it. You can't think that you were to blame for what happened?'

Phoebe shook her head and pulled her arm away. She had lived so long with the knowledge of her guilt that she had no energy to see it any other way. 'It's all right,' she said in what were, even to her ears, wooden tones. 'I've spent enough time with Paul to know that faith in Christ has made everything new. I have died and risen with Christ, the old has gone, the new has come. I know all that. Let me tell you what happened next.'

Prisca sat back and gestured to her to go on, but the look on her face indicated that Phoebe had failed to convince her of anything. She might know the right words but they clearly meant little to her.

'The more restless I became, the more I needed to walk. Day after day I walked and walked, often into Corinth and back. Then one day as I was walking through the marketplace, I heard Chrestus's name, or so I thought. It sounded odd. The man had flung open his arms and in nearly every sentence said something that sounded like *Iesous*, and then *Chrestus*, and sometimes he added *kurios* too. I couldn't work out what on earth he was saying, so drew nearer to hear more clearly. There it was again: *Iesous Chrestus kurios*. It wasn't long before I realised my mistake. He wasn't talking about Chrestus at all, but about someone called Jesus who he said was anointed (*Christos*) and was Lord (*kurios*). This latter upset various people in the crowd who cat-called and jostled every time he said it. In the end the crowd became violent, though it wasn't those objecting to the term Lord who rioted (these were nearly all in Roman dress and slunk quietly away when trouble broke out). It was the Jews who became angry and looked as if they were about to attack the man speaking. What drew and kept my attention, however, was that he seemed entirely unconcerned by their anger, and continued speaking loudly over the top of them.'

Phoebe observed Junia and Andronicus catching each other's eye and smiling at this. Clearly, this was a familiar scene to them.

'Do you remember that time I was hit right in the face by those rancid food scraps? I smelt terrible for days,' said Junia. 'I could have sworn they'd been saving them specially.'

'Who could forget?' Andronicus replied. 'I still think the moment when that slave emptied a full chamber pot over my head from an upstairs window beats that though. Who knew such a small pot could hold so much?'

Phoebe watched them with a mixture of bemusement and amusement as Junia and Andronicus vied gently for the prize of who had suffered the greatest indignity for the sake of the Gospel. With a twinge of nostalgia, she thought again of Paul; how he would have loved to have been here, joining in the competition of catastrophe – she had no doubt at all that had he been here he would, of course, have won. Immediately Phoebe wondered how long it would really be before he reached Rome. She couldn't imagine that Paul would get to Jerusalem and then turn around for Rome all in the space of a month, as he had promised, but he had seemed so adamant, and she had so many reasons to want to believe him.

Chapter 12

'Doesn't it upset you when people get offended?' Phoebe asked.

'Why should it? The message of Jesus *is* offensive.' Junia shrugged. 'For those who love success, he represents failure; for those who are comfortable, he brings disquiet; he topples those who know themselves to be right; he disturbs those who are pleased with themselves. I'd be more upset if they weren't offended. I sometimes wonder what the Good News of Jesus will look like when it doesn't upset people any more.'

'You have to admit, though, that you do love a good argument,' said Andronicus. 'You and Paul are just the same.' He broke off under the fierce gaze of his wife, and held up his hands as though in surrender. 'I quite enjoy a good quarrel myself, but I imagine it feels different for people less fond of a juicy dispute.'

'I always wondered whether that was why Barnabas really left Paul,' said Prisca. 'He's such a gentle soul. When I heard that they'd parted company it made me wonder whether Paul had upset him one time too many.'

'Maybe he did, and maybe he didn't. What I do know is that I want to know who this other lover of an argument was,' said Aquila, skilfully steering the conversation back to Phoebe's story.

Aware, at one and the same time, of how easily these four old friends could stray to discuss old acquaintances and their motivations, of how tired she now felt, and of how desperately she needed to finish her tale, Phoebe happily picked up the thread of her story that Aquila had just held out for her.

'It was Quartus,' she said, and then swiftly carried on over the chorus of appreciative noises expressed for an old friend. 'I discovered later that he was well accustomed to riots. That day I joined the respectable Romans as they slunk away from the trouble, but there was something that kept on drawing me back. Perhaps it was simply to hear – or mishear – Chrestus's name. Perhaps it was for the joy of not feeling isolated, but jostled in a crowd – albeit an unruly one. Perhaps it was because of the odd combination of deep calm and utter passion that I saw in Quartus. I had no idea why I went, but day after day my feet took me there, and day after day I stayed until the crowd became too rowdy and I was forced to leave.

'One day, as I was shouldering my way out of the crowd, I heard a voice behind me, "You come every day, don't you? I've seen you here before." '

'I wheeled around and found myself looking into the eyes of someone who was dressed as I used to be in my days as a kitchen slave. Her clothes were simple and in places worn through. I took a step back, the training of the slaves in my house having rubbed off on me – maybe she would chastise me for being too friendly? But she didn't. In fact, she barely noticed my finery. She was too intent on talking to me. Her name was Miriam; she was a slave in the house of Chloe. A number of the slaves in that household believed that Jesus Christ was Lord. She had noticed me listening to Quartus's words, and wondered whether I wanted to come the next day – the first day of the week – and break bread with them. Part of me was shocked that a mere slave would invite me, a fine lady, to break bread with them – didn't she know who I was? The moment the thought came into my mind I realised how ridiculous I had become. Of course she didn't – why would she? The other part of me, the part that had been drawn day after day to listen to Quartus for no obviously good reason, simply couldn't resist. In the end, that part of me won. That part of me had been restlessly waiting for something for years; that part of me yearned for inclusion, for trust, for peace. It was a part of me I had simply not known what to do with, so had ignored, but now it took over, and I was delighted to accept the invitation.

'I arrived early the next day, but Miriam assured me it didn't matter. Chloe was absent, had been for months, so they had no need to cook or serve a fine dinner. Chloe's absence meant that the group met in the garden at the back of the house. My luxurious lifestyle of the previous ten or so years made me yearn to recline in the comfortable-looking dining room I had glimpsed as I was led towards the back of the house, rather than crouch down on the ground among a crowd of people I had never met before. It wasn't long, however, before I had forgotten that ungrateful thought, as food was passed around and the conversation began to flow. There were about twenty people there, far too many to fit into the dining room. Some were clearly slaves or servants; some craftspeople arriving at the house still grimy from a day's work. Hardly any were dressed as finely as I was, but no one paid any attention to this – they treated me exactly as they did Miriam or any of the other slaves from the household. I wrestled briefly with a sense of outrage, before realising that their lack of preferential treatment was giving me the gift of easy solidarity I had so missed in recent years.

'After a while the conversation turned serious. They read from something they called "Scripture"; it was about God – they didn't say which one – wanting to comfort his people. It sounded very un-godlike behaviour to me; everyone knows that the gods treat us human beings as their own playthings, changing our fates on a casual whim – you only had to look at my life if you wanted proof of that. Then they talked about the passage, and what it meant for them now they were "in Christ". I had no idea what they were going on about, but I realised I didn't care. I felt safe and at peace for the first time in a very long time, and even when people in the room started inexplicably talking in languages I had never heard before or declaring what they said was God's vision for the world, that feeling did not waver. Later on, they took bread and a cup, and talked about Jesus: how he had died for us, how his last command had been to do this in remembrance of him, and how we now did this to proclaim his death until he came again. That was the moment it all changed for me. I didn't understand what they meant, but for the first time, I did understand something about me. As I ate the bread and drank the wine, something in me shifted. I knew myself to be loved with a love so great I could barely comprehend it. I knew then that I had to know more about this Jesus Christ. I wanted to come back to spend time with this generous, warm group of people. For the first time I belonged, and wanted to belong more.

'Over the next months and years, I slowly began to understand what they were talking about. Their Scripture – the Jewish Scripture – told about God, the one God, who created the world and loved it into being. It told about how human beings turned away from God, and how God tried everything to draw them back to his love. It told how human beings were so caught in a trap of their own making, a trap strengthened by greed and arrogance and power, that they simply couldn't stay faithful to God. When they laid the Scripture down, they began to talk about Jesus Christ. He was God's Son, they said. In the end God had sent him into the world to fix what nothing and no one else could mend. He was faithful, as no one else could be, and when he died, broke the power of sin, the power that had kept people from God for so long. And when he rose again, he recreated God's relationship with the world – they used a special word for it: "covenant" – the Jews were particularly keen on that word. They went on to talk about something they called baptism. In baptism, they said, we could join with Christ, die and rise with him, and live a new life, becoming more and more like him in everything we think, say and do.'

Phoebe broke off. 'I don't know why I'm telling you. You know all this already.'

'Well, yes,' said Aquila, 'but I never tire of hearing how it sounds to someone else. It clearly made a great impression on you.'

Phoebe flushed. 'It did . . . but, I'm ashamed to admit, for a long time it made no sense to me. It sounded crazy. Sheer madness. But I heard one thing. It lodged in my heart and never went away.'

'What?' The chorus of voices spoke in almost perfect harmony.

Phoebe looked at them. 'That God loves me. That's what I heard. It's what made sense. The rest bewildered me. It seemed to be answering a whole load of questions I'd never asked. Later I saw that the rest was like an enormous set of clothes. I needed to grow into them if I was even to understand why I needed to know what they were telling me. Eventually, bit by bit, much of it *did* begin to make sense. Bit by bit I understood why it all mattered. Bit by bit I realised that the clothes were bigger than I had appreciated They got even bigger when I met Paul, and I'm not sure I'll ever quite grow into them! To begin with they were just words; now those words tell me who I am. But knowing God loves me has kept me going through it all. For the first time in my life I know myself to be loved, truly loved, and it's a love that will never fail – I won't be snatched from it; it won't withdraw; it won't turn brutal and sadistic; it won't lie to me. This love pulses beneath everything I am. It is enough. I've finally worked out what my freedom is for – it's to be loved and to love in return, as simple as that.'

Andronicus, Junia, Aquila, and Prisca smiled broadly at her. One of the revelations of Phoebe's life as a follower of Jesus was the sudden ease of loving. It wasn't as though love was absent before. Nor did it mean that certain Christians were easy to love (far from it). It was that together, in community, love was present. Here, for example, with these four strangers, she felt held in an embrace of love. She didn't know them, they didn't know her, but somehow there was love. She remembered something that someone who had passed through Corinth had said. There were so many it was sometimes hard to remember precisely who said what, but someone had told her of something Jesus used to say: 'Wherever two or three are gathered in my name there I am in the midst of them.' Was that what it was? Jesus who was Love was here? She shook her head slightly. She really was getting sentimental and fanciful in her old age.

'But there's something still not right?' Prisca prodded gently.

Phoebe had known Prisca had picked up on something earlier on. This was something else that caused her deep shame. Maybe her new life in Christ was all a sham. Paul had been clear time and time again that, in Christ, the old was left behind so that you could live a new life in Christ. And she had tried so hard to turn her back on everything that had happened, shut it away deep inside, but the prospect of coming to Rome had caused it all to come tumbling out again. She nodded, her face flushing crimson yet again.

Prisca took hold of her hand. 'We aren't criticising you, dear; we just want to help.'

'I know it's stupid. I really couldn't tell Paul. He would be horrified at me. I'm clearly a terrible Christian, but I just couldn't shake off the need to come back. I know I should have left it all behind. It should have died with the old life, but it hasn't. Something has driven me back here. I don't even know why . . .' Her words stuttered and failed, and she looked helplessly at the four kind faces in front of her. The problem was she had ignored this feeling for so long that she hadn't even asked herself why she had really come. Paul had sensed her eagerness to return to Rome, and had, unquestioningly, plied her with tasks to do – she should take the letter to the Romans, take money and prepare for his Spanish mission. She was clever, articulate, and wealthy – she was the perfect person to do it.

The problem was that neither of them – Paul because she didn't tell him, and she because she couldn't admit it even to herself – had any idea of how she would deal with the other reason she had come.

Prisca squeezed her hand – Phoebe had forgotten she was still holding it. 'We'll work it out. Together, we'll work it out. We'll pray, we'll talk, and then we'll work it out, but first we'll eat!'

Chapter 13

Prisca rose and started bustling around the workshop. Phoebe sat back exhausted and felt herself soothed by the hum of activity. She was surprised to notice that the employees who had helped Felix take her belongings upstairs were in the room. How long had they been there? How much had they heard? Aquila noticed her anxious look and read her mind. 'Faustus, Hortensius, come and say hello to Phoebe. I don't think you've been introduced.'

The two burly young men made their way across the room and greeted her shyly. One of them, with impressively wide shoulders and curly black hair, who identified himself as Faustus, said quietly, 'Please let us help with anything you need. We'd love to help, wouldn't we?' This to Hortensius, who eagerly nodded his agreement. 'Ask us to help with *anything*.' The emphasis he placed on the word 'anything' indicated that they had heard her story, but, like the other four, did not appear to think any less of her for it. It seemed that she had gone from not uttering her story to a soul – not even in the depths of her own heart – to telling it to six total strangers.

A slight pressure on her thigh made her look down, and there was Felix curled up next to her, his head resting on her lap. She had no idea how long he had been there. A quick look at his face told her that she had not told her story to six strangers, but to seven, and that it had struck a chord with him. 'Felix,' she began, but he shook his head and buried his face in her lap. Clearly now was not the time to talk, and she was struck by a wave of tenderness. She placed her hand gently on his head and turned to talk to Andronicus, who sat next to her.

'Where's Junia?'

'She's popped out to get us some hot food from the stand at the corner,' he replied.

'You should have let one of us go,' said Aquila. 'If she meets someone to share the Good News with she could be hours.'

'If she's not back in ten minutes I'll go myself,' said Andronicus.

'No,' a chorus of objection bounced around the room, 'you'd just join her.'

'If she's not back in ten minutes, Hortensius will go,' said Prisca. 'He's so shy he doesn't speak to anyone.'

Ten minutes came and went with no sign of Junia, so, as promised, Hortensius went to get hot food. On his return, he reported seeing Junia in deep conversation with a tradeswoman halfway between the workshop and the stand.

'As I passed I heard her telling the woman that God loved her,' he said, looking directly at Phoebe and smiling shyly. 'I think she, like the rest of us, loved what you said about that. It reminded me of something I heard in Paul's letter. What did he say? "Nothing can separate us from the love of God"? Was that it? I didn't understand a lot of what he said, but that made sense to me.'

'Hortensius, you've become quite chatty!' exclaimed Prisca. 'I've barely heard you say so many words together before.'

'Leave the poor boy alone,' said Aquila. 'Who here ever gets a chance to speak with you around? What did the woman say?'

'She said, "Which one?",' chuckled Hortensius. 'I think she was asking which of the gods loved her. She seemed to be quite excited by the idea.'

'Oh dear. I think Junia's going to be a long time,' said Andronicus. 'Let's start eating.'

The evening unfolded happily but gently, with no more intense conversation, and lots of laughter. Junia finally arrived back at the workshop three hours later. The woman she had been speaking to thought that Junia was a prophet, and had hoped that Jupiter was the god who loved her. She was, apparently, voluble (this caused laughter around the room at the thought that Junia had found someone who could out talk her), and talked for hours about the hero she would give birth to once impregnated. The conversation had, to put it mildly, not gone the way Junia hoped, and she returned ruffled and a little put out, though after a while was able to join in the uproarious laughter that her tale evoked, even to the extent that she began to mimic the woman and some of the lewder things she had said.

The evening ended with Phoebe falling into her bed and sleeping soundly and peacefully till dawn.

The next few days passed uneventfully. Various people, whom Phoebe had seen on the first night or met on the second day, dropped by to take her out and about around Rome: with Herodion she saw various synagogues and the places where Jewish Christians gathered to break bread together; with Patrobas she saw numerous Roman or Greek shrines and temples; Aristobulus's steward, Blaesus, took her to see the magnificent Roman forum where so much politics played out; Felix was her indefatigable shadow, and, when she was not being shown other sights, he would guide her to see a beautiful building or the activity down at the harbour of the River Tiber. In all these visits, no one mentioned Paul's letter, what it might have meant, or whether it made them angry or not. She got the feeling that they had been firmly instructed (she could hear Prisca doing it in her imagination) to give her a break. Half of her felt pleased; the other half, knowing the questions would come again, wanted to face whatever was thrown at her. Nevertheless, her companions quietly and courteously avoided any serious issues and instead dedicated themselves to entertaining her and making her feel welcome.

It came as a great relief that none of them took her to the area where Titus and Quintus had lived; that might have proved challenging to her emotions, which still felt somewhat raw and bruised after telling the story that had remained untold for so many years. And that was the only part of Rome Phoebe had known then. She had been a slave, after all. Even pampered slaves are not often taken to see other parts of Rome, so these few days were a revelation. Rome was a city of contrasts – magnificent architecture and crumbling tenements; immense wealth and gripping poverty; dreams and despair; life and death. The size of the city made the contrasts more vivid, and Phoebe found her senses assaulted with the variety of it all.

Eventually the week passed and the first day of the next week approached. Prisca suggested to Phoebe that this week she should break bread and commemorate the Lord's death with the believers who met in their workshop with them, but in future weeks perhaps she would like to visit the many other small groups that met elsewhere. Many of them were in Transtiberium, where Prisca and Aquila lived too; it wouldn't take long for her to get there. She readily agreed. In Corinth, the different communities had all worshipped on the first day in slightly different ways, and she was interested to see whether the same would be true in Rome. She suspected it would be. She couldn't imagine that the deeply Jewish Herodion worshipped in the same way that Patrobas did.

In many ways, the meeting at Prisca and Aquila's house was very familiar to Phoebe – they read Scripture together, they remembered the Lord's death, they prayed, and, of course, they talked about Paul's letter – extensively. Although many of the ideas, like dying and rising with Christ, had been very familiar to Phoebe, they were entirely new to some of the people there, and needed careful explaining. Phoebe found herself, alongside Prisca and Aquila, enjoying describing Paul's view of humanity, based on the Jewish Scriptures: how he saw them all as descendants of Adam, and therefore locked into Adam's way of being (a way marked by sin and rebellion against God) and helpless to live any other way. The only escape from being like Adam was death – a death that would come to them all in the end, but was somewhat final. Jesus Christ offered a new way of being. He had died and risen on behalf of them all, and everyone who believed in him could join him in dying to their old way of life and rising to new life. They were freed from sin and freed for new life in Christ. This new life was shaped by Christ himself, and they were called to be transformed into his likeness.

Phoebe found, as she looked around the people gathered there, the usual range of expressions on people's faces. Some were animated, excited by the ideas that they were talking about; some puzzled, struggling to get their heads around Paul's very particular view of human beings, a view that was alien to them; and some were entirely uninterested, and kept asking loudly why they had to talk about that boring old letter – couldn't they have a story about Jesus instead? In the end, for them, Prisca relented and told them a parable by Jesus – one Phoebe had never heard before. It involved a rich man and a poor man called Lazarus. Paul's companion Luke had told it to her once, she explained.

The biggest difference that Phoebe noticed between what had happened back in Corinth and what happened here was the quiet. Worship in Corinth was a riotous affair. It was noisy, with people speaking in tongues, people prophesying (sometimes over each other), songs would break out at any moment – even when they were in the middle of remembering the Lord's Supper. It was vibrant, full of life, always unexpected, and often uncontrollable. Paul had tried to impose some order on them all, but only with varying success. This was completely different. People waited for one person to finish before they began. There would even be long periods of silence while people thought or prayed before they spoke again. It was very new to her, and Phoebe couldn't yet decide if she liked it or not. They even finished relatively early. In Corinth, the meetings went on long into the night as the Spirit directed; here Prisca called a halt after a couple of hours, explaining that many people had to begin work at dawn and needed to return home to sleep.

Slightly bemused, Phoebe asked Prisca whether the Spirit didn't fall on these meetings as had happened in Corinth. Prisca smiled at her.

'It can be hard for Corinthians when they worship with us here. It's not the same, is it? The Spirit is fully present, but in a different way. Have you ever heard Paul talk about the fruit of the Spirit?'

'Yes,' said Phoebe, 'love, joy, peace, patience, kindness, generosity, faithfulness, gentleness, and ... oh, there was another one as well. I can't remember what it was.'

Prisca laughed. 'You're missing self-control. I don't imagine that was all that popular in Corinth? Sometimes their gatherings are distinctly lacking in self-control.'

Phoebe felt herself bristling at this, as the Corinthians were, after all, her family in God. Prisca's light-hearted poking of fun at the Corinthians made her want to leap to defend them. Even as she opened her mouth to speak, however, she realised that it would be hard to mount much of a defence. Her Corinthian family loved excess in every way. Some of them had even claimed that they had been raised from the dead already. If it was possible to go 'too far', there was always someone who would go there. She took a breath and decided not to challenge Prisca after all, and in any case Prisca had carried on talking: 'Think about this evening. Did you notice the fruit of the Spirit?'

Phoebe had to admit that she had seen a lot of evidence of it in the gathering.

Prisca said, 'When we lived in Ephesus, I used to spend time with John, the apostle. You should meet him one day. He is inspirational. He spends his days reflecting on everything he learnt from Jesus. I told him he should write it all down. Maybe he will one day. One of the things he told me was Jesus used to say that the Spirit blows where it wills. The Spirit is as the Spirit is. You can't control it. The Spirit falling on you in Corinth had certain characteristics. The fact that they are missing here doesn't mean the Spirit is absent, just that it works in us in a different way. You just need to look for its work.'

Phoebe wrinkled her forehead. 'But how will I know what that looks like if it looks so different?'

Prisca laughed again. Phoebe thought she must spend much of her life laughing – the lines around her eyes certainly suggested so. 'The Spirit brings life. God's Spirit brought life at creation; God breathes his Spirit into every human being; the Spirit certainly brought life in Corinth. Look for life bubbling up around you, then you'll see the Spirit's work. When you know what you're looking for, it's easy to see. You just have to look. You know you said a few days ago when you were telling us your story that something had driven you back here?'

Phoebe nodded.

'Could it have been the Spirit?'

'I don't think so,' Phoebe said slowly. 'There's no life in that story I told you.'

'That's my point,' Prisca insisted. 'Maybe the Spirit is driving you to find fullness of life in an area that has brought so much death for you. Now we really must retire for the night – you've all got lots to do tomorrow.'

'Have I?' asked Phoebe.

'There's something Paul sent you to do. Perhaps you should begin? I'll send Felix to wake you at dawn.' And with that Prisca left Phoebe with lots to think about. So much in fact that it felt like only a few minutes after she had drifted off that Felix was gently patting her hand to wake her up.

'Phoebe, Phoebe . . . Felix and Phoebe have jobs to do, *come on!*'

Chapter 14

It took her a while to emerge from sleep, but when she had, and had dressed and come down to the workshop, Phoebe found a dozen or so people gathered quietly together. She looked around them, a little startled.

'We like to gather together in the morning to pray,' said Aquila.

'Why didn't you tell me before?' Phoebe guiltily thought of all the mornings in the previous week when she had slept well past dawn and breakfast time.

'We thought you needed the sleep,' said Prisca, 'but today you have so much to do we thought some time spent in the presence of Jesus would be time well spent. Come,' she gestured to a space.

Phoebe settled into it with slight hesitation. The community in Corinth hadn't had gatherings like this in the morning – or at least not that she had been aware of – and she wasn't at all sure what to expect. She needn't have worried.

It was very simple. They talked, read a psalm, and prayed for all those they knew. Phoebe found herself relaxing, and before long felt enfolded in a strong sense of peace, bound together with the others around her. In fact, she had to own up to a sense of disappointment when, what felt like a few moments later, the gathering scattered. She didn't have long to think about it, however, because no sooner had they departed than Felix stood before her, his eyes bright with excitement.

'Today,' he declared, 'Felix and Phoebe make preparations for Paul.'

Phoebe: A Story

On a number of occasions during that particularly hectic day, Phoebe found herself remembering and being grateful for that early haven of peace, as Felix hurried her from place to place – from the harbour to the market; from one workshop to another. She had no idea what they were doing, and when asked, Felix responded with relish, 'Finding out!'

As evening fell she found herself to be dizzy with the sights, sounds, and experiences of the day, and sank gratefully into a seat in Prisca and Aquila's workshop.

Aquila chuckled as he looked at Phoebe's weary face. 'I see you've been Felix-ed.'

Phoebe looked at him with incomprehension.

'It's happened to us all,' he smiled. 'Felix is a bundle of determination and energy, and forgets we aren't all as young and vigorous as he is. Do you know what you need now?'

'No,' said Phoebe. 'After today I have even less idea of what I'm doing than I had before. I've no real idea of what it is that Paul *does* need. I never really thought it through. I had other things on my mind, as you know.' She looked tentatively at Aquila for assurance that he knew what she meant. He nodded and patted her hand. 'And in any case, I assumed that Paul would come and take over, and so it wouldn't matter.'

'He'll do that, have no doubt,' said Prisca tartly as she crossed the workshop to join their conversation. 'Paul has never been one to tread lightly around the feelings of others, especially when they've gone out of their way to make the best arrangements they can.'

'One of these days you will have to let that go,' said Aquila.

'Maybe one of these days I will,' said Prisca archly, 'but this day I'm still cross, and will say so if I like.'

'What did he do?' asked Phoebe, intrigued.

'You had to ask,' Aquila said, rolling his eyes in mock desperation, before getting up and beating a retreat to the other side of the workshop.

Prisca took a deep breath, sat down next to Phoebe, and in laborious detail told Phoebe of the time when they had just left Corinth. From Corinth, they had travelled to Ephesus, and, on Paul's instructions, Prisca had spent a long time finding the three of them the perfect workshop. It was large, spacious, and on the major route into the city. It hadn't been easy to find, but it was perfect both for tent-making and for being a space in which to gather, pray, and worship. It was just what they all needed. Paul had been in the synagogue all day talking with the Jews there. In the evening, he caught up with them in the new workshop, took one look at it, and declared that he was called onwards to Antioch and Caesarea. Just like that. No thank you. No explanation. Just the simple statement that he was moving on. He went the next day, and they'd not seen him since. Prisca's story took a long time to tell, punctuated as it was with expressions of outrage and hurt. From time to time Aquila attempted to break in, Phoebe assumed to tell Paul's side of the story, but each time, with a wave of a hand or turn of the head, Prisca brushed off his attempts to interject.

'But I thought you loved Paul?' said Phoebe. 'You defended him to Herodion when I first arrived.'

'Of course I do,' said Prisca. 'Loving him and being irritated with him are two completely different things. All I'm saying is that Paul will do what Paul will do. He will change every single one of your plans if he feels called to do something else. It shouldn't stop you making the plans. You just need to know that he will not take account of your *feelings* when he decides what to do.'

'Why would he?' Aquila exploded with irritation. 'He is proclaiming the Gospel, not hanging around waiting to make you feel better.'

'I know that. I simply fail to see why his calling has to make him so insensible to the feelings of those around him.'

It was clear that this was a well-worn argument between them and that each of them was saying, again, what had been said many times before. Aquila looked as though he was about to speak again, so Phoebe jumped in. It was unlikely that rehearsing it one more time was going to change how either of them felt.

'I know I need to get started. I honestly don't mind if Paul changes it all, but I promised him I'd make plans, so plans I will make. I just don't know where to start.' It was true, she didn't. The day of hurrying from place to place with Felix had only compounded her feeling that this task was beyond her. They had gone to many places and visited many people, but she now felt less clear than ever about what they needed to do.

'What you need,' said Prisca, returning apparently effortlessly to her usual good mood, 'is Stachys. Do you think he'd be free?'

'That would depend on whether he's still making copies of Paul's letter,' Aquila said. 'Let's find out. Now where's Felix?'

'Felix is here!' A small shadow emerged from one of the corners of the room, and Phoebe made yet another mental note of his miraculous ability to lurk unnoticed in corners. It was a skill learnt by many slaves, and she would need to be careful to remember that it was always possible he was listening in, an unseen but ever vigilant shadow.

'Would you go to Stachys' shop and find out if he has time to come and help?'

Felix's face fell. 'Felix is helping. Felix does not need Stachys.'

Phoebe's heart went out to him. He was giving his love in the only way he knew how – by helping. He clearly felt that the suggestion of the need for someone's help was a rejection of the precious gift he was offering. She reached to put her arm around him, but he bristled and pulled away. She found herself wondering yet again what it was that could have happened to give him such a tough shell alongside such self-doubt. She feared that she could guess. Her own story revealed how precarious the life of a slave could be. She shuddered at the thought of what could have happened to turn Felix into this bundle of prickly insecurity. She reached out again, but this time just with words.

'Felix, dear Felix. I can't do it without you. Without you it would all be impossible, but I need extra help to get it done right.' Felix's stiff little body relaxed somewhat at this, and he looked at Phoebe, Aquila, and Prisca with such vulnerability that Phoebe felt like crying. 'I can't do it without you,' she said again, feeling frustrated that she couldn't think of a better way of saying it, 'but I think I might need Stachys' help too.'

Felix hesitated, but then straightened himself up. 'Felix will make him come!'

'No, no, that's not what we meant,' said Prisca, slightly horrified. 'You can't just summon him. Stachys is one of the best scribes in Transtiberium. People wait for months for his services. We can't just command him and expect him to come. We ask tentatively, respectfully, and wait patiently for him to fit us in.' Her speech, however, fell not so much on deaf ears as on no ears at all, since Felix was halfway down the street running as fast as his legs would carry him.

In very little time at all Felix was back, panting in such a way that indicated he had run there and back at full pelt. There was no sign at all of Stachys, or anyone else, and Phoebe looked anxiously at Prisca and Aquila, assuming that Stachys had been so outraged at the summons that he had refused to come.

Felix must have seen the look, and announced proudly, 'Stachys is coming. He is gathering some useless stuff and will be here soon.' His tone of voice communicated disdain for the slow workings of adults, who not only did not run from place to place, but felt the need to bring additional equipment too.

Before long Stachys arrived, a bag over his shoulder containing a scribe's essential equipment, and an eager look on his face. He cut short the stream of apology from Prisca and Aquila for his peremptory summons.

'Felix was quite right,' he said, and, turning now to Phoebe, 'Paul asked us to help you, so here I am ready to lend any assistance I can.'

'What about the copies of Paul's letter?' asked Prisca.

'Finished days ago,' said Stachys, 'and successfully sent to all the gatherings in Rome. Even Herodion accepted one, after a little persuasion.' As he said this, his features appeared to melt before their gaze, reforming in an uncanny imitation of Herodion's face, riven with outrage and disdain.

'And your other clients?' said Aquila.

'They can wait.' This was said with the confidence of a master craftsman who knew that his skill would always outweigh the irritation of any clients who were forced to wait to receive his services.

Phoebe wondered at this. She couldn't work out what a scribe could possibly do that would lend Stachys such a confidence in himself. Even the most skilled scribes of her acquaintance, those who could be given the merest brief outline of the content for a letter and turn it into a polished, rhetorical masterpiece, wouldn't warrant this level of confidence.

She soon found out.

Before being given his freedom, Stachys had been the slave of a prominent Roman general who had successfully fought in many campaigns. Stachys had organised them, buying provisions, identifying routes, and even occasionally arguing a military strategy. As well as all of this, he had mastered the 4,000 characters of Tironian shorthand, and could even write at the same speed that the voluble Prisca could talk. He was nothing short of a genius. All of this he could do while acutely observing and mimicking the facial expressions and mannerisms of those around him with such accuracy that Phoebe found herself, somewhat guiltily, helpless with laughter. Under Stachys' skilful but humorous touch, the impossibly large job of organising Paul's trip to Spain became, if not easy, then certainly achievable.

Chapter 15

The next three weeks sped by in a haze of activity. After a morning's discussion with Phoebe, Stachys had begun to work out what Paul would need for his trip to Spain. By the end of that day he had produced a long list of what might be required. This he organised into sub-lists of priority and importance, and, before long, Felix had been sent off on a string of errands that kept even his effervescence fully employed from morning until night. From time to time, the willing Faustus and Hortensius were permitted by a reluctant Felix to help, but normally only if an object was twice his size and impossible for him to move alone.

Phoebe was kept fully employed too, but in the workshop. Day after day, Stachys interrogated her about what Paul had in mind: where he wanted to go, when he wanted to set off, what he wanted to achieve, and how quickly. The primary effect of these questions was to force Phoebe to acknowledge her over-whelming naivety in setting off on such a big venture without having much of a clear sense of what was in Paul's mind. If she was honest, she had barely thought about it. She had felt drawn to Rome by a sense of unfinished business. Bringing the letter and preparing the Spanish trip for Paul had been a handy excuse. Stachys' military precision brought home to her how little she knew about the trip she had supposedly come to prepare for.

However, his supreme efficiency, coupled with a wicked ability to mimic the facial expressions and mannerisms of everyone they knew, met or passed in the street, kept her in equal measure reassured and in stitches of laughter. This combination was effective in keeping her anxiety and introspection at bay, though she suspected that this was also partly due to having unburdened herself of her shameful story, and to the prayers she shared with Prisca, Aquila, and the others each morning. Every so often, when she had time to think about it, she noted with a mild twinge that neither Prisca and Aquila (whom she saw all day, every day) nor Junia and Andronicus (whom she saw a lot, but more sporadically) had mentioned her story again. Maybe they had found it dull? Maybe they had just humoured her desire to unburden herself? Maybe they were so horrified they couldn't bring themselves to mention it? Her overactive imagination constructed ever worse explanations for their silence on the subject; so it was good that she was busy, since this limited the number and extent of the scenarios she could envisage.

The more she worked with Stachys, the more she marvelled at his ability to break down, understand, and organise the details of the trip into small achievable tasks. He produced list after list that enumerated exactly what was needed and when. There was even a list of his lists. Phoebe knew that she would never have had the patience nor the eye for detail to achieve what Stachys could.

Over those three weeks she learnt a little more about Stachys' story. He had been a slave for far longer than many slaves because he was so good at his role. He had amassed quite a fortune from tips given to him by grateful suppliers and soldiers, but this had also worked against him. He was so good at what he did that his master had been reluctant to give him his freedom, even though he had saved four times the amount of money that a slave would normally need to buy freedom. Eventually, his master had relented – Stachys suspected under pressure from his colleagues, who had noticed that Stachys had remained a slave far longer than he ought to have done – and had given him his freedom, begging him to stay on and continue to work for him. But Stachys had had enough, and turned his back on the constant travel to ever further flung parts of the empire to settle in Rome and open a business as a scribe.

As Phoebe watched Stachys work, she began to appreciate the depth and breadth of his gift, and remembered, to her shame, scoffing at something Paul had said to the church in Corinth. He had argued that God gave gifts to the church, and has given a list of those gifts. He had put the gift of helping alongside the gift of healing. She had laughed when she had heard it, wanting to know who would admit to having gifts of helping, when others could teach, prophesy or heal. Seeing Stachys' supreme abilities in this area she accepted that she had been quite wrong. 'Helping' may not have been glamorous, but there was no doubt that it was a valuable gift, and one that had been bestowed on Stachys in abundance.

In three short weeks, Stachys and Felix between them had procured almost everything they needed: from the promise of a passage to Spain, to the supplies that Paul would need for the trip. Stachys had even managed to get hold of a dog-eared but much prized sketch of the land that would provide Paul with some directions of what routes to take. Only two things were outstanding – someone who knew the land and its language, and Paul himself. The problem with the first was that there were no Christians currently in Rome who had been to Spain (she knew because she had been and spoken to them all). She was beginning to think that Paul would have to settle for some-one who spoke Latin but had never been to Spain, but Paul didn't settle easily for anything, and she knew that she had to wait for him to arrive to make that decision for himself.

So it was that after three weeks of focused, slightly frantic activity, Stachys, Felix, and Phoebe looked at each other and at the large pile of supplies that was taking up a good amount of space in Prisca and Aquila's workshop (something that Aquila bore with his usual, slightly sardonic good humour, and that Prisca bore with far less good grace) and declared themselves ready – or as ready as they could be in the absence of Paul. All they had to do now was to wait for him to come, then they could hand over all the plans and return to life as it had been.

Phoebe had been so busy – and so content in her busyness – that she had completely forgotten (or so she told herself) that she had come to Rome for anything other than these preparations. Her initial hurt at the silence from Prisca, Aquila, Junia, and Andronicus on the subject of her story had faded, and she decided that the best thing to do was to make plans to return home to Cenchreae with a job well done. Whenever she was honest enough to listen to herself, she was aware that the itch that had brought her to Rome in the first place remained unscratched, but whenever this thought arose, she quickly squashed it. Surely having had the courage to tell her story at all was such an achievement that she could be allowed to rest now, return home to how things were before? All they needed was for Paul to arrive.

After a while, Phoebe began to wonder what had happened to him. He was such a prolific letter writer that she had more than half expected a letter to follow soon after her, reminding her what she needed to do for him. His personal letters were often like a brisk walk on a windy day. In his public letters, Paul often drew on his rhetorical training, using structure and elegant language to argue his points. These letters might reveal his irritations, but they were carefully and stylishly constructed. In his personal letters he often forgot all niceties, getting to the point quickly, and ramming it home as hard as he could. Phoebe had been braced for such a letter, but nothing had come. As she acknowledged the oddity of this silence, a small chill of fear crept its way up her spine, making the hairs on her neck stand upright like the hairs on the back of a cornered cat. She took herself quickly in hand. She really did have the most ridiculous way of expecting the worst. Paul *was* coming. He was just delayed. The fact that he hadn't written meant nothing at all. All they had to do was wait.

She told herself this through the whole of the following week. She repeated it for the next three weeks to Felix, Stachys, Aquila, Prisca, Junia, and Andronicus. Then for the next three months to the rest of her friends in Rome, including Herodion and Patrobas, of whom she had become very fond, even as they continued their regular arguments about Jews and Gentiles. Eventually, however, even she had to admit that something was wrong, and that Paul was more than just a little delayed. She had no idea where Paul was.

Even as she admitted this, a letter came from Paul's sister in Caesarea. The news of its arrival spread quickly among Phoebe's new friends in Rome, and before long a familiar crowd of Christians from many different backgrounds was crammed into Prisca and Aquila's workshop to hear the news. Stachys was there, and, as so often, took on the role of reader.

In the letter, Paul's sister explained what had happened. After parting from Phoebe in Corinth, Paul had travelled onwards to Jerusalem, eager to give the Christians there the money he had collected for them. On the way, he had received prophecy after prophecy that when he arrived he would suffer in prison. Paul's companions became more and more worried about what would happen. When Agabus, the prophet, travelled from Judea to meet them in Caesarea and to prophesy that Paul would be imprisoned by the Jews in Jerusalem, they became so concerned that they begged him not to go on. But Paul refused to be dissuaded (Phoebe noticed Prisca rolling her eyes at this), and continued onwards to Jerusalem.

After meeting James and the other Christians in Jerusalem, Paul went at their request to the temple to be purified. James had been worried about whether Paul would be accepted in Jerusalem – given both his reputation and the fact that he had lived for so long outside of Judea – and had come up with the plan of Paul undergoing public purification in the temple (alongside four Nazirites) to reassure the Jews that there was nothing to fear from him. James's plan had backfired spectacularly. Rather than reassuring the Jews of anything, it placed Paul in full view of all those whom he had so alienated over the years.

The Jews from Asia – places as far afield as Ephesus and his hometown of Tarsus – egged on by Paul's former fellow Pharisees, whipped up a willing mob, citing the trumped-up charge that Paul had taken a Gentile into the court of the women. Paul's sister claimed that Paul had not taken Trophimus from Ephesus into the temple – never had and never would.

Prisca broke in at this point. 'And I'd believe him. Do you remember Trophimus, Aquila?'

'Not sure I do.'

'Quiet man, a silver worker. Lived in the centre of the city. His sister was baptised while we were there. She was married to . . .'

'Do we really need to rehearse his whole family tree?' asked Herodion with irritation.

Prisca subsided, clearly annoyed, 'My point, ably illustrated by my husband, who can't remember him, is that Trophimus is a retiring, self-effacing man who would never knowingly seek out trouble.'

'Shall I go on?' asked Stachys.

Prisca nodded her head.

'The mob became angrier, and more and more violent, and were intent on ripping Paul limb from limb.'

A gasp went around the room at this news, and Phoebe felt herself go weak at the knees. Her voice trembled as she asked the question on everyone's lips.

'Is he dead?'

Stachys shook his head. 'I don't think so, but let me read on and we'll find out what did happen.'

Stachys read on and it soon became clear that Paul was far from dead. He had been rescued from the crowd by a cohort of Roman soldiers, had claimed Roman citizenship, and was being protected from the irate crowd by the Romans themselves.

'Well,' came Andronicus's voice from the corner of the room, 'I never expected to receive the good news that Paul was saved by the Romans by being put in prison.' He shook his head in mock bemusement. 'I've heard it all now.'

'I don't think you have,' said Stachys. 'It gets worse.' He continued the tale.

Forty Jews had, apparently, made a pact not to eat or drink until they had killed Paul. Their plan was to ambush Paul as he was led down to the council, and to kill him. But his nephew Jacob (the son of Paul's sister) had overheard the plan and reported it to Paul, who, in turn, sent Jacob to the Tribune. When the Tribune heard this, he sent Paul, under cover of darkness, to Felix, the governor who was staying in Antipatris.

As the assembled gathering tried to take in this information, an uneasy silence fell on the room.

A silence that was eventually broken by Prisca. 'I've known Paul for years, and he never mentioned that he had a sister.'

Chapter 16

'You didn't know Paul had a sister?' Aquila rounded on his wife. 'After everything we've just heard, do you really think that the most helpful comment to make was that you didn't know Paul had a sister?'

Phoebe could have sworn she saw Prisca give Aquila the merest hint of a wink. A moment later she was confident that she had been right. Aquila suddenly relaxed, chuckled, and said, 'Now you mention it, I didn't know he had a sister either. Did anyone else?'

Over the past few months Phoebe had learnt to trust Prisca's instincts. What she seemed to be doing here was diverting attention from the frankly catastrophic news in the letter from Paul's sister. Lightening the mood might mean that they could discuss it with less immediate, emotional charge.

Help came her way in the unlikely form of Herodion.

'I did. I met her in Jerusalem once. She is remarkable. Clever, quick-witted, and very, very funny. Her name is Miriam.'

'I could have told you that,' said Stachys, waving the letter above his head, apparently a little disgruntled that his role as bringer of news had been usurped.

'Do she and Paul share many family characteristics?' asked Aquila, his eyes twinkling with mischief.

'She writes shorter and less complex letters,' observed Stachys.

'No idea,' said Herodion. 'As you know, I've never met Paul.' He sniffed with satisfaction as though he intended to keep it this way.

'I think,' Prisca said, 'that my mischievous husband is asking whether Miriam looks like her brother.'

'I put it more elegantly than that,' said Aquila.

'But you meant it nevertheless.'

'What is wrong with you?' burst out Junia, who had been sitting in the corner of the room, precariously balanced on some of the provisions gathered by Stachys, Phoebe, and Felix a few months before. 'We have just heard that Paul – like Jesus before him – has been imprisoned by the Romans, with a crowd baying for his blood, and all you can talk about is whether Paul's sister has eyebrows and a nose like her brother or not.'

Andronicus put his hand on her arm. 'It's all right, dear one. Prisca and Aquila care as much as you do; they were simply trying to distract us all for a moment.'

'It was in poor taste. Totally insensitive. Can't believe you're defending them . . .' Junia grumbled away, her voice getting fainter and fainter, though it was quite clear that she had plenty more to say, and continued saying it, if only to herself.

'What I'd like to know is what we are going to do now,' said Stachys. 'We've made all these plans – were they all for nothing?'

'Well, there is no point in carrying on without Paul,' said Blaesus, Aristobulus's steward, who stood propping up the wall on the far side of the room.

'Can we return everything?' This was from Faustus, Prisca and Aquila's servant, who, with Hortensius, had brought the bulkier items to the workshop.

'I suppose we could try,' said Stachys hesitantly. 'Or failing that, sell them on to someone else.'

'Such a shame,' said Andronicus. 'Taking the Good News to Spain was so important, and Paul was so passionate about it.'

A buzz of conversation began around the room at that point, from which phrases here and there floated over to where Phoebe was sitting. 'I always wish I'd met him'; 'those churches in

Phoebe: A Story

Greece and Asia Minor will feel his loss'; 'totally his own fault; he's only himself to blame'; 'I didn't agree with him, but he was quite something, wasn't he?' On and on the voices went.

Phoebe, already feeling a little sick at the knowledge that whatever plans they had made were now in severe jeopardy, could contain herself no longer. 'Stop!' she shouted. 'Just stop!'

Everyone fell silent and turned to look at her. She noticed that, whereas a few months ago this would have caused her to blush and feel awkward, now, if anything, she grew in stature.

'He isn't dead,' she said.

'Yet,' Herodion said.

'My brother is right,' said Patrobas (Phoebe thought wryly that only news as bad as this could unite these two). 'He might as well be. We all know what happens in Jerusalem when the Jews want someone dead. The Romans will give them what they want. They're too frightened of riots to do otherwise.'

'Not Jews, brother – mobs.' Herodion rose to stand beside him. 'No good will come of it if you Gentiles start lumping all of us Jews together and blame us for Jesus' death. The real culprit was the mob. Something happens when crowds are stirred up. Normally sensible people lose all track of who they are, and bay for blood. What happened with Jesus has happened with Paul. The mob has been let loose, and there can only be one outcome.'

Patrobas inclined his head in acceptance of what Herodion had just said. They may be sparring partners, but, Phoebe had come to see, they held each other in great respect – possibly even affection. It was almost as though they each needed the other to give them a real sense of who they were.

Patrobas said gently, 'The rest of what I said still holds. The Romans *are* terrified of mob riot, and Paul *is* as good as dead. We might as well accept that now.'

Phoebe bristled. 'I don't need to accept anything. What happened once is not what happens every time. If I have learnt

109

anything, it is the importance of hope. The world we live in always tells us to give in, to accept that evil always wins, that despair and darkness is all there will ever be. But it's wrong. Don't we know that God is greater than all of this? That love never ends? That nothing can separate us from that love?' She turned to Patrobas. 'You can accept that Paul is as good as dead if you like, but I will hope. I will light my candle in the darkness and refuse to give in. And even if he does die, I will still hope and trust in the God of love and of life. I don't know what is going to happen, but I do know that giving in is not the answer.'

Aquila started to snap his finger and thumb together by way of applause, and bit by bit the whole room joined in.

'I've never seen you so passionate, Phoebe,' he said.

Phoebe laughed, a little self-conscious now the fire had faded somewhat. 'Neither have I. I'm not quite sure where that came from.'

'We are,' said Prisca. 'From the heart and . . . from somewhere else too.'

'Where?' Voices all around the room asked the same question.

'The Holy Spirit,' Prisca replied matter-of-factly, as though she had just told a customer they made their tents out of goat skins. 'We were on the brink of giving up, and we needed reminding of who we are and what we believe in. The Holy Spirit intervened at just the right moment.

'What we need to do now,' she looked around the room, 'is to pray. We don't give up. We don't lose heart. We pray.'

'So we just pray, and God frees Paul, and he comes to Rome tomorrow?' The cynical voice of someone Phoebe had not met before brought them up sharp.

'Of course not,' said Prisca, 'but just a moment ago you had given up. I do think that praying would be very much more useful than sitting around the room declaring Paul to be dead before his time. What I'm suggesting is that with the Holy Spirit the most surprising, delightful things can happen. Prayer isn't like giving in your order for hot food: submitted one moment and delivered the next. But prayer does place us in God's presence. Prayer opens us up to see what God is already doing. Prayer invites God to be present at the heart of what we're worried about. Sometimes,' she continued looking pensive, 'I think that although God could do it anyway, He really does like us to ask.'

'What if we're not sure what to ask?' asked the quiet-voiced Hortensius.

'I liked that bit in Paul's letter,' said Phoebe, 'about the Spirit.'

' "When we do not know how to pray as we ought",' joined in Stachys ' "the Spirit intercedes with sighs too deep for words." Yes, I liked that too. We can let the Spirit ask for us.'

And with that the whole room began to pray: some out loud; some in silence; some in languages Phoebe recognised; others in languages she had never heard before. Of course, nothing happened. Or nothing that any of them in that room could see. What shifted was their own spirits. There was a discernible mood of hope, where before there had been only despair. They carried on praying for Paul, day after day, week after week, month after month.

Tiny snippets of information made their way to Rome. Paul was not dead. He had not been lynched by the mob. The pact to kill him had failed and was not revived. Phoebe couldn't really work out if it was an answer to prayer or not. It certainly wasn't an answer to her prayer. Her prayer was clear and simple. Paul should be freed and arrive safely in Rome ready to undertake the Spanish mission that they had agreed upon and prepared for. Nevertheless, the hope she had evoked in her passionate speech in Prisca and Aquila's workshop continued to flicker and burn. No one had any idea what was going to happen, but they never even got close to the despair that had overwhelmed them all when they had first received Miriam's letter.

As weeks slipped into months, Phoebe felt as though she had lived in Rome for ever. She had accepted Prisca and Aquila's invitation to stay above their workshop with them, and now often made herself useful. She was happy now to talk to a wide range of people, and discovered that she was quite good at helping new customers work out what they needed so that Prisca and Aquila could concentrate on making the tents. She also aided Stachys with his business. He had far too many clients and she helped him identify and train new scribes to take on some of the simpler tasks. To Phoebe's great joy, one of these new scribes was Felix, who picked up the skills of reading and writing with incredible speed, and demonstrated himself to be highly adept at some aspects of the scribal role (so long as he could run errands regularly – his legs wouldn't stay still for long). From time to time she even dropped by Aristobulus's elegant house, especially when Blaesus was tasked with organising a large feast, and used her skills, learnt as a slave with Chrestus, to smooth the preparations.

She also oversaw the distribution of food to the widows and orphans – as she had in Corinth – carefully ensuring that no one received less than their fair share. On the first day of the week she visited each of the Christian gatherings in turn, talking with them about Paul's letter, explaining some bits, defending others. Slowly, over time, the pile of provisions for Spain, which she, Stachys, and Felix had worked so hard to collect, began to dwindle. When she enquired after them, Aquila explained gently that they hadn't given up, but they did need the space. They had shared them around the various houses of fellow Christians ready to be gathered again the minute Paul arrived.

Before long Phoebe realised that she had been in Rome for a whole year. She also realised that, comfortable though her new life had become, there was very little purpose to it. She enjoyed helping her new friends but this pattern of living couldn't go on for ever. She also missed Julia, who had been looking after her villa in Cenchreae and her family in Christ in Corinth. She had no clearer idea now than when she had first arrived in Rome, about why she had felt such a need to come, and so began to make quiet enquiries about going home. To her surprise these enquiries took shape far quicker than she had expected. She found passage on a ship leaving in a few weeks' time. She collected together her belongings, and prepared to begin her farewells.

After much thought, she decided that there were various, particular friends that she needed to tell all at once, so she gathered them together in Aristobulus's house one evening. Aristobulus was away again, and Blaesus argued that she had become so vital to the household that she deserved a fine meal in the dining room. There was really only room for nine of them, but Blaesus argued that he never reclined for a meal anyway, so he could count as an extra. She looked around the room at her dear friends – Prisca and Aquila laughing quietly together over something Aquila had just said; Andronicus and Junia bickering gently about something that had happened that day; Stachys and Felix, who were studying a manuscript that Stachys had brought in his bag; Herodion and Patrobas arguing as usual about some matter of doctrine. Blaesus was a little delayed – Phoebe assumed there was a crisis in the kitchen – so she waited for him to join them before she made her announcement.

At last he appeared, and Phoebe signalled for silence.

'Friends, dear brothers and sisters in Christ, I have something I want to tell you . . .' She opened her mouth to continue, but, before she could, Blaesus cut her off.

'It's Titus,' he declared, his usual suave manner lost in the urgency of what he had to impart. 'Titus Cloelius Cordus is back in Rome.'

Chapter 17

The reaction to this news around the room was, unsurprisingly, mixed. Prisca, Aquila, Junia, and Andronicus appeared to be entirely unsurprised by the news, and smiled at Phoebe, their love and support evident on their faces. Blaesus, who had delivered the news, clearly knew it was important, but had no idea why. The others looked blankly around the room. It was Felix who, with his characteristic flair, broke the tension by throwing his arms in the air and announcing with delight, 'Now you can't leave after all!'

Phoebe looked at him, confused. 'I never told you I was leaving. How could you have known?'

'Felix knows everything!' he replied, a glint in his eye indicating that he was far from pleased with her. 'But Felix *was* waiting for Phoebe to tell him.'

'As indeed were we all,' said Aquila.

'You all knew?' Phoebe looked around the room in astonishment.

'"Suspected" would be a better word,' said Stachys, 'and we've all been wondering when you were going to talk to us about it. We are your friends after all.'

'Indeed we are,' said Patrobas, 'and that is why we would like to know why you would care whether Titus Cloelius Cordus was in Rome or not. It feels as though there are other things you haven't told us too.'

With that a hubbub broke out, with lots of questions, exclamations, and general confusion. In the end, Aquila's quiet voice calling for order cut through the uproar with the suggestion that, if Phoebe felt comfortable, she should tell her story for the sake of those who didn't know it yet and that at the end of it Aquila would explain what had happened next.

And so Phoebe did. This time her story came more easily. The feelings of shame and misery, though still present, were less potent than they had been, and the love that she felt within the room bore her up through the more difficult parts of her narrative. She ended her tale as she had before, with the admission that bringing the letter and organising the Spanish mission were not the only reasons she had come, that she had felt drawn to Rome by a sense of unfinished business but, once here, she had realised just how ill-formed her plan had been, and that she had no real idea of what she had hoped to achieve. She also admitted that now Paul's Spanish mission was at best on hold, and that though she loved them all dearly, she felt like a spare part in Rome and had booked her passage home.

Felix bristled with an odd mixture of pride and resentment at this. 'Felix told you she was going,' he announced to the room, and then, with hurt to Phoebe, 'Why didn't you tell us you wanted to go? Felix would have come with you.'

Phoebe realised, with a twinge of guilt, that over the years she had learnt to hide her emotions so well, sometimes even from herself, that it had never even occurred to her to share what she was feeling with these people she purported to love.

'Don't worry, we're not cross with you,' said Junia.

'Felix is,' said Felix.

'Yes, Felix may be, but the rest of us aren't, and we're sorry that we didn't tell you what we had planned after you told us your story the first time. We could see how hurt and bewildered you were. As we talked about it we thought that seeing Titus again might help heal something for you. We didn't say anything, because we didn't want to get your hopes up unnecessarily, but we used our networks in Rome and beyond and found out that Titus had moved to Ephesus. Then, soon after that, we heard that he had made plans to return to Rome. We should have told you then.' Andronicus raised his hands at this, indicating that this was precisely what he had said. 'But,' Junia went on, frowning at him, 'we wanted something firm to tell you. A list of maybes wasn't going to help.'

'Phoebe returning to Corinth before he got back wouldn't have helped either,' said Andronicus.

Aquila cut in quickly, 'Now all is well. Titus is back, Phoebe is here. All we have to do is work out what we do next.'

Phoebe felt her stomach lurch. Her desire to come to Rome had been entirely ill-formed and un-thought through. She hadn't come to Rome to *do* anything about it. She had felt a strong inner pull, and Paul had been so keen for her to take the letter. She had never thought about what would happen if she met Titus again after all these years. She looked around the room desperately, with no idea whatsoever about what to say, or what, even, to think.

It was Stachys who came to her rescue. 'No good plans,' he said, 'can ever be made in a rush. I think Phoebe needs time to think and pray, and, if she wants, to talk about it. Then, when she's ready, she can tell us what she wants to do. No one wants her to look quite as scared as she does right now.' He winked at her, and with his usual skill, allowed his face to dissolve and reform into a look of utter terror and panic.

Phoebe couldn't help but laugh, her laughter tinged with a mixture of gratitude and relief. At that moment, Blaesus began to bring in the food, and the evening unfolded into one of the happiest, most relaxed times Phoebe could ever remember having. As she looked around the room, she wondered how she could have thought that leaving these dear, kind friends would be at all easy. From time to time she caught Felix's eye, and felt herself thoroughly chastised that she had intended to leave without talking to him first. She was aware, yet again, that she had much to learn about healthy, loving friendship, and that it was possible she could learn it best in the company of these people.

The next few days brought a maelstrom of confusion and anxiety to Phoebe. Should she try to see Titus? Or would it be better to leave well alone? Her friends popped around on a regular basis, all eager to help her talk it through, but each time Phoebe found that she simply didn't have the words to communicate what she was feeling. And each failed attempt to articulate her emotions made her feel even guiltier. She couldn't help feeling as though she was letting them down.

In the end it was Stachys who impelled her into action. He sat her down, and, with his usual military precision and lack of emotion, laid out the different scenarios available to her. As he did so, Phoebe began to realise that she had known all along why she had come back to Rome. She just hadn't had the courage to admit it – even to herself. The real reason she had come back was to see Titus again, and – she barely had the courage even to admit to her deepest fantasy – her daughter. She might not have known it at the time, but this was her heart's desire, and it had pulled her back.

As soon as she acknowledged this, she also realised that only one course of action was available to her. She had to go to see Titus. Phoebe knew that what she needed to do was to fall on her knees before him, repent of all her selfishness, and see whether, by any chance, he might be able to forgive her. Then, and only then, she might be able to ask him about her daughter. The thought of having to do this made Phoebe feel sick to her stomach, but the more she thought about it, the more she knew that this was really why she had returned to Rome in the first place. Her instinct had guided her far more surely than her conscious thought had done. Even as she told Prisca this, she knew that Prisca would respond with 'or the Holy Spirit?', and she did. Phoebe hesitated to accept this explanation, as it implied that she had prayed about it far more than, in fact, she had. When she hinted at this to Prisca, Prisca merely shrugged, smiled, and declared that she thought the Holy Spirit needed far less invitation than Phoebe seemed to think.

So it was that early one morning, at the time when clients began to line up outside their patrons' houses, Phoebe and Blaesus set out together for Titus's house. There had been many long arguments about who should go with Phoebe to the house. If everyone had been given their way, then a great crowd of them would have arrived on Titus's doorstep. In the end, Phoebe put her foot down. Blaesus would guide her to the house and leave her there. This was something that Phoebe needed to do for herself, and she needed to do it alone. Having decided to go, Phoebe put all her nervous energy into walking there – so much so that Blaesus had to break into a run from time to time to keep up with her.

Soon the now familiar sights of Transtiberium faded away as they journeyed into the part of Rome dominated by the larger villas owned by the wealthy Patrician families. They turned a corner, and Phoebe stopped stock still, causing Blaesus, who had been hurrying head down to keep up with her, to bump into her. It was nearing twenty-five years since she had last seen Titus's house, but there it stood before her, hardly changed at all from what she remembered. She joined the queue of clients waiting patiently on a bench outside. The queue was short – Phoebe assumed that this was because Titus had only recently returned to Rome. Blaesus, according to their agreement, left her at that point, glancing back anxiously over his shoulder as though hoping for a sign from her that she would like him to stay. Phoebe remained resolute. Much as she would have liked his company, this was something she had to do alone. So she gazed straight ahead, and refused to catch his anxious eye. In what felt like no time at all, the clients were issued into Titus's large and, for Phoebe, achingly familiar house. As she entered the atrium, she stumbled as she caught sight of Titus sitting on the other side of the pool, facing the doorway.

In some ways, he looked almost exactly as she remembered him: his Patrician nose dominated his face; his curly hair, though now completely white, had lost none of its fullness; his gentle brown eyes twinkling with kindness. In other ways, he was transformed. There was something about his bearing that communicated a deep, worn-out sadness. The lines on his face gave him a haggard look. Nevertheless, Phoebe would have known him anywhere, and, recovering from her stumble, she took an involuntary step forward towards him.

The movement – either of the stumble or of the step – caught Titus's attention, and he turned, looking right at her. The moment their eyes met, he paled and rose to his feet, causing his steward and the other slaves to cluster around him as they offered their help.

'Phoebe.' The emotion in his voice barely allowed the word to sound. 'Phoebe, is it really you?'

He lurched towards her. Phoebe realised that the clustering of the slaves was due to the fact that Titus was too frail to walk unaided, and needed the shoulder of a strong young slave boy to lean on in order to get around. Despite that, and breaking all the customs of nobility, Titus rushed as fast as his frail legs allowed towards Phoebe.

Phoebe had come with what she wanted to say prepared. She had spent hours, with the help of Stachys, writing an elegantly worded speech in which she poured out the depth of her regret and shame, but she got no further than her opening words before being enveloped in Titus's embrace. Before long her face was wet with tears, though she couldn't tell whether they originated in her eyes or those of Titus. Soon the rush of energy that had brought Titus to her in such an undignified manner faded, and he needed to be helped back to his seat. Even then he refused to let go of her, and she followed behind, pulled along in his wake. Titus insisted that she sit next to him on his patron's seat, holding both her hands, and gazing at her as though he feared she would disappear if he allowed himself even to blink.

His loyal slaves ushered the bewildered clients from the house, passing out money, food, and wine in a bid to hurry them from the scene. Eventually all was still, and Phoebe could at last begin to say what she had come to say.

Somewhat inevitably the polished words that she had practised for so long with Stachys deserted her when she needed them most. Instead her words of regret and sorrow tumbled out over each other, almost incoherent in emotion. In the end, it didn't matter. Titus stopped her after only a few sentences, refusing to listen to any more.

'No, dear Phoebe, the fault was all mine. I wounded you when Aelia died; failed to protect you from the man I knew Quintus to be. I should have fought harder to get you back. I was weak, self-centred, and thoughtless. You have nothing to be sorry for.'

Phoebe barely heard him. She had lived for so long with her shame and sorrow that his words bounced off her, like arrows from a shield. Perhaps they had left a few cracks behind, however, because she found herself uttering the very thing she had sworn she would not say at all on their first meeting: it was too important, her hope too fragile, she had thought, to blurt out when she had only just met him again. Ever since Chrestus had told her that her baby had not died, a stubborn spark of hope had lodged deep within her heart. No matter how hard she tried to extinguish it – knowing that life was too harsh, too cruel for such hope to be true – still it flickered and burnt. The news that Titus had returned had fanned that spark into a flame. She had become accustomed to living with this hope, and, she had told herself, wasn't yet ready to know for sure what had really happened. Despite her resolve, however, she heard herself saying: 'But you redeemed everything.' She looked up. 'Chrestus told me just before he died. You saved my baby, my daughter.'

No sooner had the words left her mouth than Phoebe wished she could take them straight back; if only she could retreat once more into the comfort of ignorance.

A look of heartbreak and grief flooded Titus's face so swiftly and fully that Phoebe was left in no doubt of the words he would have uttered had emotion allowed him to speak. It was that look that made Phoebe realise with horror something that she had not acknowledged until now: Chrestus's deathbed words had kindled in her a spark of hope; a spark that had flickered into life, and burnt silently, deep within her all these years. The look on Titus's face extinguished this flame once and for all. As Phoebe slid from the seat to the ground, she was forced to admit not only that it had cast its brave flickering light inside her for many years, but that, now it was gone, the darkness it left behind was suffocating.

Chapter 18

Later Phoebe was unable to say how long she had sat on the cold mosaic floor sobbing out her pain, loss, and heartache. It could have been minutes or hours; for all she knew it could have been days. The final snuffing out of her lingering hope broke down the barriers that Phoebe had so carefully constructed around her battered heart, and she wept as though she would never stop.

Eventually, however, she became aware of a light but persistent pressure on her knee. She looked down to see a chubby starfish of a hand of a size that could only belong to a small child. The owner of that hand was crouching down beside her, her head tipped upside down so that she could look upwards into Phoebe's face. She had a mop of auburn curls spinning defiantly in all directions from her tiny head. Her forehead was wrinkled into a solemn look of concern that would have been more appropriate on the face of an elderly steward struggling to balance his master's books.

'Lady sad?' she said. 'Lady cry?' She had a piece of cloth in her hand, and began to pat it ineffectively at Phoebe's face. 'Lady fall over?' she asked. 'Lady hurt?'

'No, Bibi,' came Titus's voice, 'the lady isn't hurt . . . at least not on the outside.'

Phoebe looked up enquiringly.

'Phoebe,' Titus said, as gently as his voice would allow, 'let me introduce you to your granddaughter, little Phoebe.'

'Bibi,' said the child imperiously, 'my name Bibi.'

'Yes,' laughed Titus, 'your name is Bibi, and this lady's name is Phoebe.'

'Not Bibi,' said Bibi, 'Phhhhhhhoebe.' She clearly struggled to say an 'f' sound, and Phoebe was liberally bathed in saliva as the small child tried to form it. She couldn't have cared less. Before her, living and breathing, was a miracle of such glory that even in her most hopeful moments she could not have conceived of its existence. She looked at Titus, her jaw hanging open, struggling even to think of words to say, let alone to form them with her mouth.

'We have quite some catching up to do,' he said.

With help from the household slaves, Titus and Phoebe withdrew into one of the more private rooms at the back of the house, while Bibi was removed by one of the female slaves, her outraged cries ringing around the atrium.

Once alone, Titus and Phoebe looked at each other, neither quite sure where to start.

Titus spoke first. 'Phoebe, I can't begin to tell you how sorry I am for what I did to you—'

Phoebe cut him off. 'You did nothing. It was all Quintus.'

'No, you are kind to think that,' he said, 'but it isn't true. I had power. I could have saved you. I had the power to protect you, and I didn't. I will never forgive myself.'

'But I turned my back on you,' said Phoebe. 'I was seduced by Quintus and his glamour. I wanted to go.'

'But you were so young. How could you have known what it all meant?'

They looked at each other, each of them locked in self-condemnation and regret.

Eventually Phoebe managed to squeeze out the question she needed to ask. 'What happened to her?'

'To Carina?'

'Is that what you called her?'

'Yes,' said Titus. 'It means beloved, and she was. Oh, she was.

'Let me start back at the beginning. When you left the house with Quintus, it was as though I woke up from a dark and bitter dream. Aelia's death had hit me harder than anything had ever done in my life before. The wise old servant Anna – do you remember her? – she had tried to warn me.'

Phoebe did remember her. Being here in this house brought back a flood of memories that she had been sure were lost for ever. Anna had been Aelia's nurse as a child, and had loved her like a mother. Phoebe had always been nervous of her. Anna's devotion to Aelia excluded everything and everyone else. She loved her with a fierce passion, and expected everyone else to do the same.

'Aelia was unwell throughout the whole of the pregnancy. Anna was furious with me. She thought it was all my fault. I suppose it was really. Oddly, it was her fury that prevented me from seeing what was really going on. I blocked it out, and with it any sense of realism of what was happening to Aelia. One day I had every-thing: a beautiful wife, a child of my own on the way, an elegant house; the next I had nothing. And I just couldn't cope.

'Up until then nearly everything had gone my way. I was the pampered only son of a wealthy family; I had a wife I loved and who loved me. Even as a soldier the gods smiled down on me. Everything I did went well. The only sorrow was that we had no child of our own. Then I found you, and felt complete. I loved you as my own. But for Aelia it wasn't enough. Her long-ing for a child gnawed and gnawed away at her, sapping her from within. She was so delighted when she was pregnant, and waved away all of Anna's concerns. She had prayed for this at the Temple of Venus for years and years; had poured more money into their coffers than I dare to contemplate. I couldn't understand it myself, but to Aelia it was everything. I wanted to believe that all would be well. So I did. And when it all came crashing down, I simply didn't know what to do.

'It's no excuse, I know. I was foolish and weak. How I've regretted withdrawing over the years. If I hadn't, perhaps you'd have loved me enough to stay . . .'

His voice trailed off and tears rolled down his cheeks once more. Phoebe was lost for words. It had never occurred to her that what had happened could be said to be anyone's fault but her own. That Titus had spent as much time as she had regretting what had happened was hard to grasp.

'I did love you,' she stuttered. 'But I had been swept along on a wave of glamour. If only I hadn't.'

Titus smiled at her sadly. 'I have uttered that phrase more often over the past twenty-five years than almost any other. But when you left, I woke up. I saw the state the house was in, realised what I'd done to you, and tried to make it right.

'There was an evil in Quintus that I didn't see right away. He was so handsome and glamorous that everyone was drawn to him, but with it came utter ruthlessness. Perhaps it was because he had never been denied anything. Perhaps his lifestyle took him step by step to the edge of destruction. Perhaps the excesses altered his mind. But he was callous, brutal, and selfish. I played right into his hands. I have often wondered whether, if I had feigned indifference, he might have got bored of you sooner, and let you go. But you were so beautiful.' He looked right at her and smiled. 'You still are, and Quintus, sensing my regret, refused to let you go.

'When you moved to his house I was beside myself. I paced up and down outside his house day after day, hoping to find you and bring you home. That was where I met Chrestus. Did he tell you I paid him to look out for you?'

Phoebe stifled a sob and told Titus of the last, disastrous conversation she had had with Chrestus on his deathbed. Titus looked stricken again. 'I ruined your life so much. I have spent all these years mourning what I did to you, and there was so much more that I didn't even know.

'Chrestus kept me well informed. He was so worried about you. Especially when he discovered that you were pregnant. By then we both knew what Quintus was like; we both knew he would kill your baby as soon as it was born. So we made a plan. Chrestus would follow the slave and if necessary bribe him to get the baby. As it happened, that wasn't necessary. The slave was lazy, and put the baby down as soon as he could. Chrestus simply picked her up and brought her to me.

'By then I knew how much I'd let you down, and I was determined to protect little Carina with everything I had. So that very day, I shut up the house and moved far away so that Quintus would never be able to find us, or her, and claim her back. He could have, you know, as your owner, and he was so capricious, I feared that if he ever saw how much I loved her, he would claim her back. So I disappeared from view, and I never saw him or you again. That was the price I felt I had to pay to keep Carina safe.'

Phoebe smiled at him with gratitude. 'It was the best gift you could ever have given me. Was she a happy child?'

Titus grinned, his face suffused with delight. 'She was the happiest, most delightful, clever and talented child that ever lived. Just like you as a child. Our house rang with singing and laughter from morning till night. You would have loved her.'

'I already did,' said Phoebe. 'From the moment I felt her first move, I loved her with every fibre of my being. She was my heart's desire, a desire that took human form and grew in my womb.'

'Little Phoebe – Bibi – is so like her,' Titus said, his eyes filling with tears again.

'What happened?' asked Phoebe.

'We were in Ephesus,' said Titus. 'After a few years of travelling around, I got tired of running and wanted to put roots down. I thought that Ephesus was far enough away from Quintus. I was right. By that stage – so my spies told me – he was so drunk for so much of the time he could barely leave the house, let alone travel to Ephesus. We found a beautiful villa, settled down, and made a home. One day, an old friend of mine from the army passed through Ephesus. He had never met Quintus, so I thought it safe enough to meet him. We ate dinner together. He brought his son Drusus with him. Drusus had just turned fifteen, and by then Carina was old enough to dine with us. I thought nothing of her joining us that evening. What happened was perhaps inevitable. They fell in love. I was careful, so, so careful. After what happened to you I was not about to allow the same thing to happen to Carina, but Drusus was the kindest, gentlest, most thoughtful young man you could ever hope to meet. He was from a noble family. His father was an old friend of mine. I couldn't ask for more. And Carina was so happy, she shone with joy.

'I was probably a little too cautious. I insisted that they wait a few years, give themselves time to grow and get to know each other. After two years, Carina started complaining that she would be an old maid soon. Then I noticed her slipping away, when she thought I wasn't looking. I knew then I would lose her sooner or later if I didn't relent. So I consented, and they wed. They were such a handsome, happy couple, and barely any time had passed before Carina declared that she was with child. Little Phoebe was born, safely and happily. Life was perfect. I relaxed. I should have known better: the gods love nothing more than to turn your life upside down.'

Phoebe opened her mouth to say something at this, but decided that this was not the moment, so she simply smiled at Titus and nodded for him to continue.

'Only a year later a terrible plague swept through the city. So many people died, and with them Carina and Drusus. I was devastated. First I lost Aelia, then you, and now your daughter. To begin with I wanted to turn my face to the wall and die, but Bibi saved me. How could I have left her alone in the world?

'A few months ago I heard that Quintus had at last died. No one knew how. Or at least no one would tell me how. There is a rumour that he died with a bad gambling debt, and that he was found one morning brutally murdered and his house stripped of belongings. But after so many years I have no desire to find out the truth of it all. What did matter was that little Phoebe and I were safe, and could come home. So we did.

'It never crossed my mind that you might be here. I had heard that you and Chrestus had left Rome, but not where you had gone to. I suppose even then Chrestus, like me, feared that Quintus might change his mind, and wanted to leave no trace. I thought about you almost every day, but didn't know what I could do to find you again. I can't believe that it is you! Every moment I fear that I might wake and find you gone.'

Phoebe reached over and kissed his wrinkled cheek. 'It really is me, dear Titus. I promise you I am no dream.'

He smiled. Tears rolling down his cheeks again. 'My old heart can barely stand the joy of seeing you again after so many years. If only my dear Carina could be here too. Then my joy would be complete—' He broke off. 'What on earth is that noise?'

He turned, fear written all over his face revealing the anxiety with which he had lived as he had hidden Carina from Quintus for all those years. The sound of someone pounding loudly on the street door could be heard clearly from their room at the back of the house.

A few moments later, Phoebe heard voices in the atrium, and chuckled. 'No need to fear. I think that my friends have come to find me.'

Chapter 19

A few moments later, the door to the room they were in opened, and there stood Felix, Stachys, and Blaesus, each one in a ferment of anxiety.

'We didn't know what to do,' burst out the usually serene Blaesus. 'You were gone for so long, and we didn't know what to think. We are sorry to disturb you, sir.' Even in the midst of his uneasiness, Blaesus's good manners reasserted themselves in the presence of someone of Titus's status. 'We knew that Phoebe was worried about this visit, and once she had been gone for eight hours, we simply had to find out if she was all right.'

Behind him, Stachys and Felix nodded their heads up and down in synchronised agreement.

Titus's patrician features relaxed into a broad smile. 'I am delighted that Phoebe has such good and caring friends. If only I had been half so caring twenty-five years ago. Come in, sit down, allow me to provide dear Phoebe's friends with refreshments.' He raised a commanding eyebrow, and one of the slaves who had been hovering anxiously in the background scurried away to fulfil his requirements.

At that moment, Bibi, who had clearly escaped from the care of her nurse and was, as a result, very pleased with herself, charged through the open door into the room. She flopped down in the middle of the room, looking from face to face with open curiosity and glee. She lifted a podgy finger and pointed solemnly at Titus.

'Tata,' then on to Phoebe, 'Phhhhhhhoebe.' Next her finger swung to Blaesus. 'Who dis?'

'This is my friend Blaesus,' said Phoebe.

Bibi worked her lips around this new strange word. 'Basus,' she managed. 'Dis?' Her finger had moved now to Stachys.

'Stachys,' said Phoebe.

'Sta—' The rest of the name escaped her, and Bibi clearly felt no need to attempt to complete it. 'Dis?' she finished off the circle with Felix.

'This is Felix.'

'Lix,' nodded Bibi solemnly. Her finger ended pointing at herself. 'Bibi,' she declared.

With that, happy that introductions were complete, she rose to her feet. 'Lix play wiv Bibi,' she asserted.

'No,' said Titus. 'Felix is here as our guest.'

Bibi's chin quivered.

'Felix wants to play with Bibi,' Felix said quickly, clearly as taken with Bibi as she was with him. He took her hand and accompanied her to the garden, from where, in no time at all, squeals and gales of laughter could be heard emanating.

In much less time than it had taken them to unfold it the first time, Phoebe and Titus told Blaesus and Stachys who Bibi was, what had happened to Carina, as well as the rest of their joint story. As they reached the end Blaesus raised his hands.

'God be praised,' he said. 'What was lost has been found.'

Their conversation continued onwards for a few minutes until Phoebe, glancing fondly at her old master, noticed him looking worn and a little grey.

'We must go,' she said. 'We have worn you out.'

Titus grabbed hold of her hand, clinging to it as though he would never let go.

'It is all right,' Phoebe reassured him. 'I'll come again tomorrow.'

'Don't disappear again – I couldn't bear it.'

'I won't.' As she said this, Phoebe knew she had never spoken a truer word.

Over the next month, Phoebe's life fell into a rhythm so happy she would have been astounded to be told it was only a few weeks old. In reality there was no one to tell her, apart from Titus, with whom she spent nearly all of her time. She rose early, before even Prisca and Aquila began to say their dawn prayers, and made her way to Titus's house with Felix at her side. She and Felix never talked about whether he should come or not – it was a decision so obvious that it needed no articulation. Bibi had welcomed Felix into her heart as though he were her long-lost brother, and Felix had responded to her in like manner. Throughout the day, as Phoebe and Titus caught up on so much missed time together, their voices could be heard around the house, clearly involved in intricate games, the rules of which would have baffled anyone outside their tight friendship. Phoebe rejoiced, not only to have Bibi's guile-less joy and love soothe her own heart but to watch it healing Felix's too. In her company he unfurled, like a spring flower breaking into blossom. Slowly but surely he became less defensive and prickly, more comfortable with who he was. One day, she asked him a question and he responded, almost without thinking, 'I don't know.' Phoebe smiled, but said nothing. The old Felix would have been dramatically expansive – 'Felix does not know,' he might have said, gesticulating wildly. It was a manner that was endearing but not comfortable. His simple, unaffected 'I don't know' spoke to Phoebe as powerfully as a long speech would have done that Felix was, finally, finding his own healing in his friendship with her granddaughter and small miracle, Bibi.

Change so often comes clothed in the smallest and most insignificant of events. Phoebe's new found bubble of contentedness ended in exactly this way. Their happiness might have continued for a long time if a small slip hadn't changed the direction of all their lives. One day, when Titus was struggling to get out of his chair, the slave whose shoulder he was using for support, twisted his ankle, which caused Titus to fall heavily and painfully. After Titus had been picked up and checked for injuries (thankfully there were none) and the horrified slave reassured that it wasn't his fault and that he wouldn't be punished, Titus turned to Phoebe and begged her to come and live in the house once more. That simple slip had brought home to him how little time he might have left, and he didn't want to waste a single moment of it. Phoebe had had exactly the same thought, and readily agreed. So it was that Felix was dispatched to Prisca and Aquila's workshop with the request that Hortensius and Faustus might bring her belongings to Titus's house as soon as possible.

They arrived back very quickly, her belongings slung between them as though they weighed no more than little Bibi herself. Phoebe entered the atrium to greet them, and thank them for their help, and stopped, startled, to discover not only Felix, Hortensius, and Faustus, as she expected, but also Prisca and Aquila there too. What is more, there was someone else with them. This someone else, though not tall, was bulky. His upper body suggested someone who had spent many hours in some sort of labouring – a labouring that appeared to have happened outside, since his face was weather-beaten, lined by years in the sun, wind, and rain. Phoebe glanced at him briefly, barely taking in his appearance before turning back to her friends in an anguish of guilt. These were her dear, kind friends, who had welcomed her into their home. They had taken her to their hearts; had supported her through the telling of her painful story; had uncomplainingly (for the most part) allowed her to store the many supplies for Paul's mission to Spain in their increasingly cramped workshop; had, unbeknownst to her, spent long weary weeks and months searching for Titus and, most recently, had rejoiced with her when he had been found. These were her friends, and she, in return, had turned her back on them, leaving them, weeks ago, with barely a backwards glance, as she revelled in the joy of the discovery of her granddaughter. Her shame signalled itself in her accustomed way with a bright red flush rising from her neck to her cheeks.

She stepped forward, wringing her hands. 'I'm so sorry . . .' she began.

Prisca laughed, her chuckle rising to fill the echoing atrium. 'What must you think of us? We aren't here to tell you off, dear one. We've come to find out how you are. We've missed you at prayers and the breaking of the bread, and we wanted you to mee—' Her voice trailed off as she gazed over at Titus, who had hobbled into the room on the shoulder of the now forgiven slave. Their eyes locked, and a look of surprised recognition passed between them.

'Do you know each other?' asked Phoebe.

'Well, yes . . . a little,' said Prisca.

'It was back in Ephesus,' said Titus slowly. 'I was still hiding from Quintus, and felt so anxious and alone.'

'And we were in the marketplace talking about Jesus, and Titus –' Prisca turned to Phoebe, '– Titus is such a common name, it never occurred to me that Titus was your Titus – arrived and started listening. I remember we talked about forgiveness for hours.'

'Yes, I will never forget what you told me,' Titus said, 'that Jesus had come to bring healing into the world, that he died for us, that his death reconciled us with the God who loves us. See, I remember it all. Phoebe, if these are your friends, do you follow this Jesus the Christ too?'

'Yes, yes I do,' said Phoebe.

'Why didn't you mention it?' asked Titus.

For the second time in only a few minutes, Phoebe flushed red again. 'Because I didn't want to lose you again. You are such a great noble Roman, and I thought you would despise me if you knew.' She paused, flushing an even deeper red. 'I am so ashamed, such a failure. I suppose Paul would say that I'm ashamed of the Gospel. Maybe I am . . .'

The stranger, who had until now stood silently by, suddenly cleared his throat at this. 'If anyone has grounds for shame in this company, it would be me. I wouldn't count what you have just acknowledged as anything more than a passing omission.'

At this, Phoebe and Titus both turned and looked again at this burly, rough-looking stranger. Just as the words were forming in Phoebe's mouth to ask who he was, Felix and Bibi tumbled into the atrium in the midst of one of their mysterious games. Felix took one look at the stranger and exclaimed, 'Peter, you've come back! Where have you been?'

This exclamation provoked a flurry of conversation in which many spoke but few listened, so that whatever answer Peter may have given to Felix's question was lost in the midst of the melee. In the end it was Titus's voice that cut through the hubbub, inviting his guests into one of the family rooms for refreshment and conversation.

'I don't know about anyone else,' he said, 'but I feel as though we have too many strands woven around each other, and it will take us a good long time to disentangle them.'

When they had all found a seat; had had extensive refreshment; had established that Phoebe was also a Christian, though she hadn't found the words to tell Titus this, and that the stranger in their midst was the apostle Peter on one of his periodic visits to Rome; after all of this, they were then ready to share their stories with each other.

They decided that they would begin with Titus and Prisca in Ephesus, and carry on from there.

Chapter 20

Phoebe found she already knew much of Titus's story, but nevertheless felt her heart constrict as she heard him laying out, again, his loneliness in Ephesus and his nagging guilt that he had failed to save her. It was this loneliness and guilt that had caused him to stop and listen transfixed in the marketplace as first Prisca, and then Aquila, announced the Good News of Jesus. What had struck him most powerfully was what they said about sin and forgiveness. He had, as far as he could remember, never heard anyone suggest that sins could be forgiven. They could be revenged. They could be overlooked in the face of an attractive business or family deal. But not forgiven. What was even more striking to him was that this Jesus that they kept on talking about had given up his life so that human beings could be reconciled with God. Titus was used to being a plaything of the gods, to accepting with fortitude whatever they might throw at him. He was astounded to hear of a god who had created him, and who loved him.

It was this that had caused him to stop and talk to Prisca for hours and to return day after day for a whole week to ask more questions and to find out more about this God of love and forgiveness. He had to admit that he struggled to understand why they needed to say he was the only God. Surely this God could exist alongside all the other gods? It had taken time, but eventually he had understood. If there were more than one god, there would be different laws governing how the world worked, and there would be competition between gods so that reconciliation was no longer possible. A god of perfect love and forgiveness had to be one. He had reflected long and hard at the wonder of this all-loving, all-forgiving God. He had been convinced, he told Prisca with a smile at which she beamed back at him, but in the end he had had to walk away.

'I never understood what happened to you,' said Prisca. After all these years her bemusement tinged with sorrow was still evident.

'It wasn't because I didn't believe,' Titus said gently. 'It was because I did. Everything you told me made sense. I craved to be reconciled with your powerful, creator God, who loves all he has made and yearns to forgive. I have over the years, since we met, prayed to him, and felt, somehow, that he heard my prayer, but I knew that if I committed to following Jesus it would take everything I had. And I just couldn't give that. This kind of god would not accept the worship I give to other gods: a sacrifice here, a libation there. This God would require my all, and I wasn't ready to give it. More importantly I wasn't ready to be forgiven. I had let Phoebe down and it felt too easy, uncaring somehow, to lay down the burden and leave it behind. Saying that my failings were in the past, over and forgiven, was a luxury I couldn't grant myself. I had let Phoebe down in the worst way imaginable; if I didn't suffer for it, it would feel as though I didn't care. I wrestled with my conscience for many days, but in the end I just couldn't do it, and so I walked away. I often wondered over the years about what would have happened if I hadn't.'

Phoebe found tears running down her cheeks as she listened to Titus talk. It had never occurred to her that this good, kind man would have tormented himself for so long over what he had done – or not done – so long ago.

'If I have learnt anything over the years,' Peter began, 'it is that wondering what might have happened if . . . is a futile exercise that gets you nowhere. Believe me, I know. After Jesus died "what might have happened if" was all I could think about. I spent so many desperate hours wondering whether I could have saved Jesus. Perhaps I could have persuaded him not to go to Jerusalem, or at least not at Passover – the crowd of people gathered for the Passover was too large and too volatile, but if he had gone another time there would have been no crowd, and therefore no need for him to die. Perhaps I could have persuaded Judas out of his anger. I had seen him becoming more and more disillusioned with Jesus – maybe I could have intervened and turned his anger away. But then I was pretty cross with Jesus myself. I couldn't understand why he wouldn't start the revolt against the Romans. Perhaps if I hadn't denied Jesus – maybe I could have stood by him in the trial and persuaded them not to condemn him. There were a lot of good people in the Sanhedrin, you know, who would have clutched at any excuse to save him. Perhaps . . . if only . . . what if. But then you have to realise that I am asking what I could have done to save the one who died to save us all.' He laughed, a body-shaking, guffaw of a laugh, and then just as quickly became serious again. 'Sometimes I wonder whether the way we talk about forgiveness is right. Forgiveness was so central to what Jesus had to say: God has forgiven us and we should forgive each other. It lies at the very heart of the Good News we proclaim. The problem is that when you talk about forgiveness as you just did, it sounds so easy, trite even, as if with a single word the past can be erased as though it had never happened. I, of all people, know that forgiveness is more complex than that.'

'Excuse me for asking,' Titus broke in, 'but I thought you were the great apostle Peter. What on earth would you need forgiveness for?'

At this Felix threw up his hands in frustration. Clearly no one was going to allow Peter to conduct the story as he saw fit; at the same time he sat forward in his seat, his eyes gleaming, for once entirely ignoring Bibi's pleas for him to come and play. Peter was about to tell one of his stories of Jesus, and this was a treat too great to be missed.

'An apostle I may be,' Peter conceded, 'but great I most certainly am not. Sometimes when I've heard Paul speak, I've thought that he seemed to be saying that when you follow Jesus, you change overnight: the old has gone, the new has come. It was never that way for me.'

'He says something different in the new letter that Phoebe brought,' interrupted Prisca. 'Right in the middle of the letter he said that he did not do what he wanted, but the very thing he hated. He talked about wanting to do good, but ending up doing the evil he didn't want to do. Maybe we've got him all wrong. Maybe he struggles with the Christian life as much as the rest of us?'

'That wasn't what *I* thought he meant,' said Aquila. 'I thought he was talking about his own struggle as a Jew before he became a Christian.'

'I heard something else,' Phoebe added. 'Sorry. I thought he was talking about what it was like to be Israel delighting in the law but unable to follow it properly. I didn't think he was talking about life in Christ at all.'

'No, he was definitely talking about himself,' said Prisca confidently.

With that Prisca, Aquila, and Phoebe all started talking at once, trying to persuade the others that what they had heard was not what Paul meant. Phoebe reflected on the change in herself as she rolled up her intellectual sleeves and entered the fray. Only a year ago she would have been horrified at the thought of doing this. As a leader in Corinth she had been quiet and retiring, admired for the care she showed to those around her, but never forceful. Now she raised her voice in an attempt to be heard above the racket of debate.

Peter bellowed, making a sound so loud it could have been heard a few streets away. Phoebe wondered if that was how he had caught the attention of those he fished with in Galilee across the other side of the lake – it was certainly effective.

Once silence had descended once more he said, 'I thought I was telling my story, not opening a debate on what Paul might or might not have said in what I hear is his most convoluted letter yet.'

'I wouldn't call it convoluted,' objected Prisca. 'More complex.' Peter fixed her with a fierce glare and she closed her mouth, looking as though she knew she had been chastised.

Aquila chuckled. 'I've always said, my dear, that in Peter you have really met your match. You can give Paul a run for his money, but Peter is something else entirely!' Prisca wrinkled her forehead quizzically, but, looking at Peter, wisely decided to keep silent.

'As I was saying,' said Peter firmly, 'I have never found being a disciple of Jesus to be as straightforward as some do. I was well known in my fishing days for speaking first and thinking later. Whenever we went to Sepphoris to trade, Andrew did the talking. It wasn't that I can't speak Greek – I like to think my Greek is relatively well polished.' He looked around the room for affirmation. Most of the room nodded their eager assent, only Titus seemed less convinced and raised a patrician eyebrow in response. Peter clearly decided not to press him for something as small as a compliment on his second language, and continued.

'The problem was that I offended too many customers whenever I spoke. I just kept on telling them exactly what was in my mind, and before I knew it the sale was off. In the end, Andrew made me lift the fish and keep my mouth shut, while he did the trade. But when I met Jesus, he didn't seem to mind. He seemed to want me to say what I saw. He asked question after question, and waited for us to work out the truth for ourselves. Occasionally, my tendency simply to open my mouth and speak whatever came out was useful. One time, I remember, we were close to a place called Caesarea Philippi, right in the north near Mount Hermon. As we walked along the road, Jesus asked us to tell him what everyone was saying about him. They were saying a lot, and we told him. People were wondering whether he was John the Baptist, or Elijah, or a prophet like that. He then asked us who *we* thought he was. An awkward silence fell. We weren't really sure. We knew he was a great rabbi and a miracle worker. We knew we would follow him wherever he went. He was Jesus, and that was enough for us. All of a sudden something popped into my head and my mouth moved – as usual – before I could stop it. "You're the Messiah," I said. No one was more surprised than I was, but at the moment I said it I knew it was true.

'Of course, I had to go and spoil it. Jesus started saying something about how he had to die and rise again. I took him on one side and explained, as best I could, why that was a terrible thing to say. Everyone knew the Messiah would be mighty and victorious. They would lose faith in him if he kept on saying he was going to die. If he wanted everyone to think he was the Messiah, he had to look like one. Going around talking about failure and death was not the way to achieve this. Jesus turned on me then and called me Satan. I had no idea why. It felt harsh to me. Of course, now I know why. Satan had tested Jesus in the wilderness, tried to get him to use his powers for his own benefit. I suppose I was doing the same, trying to persuade him to be who he wasn't called to be.'

'That doesn't sound so bad,' said Titus encouragingly. 'I can't see why you would feel ashamed about that. Surely it must have been hard to understand who Jesus really was back then. We have an advantage – we have the whole story. Back then you had to work it out as you went along.'

Peter laughed, his huge belly-laugh bouncing off the walls and ceilings, sounding far too loud in that enclosed space. 'Bless you, but that isn't what I feel ashamed about. If only it were. What I did later on was much, much worse.'

Chapter 21

Phoebe knew exactly what Peter was going to say. She had heard the story before back in Corinth, but hearing it again, and this time from the lips of Peter, made her feel queasy in anticipation. The room fell silent. Peter licked his lips, clearly struggling even after all this time to speak about what happened.

Titus prompted him, 'You mentioned earlier that you denied Jesus . . .'

'Yes,' Peter looked up, his eyes full of tears, 'yes, I did. And even after all these years I still can't tell you why. I was so confident. So sure of my loyalty and love. I even told Jesus to his face that I'd never desert him. But he knew I would. He even told me when it would happen, but I was so sure, so arrogant, so self-reliant, that I barely even listened to what he said. Maybe that was where it all started. If I hadn't been so arrogant, maybe I could have stopped what happened next. I told him I would never leave him as we were walking from our last meal to Gethsemane. He seemed troubled by something, but the evening was so beautiful – the evening sun on the olive trees cast a golden light upon us all – and I was distracted, so that I only noticed his distress when I looked back on it later. We'd been busy in that run-up to the Passover, and, with the Passover meal lying heavy in our stomachs, when he asked us to pray with him, we all dropped off to sleep one by one. I didn't mean to, but my eyes simply wouldn't stay open.'

Titus looked as though he was about to speak again, but Peter stopped him. 'If you're about to tell me that that doesn't sound too bad either, let me stop you. That is not what I'm ashamed about either. Well, maybe I feel a small twinge of shame. Jesus was distraught, and all we could do was snooze. Again, as I look back, I wonder what would have happened if I hadn't slept. If I'd stayed awake and prayed. Maybe that would have changed everything. Jesus woke us up, and as we woke I realised the sun had set and it was quite dark. Through the trees I could see many lit torches winding their way towards us. As they got close, I realised Judas was with them. My sleep-befuddled brain couldn't work out what was happening. I hadn't even noticed Judas wasn't with us any more. For a moment I wondered whether Judas had brought some new followers to listen to Jesus' teaching. Then I saw they all had swords and clubs, and I assumed that he had rounded up an army for Jesus to lead against the Romans. I looked again, and realised that they were temple guards. As I sat there on the ground, still desperately trying to work out what they had come for, Judas stepped forward and kissed Jesus.

'At that moment the world went mad: the soldiers stepped forward and arrested Jesus; Judas stumbled past me and ran away with a wild look in his eye; someone, I've no idea who, took out a sword and cut off the ear of a slave. In the press and the madness of a world turned upside down, fear took over, and I did the only thing I could think of – I ran and ran and ran. I had no idea where I was going or why. I just knew I had to get away.'

Peter paused, clearly reliving the events of that terrible night over again in his mind.

Titus looked at him with compassion. 'I still think that what you did was understandable – any of us here would have done the same.'

Peter looked at Titus and smiled ruefully. 'You are an immensely kind and compassionate man, and I thank you for that, but we're still not there. There's more.

'Eventually I stopped running, and felt a wave of shame wash over me. How could I have run away? I knew that the only thing to do was to go back. So I did. I turned around and ran and ran, back the way I had come. Before long I caught up with the large, slow-moving crowd, and I followed them at a distance until I saw them taking Jesus into the high priest's house.

'By then the sun had long set and the evening air was cold. There was a fire burning in the courtyard of the house, and I pressed towards it, hoping to warm my hands. As I sat down, various people turned and stared; some spoke behind their hands to their neighbours; a couple pointed at me and whispered. The panic returned. And when a servant girl who had been watching me with a hostile stare from across the fire pointed and said, "This man was also with him," my mouth moved on its own: "I don't know him," I said. This kept on happening. I hadn't realised that people had noticed me with Jesus, but twice more people pointed me out as being one of his followers; even the day before, this would have filled me with pride, but now it brought terror. What would happen if they realised who I was? Would I be arrested too? I had to get away, to save myself. So the third time it happened I burst out: "I don't know what you're talking about." My voice must have floated over to the other side of the courtyard, where Jesus was being held, because he turned and looked me in the eye; at that moment a cock crowed, as Jesus had said it would, and my heart nearly broke in two. I had done the very thing I swore I would never do, and Jesus knew.'

Peter's flow of words came to an end, and he looked at Titus as though daring him to speak compassionate words one more time. Titus shrugged defeat, acknowledging that there was nothing he could say to ameliorate Peter's terrible tale. Then an idea struck him: 'At least you didn't do what Judas did.'

Peter tipped his head on one side. 'You really are a kind man. I've thought about it long and hard over the years. What I did was no worse, but certainly no better than what Judas did. We both betrayed him in our own ways. True, Judas's betrayal led directly to Jesus' death, but maybe mine contributed to it. If I had stood beside him, argued for him with the Sanhedrin, who knows, it might have made a difference, and even if it hadn't, I wouldn't have left Jesus so entirely alone at his moment of greatest need. I liked to think I was his friend. A fine friend I turned out to be.'

'What happened to Judas?' asked Titus.

'No one really knows,' said Peter. 'None of us ever saw him again after that night. He died, but I don't know how. Some say he was overwhelmed with remorse, and killed himself; others say he bought a field with his ill-gotten gains and had an accident, falling so badly that his innards spilled out. Whenever I think of him I'm filled with sorrow; however he died, he died despairing and alone. I can't help wondering what the risen Jesus would have said to him if they had met. I like to think he would have forgiven him.'

'Like he did with you?' prompted Felix, who, until this point in the story, had sat as still as a mouse.

'Like he did with me,' agreed Peter.

Phoebe sat forward at this point; she had never heard this part of the story. Thus far, other than hearing it from Peter's own lips, there was nothing new in what she had heard, but she had never heard about Peter's forgiveness.

'After Jesus rose from the dead I was as amazed and ecstatic as anyone. As a group, we moved from despair to incredulity, to wonder, and finally to joy within the space of a couple of days. Once we knew that Jesus really was alive, the bleakness of the previous days felt like nothing more than a dream. He had, of course, told us that he would rise again, but I don't think any of us really knew what it meant. We certainly forgot it in our despair after his death. So, with the others, I was jubilant at his resurrection, but at the same time every time I looked at him I was overwhelmed with a shame so potent that I could barely stand to be in his presence. I made sure that I was never alone with him, that I never caught his eye. Where everyone else surged forward in his presence, I sank back.

'After his resurrection, we had gone back to Galilee. After the turmoil and uncertainty of everything that had happened, it was comforting to return to the familiarity of home, and the things we knew well. One morning, I was so restless in my shame that I had to do something; only activity would calm my agitated heart. I told the others I was going fishing. They all decided to come too. We were all desperate for something to do to take our minds off what we couldn't understand. But their presence was a mixed blessing: having Andrew at my side, just like the good old days, was a balm to my soul, but Matthew – the former tax collector – was a liability, and nearly capsized us a couple of times.

'It was a terrible night for fish. We fished all night and found nothing. I was fit to scream with frustration. We had done everything right – everything – but there was not a single fish to be found anywhere. Much as I'd have liked to blame the hapless Matthew, it wasn't really his fault, especially after I sent him to untangle a knotted ball of rope in the stern of the ship. Just as the sun was rising and we had given up hope, we noticed someone on the shore. I couldn't see who it was. The rising sun was behind him, and all I could see was his outline. He called out to us and told us to put the net down on the other side of the boat. I was furious. A stranger. On the shore. Telling *me* how to fish. But as my irritation rose, I remembered another time a few years before. It was one of the first times I had met Jesus. I was irritated then too. In fact, it was the irritation that reminded me.

'We had fished all night then too and, just like now, had got nothing. We were bone tired and our nets had snagged on something and needed mending. Then this rabbi had come along. I'd heard about him from other people. He'd nearly been lynched in Nazareth for his controversial teaching. But the crowd was huge, and he wanted to go out in my boat a little way to talk to the people. I was intrigued. I've always enjoyed a bit of controversy. So I let him use my boat. I was amazed by him. He didn't seem controversial to me – just wise and compassionate. The more I listened, the more I wanted to see the world as he did; to love it as he did. At the end he told us to put our nets out again. The cheek of the man! He was a carpenter and now a teacher. I'd been fishing for the whole of my life, and he was telling *me* how to fish! Besides, it was daylight, and everyone knows it's hard to catch fish in the daylight. I was furious, and threw my nets in the sea to calm myself down a little, but then the oddest thing happened. The minute they sank beneath the surface, it felt as though they were full to bursting. Andrew and I pulled and pulled, but the nets were too full, so we had to get the other boat to come and help us. I had never in all my years of fishing had a catch so huge.

'All of this came back to me in a flash as my irritation rose, its taste familiar in my mouth. I'd been wrong then, so maybe I was wrong now. It was worth a try. So I used all my fury to throw the nets on the other side of the boat. Just like the last time, the minute the nets sank beneath the surface, they became full to bursting. Someone behind me, I didn't see who, said, "It is the Lord." But I didn't really need him to say it. I already knew. And as I knew, something burst deep within me. My shame, humiliation, and horror tumbled out, and I jumped into the sea there and then. I swam right up to him. Got out and looked him right in the eye, just as I had done in the courtyard when I denied him, and in that moment I knew I was forgiven.'

Chapter 22

'You must have been so relieved,' smiled Titus, his kind heart rejoicing for this person he had only just met.

'Oddly, no I wasn't,' said Peter. 'That is what I wanted to tell you. Forgiveness is far more complex than at first you might think. Take Phoebe, here. She forgives you for all the wrong you did to her, don't you?' He looked earnestly at her.

'Of course I do,' said Phoebe, 'except I don't think he did that much wrong to me in the first place. It was more my fault.'

Titus looked as though he was going to jump in with his now well-worn objections to this, but Peter raised his hand. 'Let's leave blame on one side for now. You are reconciled. You have poured out your sorrow and regret. Phoebe has forgiven you.' He looked expectantly at them.

Titus and Phoebe both nodded their agreement.

'So the past is gone? All wiped out? Forgotten now? And you, Titus, you have no more regrets? What about Quintus? How do you feel about him?'

Titus opened and closed his mouth a few times, his brow wrinkled as he thought through what needed to be said. While he did, Phoebe looked long and hard into her own heart and realised that lurking deep within was a fist of rage that clenched every time she thought about Quintus and all that he had done; a rage that, until this moment, she had never even acknowledged existed.

Peter smiled at them. 'It's all right. You don't need to say it out loud unless you want to? I didn't think so. I of all people know that forgiveness is complex. It's like a huge tangled ball; like one of my nets after a particularly frustrating night at sea.

One moment. One phrase, "I forgive you", might loosen one of the threads, but the rest remains, and takes much, much more work. Jesus knew that too.

'After breakfast we had a chat, he and I. And at the end of the chat, do you know what he said to me? "Follow me." Just like that, "Follow me." Just as he had when I first met him. He was telling me, then, the slate was wiped clean. I could go back to the beginning and start all over again. But before he said that, he said something else.

'He asked me three times if I loved him. I was grateful at first. I had so wanted to tell him that I loved him, that I hadn't meant to deny him, that I had made a terrible mistake. So it came as a relief to be able to say so. The second time he asked, I was confused. Did he doubt me? Maybe he thought I didn't mean it? The third time, I was hurt. Why would he not believe me? Later, though, I understood. He was giving me the chance to undo, phrase by painful phrase, the three times I had claimed that I didn't know him. He was working at that knotted, muddled ball, and allowing me to unravel the knots for myself. It was a long, painful process, but little by little the knots started to come free. The other thing was that each time I told him I loved him, he asked me to care for his sheep. Now, when the feelings of shame and despair descend again, I remember what he asked me to do, and I know that every time I care for his flock, every time I feed his lambs, I am undoing what I did.'

'Are you saying,' Phoebe stumbled, looking for the right words, 'that he didn't really forgive you and you still have to work to make it right?'

'No!' said Peter. 'I was always forgiven. Do you know, I even think he had forgiven me the moment those words came out of my mouth. When he looked at me in the courtyard, it wasn't a look of anger or disappointment; just of concern and love. I was forgiven the moment I denied him. The problem wasn't him. It was me.'

'I'm sorry, I don't understand.' Phoebe was relieved that Titus had taken the words right out of her mouth. '*What* was you?'

'Being forgiven and accepting that you are forgiven are two very different things. Jesus forgives. That is his nature. Receiving that forgiveness, living it out day by day and then forgiving others – that is what is hard. I still struggle with it,' said Peter. 'Don't look like that!' His huge laugh bounced around the walls again. 'From your faces anyone would think I'd just admitted to murdering my mother.'

'But . . . But . . . you are Peter, the great apostle,' stuttered Phoebe.

'We've been through this already,' twinkled Peter. 'Apostle? – yes. Hopelessly flawed disciple? – certainly. Human being living out my faith one step at a time? – definitely. Great? – that remains to be seen. You see, forgiveness isn't a one-off event. It's a way of life. I think it's what Jesus meant when he said we had to forgive seventy times seven. Forgiveness comes as a bundle: we are forgiven, we accept that forgiveness, and so we forgive. Forgiveness is not a magic trick that means we forget all the wrong we have done, or indeed the wrong others have done. We can't undo the past. I can't un-deny Jesus. What has happened has happened. It even makes us who we are today. We can't pretend it didn't happen. Forgiveness is not about forgetting – it's about refusing to be chained up by the past; accepting that a door has been opened for us, and walking through the door to freedom. I think,' he looked in turn at Titus and Phoebe, 'that you both need to let go. You will probably need to return to this moment again and again. Like me, you will need to live forgiveness every day of your lives. There will be days when you simply don't have the strength to forgive yourself or others. There will be days when your demons return to haunt you. There will be days when you will have to cling to your knowledge of forgiveness with the very tips of your fingers. Living forgiveness is a long and winding road. Navigating it takes courage. It takes determination. It requires you to love yourself as well as others.' He paused, smiled, and said, 'Sometimes it helps to say it out loud, so I will: your sins are forgiven, be free.'

It is only when you stop carrying a heavy load that you realise how heavy it has been.

Phoebe suddenly realised how heavily the twin burdens of her shame and her anger towards Quintus had been weighing on her. But could she really lay them down now? She had been carrying them for so long – she wasn't even sure she knew how to let them go. She squeezed her eyes tightly shut, hoping she could keep herself from weeping. As she sat fighting off tears she realised that she was ready – ready to try at least – to lay her shame down, and her anger too. And in that moment she felt aware of a sense of relief: of lightness and of freedom.

When she opened her eyes, she was astonished to find only Titus sitting in the room.

'Where did they go?'

'Peter needed to visit some people. He said goodbye, but I'm not sure you noticed. He didn't seem to mind though. I suspect he is used to the effect his story has on people.'

They spent the rest of that day and evening together in almost complete silence, as Phoebe came to terms both with the weight of the burden she had carried for so long and with the realisation that, at last, it had been lifted. She looked sideways at Titus and guessed he was feeling the same, so, other than smiling at him, she did nothing. She found Peter's advice both timely and helpful. She had lived with her guilt and shame as a constant and dogged companion for so long that it just couldn't be shaken off straight away. Several times, even during that first day, she found she needed to remind herself of forgiveness, hope, and freedom, deliberately laying down the feelings with which she was so familiar. Living her forgiveness was going to be no easy task, but she knew now why it was so important. Despite everything she had said to Prisca, Aquila,

Andronicus, and Junia, she had been living half a life of freedom, with one foot in the past. The time had come, at last, to
plant both her feet joyfully and trustingly in the present. It
would not be easy, but it had to be done – for Titus, for Bibi, for
Felix, and for all her friends. Now she could acknowledge the
wisdom of Prisca's suggestion that it was the Spirit who had
driven her back to Rome. Fullness of life was on offer; she
simply had to find the courage and determination to receive it
and live it with joy.

The next morning, after the clients had come and been allo-
cated tasks, had been soothed or advised, Titus came to find
Phoebe, full of enthusiasm.

'What are we going to do about it?'

'About what?' she asked.

'God has forgiven us. Gods always expect something in return
for their good favour. When Peter was forgiven, Jesus sent him to
care for his flock . . . Surely we ought to do the same?'

'I'm not sure it works like that.' Phoebe spoke slowly as she
tried to work out what to say. 'Peter isn't working to pay God
back for his forgiveness. He is just . . . forgiven; just as we are.
What he does now, he does with joy in his heart, not to repay
anything.'

'But we must do something; it can't just be free.'

Phoebe felt a wave of joy wash over her. 'It really is. Paul
would call it grace. It's a gift, totally free, totally undeserved.
That's what Jesus' death achieved. We are all forgiven; all we
have to do is accept it. Paul talks about it a lot in that letter I
brought to Rome. You should read it. It's complicated, really
complicated, but worth it.'

As she said this, she noticed a restless uneasiness come over
Titus that caused him to examine a fingernail in great detail,
and to avoid her eyes completely. She wondered whether to ask
him what was wrong, but something told her this was not the
moment. So instead she just continued. 'What Paul said in the

letter is that we don't need to earn anything, but in baptism we die with Christ and rise again, with him, to a new life. If we do anything, it is because we are living that new life, not because we feel we should pay anything back. The key is learning to live that new life, in Christ, to all its fullness. Peter made me see that I haven't been until now . . . I've been living half a life, but from now on all that's going to change.'

Titus's restlessness had now gone. Instead he looked pensive.

'Is everything all right?' asked Phoebe.

'Of course,' said Titus. 'I was just thinking that I would like to be baptised. I remember Prisca talking about it all those years ago in Ephesus. I want to declare my allegiance to this Jesus Christ. Before, I thought following him asked too much. Now I know it doesn't ask anywhere near enough. Such love, such forgiveness, such freedom, demands my all. I cannot rest until I have pledged that.'

Phoebe beamed at him. 'I think we need to send for Prisca and Aquila,' she said.

'Why can't you baptise me?' Titus asked, looking crestfallen.

'That's not the point,' said Phoebe. 'The point is not who baptises you. The point is that you are baptised into the body of Christ, the family of God. It would be odd if that family were not present. You're joining them in the new life in Christ, after all.'

Titus beamed his acceptance. 'A few days ago, there was just me and Bibi; now I have a huge family. A few days ago I felt alone and adrift; now I am loved and forgiven.' He shook his head in delighted wonder.

Phoebe called for Felix, who, like her, had moved into Titus's house the day before. When he didn't appear, she wrinkled her forehead in frustration. 'Where is that boy?'

Titus chuckled. 'I think that now little Bibi has ownership of his heart, you have been bumped to second place.'

Phoebe, hearing the sound of happy voices playing in the garden, acknowledged his point and opened her mouth to call again.

'Leave him alone,' said Titus. 'You shouldn't use him as your errand boy anyway, if, as you claim, you see him as family. One of my slaves can go.' Titus's favourite slave, on whom he preferred to lean whenever he moved from room to room, appeared as he said that. For the first time in a long time Phoebe thought fondly of Chrestus. He loved to do that too. He would wait like a cat preparing to pounce on a mouse, listening to his master's conversation. Even before his master had finished a sentence expressing a wish, he would be in motion ready to fulfil the command. How she missed him. How she grieved that in her hurt and anger, she had banished even these happy memories from her mind.

As Titus issued his instruction to the slave, Phoebe reflected with shame that, although Felix was not a slave – not even her servant – she had treated him like one, assuming he would hang around waiting for his next errand from her. Now his broken heart was healing, aided by Bibi's joyous friendship, he no longer needed her as he used to. His need had shown itself in wanting to be helpful. Phoebe had found it delightful (and if she was honest, useful too) and had not stopped to question his voracious need to be wanted. Titus was right: she needed to let him go. She had to let him find himself and not to be dangling forever on her every wish. She sighed. This living a life of forgiveness was going to be more onerous than she had imagined. When Peter had talked about it, she assumed he meant that she needed to spend all her energy giving and accepting forgiveness for the past; what she hadn't realised was that the present would throw up even more things that needed forgiveness. Added to the ball of rage that she was now able to admit to feeling towards Quintus, she recognised that confessing her own sins and living forgiveness was going to be quite a time-consuming business.

Chapter 23

It wasn't long before Titus's slave returned, but when he appeared, he was alone.

'Where are they?' Titus asked sharply. The slave shifted from foot to foot uneasily. He clearly was not looking forward to imparting the news he had to share.

'Not coming,' he mumbled.

'What?' Titus's voice was harsh, and not a little outraged. Phoebe twitched. She had forgotten, but now remembered with full force, how frightening Titus could be when thwarted. She didn't think he meant to be; he had just lived a life in which everything was arranged for his convenience. Like anyone who lived thoroughly at the centre of their own lives, he found it hard to accept when what he wanted did not happen as swiftly and satisfactorily as he thought it should.

'They cannot come right now,' the slave clarified, his face pale with fear.

'Can you tell us why not?' asked Phoebe as gently as she could, trying not to add to his terror unnecessarily.

'There was a widow – I think they said her name was Flavia – who was very ill. They were going out as I arrived. They said they were going to care for her. Peter was going too. They thought she might die, and weren't sure whether she would still be alive when they arrived.'

'Don't they know who I am?' thundered Titus, but Phoebe, feeling stricken, laid her hand on his arm to quieten him. In the year since she had been in Rome, she had taken over the task of overseeing the care of the widows and orphans. Each day they had arrived at Prisca and Aquila's workshop, and each day she had noticed who was present and who not, and later she would send Felix to enquire after those who were absent to ensure they were all right. Then she would ensure that each one had food enough for the day or days ahead. She knew them all by name; knew what was happening in each of their lives; cared for them, and made sure that no one suffered alone.

She had overseen something very similar in Corinth. The earliest disciples, in those heady days after the sending of the Spirit, had done far more than just care for those with no income. They had shared everything they owned together. Wonderful though this vision had been, it had quickly thrown up as many problems as it had solved – problems that came to a head with the lies and subsequent deaths of Ananias and Sapphira. Phoebe remembered listening agog to the tales of what had happened twenty years before in Jerusalem. Now most communities like theirs shared what they had by caring for those who had nothing. All those who had enough to live on (although regular arguments had arisen in Corinth about who that was) shared with those who did not (even greater arguments had arisen about who that was). The question as to who qualified as a 'widow' rumbled on and on. Technically Phoebe was a widow, but she would never have dreamt of asking for support from others. In Corinth there were a couple of women who some felt did not really deserve the help, but they had never agreed on what to do about it. Troubled by the argument, when she had begun to care for the widows in Rome, Phoebe had asked Prisca what she thought.

Prisca had just smiled her twinkly smile and said: 'When I think of what God has given me, deserving or not, I don't really feel the need to find out who deserves help and who doesn't. I'd prefer to be generous like God, and not worry about it.' Phoebe had agreed, and had happily laid down her questions.

Now, she realised to her horror that in the past few weeks of glorious happiness she had forgotten about the widows entirely.

She had been sucked into a self-contained bubble of joy that only held herself, Titus, Bibi, and Felix, and no one else. She had forgotten everyone else. And now Flavia was dangerously ill. She might have been for some time, and Phoebe hadn't even known. She got rapidly to her feet and began to dart around the house, collecting food, herbs, and anything else she could lay her hands on.

'Phoebe!' Titus's baffled voice echoed around the house after her.

When she eventually returned to the room in which he sat, she saw on his face a mixture of frustration and confusion.

'What on earth are you doing?'

Phoebe spilled out her tale of guilt as she quickly explained what she had done, and, more importantly, not done, and why she now needed to rush to Flavia's side.

'Stop! Stop!' Titus eventually implored her. 'Take a breath, sit down, and let us talk this through.'

'But I have to go.' Phoebe nearly wept with frustration. 'I forgot about her, and now she's going to die.'

Titus stroked her hair and smiled a gentle smile. 'You always did have a flare for the dramatic, dear one. I still don't see why they can't just come when I summon them, but they haven't, and now they are there with her. She is not alone. Yes, you should not have forgotten her – nor indeed any of the other poor widows you cared for – but you did. So now remember that forgiveness Peter spoke about only yesterday. You can apologise your heart out later. But for now, crowding Flavia's apartment with yet more people is hardly going to help anyone. I'll send to find out if they need anything and we can then send what they need – not,' he eyed her randomly selected bundle of odds and ends, 'whatever you have managed to scrape together in five minutes.'

Phoebe looked up, and the slave who had taken the message earlier was already in the doorway, waiting expectantly for his errand. Titus, having found out where Flavia's apartment was from Phoebe, gave him directions. The well-trained slave's face grimaced with horror when he heard that it was to be found at the very top of a tenement building in the worst part of Transtiberium, but he said nothing and disappeared silently and efficiently.

He reappeared around two hours later, this time with Prisca, Aquila, and Peter all in tow. Phoebe rushed to greet them, her misery written all over her face. 'You shouldn't have come. You should have stayed with her. She shouldn't be alone.'

'She has gone to be with Christ,' said Peter gently. 'Flavia will never be lonely again. You should have seen her face as she died. She glowed. The last word on her lips was "glory". She died ready for resurrection, and all the joy it would bring.'

Phoebe sagged, the familiar feelings of misery and self-loathing washing over her.

Prisca turned to her. 'Whatever is the matter with you? Flavia was ready to die. Over the past few weeks she had become so frail and so riven with pain. All she could talk about was the resurrection and having a body no longer wracked with agony at every movement. I've never seen her so joyful as in the moment she took her last breath. The lines of pain all melted away, and she radiated peace. I can't for the life of me think why you would begrudge her the release.'

Titus helped her out. 'I think Phoebe feels that she let Flavia down. She was so caught up with her life here that she forgot about the widows completely. She feels responsible, I think.'

Phoebe nodded miserably.

Prisca flung her arms around Phoebe and gave her a hug so vigorous that she squeezed the very breath out of her. 'What you need to remember, dear one, is that you are a far worse critic of yourself than any of the rest of us.'

Peter let out one of his bellows of a laugh. 'Do we need to have that talk about forgiveness again? Perhaps I should tell you my story every day until it sinks in? We followers of Christ deal in grace not blame.'

'Well, most of us do,' said Aquila, 'most of the time,' his innate honesty forcing him to acknowledge the reality of the ideal. 'But you must know that we understand, Phoebe? Finding Titus again after all these years, and discovering Bibi, has turned your life upside down. You would have been inhuman if it hadn't taken you time to adjust in the light of news as big as this. We were leaving you alone, giving you time. We might have raised questions in a month or so if you had still not reappeared, but for the time being we were all rejoicing with you from afar. None more so than Flavia,' he added. 'She was voracious for tales of what had happened, what Titus was like, what Bibi looked like. We spent most of her final week talking about you. She was so happy for you!'

'But there was no one to look after all the widows,' Phoebe burst out, trying, but failing, to lay down her self-recrimination.

Aquila raised a quizzical eyebrow. 'When did you become the only Christian in Rome? The point is, we are a body, all of us together, a body of Christ. When one member is weak, the rest of us bear them up; when one can't act, the rest help out. We've been looking after the widows between us, all this time.'

'So they're all right?' asked Phoebe.

'Of course they are all all right,' said Prisca indignantly. 'You aren't indispensable, you know. We coped without you before, and we have done so again.'

Phoebe recoiled slightly. While she had believed Prisca when she had said that she wasn't criticising her, there was a sharp edge to her voice, and it did feel as though she had landed a harsh blow.

'Don't worry,' smiled Aquila. 'It's me Prisca's cross with, not you. Apparently I didn't help enough. I just did the jobs she asked me to do and then stopped. Apparently I was meant to use my imagination and carry on.'

'Do you think,' Titus chipped in here hesitantly, 'that Phoebe and I might carry on that task now? Could we do it from here perhaps? I can't get around much, but I could use my house to care for anyone who needs it, if you thought that would be all right?'

'That is a generous and thoughtful offer,' said Aquila. 'Let me ask the others and let you know what they say. It's a long way from Transtiberium; it may be too far for people to come.'

'What I want to know,' said Peter, 'is what you wanted us for. Marcus here was insistent that we had to come, but wouldn't say why.'

Phoebe was momentarily confused. She couldn't think who Marcus might be, until she looked around and saw Titus's favourite slave acknowledging Peter's gesture with a smile and a nod. Again, with a flush of shame, she realised that she had never taken the time even to ask his name. He was 'a slave', even 'Titus's favourite slave'. She had never thought beyond that to see him as a person in his own right. How easy it was to slip into uncaring patterns of behaviour, even when she, of all people, knew how demeaning and demoralising that was when you were on the receiving end of it. In contrast, Peter, who had only met him twice, already knew his name and was talking to him as though he knew him. Phoebe sighed. Living this new life of freedom and peace was turning out to be very hard work.

The room had gone quiet, and Phoebe, caught up in thoughts of her failure, took a while to realise that everyone was looking at her.

'Ask Titus,' she said. 'It's his story, not mine.'

All eyes turned expectantly to Titus.

'I . . .' Titus started and then stopped. For the first time in her life, Phoebe saw Titus's patrician features, which seemed permanently set into calm superiority, twitch with nervousness.

'Go on,' she urged. 'You are among friends.'

'I would like to be baptised. I want to become part of God's family – to be brothers and sisters with you all. I want to follow Christ.' He looked over at Prisca. 'I'm ready now to give my all.'

'Blessed be the God and Father of our Lord Jesus Christ!' exclaimed Peter. 'We will baptise you on Sunday in the Tiber.'

'The Tiber?' Titus looked horrified. 'I thought we might do it here. Do you know how muddy the Tiber is?'

Peter laughed. 'I'm a fisherman. I'm used to mud.'

'And the smell!' said Titus.

'Have you ever smelt a boatful of fish?'

Titus had to admit that he hadn't, but acknowledged that it might be worse than the Tiber, even on a hot sunny day.

'And . . .' Titus's voice trailed off. He was arriving at his key objection, but had no idea quite how to say it. 'It's quite public . . . everyone will know.'

'That's the idea,' said Peter. 'What is the point of a public declaration if no one can hear it?'

Titus had gone pale. 'That is rather more "all" than I had in mind. My reputation will be ruined. I will be the laughing stock of the finest families. Cast out, most likely, from society. Are you sure we can't do this in private?'

Chapter 24

Peter looked at Titus sympathetically but firmly. 'Following Jesus is so hard when you have a lot to lose. I remember a young man coming to Jesus one day. He was the kind of person who stuck in your mind: thick, curly hair; fine features; his clothes finely woven and expensive. I remember thinking as I saw him talk to Jesus that he was used to getting whatever he wanted, whenever he wanted it. This time what he wanted was a little more complicated – eternal life. He had come to Jesus to see how to make sure he got it. He and Jesus had quite a long conversation. The young man was passionate, full of life and zeal. I could see Jesus warming to him as they spoke. He was rich, but he was also committed. He kept all the commandments as well and as carefully as he could, but he was still restless; he felt that he was missing something. You could see it in his eyes – the hunger for more. Jesus saw it too. He put his hand gently on his shoulder, looked him deep in the eye, and said quietly: "Sell all you have and give it to the poor."

'The young man shrank before my eyes. He reminded me of one of my old boats on Galilee that gets a hole in the bottom, and, if you aren't careful, quietly and quickly sinks from view. I often wonder what happened to him. He went away so sad. He had too much to lose. At that moment I knew why Jesus kept on saying how much harder it is for people with riches and power to follow him – the less you have to lose, the easier it is. Following Jesus asks so much of you. The more you have to start with, the more you have to give up. You bring that young man to mind, Titus, as you have much to lose too. The question is whether you can see that what you gain makes it worthwhile.'

Titus put his head into his hands, the enormity of his decision weighing heavily on him.

'I think,' said Peter, 'that we need to leave Titus to think this through. We should admire him. He knows the cost of what he is about to do. He just needs to decide whether he wants to pay the price or not. Now I think about it, Jesus told a parable about this.'

This announcement produced a ripple of excitement around the room. They all turned their attention from Titus and settled down in the expectation of hearing it.

Peter laughed. 'I wouldn't get too comfortable, it isn't long. It was one of Jesus' shorter and less dramatic parables. It went like this: if you were going to build a tower, you would sit down and calculate whether you had enough to build the whole thing; or if you were a king going to war, you would sit down and work out if your ten thousand troops could win a battle against the twenty thousand of the other side. In the same way, if you want to follow Jesus, you need to decide if you can bear the cost. As you know, I ploughed ahead in my usual style and realised later that I couldn't pay the cost. Look where that got me. Titus is being far more sensible. He knows what it will mean for him. The question is whether he can pay its cost. I suggest we leave him to mull on it.'

Over the next few days, Titus was quiet and withdrawn, his face creased into a permanent frown. Phoebe hesitated to talk to him, so caught up was he in what appeared to be a mammoth internal battle. She busied herself instead with catching up with old friends, and was overwhelmed by the joy she felt, and was expressed back to her by Blaesus, Faustus, Hortensius, Junia, Andronicus, Herodion, Patrobas, and, of course, Stachys. While she was visiting Stachys, the conversation turned to Felix. Stachys reminded Phoebe that Felix had been apprenticed to him as a scribe, and had shown all the signs of being excellent at the trade. If he was to live with Phoebe in Titus's house, perhaps he wouldn't need to be a scribe? But perhaps it might be wise for him to learn a trade, as who knew what the future might hold? As they talked, Phoebe realised that it wasn't just she who had been caught up in a bubble of unreality. Felix had too, and perhaps he needed to begin to turn his attention outwards again.

Last but not least, Phoebe dropped into Prisca and Aquila's workshop when she knew the widows and orphans would be gathering for the distribution of food and other provisions. Her arrival prompted, not a ripple of disapproval as she had feared, but an explosion of delight. Each person there, woman or child, knew first-hand the bitter sorrow of bereavement and grief, though they had the added burden of facing a life with no income or security. It appeared, however, that they did not begrudge Phoebe her good news. Far from it, they appeared to derive vicarious joy from her discovery of her previously unknown family.

They fired questions at her about Titus, his house, her lost daughter, her found granddaughter. As they talked, Phoebe felt herself overwhelmed with love. To begin with she had wanted to clutch her new-found love to herself, to keep Titus, Bibi, and Felix firmly protected within a cocoon of safety and security. What she had overlooked was that love breaks your heart open. The more you love, the more love there is to give. Phoebe felt herself gladly opening her heart to these courageous, kind women, where before she had simply cared for them because she should. In very little time at all, they had agreed that from now on they would make the journey to Titus's house. It was a little far from the rough tenement blocks in which they lived, but they greeted the prospect with delight. Only two were too frail to make the journey, and it was agreed that the others would take it in turns to bring food back to their houses, and that Phoebe would visit regularly so that no one would ever face the prospect of being entirely alone.

Phoebe returned to the house with a spring in her step – a spring that diminished the closer she got to home. She simply had no idea what to say to Titus. She knew what she hoped he would do, but she had never lived with the honour and respect with which he had lived. In fact the honour that she had received in Corinth had sat uncomfortably with her, and she had given it up with a certain level of relief. But honour was all that Titus had ever known. Becoming a follower of Christ, and doing so publicly in the murky waters of the Tiber, meant that he risked losing all the honour he and his family had meticulously accrued over so many years. He would place himself for ever on the outside of the society in which he had grown up. It was a hard decision, and nothing she could say would make it easier.

As she entered the atrium, she was startled to hear the bellowing laugh of Peter echoing out of Titus's private study, entwined with Titus's far more gentle but nevertheless delighted laugh. She opened the door and looked in hesitantly.

'Phoebe,' Titus greeted her, his face suffused with joy. 'How would you feel about us throwing a grand feast for everyone on the first day of the week, after I have been baptised in the Tiber?'

Phoebe looked from Titus to Peter and back again. 'You have decided then? You're going to be baptised? In the Tiber?'

'Yes. Yes, and yes! You see, I was looking at it all from the wrong angle. I was asking what I was going to lose . . . What I forgot to notice was all that I have already gained. When you look at it like that, there is really no choice to be made! Now, if you will excuse me, Peter is teaching me about the faith, and he will be leaving on Sunday, so I really have no time to lose.'

'You are leaving?' Phoebe was surprised how sad she felt. She had met Peter over the past few days no more than a handful of times, but already he felt like family. The Christian community in Rome had shifted, swiftly expanding to include him, so much so that when he left he would leave a hole. In his case, a very big hole. That was the thing with love, she reflected: it called upon you to expand your heart to greet each new person, but, having expanded, when they left, they left a hole.

'Yes,' Peter said, 'I'm an apostle. It's what I'm called to do. I'm called to journey onwards, bearing the Good News with me as I go. I'll be back. I always do come back, but for now I think I need to travel to Jerusalem to find out what is happening with Paul. I gather he's still in prison. I'm hoping Junia and Andronicus will come with me. They are so well known and well loved among the apostles that I think it is high time we all met together to see if there is anything that can be done.'

'We'll miss you.' The words were woefully inadequate to communicate the emotion Phoebe felt, but as she looked at Peter she realised she had no need to say more. He saw and understood.

'We are bound together with a bond far stronger than physical presence,' Peter said. 'We are bound together in Christ. I may be absent, but we will always be together in Christ. Pray for me. My journey is not always an easy one, and loneliness is not something I have ever got used to.'

Phoebe nodded and found the need to leave the room swiftly.

The next few days were caught up with arranging a feast of celebration for Titus's baptism and of farewell to Peter, Junia, and Andronicus. It was a task made harder by the fact that the household had decided to fast with Titus as he prepared for baptism. As a result, the sweet smells of cooking were even more tantalising than they would normally have been.

In all the busyness of preparation, it took Phoebe a few days to find the time to talk to Titus about Felix. She wanted to consult him in his wisdom about sending Felix back to Stachys as an apprentice. Titus listened carefully, nodded thoughtfully, and then smiled.

'I agree. Felix should learn his trade with Stachys, but not for the reasons you think. I have decided that I should like to adopt Felix as my heir.'

Phoebe felt her mouth drop open in astonishment. So robbed of words was she that she just sat and stared at Titus for a few minutes. On the heels of her astonishment came a maelstrom of mixed emotion: joy for Felix and all this could mean; anxiety for Bibi at the loss of her own inheritance; concern for their relationship in the future. In the end, the only words she could squeeze out were, 'What about Bibi?'

Titus appeared to understand at least most, if not all, of her concern. 'Don't worry about Bibi. I will make sure she is provided for, but she can't be my heir. I know you inherited from Chrestus, but his master wasn't from an old family, and, in any case, you were freed slaves living in Corinth. I need someone who will inherit the family name and all that comes with it. Women just can't do that. We're talking about a life in the public sphere; honour in society; status and power. It is something only men can do. I'd like Felix to be trained in running a household – Stachys could help him with that. What do you think?'

'I think . . .' Phoebe struggled to work out what she thought, astonishment kept on getting in the way of clear thinking. 'I think it is a wonderful idea.' She realised at last that she was delighted, overjoyed in fact. 'But won't people question your choice? Shouldn't you find a son of an impoverished noble family? Wouldn't that be a better idea?'

Titus chuckled. 'I'm about to be immersed in the Tiber in full view of everyone. I've decided not to worry too much about what other people think of me. Besides, I want to leave my estate to someone good. I've seen how he treats you. There is no one I would trust more. I've seen how wealth and power twisted

Quintus into something grotesque. When I die, I want to know that I am leaving everything I am and have to someone who will use it well.'

'Shall we tell Felix now?'

'No. I think we should wait until after the baptism. All this fasting is making me a little light-headed. I want to be as clear as I can be when we tell him. Right now I would like to be quiet and pray, and prepare myself for tomorrow.'

Phoebe nodded, rose, and slipped quietly out of the room. Titus's decision to be baptised in the Tiber in public was a courageous one, and, as with all courageous decisions, Titus still needed to find his own peace with it.

Chapter 25

The day of Titus's baptism was one that Phoebe would never forget. It was a day of joy, spliced with the sadness of knowing that Peter, Junia, and Andronicus would be leaving them soon after it. The word had gone around the numerous different churches in Rome, and quite a large crowd had gathered on the banks of the Tiber to witness the momentous event. After much discussion, it was decided that Titus should arrive in a litter. Titus was worried that this would be interpreted as him proclaiming his wealth and status, but Peter, far more pragmatically, argued that he would turn any hint of this on its head when he was baptised in the Tiber, and, given his frail state, it would be better if he saved his energy for standing in the river itself. In the end, Titus conceded, though reluctantly.

Phoebe was greatly concerned about Titus's frailty, and found herself gripping tightly to the hands of Felix and Bibi, one on each side, as she watched him shuffle to the water's edge. Both expressed their discomfort at the tightness of her grip by wriggling their hands around in hers, trying to get free. In the end, Phoebe need not have worried. Peter's strong arms, so accustomed to hauling in vast nets of fish, supported Titus so well that there was no suggestion of him falling as Peter dipped him beneath the murky waters, declaring him to be baptised in the name of the Father, the Son, and the Holy Spirit.

As Titus, with Peter's help, made his way back to the shore, his face shining with a serenity that can only come after an internal battle is fought and won, Bibi somehow managed to elude Phoebe's tight grip and darted into the water next to Peter.

'Now Bibi,' she declared.

Phoebe rushed forward in horror. 'No, Bibi. This is just for Titus.'

Bibi's face crumpled. 'Why? Bibi love Jesus too!'

Phoebe found herself struggling to find words that might explain why Bibi could not expect to be baptised as Titus had been. Phoebe looked around for help, and found Felix standing at her shoulder grinning from ear to ear.

'I've been telling her stories about Jesus. All the best ones I learnt from Peter. I tell a good story, you know.'

'I do know!' Phoebe had seen Felix in story-telling mode often enough to know that Bibi had learnt from the best.

'Bibi understands, she really does. Ask her. She probably knows the stories better than you do.' He turned to Peter. 'Didn't Jesus say something about the kingdom and small children?'

Peter threw his head back and guffawed. 'You're a wily one, you are. I'd give up now if I were you,' he said to Phoebe. 'He has you wriggling on a hook. They both do. You might even imagine they had planned it.'

Felix and Bibi smiled back at him, their faces a study in innocence.

Peter's face became reflective as Felix's question brought to mind a memory (as no doubt Felix had intended).

'There were many occasions when Jesus welcomed children. In fact, one time I stupidly tried to stop some parents bringing their children to Jesus. He was teaching, and I thought he wouldn't want to be bothered by them, so I got in the way and tried to send them home. It is a mistake I will never make again! That was one of the few times I saw Jesus truly angry. So if Bibi wants to come, I cannot in all conscience stop her.'

He bent down, trying to fold his enormous frame up so that he could be on eye level with the tiny Bibi.

'Bibi, would you like to be baptised?'

'Yes,' she said firmly, her small face filled with determination. 'Bibi be baptised too. Bibi love Jesus just like Jesus loves me.'

So Peter gently immersed her as he had a few moments ago with Titus.

'Bibi, I baptise you in the name of the Father, and of the Son, and of the Holy Spirit.'

As she emerged up from the murky waters of the Tiber, her face a delighted picture of joy, Phoebe discovered that she had tears pouring down her face. *I never used to cry*, she thought to herself wryly, *now I barely stop*. Almost anything would make her cry these days. She cried when she was overtaken with sorrow. She cried when she was gripped by joy. She cried when her rage with Quintus swept over her, and what felt like her futile battle to forgive him defeated her one more time. She cried with regret at so many years lost to numbness and pain. Some days she just cried, and had no idea why. The walls around her well-defended heart had been broken down and tears would flow at the smallest of excuses. She had given up trying to stop them. Whatever she did, they came anyway. She just let them flow, and smiled through them.

After Bibi, Marcus, Titus's favourite slave, came forward asking Peter to baptise him. Listening in to his stuttering account of faith, Phoebe realised that Peter had spent time with him, sharing the Good News of Jesus and what it meant – and not only with Marcus but with the rest of the household too. One by one, each member of Titus's extended household followed his lead, professing their faith and being baptised.

So it was that they all arrived back at Titus's house – the whole household wet and reeking most unpleasantly of the Tiber, though in the midst of their joy no one appeared to mind. The feast was joyous and lengthy; so much so that no one noticed Peter, Junia, and Andronicus slipping off halfway through. When, at last, she realised they had gone, Phoebe stopped and prayed quietly for them. The life of an apostle was a noble calling, but Phoebe had seen in Peter's eyes how very lonely it made him. She was glad he had Junia and Andronicus with him for this next stage of his travels, though she knew she would miss their lively, vibrant presence in Rome.

The days after the feast were quiet. The effort of getting into the Tiber had worn Titus out, and Phoebe declared he should rest as much as possible in order to recover his strength. On the fourth day after the baptism, however, the peace of the household was broken by the arrival of a delegation. It consisted of four men, all dressed in senatorial togas, with a large entourage of slaves and clients, who filled up Titus's atrium and spilled out into the street. This was clearly a 'visit', and Phoebe sent Marcus scurrying to find Titus. At the same time, she melted away, into the private areas of the house. She knew enough about aristocratic culture and expectations to know that she needed to wait to be introduced to these noble guests. She waited and waited, but Titus did not send for her as she had expected. After a couple of hours, she crept forwards again into the public parts of the house to find Titus slumped miserably, all alone in his study.

'I didn't expect it to start quite so soon,' was all he said.

After a while the story came tumbling out. As he had known it would, the tale of Titus's public baptism had circulated swiftly among the noble families of Rome. These were families who traded in honour. They could recite the long line of their family trees that stretched backwards, bathed in glory, to the time of the republic and beyond. Members of their families had been present at – and benefited greatly from – the greatest Roman military victories; if any had been present at a defeat, this fact was swiftly forgotten. They sat day after day in the Senate, wheeling and dealing in honour and insults, constantly seeking to ensure that the biggest insults landed on others less fortunate than themselves. Honour was the major business of the nobility, and, according to Titus, they had listened with incredulity when they heard that Titus had demeaned himself, and in public too. The delegation had come to ascertain the veracity of what they had heard. Did this mean that he had joined that weird, troublesome sect? Apparently lurid tales of their goings-on circulated at the best feasts and dinner parties. Weren't they the cannibals who ate their own god? Weren't they haters of humanity? What were they called? Adherents of the Christ, that was it, Christians.

Dressed up in the elegant clothing of their concern about him, Titus's noble visitors had thrown down a challenge. The next week was the birthday of Emperor Nero, and for it the usual sacrifices and celebrations would be taking place. They expected to see Titus there, joining in with everything that was going on. As he reached that part of his tale, Titus put his head in his hands and sighed with despair.

'I am ruined. There is nothing, nothing at all that I can do.'

Phoebe simply couldn't understand what the problem was. 'Can't you go and not join in? Or not go at all? Surely no one would notice if one person were not there.'

Titus smiled wearily. 'Everyone will notice. They always do. They will notice who is there, and who is not. They will notice who shows the greatest eagerness, and who reluctance. They will notice who eats, and who does not. And what is more, all this will be reported directly to the emperor himself by his network of spies. He is convinced that someone wants his power, and is paranoid that any small slight will be the beginning of the end. In fairness, he isn't wrong. Here in Rome we have seen it happen time and time again. His own adopted father, Claudius, was probably killed by his own wife, Nero's mother. Nero never forgets a slight, intended or not. He can't afford to. There are some who say he has gone quite mad. If he can kill his own mother, he can kill anyone.'

'His mother?'

'You haven't heard?'

Phoebe shook her head. Recently she had been so wrapped up in her cocoon of bliss that she had not even listened to the usual gossip that flowed around every fine household on the nimble lips of servants and slaves.

'He murdered her and pretended it was suicide. The word is that he had been trying to get rid of her for weeks. He said that she had tried to kill him. No one believed it, even though we had to pretend that we did. We think that he felt she was watching him too carefully, and he, in love with his new mistress Poppaea, wanted her gone. To begin with he just banished her from the palace, but soon even that wasn't enough. Three times he tried to poison her; three times she escaped. Then he stepped up his efforts. You have to give him credit for ingenuity and effort. They say that he built a collapsible boat that would disintegrate and crush her as she travelled home, but she got free and swam for safety. In the end, he sent assassins to beat her to death. We all know what we have to say. We are to say we believe it was suicide, and in public we do, but in the privacy of our own hearts we see it for what it was – murder. If he will kill his own mother on a whim, heaven help someone like me who crosses him. I had forgotten what happens when imperial fever grips the city. When I lived away for all those years, I yearned for home. I missed Rome's beauty and glory; I missed the majesty and splendour. What I forgot about was its evil underbelly. From time to time the grip of power becomes so toxic that everything and everyone falls under its sway. All of us at the centre are ruled, above all else, by fear, and my so-called former friends would not think twice about casting me in the path of Nero's madness if they could save their own skins.

'That's why, in the end, I had to turn my back on it all and turn to Christ. His way is gentleness and love; Rome's is terror and power. Jesus' peace comes from wholeness; Rome's from brutal suppression. Jesus poured himself out in love; Rome and its rulers fight tooth and claw to protect what they have or want. It was the right choice to make, but now I know what Jesus meant about taking up your cross to follow him. It's a choice that comes with consequences. I made that choice, and now the consequences are crowding in, I just don't know what to do.'

'I still don't understand what is so wrong about joining in with the celebrations.' Phoebe was confused, and was struggling to keep up with the cause of Titus's despair.

'Bless you and your innocence, my dear.' Titus patted her hand gently. 'If I joined in, I would have to declare that Caesar is Lord. I would have to eat the meat they had just sacrificed to idols. Joining in means declaring something that I can't. I simply can't do what they are asking. They know that, and that is precisely why they asked me. They have set a trap, knowing that all I can do is walk right into it.'

He sighed then, a long weary breath that caught at its end with the hint of a sob.

Chapter 26

Phoebe felt as though she was floundering. Thoroughly out of her depth, she had no idea what to advise Titus to do. Then, with a shudder of horror, she realised why Titus had been so agonised before his baptism. She had assumed that he was struggling with the enormity of the commitment that lay before him. Now she realised that Titus had known, as she had not, the shameful implications of his decision. Even then, Phoebe suspected that he hadn't appreciated precisely what that would feel like. It is one thing to entertain a vague theoretical idea of what something could mean; it is quite another to live it.

He desperately needed advice, and Phoebe had no idea what to suggest. They needed help – as much as they could get. So she sent messages to all her dearest and closest friends. Not for the first time since the baptism, she felt a twinge of loss that Androncius and Junia would not be there, but she sent messengers out to the others, and within an hour, they were all gathered in the familiar setting of Prisca and Aquila's workshop – Blaesus, Stachys, Herodion, Patrobas, Faustus, Hortensius, and even Felix, who, sensing the import of the occasion, had left Bibi to her own devices and accompanied Phoebe behind Titus's litter. Titus had begged Phoebe to join him in the litter – to ride as a noble lady would through the streets of Rome – but Phoebe, still not comfortable with such status, decided to walk alongside.

Once arrived, it took a while for them all to get settled. While most of their friends were accustomed to perching on any available surface, Titus, in his frail state, was unable to do so, and his slaves, led by Marcus, spent some time finding the right chair, filling it with cushions, and solicitously ensuring Titus's comfort, before withdrawing discreetly to wait with the litter outside in the street. Titus opened his mouth to speak, but Prisca cut him off peremptorily.

'We can't begin without Marcus and the rest of your household, who are currently waiting patiently outside.'

'They don't mind,' said Titus. 'They are quite used to it.'

'That is not the point. When they were baptised, they became part of the body of Christ. They are a part of us now. One of the family. In Christ there is no Jew or Greek; slave or free, male and female. We are all one in Christ Jesus. We can't just declare it to be true; we have to live it too.'

Phoebe was struck by what Prisca said. Although she had never heard those words before, she thought that they sounded like a saying; not something Prisca had just made up, but something repeated many times before. The words to ask where the saying had come from were on the tip of her tongue, but just then she was distracted by Felix jumping up and running outside to summon the household to join them.

The slaves appeared at the door, exuding reluctance. She turned and looked at Titus, and couldn't decide who appeared to be more uncomfortable – Titus, or Marcus and the other slaves. She remembered the feeling all too well, and from both sides of the experience. The world of slaves and servants was a sealed unit; the rich and powerful may command them, but may never join it. The gap was further compounded by the rich and powerful spending most of their lives oblivious to its existence. Bridging the gap was a long and complex process, and would take far, far more than a simple declaration that it no longer existed. The palpable sense of discomfort that entered the room along with the slaves declared the depth and breadth of the chasm that existed far more powerfully than words alone could have done, but Prisca was firm, and refused to allow any of them to back away from the dis-ease it evoked.

As a result, another hiatus ensued as the newest, and least willing, members of their group found a space in which to sit or on which to perch. Of all of them, Marcus was the most reluctant to join in. He claimed it was because he was concerned that a foray this deep into Transtiberium (an area that he viewed with huge suspicion) could only result in the theft of Titus's ornate litter, borne off by the riffraff that passed by the workshop. Prisca's demeanour became increasingly frosty as Marcus expressed, at length, his low opinion of the street on which she lived. Eventually, even he noticed her froideur and subsided, folding himself onto a window ledge from which he could survey both the street and the room. He contented himself with leaping from the window at regular intervals to the street outside, startling any passers-by whom he deemed to look 'suspicious'. It turned out that this was most of them. Watching his antics, the peaceable Aquila chuckled and said, 'Well at least he won't suffer the same fate as Eutychus.'

As intended, his statement drew attention away from the clash between Prisca and Marcus, and on to a new subject.

'Who was Eutychus?' asked Phoebe, realising as she looked around the room that she wasn't the only person who had never heard of him before.

Felix smiled. 'Allow me?'

Aquila nodded encouragingly, and Felix, with his usual relish at storytelling, began: 'He was a young man from Troas. One time when Paul was passing through, he got into a long discussion after the breaking of the bread. As here, the room was full, and people were perched wherever they could find a space. Like Marcus here, Eutychus had chosen the window. Let us just say that Eutychus found the conversation somewhat less than exciting and he dropped off – literally: he fell asleep and out of the window.'

At this, Marcus fell dramatically out of the window, reappearing moments later, his face split into a grin. Even Prisca thawed at this, and allowed herself the tiniest of smiles.

'I think it is time,' she said to Titus, 'to tell us what is troubling you.'

Titus sighed and began to recount what had happened that morning. As his tale unfolded, the faces of those around the room who knew more about Roman life and culture grew increasingly troubled. They all appeared to understand how difficult a situation Titus was in.

In the end Patrobas could contain himself no longer.

'Now do you see what I have been trying to say all along? I knew it would come to this, but would you listen? No, of course not! If I have said it once I have said it a hundred times, that if we are not careful we will come to the attention of the authorities. No good ever, EVER,' he raised his voice here and bellowed, 'comes of being noticed in Rome. Just look what happened to the Jews under Claudius. They rioted – making a nuisance of themselves – got noticed, and were evicted. Living in peace in Rome means making no waves, causing no trouble, doing nothing out of the ordinary. Titus will cause us trouble, just as I've said time and time again that you women running about in public will cause trouble too.' The stony look Prisca gave him at this made her froideur towards Marcus only a few moments earlier appear positively warm. 'As we all know, in proper society, women are rarely seen. They occupy the rear quarters of the house, and only appear when expressly invited.'

Prisca looked as though she was about to explode, but Patrobas hurried on. 'It is one thing for you women to take a part in our gathering together in the safety of our own houses. We are, after all, one family under God, so the usual rules do not apply when we worship together. But it is quite another thing for Junia and Prisca and others . . .' he glared here at Phoebe as though he suspected her of secretly following in Junia's footsteps and getting into public arguments outside pagan temples, '. . . to swan about the city causing trouble and dragging our good name into disrepute. Now Titus here has caused the very best, the very finest families to notice us. It is nothing less than a catastrophe. Mark my words: no good ever comes from being noticed.'

'I'm not sure you are being quite fair,' Aquila's measured tones broke in, soothing the ruffled atmosphere of the room. 'I think we have long been noticed. Just think back to what happened under Claudius. The question is not whether we are noticed. The question is whether it suits someone in power to cause trouble for us. In recent years we have been blessed that no one has found it necessary or helpful to make any difficulties and so we have lived a quiet, untroubled life. Blaming women, slaves – current or former – Jews, or the rich,' he gestured around the room at various people as he mentioned each category of potential problem people, 'avoids the central and most important issue of all. The call to follow Jesus is not the call to a quiet life. We can't help but be noticed. We can't help but cause trouble. The very person of Jesus threatens those with power in our world. It would be odd if we didn't upset them.'

'But,' Patrobas's voice began to sound desperate, revealing the deep-seated fear within, 'can't we just be a little bit sensible? Why can't we just keep our heads down? Avoid upsetting anyone. Live a quiet life. It would be so much better.'

At this, a loud hubbub broke out in the room, with angry claims and counter claims fired back and forth. It almost felt, to Phoebe, as though she were back in her beloved Corinth. An argument raged around her such as she had never yet heard in Rome.

'Excuse me.' Marcus's rich deep voice cut through the noise and ushered in a startled silence. Phoebe realised that Marcus spoke so rarely, and, when he did, in such a humble manner, that she had never guessed how strongly melodic his voice could sound.

'Excuse me for saying so,' he said. 'I know I am new to all this, and I only know the stories told to me by Peter, Titus, and of course Felix.'

Felix glowed with pride here, his demeanour suggesting that he thought he had told them best of all.

'But I don't understand the problem. The stories I know – and love – all tell me that Jesus did not keep his head down to avoid trouble. Granted, he didn't seek out trouble, but he didn't avoid it. If Prisca is right and we are all one in Christ Jesus, then isn't keeping up appearances to avoid upsetting our Roman neighbours the very last thing we should do? Shouldn't we be encouraging Titus to go to the emperor's birthday feast and be who God has called him to be? I've read and re-read the letter Paul sent to you all, and I think he would say it doesn't matter whether Titus eats the meat offered to idols or not. I think he'd agree that the idols aren't real, and are just lumps of wood, but didn't he say that we should care for each other? Seek what pleases our neighbour? Whatever Titus may or may not think himself, he now knows it troubles Patrobas, and so he can't eat any meat that has been offered to idols.

'I don't understand why you are making it so hard. Isn't it, actually, very simple? I think Titus should go to the celebrations just as he was invited to, but, when he does go, he only does what he feels he should do: he doesn't say that Caesar is Lord, and doesn't eat the meat. And when they ask him why, he can tell them.'

As he spoke, Marcus had become more and more animated, his face lit with a passion from within. He spoke with a natural authority such as Phoebe had never even glimpsed in him before. As he came to the end of his impassioned speech a silence fell on the room, as she and the others in the workshop stared at him, their mouths hanging open slightly in surprise.

Chapter 27

'Marcus,' Phoebe eventually squeezed out, 'I've never seen you like this. What haven't you been telling us?'

'I suspect,' Titus said, 'that the issue is less what he has told and more what you haven't asked. Marcus came to me a few years ago. I bought him from a slave market in Ephesus. I got him cheaply because he was in a terrible state, thin and ill-nourished, but when I looked into his eyes I saw something, and knew that he was the intelligent fellow you see before you today. It didn't take long before I was proved right. A diet of healthy meals, a good dose of care and consideration, turned Marcus into a strong and vibrant young man. A few months later I came into my study and found him reading one of my books. He isn't just clever, but literate too.

'But I should let him tell his own story, as you can tell he is perfectly capable of doing so.' All eyes in the room turned to Marcus, and he began to tell his tale. Like Phoebe, he had been taken as a child from his home. Unlike Phoebe, he had then bounced around a few slave markets until he had been bought by a curmudgeonly old man in Ephesus. He had been a cruel and brutal taskmaster, but had, nevertheless, recognised Marcus's intelligence – as Titus had a few years later – so he taught him to read, beating him savagely every time Marcus made a mistake. Fortunately Marcus's intelligence saved him from too many beatings, and before long he could read, write, and count efficiently. He soon became invaluable to his master and was beaten less.

Then, one day, his master's temper got the better of him, and he picked a fight with a couple of legionaries. He died, Marcus gleaned later, in a gutter, beaten to death. Thus began three of the worst years of Marcus's life: sold on from person to person, each time for a lower amount of money; each time fed less and less, so that it became highly unlikely that anyone would ever want to own him. But then Titus had come along, found him, and nurtured him back to life.

At this point Titus indicated that he wanted to take over the story. 'What you don't know is that Marcus protects me from a secret shame I hide. You see, I can't read. As a child I tried and tried – and was beaten for my failure – but when I look at a page the words swim around or bunch together. I just can't see what they say. Until I met Marcus I never told anyone. I just learnt to pretend I could read. It's amazing what you can do when you have money. But now Marcus reads and writes for me. He tells me what I need to know, and no one need know that I can't do it for myself. He has saved me from public disgrace time and time again. Everyone thinks my memory is bad, as I get Marcus to "remind" me what they wrote. Today, however, I decided to admit it to you. If I am to live a life in which I face shame head on, you might as well know the whole story.' He turned to Phoebe. 'Marcus read Paul's letter to me. It's why he knows it so well.'

Phoebe felt a flood of shame wash over her. She of all people knew what it felt like not to be seen, to be regarded, at best, as a piece of furniture that exists for the comfort of someone more important than her, but never as a person in her own right. And she had done exactly the same with Marcus. She had seen him as Titus's strong shoulder to help him get around, his silent shadow always ready to do his bidding, but never as Marcus – clever, determined Marcus whose passion for life burnt strongly. She had looked, but never seen him, and she felt ashamed.

She glanced around the room, and realised that she was not alone. Marcus had arrived in their midst as a slave, and no one had ever taken the trouble to see past that label to the person beyond. A murmur of apology began to rise, passed from person to person. Marcus's face split into a broad grin, and he bowed his acceptance of their embarrassment.

'You see,' he declared cheerily, 'we didn't need to come all this way for advice – I could have given it at home.'

'You could,' said Aquila, 'but we would have been the poorer for it, so I'm glad you didn't. You are quite right, Marcus, it is clear what he must do. It is simple, just not easy. In coming here, Titus has given us the gift of knowing quite what a challenge he faces so that we will do all we can to help him face it.'

This was exactly what Titus, and all their friends, did. Titus faced the challenge with quiet determination, and the whole community prayed with him and supported him. When the fateful day of the emperor's birthday came the following week, Titus set off to it in his litter, accompanied by the faithful Marcus. His face was set in grim determination, but he allowed himself a glimmer of a smile as he waved to his friends gathered by his front door. After he left, they all dispersed to their own lives, but returned at the end of the day, anxious concern written all over their faces.

Finally, Titus returned too. To begin with all he said was, 'It is done,' before sitting down wearily in his chair and gratefully accepting the goblet of wine offered to him by one of the slaves. It was Marcus who filled them in. Titus had done as they agreed. He had attended the celebrations, but declined to take part in the sacrifices, to join in the accolades given to Nero, or to eat the meat that had been sacrificed. He acted throughout with gentle, unswerving dignity, and his snubbing by those present was as blatantly obvious as it was unstated. Titus had been excluded from the best society. His words 'It is done' summed up the situation precisely. His decision had been made and enacted, and there was no turning back now.

'Well at least the worst is over,' said Aquila, optimistically.

Titus smiled at him, a smile that though gentle spoke of deep exhaustion. 'Dear friend, it has only just begun. Just you see. Much of it you won't see. Invitations to dinner parties and feasts will dry up. Clients will seek patronage elsewhere. Business will become more difficult, and decisions that would have naturally gone my way will mysteriously go another way instead. *You* won't see much of a change, but *I* will.'

At that moment a knock on the door announced the arrival in their midst of the silver worker who lived and worked in the shop on the street in front of Titus's house. He looked uncomfortable, and Phoebe thought she could see the beginnings of a bruise on his cheeks. He shuffled from foot to foot and mumbled under his breath so that Marcus had to lean in to hear him.

'He says,' Marcus reported, 'that he finds he no longer needs to rent your shop, and will clear his stuff out by the end of business tomorrow.'

Titus leant forward, concern on his face. 'Are you sure? I don't want you to be out on the streets because of what I've done. Let me take care of you . . . please!'

But the silversmith dumbly shook his head, his eyes firmly glued to the ground, as he silently backed out of the house. Titus shrugged and looked helplessly around.

There was little anyone could do to help, so after a while they drifted quietly away, all sobered by the swift manner in which Titus had been excluded from the life he had once lived. Titus, grey with exhaustion, went to lie down for a while, but only half an hour later Marcus came running to find Phoebe.

'He wants to talk to you and Felix,' he said. 'I'll go and find Felix,' he threw over his shoulder as he ran past her on his task.

Phoebe was still making her way to Titus's bedchamber when she heard Felix and Marcus behind her.

'I was practising my shorthand,' he declared, grinning broadly. 'Stachys is showing me how. It is so much better than writing normally. I don't have to stop my brain while the writing catches up! My hand and my brain can go at the same speed.' He prattled on as they made their way to Titus's room, apparently entirely unaware of the foreboding air that seemed to have descended on the house since Titus's return from the celebrations. Phoebe watched Felix as he talked. Gone was the closed-in, prickly, small boy she had first met, and in his place was a quietly confident young man. He had begun to shoot up, and already equalled her in height. Far more remarkable than any of that, however, was the fact that he was now at ease in himself: he no longer referred to himself in the third person; he looked her full in the eye as he spoke, eager to see reflected back her pride in him.

They smiled at each other, their unspoken language as articulate as the time they had first met. She offered homage to his grown, adult self, and he returned it with the gratitude he felt for the gifts of love and a family. They paused at Titus's door for a moment, but then, urged by an anxious Marcus, opened it and went in.

It was clear that Titus had not slept at all, even though he had claimed to be going to rest. His skin bore a worryingly grey tint, and his eyes were full of anxiety. Phoebe rushed to him, but he batted her away, signalling that she should sit and listen. She sank onto a bench with Felix next to her and waited anxiously for him to speak.

'Today, I realised the enormity of the task ahead of me,' he said slowly. 'I knew it would be hard, but had no idea it would be this hard, and my strength is beginning to fade. No, no dear,' he interjected to prevent Phoebe from rushing to him again, 'this is the best battle I will ever face. I am loved with a love greater than I imagined could exist. What is the loss of a little status in the face of that? But I am an old soldier, and I remember what Peter said about a king going into battle counting his troops in advance. I have counted what I have – my strength

– and I fear I do not have enough to see me through. I will use every last bit of strength I have to shine the light of the Good News of Jesus in all the finest families in Rome. It is my calling, I know that, but, like any general going into battle, I need to plan my strategy, and know what I will do. So today I have an important task.'

He turned to Felix. 'Young man, come and kneel before me.'

Felix looked from Titus to Phoebe, confusion all over his face. Phoebe shooed him with her hands, her face breaking into a broad grin. She knew what Titus was about to do, and felt delight run through her at the thought. Titus took both of Felix's hands in his, and Marcus appeared at his side – he clearly also knew what was about to happen.

'Felix,' Titus said, his voice becoming formal, his tone as Phoebe imagined it might sound in the Senate, 'from this day forth you will be my son, my legal heir in all things. I adopt you into the Cloelius Cordus family. From this day onwards you will be known as Felix Cloelius Cordus.'

And Felix – the dynamic, articulate, chatty Felix – was, for the first time since Phoebe had met him over a year ago, completely and utterly silent.

Chapter 28

After what felt to Phoebe like a lifetime, Felix got up very slowly from his knees and walked out of the room without saying a word, his shoulders hunched and his head bowed. Titus and Phoebe looked at each other in bemusement. It was not like Felix to be so very rude. A few minutes later, Phoebe followed, and found him sitting by the pool in the atrium, his shoulders heaving in huge racking sobs. Bibi, who had been playing one of her mysterious games (which in this instance involved running as fast as her small legs would carry her from the far end of the garden to the doorway that opened onto the street and back again), was standing in front of him, her small face crumpled with anxiety. She looked at Phoebe and then back again at Felix, her bright little eyes flitting backwards and forwards as though seeking stability in a suddenly rickety world.

'Lix?' she said hesitantly, but possibly for the first time since she had met him, her beloved friend and playmate was incapable of saying anything at all.

'Bibi,' Phoebe knelt down and took her in her arms. 'Felix is sad. Maybe you can find him some treasures to cheer him up?'

'Yes,' nodded Bibi, 'Bibi give tweasures.'

Despite her anxiety for Felix, Phoebe felt her heart give a small somersault of love as her granddaughter tried so hard to wrap her lisping lips around that long, difficult word. Bibi trundled off, determination oozing from every pore, as she set out on her task to find treasures worthy of distracting Felix from his paroxysm of grief. Bibi was small, but she was not light on her feet, and her resolute footsteps could still be heard long after her diminutive form had disappeared from view.

Phoebe sat quite still next to Felix. She knew from her own experience that when a well-defended heart was overwhelmed by love, it took a while for its owner to find sufficient equilibrium to speak. In the silence that ensued, Bibi's little voice could be heard trying out her newly learnt word as she journeyed from room to room, 'tweasures', 'tweasures', sometimes sung high as a bird's chirruping call, and then proclaimed low and loud – or as low as her small vocal cords allowed. Eventually, when one of these low utterances somehow mangled itself into a sound reminiscent of a frog's croak, even Felix lifted his tear-stained face and allowed the faintest of smiles across his face.

'I never thought I would ever be anyone's son,' he began slowly. 'My old master, the one who used to beat me, told me I was a nobody. He said he could beat me to death if he wanted to, and no one would care. He was right. No one would have cared. I doubt that anyone would have even noticed. I was rubbish. As disposable as a shard of pottery, maybe even more so – at least you can write on shards of pottery, reuse them again and again.

'Each time he beat me, he would say, "Perhaps today will be the day." I never questioned it. I knew I was nobody. It never occurred to me to think anything else. When at last my master died and I was turned out onto the street, I was strangely relieved. Maybe I could just curl up quietly and die. But then Herodion found me and took me to Prisca and Aquila's house. I couldn't live with him, he explained kindly, as I was a Gentile and would make him unclean. I had no idea what he was talking about, but I didn't care. I learnt to make myself useful. I was no longer a nobody, I could be somebody. Then you came along, and I knew I had found someone who would care for me, but I was happy to be your servant, really I was. I never thought

I would ever have anything more . . .' He trailed off, too over-whelmed with emotion to speak.

'But you heard Paul's letter,' Phoebe said. 'Surely you knew you were a child of God? God's heir? You are already someone's son. You have already been adopted. You have a family. I know this is big news, but it isn't that new.'

Felix shook his head. 'I knew he didn't mean me. A slave is a slave, and always will be. The sooner you accept that, the easier life is. He was talking about you free people, not people like me.'

'You're quite wrong, Felix. He did mean you. He meant exactly you. I'm sorry you didn't believe it. Don't you remember what Prisca said about Marcus and the others: "in Christ there is no slave or free"?'

'But elsewhere Paul calls himself a slave of Christ, so surely he means "in Christ there is no slave or free", only slaves? If we are all slaves, of course there is no slave or free.'

Phoebe shook her head in the vain hope it might shake her thoughts into a clearer order. A few times recently she had noticed that Felix could outstrip her in an argument without even trying. It wouldn't be long before she would lag behind him intellectually, just as she already did physically.

'No,' she said. 'I think he means quite the opposite. In Christ we are free. We are adopted and full members of God's family by right. This freedom – the greatest freedom imaginable – invites us to choose to become slaves of Christ.'

'That's mad.' Felix's face grimaced in disgust. 'Whoever would choose to be a slave? You can't choose. It's forced on you, and after that, everything else is too.'

'I think that's the point.' Phoebe felt herself struggling to make herself clear. 'Choosing to be a slave is nonsensical. It *is* foolish, just like dying on a cross. It is the maddest thing you can do, and at the same time the most sensible. Choosing to be a slave to the one who is love itself is the wisest decision you can make in your life. Choosing to be a slave of Christ is the choice for freedom. Think about it . . . but maybe not right now. How about we go back to Titus? He must be wondering what has happened to you.'

They went back to Titus at that point, who, as Phoebe had predicted, was waiting anxiously in his room. The broad grin on Felix's face told him everything he needed to know. He was about to speak – probably to say something formal and fitting – but he was interrupted by Bibi, who burst into the room behind them bearing, as though it were the most precious jewel in the world, a slightly dirty, smelly piece of cloth.

She presented it to Felix, declaring, 'Bibi's tweasure for Lix.'

Felix, who, until this moment had become dry-eyed again, burst into sobs once more. When he could speak again he explained to a puzzled Titus that Bibi had given him her 'bobo': her most precious piece of cloth, which she carried everywhere, held next to her cheek as she slept, and from which she refused to be parted. Her nursemaid reported that Bibi had searched the whole house, picking up and discarding many objects. In the end, only one thing would do to be her treasure: this, her most precious object. Smelly or not, there could be no greater sign of her love. Having presented her bobo to Felix, Bibi stayed close, eyeing it anxiously, torn between the love she wanted to show and a sudden anxiety about what she would do without it. Felix cleverly suggested that she might look after it for him, so he would know it was safe. Relieved, she scampered away, bobo clutched tightly to her chest, to return to one of her complex games. She stopped at the door, turned back, and beamed in turn at Titus, Phoebe, and Felix. Her world – which a few minutes ago had turned itself upside down – had righted itself again, and she wanted to show them how pleased this made her . . . lest they should think to make a habit of it.

Over the next few days, their lives began to settle back into a familiar routine: Titus would receive his increasingly few clients in the morning before going out to the Senate or to visit other noble families; Felix, after much discussion, decided to return to his training with Stachys – he no longer needed to, but decided he enjoyed it so much he would choose to continue; Bibi did . . . well, whatever it was that Bibi did – only Felix could have told them, but he was with Stachys, and so her games remained a mystery; and Phoebe cared for the widows and orphans, and visited anyone who was sick or who wanted to talk more about the complex and confusing letter from Paul. On the surface, everything settled back to normal, but underneath everything felt different. After the emperor's birthday, a shadow had fallen over their lives, and, at the risk of being melodramatic, Phoebe couldn't help thinking that things would never be the same again.

One morning, a few days later, one of the widows – Mary, who had been greeted by name in Paul's letter – took Phoebe aside at the end of the daily distribution of food. She was uncharacteristically nervous, shifting her weight from foot to foot. Phoebe was aware that the other widows were watching her expectantly, as though they had sent her to say something. She signalled to them all to come and sit down in one of the more private rooms, and asked what she could do to help them. Eventually Mary got over her diffidence, and as soon as she started speaking Phoebe understood the issue. The widows were grateful for everything that they were given – really grateful – and they didn't want what they were about to say to detract from that gratitude, but before they were widows, they were wives and daughters. They were people. Constantly receiving 'help' from the community felt demeaning to them. They had talked about it – at length – and they wanted to set up a business. They were all fine needlewomen. They would like to sew and sell what they sewed to earn their own money. But they were women, and not allowed to have their own business. They wondered whether Phoebe would ask Titus if he would own the business and let them work.

Phoebe told them to stay where they were. Titus was still in the atrium, having just finished with his last client of the day. Phoebe spilled out Mary and the other widows' plans, and, as she did so, Titus's face split into a wide grin.

'Yes of course! And they can have the workshop now vacated by our errant silver worker. But they will need help, selling their wares and running their business.'

A gentle clearing of the throat beside him drew their attention, as intended, to Marcus.

'Would you allow me to help? As you know, I can read and count. I know the city well. I could still come out with you on your visits, but during the rest of the time I could help establish the business.'

And so it was settled. In what felt like very little time at all, the women were comfortably set up in the old silversmith's workshop. When they said they were 'fine needlewomen', they had not exaggerated. Not only could they sew clothing and furnishings, some of them could embroider exquisitely, and one woman used bobbins to create the most beautiful tassels. Their presence in the workshop also lent a happy hum to the front of the house. The room never had fewer than ten women in it, and, if anyone were listening anywhere else in the house, they would claim that there was never a gap in the constant hum of conversation. Marcus also flourished. He turned out to be an excellent businessman, and before long had established a chain of suppliers and buyers that ensured the women had a steady stream of work making its way to a grateful noble lady the moment it was finished.

It wasn't all plain sailing: on hearing in whose house the workshop was to be found, a good number of suppliers suddenly announced that their bales of material, which they had shown to Marcus only the day before, had suddenly disappeared. But it was Rome, and there were plenty of suppliers, many of whom cared more for good money than for social standing. In spite of those families who had turned their backs on Titus, Marcus could always find ready buyers (even in the houses of those noblewomen who, purportedly, would have nothing more to do with the Cloelius Cordus family – the goods just went in the back entrance rather than the front).

Titus's formerly quiet house became a hive of activity. Through it all, Titus endured. He went regularly to the Senate, and regularly he tried to visit the families who used to be his friends. He was often rebuffed, often ignored, and often reviled publicly, but still he continued; his gentle face set in determination. Phoebe watched him with awe. She had feared the effect that this would have on him, but, other than an increased weariness at the end of the day, she saw no ill effects at all. Occasionally she asked him how he managed it, and his answer was simple: hope. There was, he said, a sentence in Paul's letter that kept him going no matter how hard the day: suffering produces endurance, endurance produces character, and character produces hope, and hope does not disappoint us because God's love has been poured into our hearts. In this hope, he said, he found strength to face each day.

Chapter 29

And so it was that weeks and months slipped by. Phoebe had been in Rome for three years, but could have sworn it was much less, until she looked at Bibi and Felix and saw how much they had grown. In the time since she had known them, Bibi had grown from a lisping toddler to a confident girl; Felix had turned into a man – a very fine man at that – and, increasingly, took over the running of the household. Mary and the other widows went from strength to strength, their needlework sought after, secretly but voraciously, by all the best families, and Marcus thrived as a businessman, but, despite Titus's frequent pleas, refused to accept his freedom: he knew who he was, he said, and without it he would feel adrift. Titus, with an extraordinary inner strength at which Phoebe still marvelled, continued to make his gentle, dignified way among his old friends, and, little by little, some of them thawed. Now, he even received the occasional invitation to a feast or private dinner, and, according to the slaves who accompanied him, often found ways to share the Good News of Jesus while he was there.

And Phoebe? Phoebe's family – Titus, Bibi, and Felix – and her many friends brought her a rich seam of joy. It was a joy that was founded on the love of God, and the grace she saw evidenced every day of her life. Living a life of forgiveness got no easier. Sometimes she felt herself overwhelmed with a rage so great that it took her breath away. Slowly, however, she began to see that she was right to be angry. Quintus had done her a great wrong, and the only response was to rage against the injustice of it. A life lived in forgiveness allowed the rage to come, but, most importantly, to go again. It didn't harbour the rage, or allow it to fester and become toxic. As she lived on, embracing forgiveness and growing into Christ, she knew that there was no other path she would choose to tread. Hard though it may still feel from time to time, she could no more imagine a life without the love of God in it than she could imagine a world without air.

She thought of Paul often, and wondered what had happened to him. They had received a few further letters after that initial dramatic one. After two years had passed, with a change of governor in Judea, Paul had asked to be sent to Rome to speak with the emperor. The various members of the community in Rome had laughed when they had heard this – no one was ever granted passage to see the emperor. It was a laugh that ended as abruptly as it had begun, as Stachys read on and declared that the new, inexperienced governor Festus had agreed, and Paul was to be sent to Rome. Another year had passed though, and they had heard nothing from him, and after a while had stopped expecting to hear either. No one said so out loud, but Phoebe could tell from the eyes of her friends that they were all thinking the same thought. The ship bearing Paul to Rome had set off at the wrong time of year, the time when the winds and tides would be against them; a ship full of prisoners would not have been able to land at Corinth (for fear of the prisoners escaping), so they would have had to sail around the perilous southern tip of Greece, notorious for its tricky tides and adverse winds. No one mentioned the fact that they had heard nothing from Paul, because to do so would invite a conversation on the topic none of them could bear to face – whether he had survived or not. Paul hovered as an unspoken presence among them all: his words still read and tussled with when they met to break bread together, but his own self not mentioned at all for fear that they would have to admit he had died.

The silence about Paul was one day broken abruptly by a

breathless Faustus, who had clearly run all the way from Prisca and Aquila's workshop to Titus's house to summon whoever was there to an urgent meeting. A quick conversation among those present concluded that there wouldn't be room in the workshop for all of them, so they decided on Phoebe, Felix, Marcus, and Mary, who hurried back to the workshop as fast as their legs would carry them. When they got there they found a travel-weary messenger whom Prisca introduced as Isaac from Puteoli. He had news, Prisca announced, her eyes dancing with delight, that would astound them all. She was right. Isaac's news did astound them: Paul had landed at Puteoli, and would be spending a few days there before travelling onwards with his Roman guard to Rome. A stunned silence fell on the room, as the many people who had assumed Paul had died readjusted their thoughts in order to take in this latest news. Before long the room was filled with a hubbub of noise. The snippets that floated over to Phoebe revealed that there was a predictably mixed response to the news, from delight to dismay; excitement to fury. What she heard challenged her to ask what she herself thought, and she had to admit that the mixed emotions in the room were almost exactly mirrored in her own heart.

When she first learnt that Paul was on his way, she experienced a mixture of delight and relief. She had, she admitted, begun to fear the worst after such a long time, and was overwhelmed with joy to discover that her dread had been unfounded. Right on the heels of that delight, however, came a further sense of dread. What would Paul say to her about the Spanish mission? Although she had worked hard on it when she had first arrived, and, with the help of Stachys, had made all the preparations necessary ready for Paul's arrival, she had not thought about it for over two years. They were no longer ready to go, and she feared that this news would not go down at all well with Paul.

Once the hubbub had died down, Prisca began to make arrangements as only Prisca could. It was agreed that a group would go out to meet Paul and celebrate his arrival in Rome. A couple of times Aquila tried to say something, but the excitement generated by Prisca's plan was so great that his words didn't so much fall on deaf ears as never made it out of his mouth in the first place. In the end he subsided, a worried look written all over his face. Phoebe wondered what it was that concerned him so much, but was soon so caught up in the tumult of excited organisation that she forgot about it until later. Eventually the plan was set. There would be two groups. The younger and swifter group, led by Felix, would head out to the Forum of Appius; the older and less agile group would go to the Three Taverns. That way Paul would have two formal welcomes on his way to Rome, and would know how honoured he was. At this Aquila's face twitched again, but this time he forbore trying to say anything. There were about a dozen people in each group, and they set out at the same time with excitement in their hearts. Phoebe stayed behind. Not, she told herself, because she didn't want to see Paul (although her nervousness about what he might say about the Spanish mission remained), but because Titus and Bibi had both caught a heavy cold, and she wanted to ensure that they were well cared for.

A few days later, news came that the delegates had returned, and Phoebe hurried to Prisca and Aquila's workshop to meet them. The mood of the returnees was not what she had expected it to be. They had left on a high of excitement, going off to offer Paul the honour they felt he deserved; they returned subdued and confused. They had clearly not received the response that they had expected. On further questioning, it turned out that Paul had greeted them, not as long-lost friends, as most had expected – whether they had met him or not – but as delegates come to honour him. At the Forum of Appius, he had received them formally in the forecourt of an inn, accepted their speeches of welcome (one of which was by Felix, and regarded by all present as the most polished of all the speeches made), and then dismissed them. The same had happened at the Three Taverns, though the meeting had lasted a little longer, at the dogged insistence of Prisca.

'I don't understand,' said Prisca, by way of summing up. 'It was as though we weren't friends at all.'

'I did try to warn you,' said Aquila. 'You have never quite understood the man.'

'What on earth do you mean?'

'Paul is a man driven by the mission given to him by God.'

'I know that.'

'Yes, but I don't think you understand what it means. Paul has no time for relationships. In fact, I don't think he would even understand why you are all upset now. He feels called to proclaim the Gospel to the ends of the earth. His arrival in Rome is a significant marker on that journey – that's why he wanted to go onwards to Spain to finish the mission. It's proclamation that matters to him, not friends. I'd be very surprised, in fact, if we hear much from him once he's settled in Rome.'

'But why wouldn't he want us to care for him? We could take him food. Look after him in his prison cell.'

Aquila chuckled. 'When have you ever known Paul to want to be cared for? He even carried on tent-making so that he wouldn't be a burden on people. Paul is thoroughly independent; the company he seeks is to help him in his proclamation, not for its own sake. You have to let him be who he is. Who he is has brought him this far, and we wouldn't be who we are without him. Let Paul be Paul; you can't change him now.'

Aquila's words, though they were badly received, proved to be true. They heard nothing more from Paul over the course of the next few days – although they did hear plenty about him.

They heard about him from Herodion, who crashed into the workshop a few days later while Phoebe was visiting Prisca, full of characteristic rage because Paul had summoned some of the Jews in Rome (though not Herodion and other Jews who already followed Christ) to his prison cell to talk to them about what had happened in Jerusalem, and about the Good News of Jesus Christ. The first Herodion knew of it was being told third-hand by the friend of a friend. It was hard to tell whether he was more outraged by Paul's invitation to the Jews of Rome, or by the fact that he hadn't been invited himself. Aquila chuckled – he seemed to be doing this even more than usual at the moment.

'Rejoice and be glad!' he said. 'Don't be offended by Paul – it could take up the whole of your life. Paul has brought new members to our number, so just be glad. Being angry is a waste of time.'

They also heard about Paul from Prisca, who, with Mary and a number of the other widows, had taken some food down to Paul in his prison cell. The soldier on duty had taken the food, his eyes gleaming with hunger, but they had been turned away. Paul was in conference with some of the Jewish leaders, and had no time to talk to them. This was a pattern that continued over the next weeks and months. Paul made it clear that his purpose for being in Rome was to proclaim the Gospel to all those who had not yet heard it. His burning ambition was to proclaim it to Emperor Nero himself. He was a man on a mission, and he simply did not have the time to spend with those who were already in Christ. Aquila reminded them all time and time again that they should not take this personally – Paul's mission was who he was, who he was called to be in Christ – but some people found it easier to take this advice than others. Prisca, in particular, struggled to accept it. She had believed that she and Aquila were Paul's friends, and was cut to the quick by his refusal to see them. Phoebe, somewhat guiltily, felt relieved. She wasn't looking forward to revealing her ulterior motive for coming to Rome, nor that she had left his plans of going to Spain sitting on a shelf festering for three years.

Chapter 30

It is remarkable how quickly 'the new' can become 'the normal'. In almost no time at all the community in Rome adjusted both to Paul's presence in their city and to the fact that they were unlikely to see much of him. What they did notice was a steady stream of people – Roman soldiers, food vendors, members of synagogues, who as a rule had nothing to do with the followers of Christ – all sent by Paul to Prisca and Aquila's workshop, having heard the Good News of Jesus Christ. Before long, their accustomed practice of explaining the faith to one person at a time, and helping people to grow as disciples, became impractical, so great was the influx of people from Paul. It appeared that his prison cell was every bit as effective a platform for spreading the Good News as the synagogues or marketplaces that he used to frequent.

Eventually Stachys suggested that they met together to offer instruction in the faith to whole groups at a time, so that as many new believers as possible could learn and grow as disciples. Felix took a lead in this. He was delighted to find large and captive audiences for whom he could weave the stories of Jesus that he had hoarded over the years, and which he loved to tell. A recent visit from Peter had filled his quiver of stories even more. Peter had brought with him, this most recent time, a quiet young man by the name of John Mark, who had accompanied Paul earlier in his ministry before leaving him abruptly in Pamphylia. His desertion later led to a falling out between Barnabas and Paul, something that John Mark still felt responsible for. Phoebe had suspected that this was the reason Peter had taken him under his wing, recognising the peculiar inner torture felt by those who thought they had let others down.

Whatever the original reason, however, for looking after him, Phoebe could see why Peter kept him by his side. John Mark shared with Felix a love of stories about Jesus. He and Felix stayed up late into the night proclaiming stories to each other, getting more and more animated as they went on. As she listened in, she sometimes imagined Jesus running around Galilee at a fast pace, spurred on by their cries of 'and immediately'. Though she might smile privately (and a little indulgently) to herself at Felix's passion for storytelling, she couldn't help admitting how valuable he was to the new followers of Jesus. He held them spellbound for hour after hour as he talked to them about the earliest disciples, Jesus' miracles and teaching, his conflicts with the high priests, scribes and Pharisees, and, ultimately, his death and resurrection. Once Felix had finished weaving his stories, others from the various communities, including Phoebe and Prisca, would join in and carefully and patiently attempt to lay out some of the ideas found in Paul's writings. Each time she took part in these sessions, Phoebe found herself glowing with the joy of helping those around her understand that little bit more about Jesus: who he was and how he had changed the world for ever.

A couple of times at the end of these sessions, Phoebe found Prisca eyeing her speculatively. The look in her eye, for reasons she couldn't understand, gave Phoebe a mild sense of nausea. Once Prisca asked: 'Do you ever think about the Spanish mission?'

'No!' Phoebe's response was a little more vehement than the question required. 'I prepared everything for Paul. It was never meant to be more than that.'

'If you say so.' Prisca twinkled her vibrant smile at her disconcertingly, and went on her way.

After Prisca had asked about the Spanish mission Phoebe

breathed a sigh of relief and looked around her for Felix and Marcus, who were waiting by the door to escort her home. She noticed that evening that there were more of Titus's slaves waiting for them than usual. She suspected she knew why.

Paul's presence in Rome meant that Patrobas's wish to remain unseen and unnoticed by the Romans became less possible day by day, as large numbers of new believers were baptised in the Tiber.

It wasn't long before Phoebe began to understand first-hand why Patrobas had been so keen to remain as unnoticed as possible. She had spent most of her life – albeit for the large part as a slave – in noble circles. Although some of her experiences had been far from happy, the world that she knew, and therefore expected to encounter, was a world of gentility and dignity. Conflict, when expressed, found a verbal form – even if that meant a disdainful silence. Titus had been deeply hurt by the verbal barbs from his noble friends, but they were simply words; words could be wounding and distorting, they could stick to the soul like burrs, but they were rarely fatal. Over the past few weeks and months, Phoebe had begun to discover that the rest of Rome expressed its feelings far more physically than Titus's noble friends. As the number of followers of Christ in Rome grew, so did the number of what Felix liked to call 'skirmishes' that broke out between them and other groups. Barely a week went by without a report of someone from the ever-growing Christian community returning home battered and bruised.

One day, when Phoebe had dropped around to Prisca and Aquila's house, as she often did for the simple pleasure of their company, Faustus and Hortensius burst through the door of the workshop as though they were being pursued by wild animals. Their clothes were muddy, smelt strongly of rotten vegetables, and appeared to have been almost ripped off their backs; blood poured down Faustus's face and one of Hortensius's arms. Phoebe suspected that it would not be long before their faces turned a mottled purple colour as bruises began to appear. There was no need to enquire what had happened, since the usually shy and reticent Hortensius turned on his friend in fury.

'I told you to leave it alone. I told you to walk on by, to rise above their insults, but you just had to respond, didn't you?'

Faustus appeared to be unrepentant. 'They brought shame on the name of Jesus. I had to say something.'

'Which was precisely what they wanted. They were baying for a reason to set on us, and you gave it to them.'

'We could have defended ourselves. Look at the size of you. Come to that, look at the size of me – we could have beaten them off in no time.'

Phoebe had often marvelled at their strength. The two mild-mannered servants of Prisca and Aquila were heavy-set, their muscles well defined after many years of lifting and carrying bales of skins – and then finished tents – in the workshop. When they stood side by side they almost filled the whole width of the workshop. Phoebe was tempted to agree with Faustus that they would have easily been able to defend themselves.

'But,' said Hortensius, dabbing ineffectually at the blood seeping down his arm, 'that is not the way of Christ. Don't you remember what Paul said? Don't pay back evil for evil; overcome evil with good. If I retaliate, if I punch back, I am doing exactly what Paul said not to – returning evil with evil. If his words mean anything at all, then I can't defend myself.'

'But what if he kills you? What if he kills *me*?' Faustus was clearly more horrified at the second thought than the first.

Hortensius shrugged. 'If I'm killed, I'm killed. I rather thought that Jesus proved that wasn't the end of the world . . . Besides, I know Lucius, the ringleader. He works for the tanners around the corner. He has a hard life, doesn't get much to eat. I thought I'd take him some food tomorrow, just like Paul said. Maybe he picks fights with passers-by because he is frustrated, hungry, and alone. Some hot food might cheer him up.'

Remembering this conversation as they walked home a few days later, Phoebe asked Marcus why they had so many slaves with them and what they would do if they were attacked. Marcus laughed, and said softly, 'I hope that the number of slaves we have with us will mean that there is no need to answer that question. *We* know that they won't retaliate if we're attacked, but I hope that anyone else thinking of attacking us won't know that.'

Phoebe joined in Marcus's laughter, wondering if that was quite in the spirit of Paul's teaching, but not sure whether she wanted to ask. Furthermore, looking around, Phoebe wasn't entirely convinced that none of the slaves would retaliate if attacked. A couple of particularly burly slaves looked ready for a fight.

'Excuse me for asking,' Marcus interrupted her slightly tortured ethical conundrum, 'but did I hear Prisca say the word "Spain"? I wasn't listening. It's just that mention of my homeland always makes my heart sing, and I thought I heard her bring it up.'

Phoebe stopped still in the street suddenly, causing the two slaves walking behind her to catapult into her back. When they had all disentangled themselves, and when Phoebe had reassured them sufficiently that she was fine, that no one was hurt at all, and when they had all begun walking again, Phoebe finally managed to overcome her astonishment.

Since Titus's baptism, she had got to know Marcus well, and in that time had learnt to trust and admire him, but in all that time had never thought to ask him where he came from. There was no reason to unless he had wanted to talk about it, which, until tonight, he had shown no interest in doing. His sudden announcement, however, brought back Phoebe's queasy sense of foreboding that had washed over her at Prisca's question earlier in the evening. When she had completed her work preparing for Paul's Spanish mission, she had completed it with only two items missing: someone who knew Spain, and the presence of Paul himself. Marcus's sudden announcement, and Paul's arrival in Rome, meant that those long abandoned plans were, at least potentially, complete. Did this mean that Phoebe needed to revisit the mission itself? No, surely not. She had made it clear all along that she was simply preparing the way for Paul, and he was still in prison. There was no need to think about it any more. Really there wasn't.

She became aware that everyone in their large party – Marcus, Felix, and a dozen or so slaves – had stopped stock still in the street and were looking at her expectantly. She looked back at them in bemusement.

Felix, seeing her confusion, came to her aid. 'You were having one of your daydreams again, weren't you? Marcus just asked you for the third time why you and Prisca were talking about Spain. Come on,' he pulled impatiently on Phoebe's arm. 'If you walk, I'll tell him.'

Phoebe walked between Marcus and Felix, but they were both so tall that they chatted happily over her head without any inconvenience at all. She listened in as Felix told, in his usual dramatic style, the story of how and why Phoebe had come to Rome; how they had spent so long making plans and gathering things together, but then had to wait because Paul had not come. All the while, an odd nagging feeling inside her tugged at her equanimity, suggesting that there was a decision to be made, one that she couldn't put off any longer.

As they entered the house, calling out greetings and blessings as they went, to Mary and the other widows hard at work in the shop at the entrance, Marcus grabbed hold of Phoebe's arms, his intelligent eyes shining with joy.

'We could do it,' he said. '*We* could take the Good News of Jesus Christ to Spain. We could go on ahead, and Paul could come after he's seen the emperor. We could take the greatest story of love to the land I love more than any other. We could do it. We could, couldn't we?'

Chapter 31

Phoebe stood stock still and stared at Marcus: her mouth was dry; her heart pounding; the nausea, which she had noticed when Prisca first mentioned Spain earlier that evening, returned in full. It felt as though a decision that she had been deliberately and determinedly evading had at last caught up with her. The moment she acknowledged this, she felt that a tsunami of questions and objections rose up within her. This was not what she had agreed to do. She had agreed to come to Rome to make preparations . . . that was all. She was not an apostle like Peter, or Junia, or Andronicus; she was not called to travel like them and proclaim the Gospel; she was called to serve her local church. She was a deacon, like Stephen or Philip. Even as she thought this to herself, she remembered that Stephen had, in fact, met his death proclaiming the Gospel to the Jews in Jerusalem, and Philip had been sent by an angel to Gaza to proclaim the Gospel to a eunuch from Ethiopia.

'Are you all right, Phoebe?' Phoebe came back to the present to realise that not only Marcus but Felix and Titus too were gathered around her, looking at her anxiously.

'What did you say?' Titus asked Marcus. 'You appear to have petrified our dear Phoebe. If I still believed in her I would say that she looked as though she had seen Medusa, the Gorgon.'

'I only said that we could go to my homeland together to spread the Good News of Jesus Christ,' said Marcus, looking bemused and not a little hurt. 'Spain is a beautiful place. There's no need for anyone to look quite like that.'

'Marcus,' said Titus, his twinkling eyes belying the sternness of his words, 'you are an idiot. You may be intelligent in many, many ways – and you have certainly saved me from shame on more than one occasion when I couldn't read something – but in other ways you are an utter fool. Phoebe has been battling with her calling ever since we first met her. Deep down she knows that, eventually, she will need to give in and go to Spain as Paul intended all along, but right now she has found a family she never thought she had. She is healing from wounds so deep that they have embedded themselves into her soul. Give her time. She'll get there, but in her own time.'

Marcus looked duly chastened, patted Phoebe feebly on the arm, and turned to go into Titus's study to continue some of the work that formed part of his daily duties. Titus leaned on Phoebe's shoulder and suggested they go to sit down. Felix came too, and sat on one side of her, while Titus sat on the other. For a long time they remained together in silence, and eventually Phoebe gave out a great sigh.

'I have to go, don't I?'

'No, I don't think you have to go,' said Titus slowly, 'but I do think you are being called to go. The question is how you answer that calling.'

Phoebe looked at him, startled.

'How long have you thought I was called to go? And why didn't you mention it before?'

'I only knew for sure when I saw your look of terror just now. It was how I felt when I knew I had to be baptised but didn't want to open myself up to the shame of it. There's no feeling like it, being held captive by God's love, while everything in you wants to run in the other direction.'

'But I haven't got what it takes. You know that. I'm no public speaker like Paul. I've had enough of adventures. I just want to settle down here, live a quiet life, serve the church as a deacon. Is that too much to ask?'

Titus was silent for a while.

'I don't think I ever told you what Peter said to me that made me able to take the plunge,' he chuckled to himself as he real-ised what he had just said, 'and be baptised. That was some plunge!'

'No, you didn't tell me.'

'He told me about Jesus' teaching, and about how he said that disciples had to take up their cross and follow him. The decision to follow always comes with a cost – a great cost – but he also said that Jesus kept on saying that "those who want to save their life will lose it and those who lose their life for my sake will find it". He was right as well. Before my baptism I held my dignity close to my chest, cherishing it like a miser. It was only when I had the courage to let it go, to lay it down and publicly sink between the dirty, stinking waters of the Tiber, that I discovered what dignity really was. You have to let it go, and when you have, you will discover what life really is. Clutch it tight to your chest, and you'll squeeze it to death.'

Phoebe felt a mighty battle erupt inside her. She knew that what Titus was saying was true. She knew – as she realised now that she had always known – that God was calling her onwards to Spain, but still she fought and fought and fought. As she fought, she felt she could hear the words of Peter ringing in her ears: 'too much to lose'. The irony was that for the first time in her life she had some-thing to lose, and not just something, but someones: people whom she loved with her whole heart, and now she was being asked to let them go. It was too hard, far too hard.

As the turmoil raged within her, a passage from Paul's letter came to her mind. After he had laid out all that God had done, Paul had said that followers of Christ should present their bodies as a sacrifice: alive, holy, and pleasing to God. The response that God required was the surrendering of their bodies. A number of times Phoebe had been asked about this as she discussed it with various people around Rome, and each time she had deflected them, drawing their attention to what Paul said next, about not shaping their minds to this world, but about being transformed by the renewal of their minds. It was easy to do, but was, she knew, a little deceitful. She had done so because she could not bear the thought of what it entailed. For years she had surrendered her body to Quintus, and the thought of doing it again – even to God – made her shiver with horror. As a result, she had held back. She had not given herself over completely to God. From time to time she was aware of a gentle, loving presence quietly waiting. It was, she knew, Jesus, waiting for her with loving patience, but still she had shied away, still she held back, unable or unwilling to give more.

Phoebe had no idea how long she sat there while she struggled with her thoughts, but what she did know was that Titus and Felix sat there with her the whole time. She could feel their prayers bearing her up as she fought on. Eventually, she heard – or thought she heard – a voice. It had a commanding authority, an authority that she knew was laced with love. It was a voice she had never heard before, but it was as dear to her as her own breath. It said quietly but firmly: 'Be still.' Straight away the raging ceased, and a deep peace spread through Phoebe, from her head to her toes. The battle was over, and in that moment of deep calm, Phoebe did what she had sworn she would never do again. She gave over her body to someone else, though this time she presented it to God, and accepted all that it meant for her present and her future. As she did so, she realised how wrong she had been to resist it. Being a slave of Christ gave the greatest freedom she had ever known; giving her body to God made her feel safer than she had ever felt in her life before. She took a deep breath, looked up and said: 'If I'm going to Spain, I had better get on with my preparations!'

'What do you mean, *your* preparations?' said Felix, indignation exuding from every pore. 'I think you mean *our* preparations?'

'But Felix, you can't go,' protested Phoebe. 'You're Titus's heir – you need to stay here with him.'

'Felix can be my heir just as well in Spain as he can here,' said Titus. 'Naming him my heir was meant to be a gift, something that freed him to be who he is called to be, not something to lock him in a gilt cage. Felix, if you want to go, you go with my blessing and encouragement.'

Felix bowed his head as he received these words. As he raised it again, Phoebe saw that his eyes were swimming with tears.

'Thank you, sir. I would have gone with or without your blessing, but to have your blessing means a lot to me. When Phoebe first came to Rome we formed a bond. At the time I was young, and I had no words to tell her what it meant, but recently Marcus found one of those stories from the Scriptures. It was about a girl called Ruth, and she said my words for me.' He turned to Phoebe as he said, ' "Where you go, I will go; where you lodge, I will lodge; your people shall be my people, and your God my God." Your God is already my God, but the rest stands. We formed a bond, you and I, so we go together.'

At that moment Marcus walked into the room.

'Go where? Where are you going, Felix?'

'To Spain!' Felix's eyes danced with the excitement of an adventure newly formed.

Joy spread across Marcus's face. 'You're going? You're really going?'

Phoebe nodded, still ensconced in a deep and secure peace. 'Yes, we really are going.'

Marcus fell to his knees before his master.

'I know I am not free to go, but would you consider allowing me to go too?'

Titus threw back his head and laughed. 'Marcus, I have been trying to persuade you to take your freedom for too long now. Please take it, and in exchange, go with them, keep them safe for me. They are both of them dear to me.' He paused reflectively, and added, 'As indeed are you too. It will be a wrench to see you go, but go you must. Take Bibi too. She needs her family around her as she grows up.'

Phoebe started forward, a look of distress on her face. 'But you will be left alone. We can't do that to you. You are old. Your strength is fading as you yourself have told us. We would be unfeeling to leave you on your own.'

Titus chuckled. 'Have you been in this house recently? I can no more be alone than I can run! There are slaves, many of them; then there's Mary and the widows, who like to look after me as though I am their own flesh and blood; there are all those who drop in to pray and to break bread together, as well as our other friends around the city. I would complain of the noise if I didn't love it so much. I won't be on my own, dear heart. I will miss you all, more than words could ever say, but I won't be lonely. I promise.'

Phoebe nodded, a sense of relief flooding over her at his mention of Bibi. She had wanted to ask whether her beloved granddaughter might come too – apart from anything else, she had no idea how Bibi would cope with being separated from her beloved Felix – but hadn't wanted to ask Titus, as it seemed too brutal a suggestion to make. She smiled as a sense of well-being lapped over her. Her greatest fear had been leaving her family behind. Now, it seemed that the moment she had surrendered to the idea of giving up her family, she had got them back again. She and Felix and Marcus and Bibi would go to Spain together, and spread the Good News there.

As she sat back, relieved and at long last at peace with herself and God, a thought suddenly struck her.

'Who is going to tell Paul?'

Chapter 32

After some discussion, various messengers were sent off not only to Paul, but also to the rest of their friends in Rome. News as momentous as this needed sharing. In very little time at all a familiar scene lay before Phoebe – the only difference being that her dear friends were gathered together in Titus's much more spacious house; not, as usual, crammed together in Prisca and Aquila's all too small workshop.

As they talked, it became clear to Phoebe that she was the only person who hadn't thought that, in the end, she would go to Spain. Everyone else – including the widows from the needle-work workshop – all gravely nodded their heads and said they were simply waiting for her to recognise it for herself. The old Phoebe – the one who had arrived in Rome all those years ago bearing Paul's letter – would have been consumed by embarrassment and shame at this; the new Phoebe was wiser. The new Phoebe knew that they had been waiting and praying for her to heal and to gain in confidence. She was surrounded with love, and she knew it. It was a new sensation – and a pleasant one.

They spent the next few hours making excited plans about the trip. Stachys, who had filed but not lost their original plans, estimated that they could be ready to leave in as little as a week. A couple of times Phoebe felt a little dizzy at the speed at which things were progressing, but she gently reminded herself that as the Spanish mission had been on hold for years, if you took the long view, its progress was far from hasty.

Towards the end of the afternoon a messenger arrived at the house, bearing a letter. When she saw him, Prisca exclaimed with delight, 'It's Timothy! I didn't know you were even in Rome!'

Timothy smiled and returned Prisca's effusive welcome. 'I've only just arrived, but Paul wanted to make sure Phoebe got his letter right away. Is she here?'

'Yes, yes I'm here! The last time I saw you was in Corinth. It feels like a lifetime ago.'

'Well, a lot has happened since then for all of us,' he said, holding out a slim scroll. 'Would you like me to read Paul's letter for you?'

'Or I can?' Stachys offered.

Phoebe felt relieved. She would prefer to hear what Paul had to say – words that she was somewhat dreading – in the voice of her dear friend, rather than Timothy's, who, gentle though he was, she knew less well. As Stachys unrolled the scroll, she braced herself for what she knew would be a telling off for taking so long to go to Spain.

'Paul, an apostle of Christ Jesus by the will of God to Phoebe, my dear sister in the faith. Grace, mercy and peace from God our Father and the Lord Jesus Christ.

I always give thanks to God for you, mentioning you in my prayers and remembering before our God and Father your faith in Christ Jesus and your immense labour of love in bringing so important a letter to the saints in Rome, so that they might be rooted and grounded in the love of God and not ignorant of that righteousness that comes from God our Father.

I was not unaware, dear sister, of the pain that you had suffered before you were in Christ and I yearned for you to find what comfort you needed in Rome. I have indeed received much joy and encouragement as I learnt of the preparations you made for me to go to Spain and now rejoice with great joy to hear that you

*intend to go ahead of me to Spain. Be bold, dear sister,
in the Lord. Do not be ashamed of the Gospel for, as
you know, it is the power of God for salvation to all
who believe. I trust in the Lord that I will come to be
with you soon.*

Greet the saints who are with you.

*To our God and Father be glory forever and ever.
Amen.'*

As Stachys' voice faded away, a silence fell on the room. A
silence that was broken by Phoebe's voice saying, 'He knew. He
knew all along.' She turned to Aquila. 'Why didn't he say? Why
didn't he tell me that he knew why I was really coming to
Rome?'

Aquila shrugged. 'I've no idea. I imagine he assumed that
you knew he had guessed. I've said it before and I shall, no
doubt, say it many times again: you should never, ever underes-
timate Paul.'

Prisca made a harrumphing sound. 'He doesn't make it easy,
though, does he?'

'Let's not start this again, dear one,' said Aquila.

'How soon will he come?' asked Phoebe. 'Does he know how
long it will be until he is released? Shall I wait until he comes
too?'

'No,' said Timothy. 'He knows nothing. He waits and prays
and proclaims the Gospel, but he knows nothing at all. You
need to know that your message brought such joy to him,
Phoebe. Ever since it arrived he has been singing from Psalm 22,
"All the ends of the earth shall remember and turn to the Lord."
He feels that at last the Gospel may spread to the ends of the
earth, that the prophecies will be fulfilled.'

'Has his singing improved at all?' Aquila asked, his mouth
twitching.

'Not much!' said Timothy.

217

'No wonder you were so keen to bring the message then.'

Timothy grinned, but forbore to answer.

So it was that a week later a small but determined party consisting of Phoebe, Marcus, Felix, and Bibi set out from Rome, first for the port of Ostia, and then, by ship, to Spain. The leaving had been hard. They all knew that it would be the last they would see of Titus, but he had quietened their anxious concerns by stating over and over again how content he was: he was surrounded by friends; he was reconciled with Phoebe; had great trust that his fine heir – Felix – would return when he was ready, and would bear with honour the noble name of Cloelius Cordus; he knew that his beloved Bibi would relish the adventure of a visit to Spain. Death was coming, he knew, but he waited for it with joy in his heart. His old bones were weary, and he was ready for his resurrection body. They went with his blessing and his love. He wanted for nothing.

Saying farewell to their other friends was less hard, but was still far from easy, not least because Phoebe couldn't shake the feeling that she would never see them again. She didn't know why – she fully intended to return to Rome just as soon as Paul had arrived in Spain – but a sense of foreboding clung to her as she said her tearful farewells.

As they journeyed out of Rome, Bibi's cheerful chatter distracted them all a little from their sorrow at leaving.

'Will we see the big fish, do you think? If I fall in the sea, will it swallow me too?'

'What on earth is she talking about?' a bemused Phoebe asked Felix.

Felix laughed. 'I've been telling her the story of Jonah. He was on his way to Spain – Tarshish, you know – when he was swallowed by the giant fish. Bibi wonders if we'll see it too.'

Phoebe smiled, her aching heart warmed by the love she felt for her travelling companions: 'Ah . . . Jonah. I've always loved that story. Like him, I've been on the run from God for far too long. It's time now to go to Tarshish and see what he has in store for us.'

They paused at the top of a hill and looked back at the great city of Rome that lay at their feet. It was such a big city, and it, and many of its people, had captured her heart.

'I will return,' whispered Phoebe. As she looked, she noticed a faint glow of red flickering and burning in one part of the city near the Palatine Hills.

'Is that a fire?' she asked Marcus and Felix, pointing to it as she looked.

'It does look like one,' Marcus answered. 'Don't worry, I'm sure they'll have it under control in no time at all.'

'And our friends will be fine anyway,' added Felix. 'Transtiberium is so marshy it could never go up in flames. Don't worry, they will be safe.'

Phoebe felt much less confident about this as she stood for a while and watched the flickering light, which was soon accompanied by billows of black smoke. The smoke hung over the city, a baleful portent – or so Phoebe imagined – of what was to come. She shook her head. She really was getting fanciful in her old age. It was just a fire. They happened all the time in Rome. As Marcus had said, it would be swiftly extinguished. She turned her back determinedly, and began to walk onwards into the future and all it would hold.

PART TWO

Notes

Introduction

Reading requires imagination. As we read, we see in our mind's eye the characters, the setting, the events as they unfold. This is why seeing a well-loved book in film or on the stage can be so disappointing; if the imagination of the director is different from our own it looks all wrong. One of the challenges of reading ancient texts – like those that make up the New Testament – is that our imaginative skills can be challenged, since most of us don't have the library of information available at our fingertips to be able to imagine what it might have been like to be there. It is harder to see in our mind's eye what the setting might have been like; harder to imagine how it might have felt for the first audience to have received whichever book we are reading; harder to understand the cultural setting and references.

It is particularly hard with the epistles – the letters attributed to authors like Paul, Peter, James, and John, and written to communities of the early church all over the Roman empire, from Asia Minor to Rome itself. In the epistles, the authors take little, if any, time to set the scene. Why would they? They were normally writing to people they knew, and who knew them. As a result it can be hard to imagine our way into the epistles, or to get a sense of what it might have been like to have received the letter for the first time. Of course, what the letter would have meant to its author, and then what it would have meant to its various recipients, is not all it can mean; the Bible continues to speak powerfully into the lives of people reading it thousands of years later. Nevertheless, being able to imagine something about the context in which and into which it was written can bring its words to life like nothing else.

What we need, therefore, is to engage in an act of historical imagination. This involves understanding as much as we can about the time, the social history, and the day-to-day life of the people writing or receiving the text we are reading so that we can think our way into what it might have been like to be those people, in the case of the New Testament, in the first century. It is when we can begin to imagine what it felt like to hear first-hand the words in, for example, Romans, that the significance of what Paul was saying begins to lift off the page and to make more sense both intellectually and emotionally.

Engaging in historical imagination – especially when the history concerned is ancient – is not easy. While we can know a certain amount about the Roman world, and what it was like to live then, we know far less about it than many other eras of history. There are many gaps in our knowledge that will never be filled. Add to that the problem that, of course, scholars do not agree about some of the details of what we do know, and the task gets even trickier. An added layer of complexity is provided by the fact that the way in which we view the world today is very different from the way in which those in ancient Rome viewed it. As a result, an attempt to imagine what it was like inevitably leads to imposing our own expectations onto a very different culture. Nevertheless, it is worth trying, while at the same time recognising the limitations that lie before us.

This book is an experiment in historical imagination. It isn't the only one. There are various examples of other acts of historical imagination; two of my favourite include Gerd Theissen's book, *The Shadow of the Galilean* (SCM Press, 2010), which attempted to bring to life historical Jesus scholarship, and Bruce Longenecker's *The Lost Letters of Pergamum* (Baker Academic, 2016), which adopts the form of a collection of letters that bring to life what it might have been like to be a Christian in the eastern Mediterranean.

What this book is and is not

It is worth, alongside this introduction, being clear about what this book is, and what it is not. It is an attempt to imagine, just a little, what it might have felt like to be Phoebe – the person mentioned by Paul in Romans 16:1–2 as a deacon of the church in Cenchreae, and a benefactor of many. Phoebe appears to have brought Paul's letter from Corinth, where he wrote it, to Rome. In Romans 16:2 he also asks that the Roman Christians help her 'with whatever she may require of you'. This opens an imaginative door begging the questions of what Phoebe was doing in Rome, and what help she might need. This is the door I pushed on as I wrote, using both scholarship and my own imagination to begin to propose some answers.

The book is not a novel. Novels are carefully crafted stories, written for the sake of the story alone, that evoke worlds and go wherever the imagination leads. This book comes, at least in part, in the form of a story, but it is not written just for the sake of the story. It is written to bring to life the characters and experiences hinted at in Romans 16, and to suggest ways in which you might imagine what it was like to be part of an early Christian community. It aims to inform as much as to entertain, and, consequently, does not fit fully into the genre of fiction.

It also can't claim to be a novel because it comes with references – notes at the end that explain some of the scholarship, indicating especially what we do know, and what we don't. You can choose to read the notes or not, as suits you. The notes are there to give you a sense of the information that I used to shape the narrative. I should say that I am aware that a book with endnotes can be annoying to the reader. I know this because endnotes annoy me too, but there is no other way of doing this kind of book. Footnotes at the bottom of the page break up the text, and are distracting. All I can do is apologise for the annoyance in advance, and hope that you find a way to be dextrous enough to flick backwards and forwards without too many papercuts. I haven't included traditional notes (with numbers in the text linking to notes at the end) because they don't work for this kind of enterprise. Instead, I've included information ordered by chapters. Inevitably there are many more notes at the start than at the end, as it takes time to set the scene. The notes are not exhaustive, but will give you a sense of the kinds of issues that are discussed in each area. Where there is more to discover, the notes will point onwards to other books for further exploration.

Probably most important of all, this book can't claim to be a novel because I am not a novelist – and to all expert weavers of stories, I offer you my admiration for your skill and my apology for the very many ways in which this story falls short of what it could be.

On imagination

My primary aim in writing this is to prod your imagination. People are familiar with imagining themselves into Gospel stories, but much less accustomed to doing the same thing with Paul's letters. This is for obvious reasons. The Gospel stories invite an imaginative inhabiting of their narrative; Paul's letters do not. Nevertheless, what I am hoping to demonstrate is that, though a less obviously fertile ground for the imagination, imagining our way into the lives of those receiving Paul's letters can give our understanding of them greater richness and depth.

I am not asking you to agree with what I have imagined. What I hope is that, in reading where my imagination took me, you might feel inspired to imagine for yourself what it might have been like to receive one of Paul's letters, and what you might have learnt from them when you did so. I have no doubt that you will disagree with some (or maybe even all) of my imaginative exercise. That doesn't worry me at all, so long as you grab the baton and carry on with some of your own.

Throughout the book I have been careful never to introduce Paul directly. The position the Romans were in when they first received the letter is the same one that we are in today. Many of them (though not all) had never met Paul for themselves. They encountered him through the encounters of others, and through his letters themselves. When this happens, who a person was or is becomes refracted through the many different perspectives of others. In this story, I have tried to reflect this a little, presenting a range of views of Paul, all evoked by the different people and the different circumstances in which they found themselves. Whenever someone tells me they just don't like Paul, I always wonder whether it is Paul himself they don't like (it may be), or whether it is the version of him depicted by someone else.

I am also acutely aware that though I have some expertise in Pauline theology, I have much less in Roman history, and so, while I have attempted to avoid anachronisms, I am sure a good number have crept in – especially in attempting to make the dialogue readable and interesting. In particular, I decided not to mimic the long, complex Greek-style sentences in dialogue, as these can be especially hard to read for people used to shorter, clearer sentences. For any glaring anachronisms that do appear, I beg your pardon and hope they do not detract too much from the overall story.

Women and the early church

I am aware that in choosing to make Phoebe the central character of this story I am stepping into hotly contested areas about women's roles in ministry generally, and leadership in particular. If you want a book that explores, in depth, the arguments involved you will need to look elsewhere. There are many books that do this, and this is not one of them. Nevertheless, my choice to weave a story around Phoebe is not accidental. As a female Pauline scholar, I have lost count of the times I have been told that Paul is 'bad for women', or something similar. You will gather, as you read, that I do not agree.

My own view is that the argument about Paul's attitude to women so often begins in the wrong place. People pull out of Paul's letters those passages (1 Corinthians 11:1–16; 14:33–36; 1 Timothy 2:8–15, as well as Ephesians 5:22–33 and Colossians 3:18–19) that appear to proscribe the role of women in one way or another, and read them all together, assuming that their presence in letters ascribed to Paul indicates a blanket situation across the whole of Pauline Christianity (i.e. the Christian communities founded by Paul and addressed by him in his letters). If you begin elsewhere, however, the situation looks different. Evidence both in Acts and in Paul's letters indicates that women were involved in various forms of leadership within Pauline communities, some as itinerant leaders, like Prisca, who, along with her husband Aquila, travelled with Paul from Corinth to Ephesus (Acts 18:2 and 18), leading a church in their house, probably in Ephesus (1 Corinthians 16:19), and another one back in Rome (Romans 16:3); others appear to have been local leaders of churches that met in their houses, like Nympha, mentioned in Colossians (4:15). Junia is mentioned as being prominent among the apostles (Romans 16:7, see page 261 for more on arguments about whether Junia was an apostle or not, and indeed a woman or not) and Phoebe is commended to the Romans as a deacon and a patron of many (Romans 16:1–2, again see page 232 below for more on Phoebe's title and role). These are not the only key women in these communities; others include Euodia, Syntyche, Lydia, Eunice, and Lois.

It is important to read the famous 'tricky' passages in Paul against a background in which women did play various significant roles in the life of the community. When you do that, the passages immediately begin to sound and feel different. As mentioned above, however, it is not the task of this book to explore those passages – they have been explored well and in depth by others. On this subject I find these books particularly helpful: Linda L. Belleville, *Women Leaders and the Church: 3 Crucial Questions* (Baker Publishing Group, 2000); Craig S. Keener, *Paul, Women, & Wives: Marriage and Women's Ministry in the Letters of Paul* (Baker Academic, 1992); Ian Paul, *Women and Authority: The Key Biblical Texts* (Grove Books Ltd, 2011). You may also find helpful Steven Croft and Paula Gooder, eds, *Women and Men in Scripture and the Church: A Guide to the Key Issues* (Canterbury Press, 2013).

In this book, I accept the view of many scholars that Phoebe was the person who carried the letter of Romans to Rome and, therefore, was most likely the one who first explained it to the Roman Christians; I also take as read that Prisca – alongside her husband Aquila – led churches that met in their house, and that Junia was, as Romans 16:7 appears to say, prominent among the apostles. The book does not mount arguments in favour of this view; it simply reflects the view that I hold after a careful reading of the text. If you disagree, you are unlikely to enjoy what follows.

Many of the details in what follows are drawn from the major commentaries on Romans. If you want to conduct further reading, you can consult them for more detail. I will only point to specific references from commentaries when they are particularly important. My four favourite (and most used) commentaries on Romans are:

- James D.G. Dunn, *Romans 1–8* and *Romans 9–16 Volumes 38a and b* (Zondervan, 1988)
- Joseph Fitzmyer, *Romans* (Yale University Press, 2007)
- Robert Jewett, *Romans: A Commentary* (Augsburg Fortress, 2006)
- N.T. Wright, 'Romans' in *The New Interpreter's Bible: A Commentary in Twelve Volumes, vol. 10: Acts, Romans, 1 Corinthians* (Abingdon Press, 2002)

Setting the scene

WHAT WE KNOW ABOUT PHOEBE

Phoebe is only mentioned in Romans 16:1–2, where Paul says:

> I commend to you our sister Phoebe, a deacon of the church at
> Cenchreae,[2] so that you may welcome her in the Lord as is fitting
> for the saints, and help her in whatever she may require from you,
> for she has been a benefactor of many and of myself as well.

Although this short passage tells us little, what it does tell us is
intriguing.

Her name

Phoebe (or Phoibe in Greek) means 'shining', and was the name
of one of the Titans (the offspring of the first gods in Greek
mythology). She was particularly associated with the moon. The
Greek mythological background of her name makes it very likely
that she was Gentile in origin – it is hard to imagine a Jew naming
their child after a Titan. Many scholars assume that she was a
freed slave. The name is relatively rare, and, where it is used, was
given to female slaves. For example, the Roman historian
Suetonius refers to someone called Phoebe who had been the
slave of Augustus' daughter, Julia. I have followed this assumption in this story, and supplied some imaginative background for
how she went from being a slave to becoming a rich benefactor.

Where she lived

Phoebe is said to belong to a church in Cenchreae, which can
also be spelt Kenchreai. Today it is called Kechries. The town
lies on the Saronic Gulf, about five miles southeast of the city of
Corinth. Cenchreae was one of Corinth's two ports. It supported

the eastern trade routes, while Lechaion served the western trade routes. Corinth was located on an isthmus, or narrow strip of land, that connected the northern region of Greece (Attica) to the south (Peloponnese). For various reasons (such as the treacherous winds that blew around the southern cape of the Peloponnese), it was simpler and safer for sailors sailing west to east (or vice versa) to remove their boat from the water and push it using logs for rollers along the *diolkos* (which was a stone ramp about four miles in length), before putting it back in the water on the other side. Various attempts to dig a canal were abandoned as being too complex or too costly, and the canal itself was not completed until 1893. Cenchreae and Lechaion, though having small populations compared to Corinth itself (which is estimated to have had a population of around 50,000), were geographically important on the trade route.

Her role as deacon and patron

One of the most striking features of Paul's introduction of Phoebe is that he calls her 'a deacon of the church at Cenchreae' and 'benefactor of many'. Both phrases require further exploration, and have been the subject of much disagreement.

The problem with the word translated as deacon (*diakonos* in Greek) is that it is a word widely used in the first century for 'servant'. The question then is whether in introducing her as a servant, Paul is attributing to her a subordinate role (as some think) or an honoured role (as others think). What makes the situation all the more confusing is the call on Christians to take humble positions (the exhortation to be as servants to each other rather muddies the water, even if in a very good way). Despite these complexities, many scholars believe that, as well as being a generic call to all Christians, the role of *diakonos* did imply a position of leadership within the church. (For more on this see the particularly helpful book by Bengt Holmberg, *Paul and Power: The Structure of Authority in the Primitive Church as Reflected in the Pauline Epistles* (Wipf and Stock Publishers, 2004, 99–102)). As a result, when Paul introduced Phoebe as a deacon of Cenchreae he expected this to evoke respect among the Roman Christians. For a further discussion of the role of 'deacons' in the church, see pages 288 –89.

The other terms *'prostatis'*, translated by the NRSV as 'benefactor', has caused even more debate than the term *diakonos*. The masculine version of this feminine noun meant 'patron' (for more on the patron–client relationship see Notes for Chapter 2), but it was often assumed (and stated) that women could not be patrons, and therefore the feminine noun simply meant 'helper', or something similar. Recent discoveries, however, indicate that women could and did offer patronage both legal and economic in the way that men did, suggesting that the best translation for the word here is 'patron'.

For more on this see Jewett, *Romans*, 946–7.

THE WRITING OF ROMANS

Where it was written

The commendation of Phoebe in Romans 16:1 to the Romans indicates that she had brought the letter to Rome from Cenchreae, one of the ports of Corinth. In addition, in 16:23, Paul sends greetings from Gaius to the Romans. It is most likely that this is the Gaius mentioned in Acts 18:7 and 1 Corinthians 1:14 as the church leader in Corinth whose house was next to the synagogue.

Some people also think that Erastus (Romans 16:23), who is described as the city treasurer, was the Corinthian official mentioned in a paving block, found by archaeologists in the 1920s, which commemorated an 'Erastus' who paid for the paving of the street in exchange for the office of *aedile* (a Roman official responsible for public buildings, the games, and the supply of corn to the city). This identification has, however, been questioned by recent scholars, and may or may not be true. For more discussion on this see S.J. Friesen, 'Poverty in Pauline Studies: Beyond the So-Called New Consensus' (*Journal for the Study of the New Testament* 26, 2004, 354–5).

Whether or not Erastus was the Erastus mentioned in the paving block, the other evidence points strongly to the letter being written in Corinth.

When it was written

The location of the writing of the letter in Corinth helps to tie down its date (a little).

Paul was in Corinth for the first time, where he stayed for eighteen months. His time there, Acts 18:12–16 tells us, overlapped with the time that Gallio was proconsul of Achaia. He was proconsul from AD 51–52. After leaving Corinth that first time, Paul travelled to Jerusalem (Acts 18:22), from there to Antioch, and onwards to Ephesus, which was the base for what people often call the third missionary journey. Most scholars argue that Paul wrote Romans at the end of this third missionary journey, and that he returned to Corinth at that point before going on to Jerusalem.

Although Acts does not report a visit by Paul to Corinth at this stage, this is not unusual: there are a number of visits that Paul made that are not recorded in Acts. Paul's stated intention in 2 Corinthians to visit the Corinthians again, and the clear evidence from Romans that it was written in Corinth, both point to a visit there just before he took 'the collection' (the money he had collected for the Jerusalem church) to Jerusalem.

After arriving in Jerusalem he was imprisoned (Acts 25:6), and held for two years before appearing before the newly appointed governor, Festus. There is discussion about precisely when Festus became governor, but it seems likely that it was between AD 59 and 61. This puts Paul in prison around AD 57–59, and therefore writing Romans somewhere between AD 56 and 58. It isn't an absolutely precise date, but it is much better than New Testament scholars often achieve.

In terms of our story, this means that the Emperor Claudius had died a few years before (in AD 54), and that his adopted son, Nero, had just begun his reign. For more on Nero's reign as emperor and how it was greeted at the start see page 258.

How do we know Phoebe took the letter to Rome?

While we cannot know with absolute certainty that Phoebe did carry Romans to Rome, Romans 16:1–2 certainly suggests that she did. The verb *sunistemi*, which Paul used in Romans 16:1, was typically used in letters of recommendation; letters that not only commended the person carrying them to the recipients, but that also designated the bearer a trustworthy representative of the author. For more on this see John Lee White, *Light from Ancient Letters* (Fortress Press, 1986, 216).

The foundations of Roman Christianity

Irenaeus writing in the second century AD associated both Peter and Paul with the foundation of Roman Christianity. Historical evidence suggests, however, that whatever their later role, Christianity was present in Rome from the late 30s/ early 40s AD (for more on the expulsion of Jews from Rome, see page 258). While this early date for Christianity in Rome seems very likely, it is almost impossible to discover much else about the foundation of Christianity.

The reality is that Christianity probably arrived in various ways in Rome via the trade route, as a result of slaves attached to households, and soldiers returning from the East. This means that by the time Paul wrote in the late 50s, there were already a number of thriving Christian communities totalling at least 200 if not more.

THE SOCIAL MAKE-UP OF PAULINE CHRISTIAN COMMUNITIES

Rich and poor together?

One of the key questions often raised by scholars is what we can know about the social make-up of the early Christian communities. In other words, were all the early Christians poor? Were some rich? What was the mix? This is an ongoing debate, and no doubt views on the subject will continue to change. The end of the twentieth century saw a proclaimed new consensus on the social make-up of the early church. It was said that until then scholarship influenced by Adolf Deissmann (a German New Testament scholar writing in the late nineteenth and early twentieth centuries) believed Christianity only to be made up of the poor.

Scholars writing at the end of the twentieth century argued that this view had now been overthrown, and that a new consensus was emerging that saw a spread of people from all classes of society (probably the most famous advocate of this view was Wayne A. Meeks in his book *The First Urban Christians: The Social World of the Apostle Paul* (Yale University Press, 1983, 51–2)). Still more recent scholars have begun to question this 'accepted' consensus. One of the fascinating issues that has arisen is the assumption that there were two – and only really two – types of people: those in crippling poverty, and the super-elite wealthy. The more nuanced position of scholars like Steven Friesen and Peter Oakes is the recognition that you cannot split society into two groups. Or

at least if you do then three per cent of the Roman population fell into the category of super wealthy, and ninety-seven
per cent into the category of poor. The reality is that then, as
now, there were gradations of wealth and social class, and
these need to be appreciated in describing the social make-up
of the early Christian communities. What I have done in this
book is to follow Friesen and Oakes in imagining that most,
if not all, early Christians were drawn from the ninety-seven
per cent, and that within that ninety-seven per cent there
were those who had moderate wealth, as well as those with
nothing at all. The picture still represents a social spread, but
a social spread that does not imagine the presence of the
super-elite.

For more arguments on this see in particular S.J. Friesen,
'Poverty in Pauline Studies: Beyond the So-Called New Consensus'
(*Journal for the Study of the New Testament* 26, 2004, 323–61),
and Peter Oakes, *Reading Romans in Pompeii: Paul's Letter at
Ground Level* (SPCK Publishing, 2009, esp. chapters 2–3).

Greek, Latin, and Hebrew

Another interesting point to notice is that Paul refers to twenty-
nine people in Rome (twenty men and nine women). Of those,
some have Latin names, suggesting that they are Romans born
and bred (like Ampliatus and Urbanus), and some have Greek
names, suggesting that they are immigrants from elsewhere in
the empire, brought to Rome by trade or as slaves (like Apelles,
Hermes, and Stachys). One person (Miriam) has a Hebrew
name, but others (like Andronicus, Junia, and Herodion) have
names that are either Latin or Greek in origin, while their
owners are identified by Paul as Jewish. This gives a sense of
the range of the community. There are Romans, Greek immigrants, and Jews in the Christian community, including Greek-
speaking Jews. This variety lies behind some of Paul's pointed

comments about relationships between Jews and Gentiles, the weak and the strong.

One of the issues in telling this story is the recognition that some Christian communities in Rome would have spoken Greek, some Latin, and some Aramaic. There may well have been many other languages spoken too. I have assumed in the story that the common language, which would have allowed all the followers of Christ to communicate with each other, was Greek, and that, when they were all together, this was the language they spoke. It would have been cumbersome – if perhaps more accurate – to have attempted to differentiate between languages in different contexts.

House/tenement churches in Pauline Christianity

Another assumption that has been accepted for many years is that the early Christians met in 'houses', which would have been typical Roman houses with a floorplan that looks a little like this:

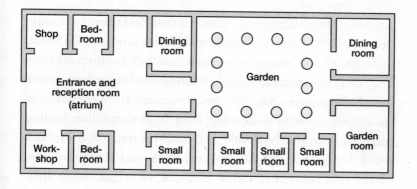

From that assumption, scholars have tried to work out how many Christians there may have been in any one community. Jerome Murphy-O'Connor famously argued for about forty, as that was the number he thought could have comfortably met in a house like the one above (Jerome Murphy-O'Connor, *St. Paul's Corinth: Texts and Archaeology* (Glazier, 2002, 156)). More recent scholars have begun to question this assumption, and, using a variety of evidence, have demonstrated that while a few communities would have met in a house like the one above, there is evidence that communities met in a range of other settings too: shops, workshops, and barns; rented dining rooms and bathhouses; outdoor gardens, and even tomb-sides. For more discussion of this see in particular Edward Adams, *The Earliest Christian Meeting Places* (revised edition, Bloomsbury, T&T Clark, 2015).

While not abandoning the range of possible meeting places, it is important to note that Robert Jewett argues that the majority of communities at the time of the letter to the Romans would have met in tenement or apartment blocks (Jewett, *Romans*, 54). This is because the vast majority of Romans lived in apartment blocks in the first century. Only the wealthiest could afford a house. This does not mean that the blocks were all run-down. What archaeological evidence can be found (given that most of ancient Rome lies covered by modern Rome) indicates that the majority of apartment blocks had workshops with attached living accommodation on the lowest floors, above which there were often very opulent apartments. The accommodation deteriorated the higher in the building it was, given the danger (and large number) of fires that broke out (for more on this see Oakes, *Reading Romans*, 89–97). It is worth adding as an additional detail that, much like modern London, far more people lived in villas elsewhere than they did in Rome. Where a simple villa would have been affordable elsewhere, the demand for property was such that the majority lived in apartments in the city of Rome itself.

In this book, I have imagined most meetings to take place in Prisca and Aquila's tent-making workshop, while at the same time giving Phoebe a villa in the coastal town of Cenchreae. As there is conflicting evidence, there is disagreement among scholars about how wealthy Prisca and Aquila were, and hence how large a house they might have had. The fact that Prisca is mentioned first leads a number of scholars to assume that she was of nobler birth than her husband. Jewett also points to the presence of the Santa Prisca parish in the Aventine district of Rome, which he claims was 'probably on the site of the original house church that was named after her', and to the Catacomb of Priscilla, which was to be found in the country estate of the Acilian family, as evidence that Prisca was of noble birth and was wealthy (Jewett, *Romans*, 955–6). Counter to this is Aquila's trade, which is relatively low status, and suggests a less noble family (Lampe, *Christians at Rome*, 195). On this point I have assumed a lower status for the couple, living out in a workshop with simple rooms above (here following Jerome Murphy-O'Connor, 'Prisca and Aquila – Traveling Tentmakers and Church Builders' (*Bible Review* 6, 1992, 40–51)).

Where in Rome were the Christian communities based?

It may seem to be an odd question to ask given how little we know about the Christian communities in the first century. Nevertheless, it is worth noting that the work of Peter Lampe has drawn together various pieces of evidence, from inscriptions to contemporaneous writings, and concluded that the majority of Roman Christians would have lived in the low-lying marshy area known then as *trans Tiberim* (i.e. across the Tiber) and now as Trastevere. If he is right, it might give one reason why Nero found the Christians so easy to blame – their houses would not have burnt because of the marshy conditions of the area.

For more on this see Peter Lampe, *Christians at Rome in the First Two Centuries: From Paul to Valentinus* (Continuum, 2006).

The size of the Christian communities in Rome

It is not easy to work out precisely how many Christians there would have been in Rome at the time of the writing of Romans. Estimates vary from only a few hundred (see Lampe, *Christians*, 82 and Rodney Stark, *The Rise of Christianity* (HarperCollins, 1997)) to several thousand (Jewett, *Romans*, 62). Jewett's challenge to the small numbers proposed by Lampe and Stark rests in there needing to be a sufficient proportion of Christians to have stimulated unrest in AD 41 and 49 and then again in the 60s AD among what was estimated to have been an overall population of between 800,000 and 1.2 million (see Neville Morley, 'The Transformation of Italy, 225–28 BC' (*The Journal of Roman Studies* 91, 50–62)).

The reality is that it is almost impossible to work out how many Christians there would have been in Rome at this point. One of the key questions is whether Paul greets everyone in Rome, just the key leaders, or those that he knows or has heard about. In this book, I decided not to attempt to reach a conclusion on this issue – having over a hundred altogether when the letter was first read, but alluding to the presence of others.

Communities and leaders

Connected to the question of the size of the Christian community is the question of how many communities there were. An examination of Romans 16 reveals that there were at least five separate communities referred to by Paul. These are:

- The church in the house of Prisca and Aquila (16:5)
- Those from among the slaves of Aristobulus (16:10)
- Those from among the slaves of Narkissos (16:11)
- The brothers and sisters who are with Asynkritos, Phlegon, Hermes, Patrobas, Hermas (16:14)
- Philologus, Julia, Nereus, and his sister, and Olympas, and all the saints who are with them (16:15)

A note on 'the slaves of' in points 2 and 3 above: the Greek is odd – literally it reads 'those from among those of Aristobulus/ Narkissos'. The best explanation of this is that it refers to those from their households, most likely their slaves.

Another intriguing feature of the list of people greeted by Paul is trying to discern who, if any, were leaders of the communities. Most assume that Prisca and Aquila led the 'church in their house'; some think that Asynkritos, Phlegon, Hermes, Patrobas, Hermas, and Philologus, Julia, Nereus, and his sister, and Olympas co-led their communities, and some that the households of Aristobulus and Narkissos created a common life together without formal leadership (see Jewett, *Romans*, 64–69 for more on this).

We also know, from elsewhere in the New Testament, that in the earliest period formal ministry was still evolving and developing. While a threefold order of ordained ministry can find its roots in the New Testament, a fully formed threefold order in which bishops, priests/presbyters, and deacons had clearly delineated and interlinked roles had not yet developed. Indeed the evidence points to bishops (or those with oversight) and deacons (or those who served a community) relating much more closely together than presbyters did. There is also very little evidence that communities were led by a single person in this period. Indeed, Brian Capper has argued that the focus on a single, designated leader within a community was a development that took place in the second century AD, once churches became too large for a domestic setting.

For more on this see Brian Capper, 'Order and Ministry in the Social Pattern of the New Testament Church' (in *Order and Ministry*, edited by C. Hall and Robert Hannaford, 61–103, Gracewing, 1996), and Andrew D. Clarke, *Secular and Christian Leadership in Corinth: A Socio-Historical and Exegetical Study of 1 Corinthians 1–6* (Brill, 1993).

What happened when people met together?

One of the great conundrums of early Christianity is the question of what worship was like when Christians gathered together. We know fragments, but not enough to have a clear idea of precisely what they would have done. They met together on the first day of the week in commemoration of the day that Jesus rose again (see Acts 20:7) and, according to 1 Corinthians 16:2, to save money for 'Paul's collection', in other words to put aside money to care for other Christians elsewhere in the Christian community. We also know that when gathered together they commemorated the last supper that Jesus ate with his disciples, using the words that he said to them at that meal (1 Corinthians 10:16–17 and 11:20–29). Just before this, in 11:1–19, Paul also talked about the proper attire for praying and prophesying, and a few chapters later (14:1–33) about speaking in tongues, with interpretation and prophesying. Elsewhere reference is made to singing hymns and psalms (Ephesians 5:20) and to instruction (Colossians 3:16). Also important was the baptism of new Christians, a practice that, like the Lord's Supper, was instituted by Jesus himself.

As well as a weekly meeting, there is also reference to the importance of ensuring that all members of the community had daily food (Acts 6:1, and James 2:15) and that they ate together, breaking bread (Acts 2:46).

Another piece of the jigsaw is the recognition that Jewish Christians would also have gone to their synagogue, where they would have prayed, read from the Scriptures (i.e. the Hebrew Scriptures, but mostly from Torah and the Prophets), and praised God for his word.

The key point to mention here is variety. The Jewish synagogues before the Rabbinic era were different from each other, with little set form of what happened when people came together, and the same would have been true of the early Christians. Those Christian communities that were Jewish in origin might well have modelled their time together on the synagogue, but those that were Gentile in origin may well have had different patterns. (A particularly interesting book on the development from synagogue worship to church is James T. Burtchaell, *From Synagogue to Church: Public Services and Offices in the Earliest Christian Communities* (Cambridge University Press, 2008), but also see the discussion about Gentile associations etc. in Meeks, *First Urban Christians*, 74–110.)

In short, then, while recognising that each community would have done things differently, key features of early Christian worship were: baptism, the Lord's Supper/Eucharist, singing hymns and psalms, thanksgiving, speaking in tongues (with interpretation), prophecy, instruction and discussion about the Scriptures, the collection of money for other Christian communities, and the daily care of members of their own community.

It is interesting to notice that Justin Martyr, writing around AD 150, reflects something very similar to this (though with no reference to speaking in tongues or prophesying):

> And on the day called Sunday, all who live in cities or in the country gather together to one place, and the memoirs of the apostles or the writings of the prophets are read, as long as time permits; then, when the reader has ceased, the president verbally instructs, and exhorts to the imitation of these good things.

Then we all rise together and pray, and, as we before said, when our prayer is ended, bread and wine and water are brought, and the president in like manner offers prayers and thanksgivings, according to his ability, and the people assent, saying Amen; and there is a distribution to each, and a participation of that over which thanks have been given, and to those who are absent a portion is sent by the deacons. And they who are well to do, and willing, give what each thinks fit; and what is collected is deposited with the president, who succours the orphans and widows and those who, through sickness or any other cause, are in want, and those who are in bonds and the strangers sojourning among us, and in a word takes care of all who are in need. But Sunday is the day on which we all hold our common assembly, because it is the first day on which God, having wrought a change in the darkness and matter, made the world; and Jesus Christ our Saviour on the same day rose from the dead. For He was crucified on the day before that of Saturn (Saturday); and on the day after that of Saturn, which is the day of the Sun, having appeared to His apostles and disciples, He taught them these things, which we have submitted to you also for your consideration.

Justin Martyr, First Apology 67

This may begin to give us a sense of the kind of worship that took place.

Finally, the names used in this book are, as far as possible, names that were used in the Roman empire. I have used people named either in Romans 16, or in inscriptions and documents mentioned elsewhere in the Roman world, and also have tried to use names that would have been used for slaves, Hellenistic Jews etc.

Chapter 1

OSTIA AND ROME

Ostia was the harbour city of ancient Rome. Anyone seeking to reach Rome by sea would come to Ostia and then travel the fifteen miles onwards to Rome itself. During the time of Julius Caesar, goods were transferred to barges and sent up the River Tiber into the heart of Rome. When travelling to Rome, Phoebe would have had to land at Ostia before travelling onwards.

Ostia Antica is a remarkable archaeological site. Its population began to dwindle in the fourth century, and it was abandoned entirely in the ninth century because of regular invasions by Arab pirates; but because it was abandoned and not further built on, the site remains as a vivid testament to what houses, tenements, and markets might have looked like.

For more on Ostia and its importance see Gregory S. Aldrete, *Daily Life in the Roman City: Rome, Pompeii and Ostia* (Greenwood Publishing Group, 2004, 23–217).

THE COMPARATIVE SIZE OF ROMAN AND CORINTHIAN HOUSES

The pressure on space and the huge comparative cost of living in Rome would have led the few who had houses to have had much smaller houses than their counterparts who lived elsewhere. Peter Oakes estimates that craft workers like Prisca and Aquila would only have been able to afford to rent about half as much space as a craft worker in Pompeii. For this reason I imagine Phoebe's house in Cenchreae to have been much bigger than Aristobulus' fictional house in Rome.

SIZE OF ROME IN THE FIRST CENTURY

As mentioned above, it is estimated that the size of the population in Rome in the first century was somewhere between

800,000 and 1.2 million (see Neville Morley, 'The Transformation of Italy, 225–28 BC' (*The Journal of Roman Studies* 91, 50–62)). There is little agreement among scholars about the population density of the city at this point, but many suggest that it had a higher density than modern Mumbai. Whether this is true or not, Rome would have felt very crowded in comparison to places elsewhere.

Nubia

The region of Nubia runs along the Nile delta south of Egypt, as far as what is now North Sudan. One of the kingdoms of Nubia mentioned in the Old Testament was the Kingdom of Kush. Although Nubia was never conquered by the Romans, the Romans made regular incursions into Nubian territory, and also had a healthy trading relationship in the region.

The different communities in Rome

As mentioned in the introduction (see page 240), Paul addresses five groups of people alongside the many individuals to which he sends greetings. This suggests that there were at least five Christian communities in Rome – though Jewett argues there were probably eight to ten. It is highly likely that these communities came together through personal connection, whether it be that they lived and worked in the same house (as with the slaves of Aristobulus or Narkissos); that they were Jewish Christians or Gentile Christians, or had a personal connection with the leaders. It seems reasonable to suppose therefore that there were groups of exclusively Jewish Christians, exclusively Gentile Christians, and those that had mixed membership.

Prisca's name coming first

One of the striking features of the appearance of Prisca and Aquila in the New Testament is that in five out of the six times they are mentioned, Prisca's name is given first (Acts 18:2, 18, 26; Romans 16:3; 2 Timothy 4:9). Only in 1 Corinthians 16:19 is Aquila's name given first. Where today, in mentioning a couple together, it would be entirely possible but less common to mention a woman before a man, in the ancient world this was strikingly unusual. The two main arguments given for this are that Prisca was of more noble birth than Aquila and hence in terms of honour needed to be mentioned first (see discussion in, for example, Meeks, *Urban Christians*, 59; Jewett, *Romans*, 956–7) and/or that she was more prominent among the early Christians at the time (see Fitzmyer, *Romans*, 735). I decided to hint at both possibilities, but do not go as far as Jewett in imagining Prisca to be from an aristocratic background.

WHO WAS STACHYS?
Stachys was mentioned in Romans 16:9 by Paul as being 'my beloved Stachys'. The name Stachys is Greek (i.e. he was an immigrant to Rome), and there are a few references to slaves called Stachys in, for example, the imperial household. I have therefore imagined him to be a former slave who used to act as a scribe/amanuensis, and someone who knew Paul well, so therefore was ideally placed both to read Paul's letter to the Romans and to make copies of it for the various communities around Rome.

THE READING OUT OF LETTERS IN THE PAULINE CHURCHES
In a largely non-literate culture, the primary way that most Christians would have engaged with any text – whether they be the Hebrew Scriptures or new letters or Gospel by fellow Christians – would have been aurally. In other words, someone would have read them out loud. By the time of the fourth century AD, there was a formal church office of 'lector', whose role it was to read out the Scriptures. There is no evidence at all that this office existed in the first century. Nevertheless, evidence

from around the ancient world indicates that some slaves were specially trained to read and write so that they could read out loud – even perform – the texts that their masters wanted to engage in.

For more on this see especially William Shiell, *Reading Acts* (Brill Academic Publishers, 2004, 1–33).

Chapter 2

PATRONS AND CLIENTS

One of the key relationships in ancient Rome was that between patrons and their clients. Although the relationship was hierarchical, there were obligations on both sides. The patron acted as the protector and benefactor of their client, and the client undertook never to bear witness against their patron or to dishonour them in any way. Clients also committed themselves to supporting their patron publicly, especially if they were campaigning for public office. A client would often line up outside their patron's house early in the morning to put their petitions to the patron when he or she had time to see them.

The patronage system in ancient Rome was based on social norms, rather than any kind of legal code. The wealthy used their money to extend influence both privately (supporting the work of their clients) and publicly (giving donations for the benefit of the place where they lived), and by doing so built up a network of relationships both public and private. Paul's introduction of Phoebe in 16:2 as a patron indicates that she had clients, and used her wealth to support a range of people, one of whom was Paul himself.

One of the big questions raised by this (and relevant to the role of the various women who feature in this story) is whether women could in fact hold such public roles in Roman society. Various Roman writers, such as Plutarch, argue for women only to be seen in public with their husbands, indicating that their influence should be kept only to the private sphere. The complexity, however, is that while numerous writers might also assert this, or something similar, there are statues to women praising their public deeds, inscriptions indicating that they were patrons, legal documents indicating that they were appointed to be legal patrons, and so on. In other words, what some Roman authors thought should be the case, was not the case. For a fascinating discussion of women and patronage see Lynn Cohick, *Women in the World of the Earliest Christians: Illuminating Ancient Ways of Life* (Baker Academic, 2009, 285–320). As she points out, the distinction between public and private has never been quite so easy to establish.

TENT-MAKING

Acts 18:3 states that Prisca and Aquila, like Paul, were tent-makers. The word used (*skenopoioi*) doesn't indicate what material the tents were made from – the two options are skins, or goat hair woven into a course cloth. The odd smell that I attribute Phoebe with noticing could come from either of these sources. Tent-making would have been a smelly job, though probably also relatively lucrative. (See C.K. Barrett, *Acts 15–28* (T & T Clark International, 2004, 863), and Ronald F. Hock, *The Social Context of Paul's Ministry* (Fortress, 1980)).

GAIUS

Romans 16:23 refers to a Gaius who sends greetings to them all. He is thought to be the same person mentioned in Acts 18:7 (as Titius Justus) and 1 Corinthians 1:14 (as Gaius) – and that his full name was, following Roman custom, Gaius Titus Justus – who lived next to the synagogue, and who was baptised by Paul. He is not thought to be the same Gaius who was a Macedonian and travelled with Paul (Acts 19:29), nor the Gaius who represented the congregation in Derbe (Acts 20:4), nor even the Gaius who received 3 John (3 John 1).

The question is, what is meant by being host to the whole church? Many commentators take this to mean that he extended hospitality to Christians travelling through Corinth who were in need of somewhere to stay. It is also possible that he had a house large enough to offer hospitality to the various groups in Corinth when they had occasion to gather together. This is the scenario I imagine in this chapter.

DESCRIPTION OF PAUL FROM PAUL AND THECLA

The earliest description of Paul can be found in the Acts of Paul and Thecla II:3, an apocryphal story about Paul that was written in the mid second century AD.

> And he saw Paul coming, a man little of stature, thin-haired upon the head, crooked in the legs, of good state of body, with eyebrows joining, and nose somewhat hooked, full of grace: for sometimes he appeared like a man, and sometimes he had the face of an angel.

Though the text cannot be demonstrated to be accurate, it is the fullest description of Paul that exists, and rings true with some of the statements that Paul makes about himself.

CORINTH AS A CITY OF FREED SLAVES

Corinth had been an ancient and proud city, with evidence of habitation from as early as 6,500 BC. During its heyday, Corinth was very wealthy, rivalling both Athens and Thebes in influence, and host of the Isthmian games (which were second only to the Olympic games), but the city was destroyed by Lucius Mummius in 146 BC, after a war with Rome.

The city was re-founded by Julius Caesar in 44 BC, and had three key groups of people: freed slaves, veterans from the army, and urban traders. As a result, Corinth gained the reputation for being the place to go to reinvent yourself: the place where people who wanted to leave the past behind could live a new life. Its other reputation, as a place of licentiousness, was due to the popularity of the cult of Aphrodite, the goddess of love. The historian Strabo maintained that there were more than a thousand prostitutes associated with the temple of Aphrodite in Corinth. Jerome Murphy-O'Connor argued that Corinth's reputation was probably harsher than its reality, and that it was no worse than any other port in the eastern Mediterranean. (See Murphy-O'Connor, *St Paul's Corinth*, 55–57.)

HERODION

Herodion is greeted personally by Paul in 16:11. His name suggests a family connection with the Herodion household, and Paul's reference to him as a 'relative', as with Andronicus and Junia below, probably refers to him being a fellow Jew rather than some kind of cousin.

ROMAN MEALS

The three key Roman meals of the day were:

- *Ientaculum* – a meal eaten just after dawn, consisting normally of barley bread dipped in oil, wine or honey, or a simple porridge.
- *Prandium* – eaten late morning, normally consisting of leftovers from the previous day's *cena*.
- *Cena* – the main meal of the day, which ranged in content depending on the wealth of its participants. Poorer people would eat a porridge made out of wheat, possibly flavoured with a fish sauce, vegetables, herbs, and meat. Richer Romans would have meals of various courses consisting of salads, meat, fish, and even desserts.

The Romans drank wine of various forms (considering both beer and milk to be uncivilised). The wine most often drunk was watered down – Romans never drank wine without water.

Prisca and Aquila, though working with their hands, appear to have been wealthy enough to travel from city to city, and to have a home in each city large enough to house a worshipping community. As a result, their food, though not lavish, would have probably consisted of more than the most basic porridge.

See Aldrete, *Daily Life* (111–113), for more on this.

Chapter 3

PETER IN ROME
Although some of the early church fathers linked Peter with Rome (e.g. Clement of Rome, Clement of Alexandria, and Irenaeus), there is considerable doubt among scholars about whether Peter ever went to Rome, let alone was the bishop there (see especially Raymond Brown, *Antioch & Rome* (Paulist Press, 1983)). Nevertheless, Christian tradition places such a strong connection between Peter and Rome (not only as bishop of Rome, but also as the place where Mark recorded Peter's eyewitness testimony to Jesus) that for the sake of this story I posit that Peter passed through on a number of occasions, sharing his stories with the Romans as he did.

PAUL AND THE LIFE OF JESUS –
DID HE KNOW THE STORIES OR NOT?
One of the surprising features of Paul's epistles is the scarcity of reference within them to the life of Jesus. Apart from the institution of the Last Supper in 1 Corinthians 11:23–26, and the numerous references to Jesus' death on the cross, there are no other clear mentions of what Jesus did in his life and

ministry. This raises the question of why this is missing. The options range from that he simply didn't know the stories, to that he knew the stories well, but assumed that everyone else knew them too and so didn't refer to them. David Wenham's very helpful book, *Paul: Follower of Jesus or Founder of Christianity?* (Wm. B. Eerdmans, 1995), demonstrates the very many latent references to Jesus' life in Paul's writings. Nevertheless, I think it likely that, when he proclaimed the Gospel, he talked more about who Jesus was and what his death and resurrection meant (as he does in the epistles) than about the stories themselves.

Hence someone like Phoebe, from a more strongly Pauline community, may not have been as familiar with the telling and retelling of the Gospel stories as a community that had been founded by other early Christians with closer links to the twelve disciples. Indeed, I am assuming that the Christian tradition that links Peter and the Christian communities in Rome had already been influenced by the Gospel stories by the time the letter to the Romans arrived.

TERTIUS AND SCRIBES IN THE ROMAN WORLD
The name Tertius means 'third', and such names were often used for slaves. Jewett suggests that Tertius was Phoebe's slave, and that she had placed him at Paul's disposal to act as his scribe, hence his gratitude to her for her patronage (Jewett, *Romans*, 979). This is something that cannot be known for certain but is certainly not impossible. The language of Tertius' greeting suggests that he too was a Christian, and thus implies (since he was at liberty to do this task) that his master or mistress was also Christian.

Scribes or amanuenses were common in the Roman world. An amanuensis could provide a range of scribal services: from direct dictation, all the way through to being given a general brief and then writing a letter in the required form and style.

Many of the letters attributed to Paul give an indication that he used an amanuensis for most of the letter before picking up the stylus to sign it off (see 1 Corinthians 16:21; Galatians 6:11; Colossians 4:18; 1 Thessalonians 3:17). Romans is the only letter in which we hear from the scribe directly.

The key question in issues of Pauline authorship is how much latitude Paul gave his scribes in recording his message. We normally assume direct dictation, but varieties in style and vocabulary might just be attributable to different scribes being given latitude in their recording of Paul's message.

PAUL AND CO-AUTHORSHIP

It was very rare in the ancient world to 'co-send' a letter. The custom was that there was one author who was listed as its sender. This custom makes Paul's habit in his letters of listing a 'co-sender' even more remarkable (though intriguingly this is often overlooked). Paul lists various people as co-senders of his letters: Timothy (in 2 Corinthians, Philippians, Philemon, and Colossians); Silvanus and Timothy (in 1 and 2 Thessalonians), Sosthenes (in 1 Corinthians). This reveals, as Thiselton observes, that 'Paul does not perceive himself as commissioned to lead or to minister as an isolated individual without collaboration with co-workers' (Anthony C. Thiselton, *The First Epistle to the Corinthians* (Wm. B. Eerdmans, 2001, 69).

The fact that Romans is an exception to the general rule (the other two exceptions are Galatians and Ephesians) indicates something significant about Paul's understanding of the epistle, and it is worth reflecting on what this is. My view is that Paul wanted to lay out his understanding of the Gospel for the Romans. The fact that he wrote the letter alone makes it clear that this *was* his vision of and for the Gospel.

Notes: Chapter 4

THAT EARLIER LETTER – 1 AND 2 CORINTHIANS

It is difficult to refer to the Corinthian epistles in any way that would have made sense to the Corinthian community. The problem is that 1 Corinthians was not the first letter Paul wrote to the Corinthian community – 1 Corinthians 5:9 refers to a previous letter he had sent. The implication is that the Corinthians responded, in whole, in part, or with a number of letters; Paul's response to that is what we now have as 1 Corinthians.

Likewise, 2 Corinthians 7:8 refers to another letter that Paul sent them (often referred to by scholars as the letter of tears), with 2 Corinthians as the follow-up to that clearly disastrous letter.

In other words, '1 Corinthians' was actually at least 2 Corinthians, and '2 Corinthians' at least 4 Corinthians (he could have written more letters as well, not referred to in the ones we now have). So referring to the letters is tricky, which is why I call them 'that earlier letter' (1 Corinthians) and 'the more recent one' (2 Corinthians).

Chapter 4

THE (NOT-SO) NEW PERSPECTIVE ON PAUL

My view of Romans is influenced strongly by the new perspective on Paul, and it is worth laying out this view of Paul's writings here.

The new perspective on Paul is no longer very new. It finds its roots in the writings of, among others, E.P. Sanders, who wrote his seminal book *Paul and Palestinian Judaism* in 1977 (SCM Press, 1977). In it, Sanders argued that contrary to popular Protestant belief (a belief largely shaped by Martin Luther and his adherents), Jews did not believe that they would be saved by doing works of the law. In contrast, they were already in a covenant relationship with God that was created because of

God's grace, and keeping the law was simply the appropriate response to God's covenant mercy towards them.

As a result, Paul's problem with the law was not, as Luther assumed, that the Jews believed that by doing the law they would be saved, but that they saw God's promises to them as exclusive. Paul's issue with the Jews was the Jewish desire to keep God's promises for Jews alone, and allied to that, to insist that any Gentile who recognised Jesus to be the Messiah needed to be circumcised and become Jewish. Paul argued that faith in and faithfulness to Jesus was all that was required to be saved.

This is a basic, probably too basic, description of the key features of the new perspective on Paul. The problem is that any description that is less basic than this quickly becomes very complex indeed, as the major proponents of the new perspective do not agree with each other on interpretation.

For more on the new perspective on Paul, see Kent L. Yinger, *The New Perspective on Paul: An Introduction* (Cascade Books, 2010), which is a good and helpful way in.

GALATIANS 2 AND PETER, AND EATING WITH GENTILES
When reading Paul's account of his dispute with Peter, it can feel as though Peter flip-flopped in his views on what was a simple subject: they had agreed that Gentiles did not need to become Jewish in order to follow Jesus, so why would Peter go back on this? The answer, as always in complex negotiations, would be a pastoral one. The agreement as laid out in Galatians 2:9–10 was that Paul would concentrate on proclaiming the Gospel among the Gentiles (the uncircumcised), while James, Cephas, and John concentrated on doing so among the Jews (the circumcised). The agreement was one of amicable division or, as Betz calls them, 'two cooperative but independent missionary efforts' (Hans Dieter Betz, *Galatians* (Augsburgh Fortress, 1979, 100)). Indeed, the only point of proposed union between Gentiles and Jews was care for the poor: a group that

appears to form a part of the Jerusalem church, since Paul spent a good portion of his time and effort collecting money for them from the Christian communities he served (see for example 1 Corinthians 16:2).

The problem was what happened when Jews and Gentiles met together, since table fellowship was an essential of early Christian worship, and Jewish purity regulations forbade Jews to eat with Gentiles. In short, the crunch question for Jewish Christians was whether Gentiles who followed Christ were still regarded as being impure. Paul thought not; James clearly thought they were. There would have been no easy solution to this conundrum among devout Jews. If they agreed with Paul, they would effectively have cut themselves off from any of the rest of their Jewish family that was not Christian. As a result, agreeing with James was far more straightforward.

The problem was that absolute separation, while easier in the short term, was not a long-term solution, nor, as Paul argued in various places, did it do justice to what they believed about faith in Jesus.

For more on this see Betz, *Galatians*, 105ff.

THE EXPULSION OF THE JEWS FROM
ROME, AND NERO'S EARLY YEARS
The Roman historian Dio Cassius reported that, in AD 41, the Emperor Claudius issued an edict that forbade Jews from holding meetings (*Roman History* 60.6.6). Many scholars believe that this was because of 'Christian agitation in the synagogues resulting in violent conflicts' (Jewett, *Romans*, 18–19), which so worried the Romans that they forbade Jews from meeting together at all. This sheds interesting light on Roman Christianity, because it means that there were Christian communities in Rome when Paul's missionary activity was in its infancy. Add to this the fact that the letter to the Romans appears to be Paul's first significant engagement with Christians in Rome

(although Romans 16 suggests that he already knew a number of Roman Christians), and Roman Christianity reveals itself to be far from entirely Pauline. Paul, therefore, had a task of persuasion to do to encourage those to whom he was writing to see things from his perspective. It also suggests that conflicts between Jews and Christians, and between Jewish and Gentile Christians, were not new in Rome.

A different Roman historian, Suetonius, reported that Claudius later expelled from Rome 'the Jews constantly making disturbances at the instigation of Chrestus' (*Life of Claudius*, 25). Although some scholars conflate this second event with the first, most see it as a separate event that took place around AD 49. This supports the Acts 18:2 reference to Prisca and Aquila being in Corinth because Claudius had expelled all Jews.

For more on this see Jewett, *Romans*, 18–20.

Claudius' reign as emperor (AD 41–54) was marked by both efficient administration and multiple challenges to his power from senators. There were a number of coups during his reign that led to the execution of a large number of senators. As a result, Nero's accession to power was hailed by many as ushering in a new golden age in which the role of Senate would be restored, and the rule of law established. This optimism lasted from AD 54 to AD 62, when Nero's rule degenerated into tyranny and extravagance. Before then Nero ruled relatively well, despite his habit of 'stalking the streets of Rome with his crowd of sycophants demanding sexual services from passers-by' (Jewett, *Romans*, 48).

THE PHARISEES

It is easy for those who only encounter the Pharisees through the pages of the New Testament to get completely the wrong impression of them. Indeed, the English-speaking world has got such a wrong impression of them that the word 'Pharisee' is synonymous with parsimonious, nit-picking self-righteousness. While there may have been some Pharisees like that, this was not the focus of Pharisaism. The Pharisaic movement had numerous phases of its life, and was sometimes more politically involved than at other times. By the time of Jesus it was largely a movement of personal piety, one that sought to evoke the expression of devotion to God in everyday life.

The Pharisees' concern with purity and food laws emerged out of this concern for everyday piety. In contrast with many who simply attended the temple three times a year, the Pharisees sought ways to be devout every day. In a way, their opposition to Jesus emerged from the fact that they both sought to encourage people into everyday devotion – the Pharisees by careful observance of the law; Jesus by living the kingdom principles of justice, mercy, and peace in everything that he did. We do know that the Pharisees' passion for the law was very attractive to their contemporaries, and two key people – Paul and Josephus (a Jewish historian writing at the end of the first century AD) – were so attracted by them that they both became Pharisees.

THE SUPER-APOSTLES

Much time and effort has been spent discussing the identity of the so-called 'super-apostles' that Paul mentions in 2 Corinthians 11:5 and 12:11. It is probable that Paul's apostolic rivals in Corinth were Hellenistic Jews, and claimed superiority over Paul in many areas including their Jewish heritage. Paul's 'foolishness speech', which begins at 11:1, appears to play them at their own game – claiming great accolades, before turning and adding in beatings, shipwrecks, and stonings. By doing so, Paul turned the whole argument on its head, reaching a climax in 12:9–10, in which he acknowledged that Christ's power was made perfect in weakness. In other words, even if the super-apostles had every superiority that they claimed over

Paul, then they would still not be 'super', as Christ's power is made perfect in weakness.

It is in the middle of this speech that Paul apparently gives in to the pressure, and boasts about his Jewish heritage.

For more on this speech, see Victor Paul Furnish, *II Corinthians* (Yale University Press, 1984, 484–556).

Chapter 5

PHARISEES AND DEBATE

The principle of debate and exploration was important to the Pharisees: pressing ideas, exploring them, and arguing about them. They were so passionate about this principle that they believed that the very same levels of study and argument went on among the angels in heaven too; they were simply doing what the heavenly court did (see Jacob Neusner, *Invitation to the Talmud* (HarperCollins, 1996, 8)). It is hard to know whether Paul learnt his skills of argument from the Pharisees, or whether he was drawn to them because he loved an argument, or both.

For more on the Pharisees see Jacob Neusner and Bruce D. Chilton, eds, *In Quest of the Historical Pharisees* (Baylor University Press, 2007), and Anthony J. Saldarini and James C.C. VanderKam, *Pharisees, Scribes and Sadducees in Palestinian Society* (Wm. B. Eerdmans, 2001).

JUNIA, ANDRONICUS, AND APOSTLESHIP

One of the most hotly contested verses in Romans 16 is verse 7, which mentions Andronicus and Junia: 'my relatives who were in prison with me; they are prominent among the apostles, and they were in Christ before I was'.

Most scholars assume that the reference to them both being 'my relatives' indicates that they were Jewish, not that they were related in any other way.

The real debate is not about that, but about Junia being 'prominent among the apostles'. Various solutions have been offered to what some think is an improbable scenario – the first that Junia was not a woman, but a man with the Greek name Junias; the second that 'outstanding among the apostles' should instead be translated as 'remarkable in the judgement of the apostles'. Neither of these explanations is particularly persuasive. The name Junia is well known in the Roman world, with many attestations; the male version Junias is not found at all, anywhere. The words 'prominent' or 'outstanding among the apostles' are written in a way that mimics other similar phrases outside the New Testament, which associates someone with being honoured among a group of people.

This is certainly how this verse was interpreted for about twelve centuries in the early church, with writers like John Chrysostom saying: 'Even to be an apostle is great, but also to be prominent among them – consider how wonderful a song of honour that is!' (*Homilies on Romans* 31:2).

The easiest and best explanation of Paul's reference is that Junia was a woman, and was honoured among the apostles – and that we should adjust our understanding of women's roles in the early Christian community accordingly.

For more on the argument about Junia see the excellent Eldon Jay Epp, *Junia: The First Woman Apostle* (Augsburg Fortress, 2005).

THE ROLE OF WOMEN IN PUBLIC AND PRIVATE
One of the big questions that arises from references to Junia as an apostle, or Phoebe as a deacon, is what roles women were allowed in the Roman empire in the public or private sphere. Almost as soon as asking the question, the impossibility of giving any kind of helpful answer becomes clear. The equivalent today would be to ask what kind of role women have in the twenty-first century. Then, as now, the answer to the question

depends on where you live, and what the cultural expectations are of the society in which you live.

There is no doubt that in many parts of the Roman empire, women were exhorted to stay at home, silently, and have no public role (see Plutarch's *Moralia*, 139c). Similar views of women in Judaism suggest that, for some at least, women's primary role was within the home. Various issues arise, however, as soon as you start pressing these assumptions. The need to state them at all suggests that there were women who did not remain silently and privately at home, and needed to be reminded to do so. Lynn Cohick also reveals a wide range of evidence, in Jewish, Roman, and Greek circles, of women who were influential as leaders of synagogues, as legal or other patrons, as educators, traders, moneylenders, and farmers.

At best, we can conclude that while many women did stay home in private, there were others who did not, and that, while no women were either politicians or soldiers, there is evidence of their role and influence in almost every other sphere of ancient life. Any assumption we make, therefore, needs to be made cautiously, and with the knowledge that there will have been exceptions to the rule. Women had little formal status: they could not be Roman citizens, and hence could not take any formal, public roles in spheres like politics. This did not mean, however, that they never emerged from the house. They could and did play roles in less formal public areas, especially if they were wealthy.

For a full and careful study on this subject see Lynn Cohick, *Women in the World of the Earliest Christians* (Baker Academic, 2009, 285–320).

THE TEMPLE OF THE DEIFIED CAESAR
After his assassination, Julius Caesar was declared to be a god, and a temple was built to commemorate him on the spot where

he was cremated. Two ramps led on each side of the temple to a large platform at its front. This was used as a speakers' platform, and was the place from which emperors often chose to speak to the people.

One of the key features of the Christian message found in Paul's writings is the proclamation of Jesus as Lord. In Rome, such a proclamation was politically charged. The emperors were known as 'Lord': Lord of everyone who lived within the Roman empire. To claim that it was Jesus and not the emperor who was Lord of all the world was directly to challenge imperial power. See for example the discussion in N. T. Wright, 'Paul and Caesar: A New Reading of Romans', in *A Royal Priesthood: The Use of the Bible Ethically and Politically*, edited by C. Bartholemew (Paternoster Press, 2002, 173–93).

PRISONS IN ROME

The prison to which Junia and Andronicus were taken might have been the Mammertine Prison.

In the Roman world, people were not imprisoned as a punishment. Time in prison was spent either awaiting trial, or, after trial, awaiting execution. The most famous prison in Rome was the Mammertine Prison, which was located at the foot of the Capitoline hill. The circular, lower room was built among the sewers underground, and known as the *tullianum*. It was where convicted criminals awaiting execution were held. Christian tradition maintains that this was where the apostle Peter was held before his martyrdom. Other parts of the prison complex were above ground, and were where people were held for trial.

THE TROUBLES UNDER CLAUDIUS

See above page 258 for a discussion of Claudius expelling the Jews from Rome.

Chapter 6

SLAVERY IN THE ROMAN EMPIRE
This note on slavery will be relevant to quite a lot of the chapters that follow.

One of the factors about the Roman world that is very hard for a modern audience to comprehend is that slavery was seen as a natural and normal part of everyday life. This does not mean that it was right, merely that it was never questioned.

The majority of slaves became slaves when their land was conquered by the Roman army. After defeat, slaves were captured and sold on by Roman soldiers to slave markets, and from there to those wealthy enough to be able to buy them. It is said, for example, that after the destruction of Carthage at the end of the Third Punic war in 146 BC, 250,000 people became slaves, debasing the 'slave' currency for a while, as so many new slaves flooded on to the market.

It is worth noticing though that there was not a rigid boundary between those who were 'slaves' and those who were 'free'; slaves could and often were freed, and those who were free could fall into slavery, often as a result of debt. It is also worth noting that there was an expectation, among some Romans at least, that slavery was a temporary condition, and that many, though not all, slaves could expect to be freed under the right circumstances.

> For many Roman slaves, servitude was a temporary situation. If they worked hard and honestly and served their master well, they could reasonably expect to be granted their freedom.
>
> Jerry Toner, *How to Manage Your Slaves by Marcus Sidonius Falx* (Profile Books Ltd, 2015, 178)

Slaves could be freed by a number of methods. Some bought their freedom. It was accepted by many Romans that it was just for slaves to save a portion of the money they earned for their master (for example a tutor might save five per cent of what they earned in tutoring) and when they had accrued their own worth in money, they could buy their freedom. Others were freed at the instigation of their masters, either in a will, or when someone inherited a household and wanted to free a childhood friend. Indeed this practice was so common that the Emperor Augustus ruled that no one could free more than 100 slaves in any one will.

Having said this, slaves were seen as the property of their master or mistress, so much so in fact that when slaves ran away they were seen as stealing themselves. This illustrates that the welfare of a slave was entirely at the whim of the person who owned them: some owners were kind, others brutal; some had favourites whom they treated like family, others were beaten or killed at will. It is also not true to say that a slave was worse off than a servant; some were, others weren't. A slave who was loved and cared for by their owner was much better off than a servant who was not owned, but who earned too small a pittance to thrive.

This story refers to a variety of slaves – some freed, others not; some well-treated, others appallingly treated – in an attempt to represent something of what it might have felt like to be a slave in the first century.

For more on slavery in the Roman world see Aldrete, *Daily Life*, 65–68.

It is in the context of the normality of slavery in the Roman world that we need to read and understand Paul's comments about being 'slaves of Christ' (a phrase often obscured in English translations, which render it 'servant of Christ'). Paul's language of being 'slaves' would have been abhorrent and repulsive in the Roman world, and never a term that would have been willingly embraced, especially by the many former slaves who made up the Pauline Christian communities.

For a fascinating study on Paul's slave language see Dale B. Martin, *Slavery as Salvation: The Metaphor of Slavery in Pauline Christianity* (Yale University Press, 1990).

THE COLLECTION

One of the fascinating nuggets of information half mentioned in Paul's letters is the collection he made for the church in Jerusalem; it is half mentioned in that he reminded various churches to contribute to the collection, but said little about how or why they would do so. He mentioned it in 1 Corinthians 16:1–4, 2 Corinthians 8:1–9, and Romans 15:25–28. From what we can glean from these passages (and from Acts 24:17), Paul collected money from around these congregations, and took it to Jerusalem to the church there, on his way to Rome.

It is worth noting, however, that Jerusalem is not on the way from Corinth to Rome, but significantly out of the way. Paul was so driven by the importance of this task that he felt obliged to go considerably out of his way in order to fulfil it. Romans 15:20–28 gives us a clue as to why this was important to him. In these verses, he indicated that he felt he had completed his mission of proclaiming the Good News of Christ where he had not previously been named ('Thus I make it my ambition to proclaim the Good News, not where Christ has already been named, so that I do not build on someone else's foundation', Romans 15:20). This also explains why he had not yet been to Rome, since Christ had already been named there. In verse 23 he made it clear that he felt there was nowhere left in the regions he had been travelling through where Christ had not been named, and so there was the need to travel onwards to what we would call western Europe.

There is a real possibility that Paul felt that this would mean he would not have the opportunity to travel to Jerusalem again in the near future, and so took this last opportunity before going west to deliver the money he had been collecting up to that point.

The reason for the collection is indicated in Acts 11:27–30:

> At that time prophets came down from Jerusalem to Antioch.[28] One of them named Agabus stood up and predicted by the Spirit that there would be a severe famine over all the world; and this took place during the reign of Claudius.[29] The disciples determined that according to their ability, each would send relief to the believers living in Judea;[30] this they did, sending it to the elders by Barnabas and Saul.

The issue seems to have been that a famine hit Judea (which was far poorer than most of the rest of the Roman empire) harder than it did other regions. As a result (and encouraged by his promise recorded in Galatians 2:10 to James, Peter, and John to 'remember the poor'), Paul had dedicated much of what is known as his second missionary journey to collecting money from the relatively well-off Christians in Greece in order to give it to the much poorer Christians in Judea.

PAUL'S VISIT TO SPAIN, AND PHOEBE'S CONNECTION WITH IT

Romans 15:20–28 set out clearly Paul's plans to travel to Spain after visiting the Christians in Rome on the way. As mentioned above, the reason for this was that Paul felt he had exhausted opportunities to proclaim the Gospel in the East, and was seeking previously un-evangelised places in which to 'name Christ' (to use Paul's own phrase). Robert Jewett argues, in my view persuasively, that the best explanation for Phoebe's visit to Rome was that she had been sent by Paul to put in place preparations for his visit to Spain, with the promise that he would follow her as soon as he could after he had delivered the collection to the church in Jerusalem.

In the story, I imagine that Phoebe had an additional motivation, which she kept hidden from Paul.

For a fully argued case, see Robert Jewett, 'Paul, Phoebe and the Spanish Mission', in *The Social World of Formative Christianity and Judaism: Essays in Tribute to Howard Clark Kee,* edited by Howard Clark Kee and Jacob Neusner (Fortress Press, 1988, 144–64).

The arrangements that Phoebe would have needed to make alongside general logistics such as how to get there, would have included finding translators. Spain, unlike the Eastern Mediterranean, spoke either its own language and dialects, or Latin. It is unlikely, though possible, that Paul, who grew up in Asia Minor and was fluent in both Hebrew and Greek, would have spoken Latin, let alone any of the Spanish dialects. As a result, an urgent task would have been to find people to accompany Paul and help him with the language.

Chapter 7

LEGIONARY LEGATE

The *legatus* (legate) in the Roman army was a general. They answered to the proconsul or provincial governor, and were drawn from the senatorial class of Rome (i.e. those whose birth made them automatically qualify to be a member of the Roman Senate). Legates received a large share of the army's plunder after a successful campaign, making the role highly sought after by those seeking to increase their wealth.

ROMAN NAMES

Roman names were made up of three parts (*tria nomina*): the *praenomen*, given to a child eight to nine days after birth by the parents; the *nomen*, the family name that identified what class someone belonged to; and the *cognomen*, an additional way of identifying someone, especially among large families. The *cognomen* indicated the branch of a family, but often took the form of some kind of nickname, referring to their (or their family's) exploits or quirks of behaviour.

The name Paul is most likely a *cognomen* (meaning small) and a part of Paul's longer Roman name that he began to use as he travelled throughout the Roman empire. Unfortunately, his *praenomen* and *nomen* are unknown, as these might have been helpful in being able to locate him in terms of class and relationship.

I have given to Titus, in this story, the *nomen* Cloelius, which was the *nomen* of a famous patrician family.

TRANSTIBERIUM

Known in modern Rome as Trastevere, Transtiberium was a low-lying marshy area in ancient Rome. It was a harbour quarter in which harbour workers as well as shopkeepers and craftspeople lived. It was densely populated, with the majority of inhabitants living in *insula* or tenement buildings.

For more on Transtiberium see Lampe, *Christians at Rome*, 48–58.

Chapter 8

MARRIAGE AND THE AGE OF WOMEN

In the Roman world, as in many ancient cultures, it was legal for girls to be married shortly after the start of puberty, around the age of twelve. As a result, while thirteen would seem to us to be shockingly young, it would not have been all that unusual at that time. In fact, numerous tombstones in Rome record the deaths of women before the age of twenty, having already given birth five to six times. Indeed it is quite possible, probable even, that extreme youth was a contributory factor in many deaths in childbirth.

Chapter 9

SWADDLING

There are votive statues depicting swaddled babies dating back as far as the second millennium BC. In particular there are many votive statues from both Greek and Roman times, indicating that the practice of swaddling was common in the ancient world. Swaddling bands were long strips of cloth, like bandages, that were tied together to make one long strip. After birth, a baby would be rubbed with oil and salt, and then wrapped in swaddling bands, both to keep them warm and to keep their limbs straight.

INFANT EXPOSURE

A father had the power to accept or reject any child born to him. Cicero described a ceremony in which a baby was placed before its father. If the father lifted up the baby, then he or she was accepted and reared within the household, if not, then the baby was either killed directly (often by drowning) or exposed. The latter practice was widespread, and ended in different outcomes.

Some people exposed babies in easily accessible places, with the expectation that someone might come along and rescue the baby; though at other times the baby would die as a result of the elements or fall prey to wild animals. There are stories, however, of people exposed as a child, but later reclaimed by their father in adulthood, and the Roman historian Suetonius tells of an expert in grammar called Gaius Melissus who was exposed at birth, but then well cared for by the man who retrieved him. He was later given as a slave to someone called Maecenas, who was kind to him. Later still, he was freed from slavery and became a favourite of Augustus.

For more on infanticide and exposure see Cohick, *Women in the World of the Earliest Christians*, 35–42.

Chapter 10

SLAVERY AND MARRIAGE

Technically slaves could not marry. They could enter into a union known as a *contubernium*, which was to all intents and purposes marriage, but their relationship depended very much on the whim of their master. The master could decide their sexual partners, and, if he chose, could split their union apart entirely. It may be hard for us to imagine this today, but it is one of those 'facts of life' for slaves in the Roman world that reveals, even in a small way, the grim reality of life as a slave. Slaves were 'property', and so were treated like other aspects of property – chairs could be moved from room to room as the master chose, and, in the same way, slaves could be moved too.

For more on marriage among slaves see Robert C. Knapp, *Invisible Romans*, 159–64.

MARRIAGE FOR THOSE WHO WERE FREE

In Rome, as in many societies, marriage was primarily about political and economic alliances. Indeed, the more aristocratic a family was, the more this was true. A marriage could be made between what we would consider to be close relatives (i.e. first cousins or uncle to niece), but both parties had to be Roman citizens; Roman law did not recognise marriage with a foreigner, a slave, or even a freedman. This didn't mean that, for example, those freed from slavery could not marry, merely that their union was not acknowledged legally.

During the period of the republic, marriages were nearly all *manus* marriages, which means that a woman was regarded as the property of her husband, and was passed from the 'hand' (in Latin *manus*) of her father to the hand of her husband. In the empire, however, this changed, and many, though not all, marriages were 'free marriages'. This meant the woman was not under the control of her husband, and retained all her own property, so that if they separated she would keep everything she owned. This is important to recognise because it shows that women could own property, could inherit, and could keep control over it.

For more on this see Aldrete, *Daily Life*, 57–62.

SLAVES, ADOPTION, AND INHERITANCE

Adoption was common in the Roman world, but it often took a form that is a surprise to the modern mind. Adoption – normally of boys as they reached adulthood – was to ensure inheritance. High levels of infant mortality, coupled with the expense of raising children, meant that young men were often adopted in order to inherit wealth and power. Indeed, many of the Roman emperors (Tiberius, Caligula, Nero, Trajan, Hadrian, Antonius Pius, Marcus Aurelius, and Lucius Verus) were adopted in order to become the next emperor. This lends Paul's language of adoption in Romans 8:15–17 a particular cultural resonance that we will explore further below.

While it was common to adopt children of other family members or close allies, it was also possible for slaves to be adopted by their masters. There are various Roman tales of slaves being adopted and named as heirs by their masters. For more on this see Robert C. Knapp, *Invisible Romans: Prostitutes, Outlaws, Slaves, Gladiators, Ordinary Men and Women . . . the Romans That History Forgot* (Profile Books, 2013, 147–53). It was not unknown, indeed, for a slave to be freed and named heir in a single will. Since the inheritance was to all the rights and property of the person writing the will, then a slave could be catapulted overnight into a position of wealth and influence.

THE WIDESPREAD NATURE OF SLAVERY

It may seem odd for a former slave to have slaves themselves. Surely, they would have hated such a practice? The reality is that Roman households (indeed the empire itself) depended completely on slaves. It is estimated that slaves made up around forty per cent of Italy's population, and about fifteen per cent of the population of the empire as a whole. Slavery was so 'normal' that it would have been almost impossible to imagine living without them.

Chapter 11

Gallio as proconsul

During the time of the empire, a proconsul was the governor of a province. The empire was split into provinces, some of which were 'imperial provinces', and others of which were 'senatorial provinces'. The imperial provinces, which were mostly found on the borders of the empire, were ruled directly by the emperor via a personally appointed governor. Most of the Roman legions were stationed in the imperial provinces. The senatorial provinces were governed by a proconsul elected for a single year by the Senate. Gallio was sent as proconsul to Achaea around AD 51–52, and is mentioned in Acts 18:12–17 where he displayed little interest in or sensitivity to Jewish complaints.

Gallio's full name was Lucius Junius Gallio Annaeanus. He was born Lucius Annaeus Novatus, and was the son of Seneca the Elder, and the older brother of Seneca the Younger. His name comes from his adoptive father, Lucius Junius Gallio, who was an influential rhetorician of the period.

The name Chrestus

The name Chrestus was widely used in the Graeco-Roman world and did originally mean 'useful'. It is quite possible that this name was mistaken for Christos (in Greek, the word for Messiah). Indeed Suetonius, the Roman historian, makes the following observation as an explanation for why the Jews were expelled from Rome during the reign of Claudius: 'As the Jews were making constant disturbances at the instigation of Chrestus, he expelled them from Rome' (Suetonius Claudius 25:4).

Scholars are divided about whether this refers to Jesus Christ or to another Jew called Chrestus. It does not matter for our story whether this was, in fact, a reference to Jesus or not. It illustrates that the names Chrestus and Christos could potentially quite easily be mixed up.

Kurios/ Lord

The statement that 'Jesus is Lord' (e.g. 1 Corinthians 12:3; Romans 10:9–13) is thought by some scholars to be a profound challenge to the rule of the Roman emperor. The emperor was known as 'lord', so to claim that Jesus is Lord was to set up a rival power to the totalitarian rule of the Romans. If the Romans heard this statement as scholars imagine they did, then they would have been offended by it.

For more on this see N.T. Wright, 'Paul and Caesar'.

Chapter 12

Barnabas and Paul

The split between Paul and Barnabas is reported in Acts 15:39, where their disagreement over whether John Mark should be allowed to accompany them became so sharp (literally the Greek says that 'it became a provocation', i.e. a bone of contention) that they agreed to part company. The question is, what was it that so annoyed them both that it was better to part? Acts suggests that it was the fact that John Mark had previously deserted them (15:38); other scholars wonder whether when he deserted them he joined those who did not eat with Gentiles, thus causing Paul's wrath (this is certainly suggested by Galatians 2:13).

As with all relationship breakdowns, it probably involved a range of factors, and a personality clash, if there was one, would not have helped the situation.

QUARTUS

Quartus is mentioned, alongside the majority of the rest of the characters in this book, in Romans 16 (16:23). His name means simply 'fourth', which may well indicate that he was or had been a slave. In some households, slaves were simply named by the order in which they had arrived in the house. What is intriguing about Quartus is that Paul singled him out for a greeting as 'the brother'. As so little is known about him it is hard to work out why Paul identified him in that way.

Jewett suggests that he was the brother of Erastus, and that the whole phrase should read: 'Erastus and his brother Quartus' (see Jewett, *Romans,* 981–84).

STATUS INCONSISTENCY, AND EARLY CHRISTIANITY

Sociologists use the term 'status inconsistency' to refer to the dislocation and isolation felt when a person transgresses the firmly held categories of status in a society. Wayne Meeks observed that one of the crises faced by the Romans in the first century was a large number of people whose status was inconsistent. He postulated that the close bonds of Christianity might have bridged some of those gaps:

> May we further guess that the sorts of status inconsistency we observed – independent women with moderate wealth, Jews with wealth in a pagan society, freedmen with skill and money but stigmatised by origin, and so on – brought with them not only anxiety but also loneliness, in a society in which social position was important and usually rigid? Would, then, the intimacy of the Christian groups become a welcome refuge, the emotion-charged language of family and affection and the

image of a caring, personal God powerful antidotes, while the
master symbol of the crucified savior crystallised a believable
picture of the way the world seemed really to work?

Meeks, First Urban Christians, 191

I have sought to suggest that Phoebe, a freed slave with now an
apparently large fortune, would have suffered some of the
pangs of status inconsistency described by Meeks, and that
relationships within the Christian community would have been
very welcome to her.

CHLOE'S PEOPLE
In 1 Corinthians 1:11, Paul refers to a group he calls 'Chloe's
people'. Scholars have debated extensively as to who they might
have been. The majority agree that they were probably slaves of
someone called Chloe who were supporters of Paul, who felt
the need to report to him disharmony among the Corinthian
community.

DYING AND RISING WITH CHRIST
The themes discussed in this chapter are themes discussed by
many Pauline scholars. One of my favourite unpackings of
them can be found in Michael J. Gorman, *Inhabiting the
Cruciform God: Kenosis, Justification, and Theosis in Paul's
Narrative Soteriology* (Wm. B. Eerdmans, 2009).

Chapter 13

FOOD STANDS
There is extensive evidence from Pompeii that the majority of
non-elite Romans did not have the means to cook in their own
houses. Pompeii is thought by archaeologists to have had in
the region of 120 taverns or *popinae*. A *popina* had a wide
storefront open onto the street, so that people could buy food

to 'take away' as well as to eat in. It is thought that most poorer Romans would have eaten the majority of their main meals this way, and would have bought hot stews, cuts of hot meat, tripe, hot tarts, and various kinds of vegetables to eat in the evening.

Taverns were looked down on by the Roman elite. Lucilius, a Roman satirist, described them as infamous, shameful vittling houses (1:11), and Juvenal as reeking cookshops (11:81).

For more on taverns see Gustav Hermansen, *Ostia: Aspects of Roman City Life* (University of Alberta, 1981, 125–96).

EPHESUS

Christian tradition records that John the Apostle settled in Ephesus after he left Judea. There is extensive debate about whether the John attributed to have lived in Ephesus by early fathers such as Papias, Polycarp, and Irenaeus (and to have written some or all of John's Gospel; Johannine epistles, and Revelation) was John the Apostle or John the Elder. Much less discussed is the overlap between Johannine and Pauline Christianity in Ephesus. I have long been fascinated by the potential theological connections between the letter to the Ephesians and the Gospel of John.

In Christian tradition, John lived into old age in Ephesus. The letter to the Ephesians, which, although some scholars dispute its authorship, is part of the Pauline tradition, may well have been received by the Ephesian community while John lived there. Once an initial connection is established, it is fascinating to compare theological themes in both Ephesians and the fourth Gospel, and to note some very interesting points of overlap.

In this chapter I have imagined that Prisca, while she lived in Ephesus, could have spoken to John and learnt parts of what can only be found in John's Gospel.

Variety in early Christian worship

In this chapter I am trying to illustrate that there was, probably, as much variety in Christian worship in the early church as there is today. Gordon Wakefield, in his book on worship, contrasts Acts with the Johannine community; I have contrasted Corinth with Rome. The reality is that there were probably different communities in each place with different styles.

> We must not think that the early Christians all agreed about worship, which seems ... to have been a combination of 'chaotic informality' and great reverence, with some contention between parties more inclined to one than the other.
>
> Gordon S. Wakefield, *An Outline of Christian Worship* (T&T Clark Ltd, 1998, 8)

Chapter 14

Spain

In the Roman world, Spain was often seen as a land of Barbarians. The inhabitants were resistant to Graeco-Roman culture, and, in addition, in the first century contained no known Jewish communities. On certain Roman maps, Iberium (the Latin name for Spain) was depicted as a peninsula at the end of the known world. Paul's decision to go on a mission to Spain almost certainly represented him going to the ends of the earth.

Paul and Ephesus

The account of Paul's visit to Ephesus in Acts 18:19–21 is brief in the extreme. They arrived, he went to the synagogue, he left. Nothing is recorded as to how anyone felt about the brevity of this visit, but it must have felt at least a little unsettling for Paul's companions on the trip.

TIRONIAN SHORTHAND

Tironian shorthand or Tironian notes was one of the first shorthand systems ever recorded. It was devised by Marcus Tullius Tiro, Cicero's slave, who worked out the system in order to make a live record of Cicero's speeches and conversations. When first developed it contained 4,000 symbols. By the time it was taught widely in medieval monasteries, it had been expanded to around 13,000 symbols.

An expert scribe like Stachys in the first century might well have been versed in Tironian shorthand.

Chapter 15

GIFTS OF THE SPIRIT – HELPING

The gifts of the Spirit found in the writings of Paul in four places (Romans 12:6–8; 1 Corinthians 12:8–10 and 28, and Ephesians 4:11) seem to be a motley collection: from what many would regard as more formal roles, like apostles or prophets, through what are considered to be more glamorous gifts, like speaking in tongues, to giving and helping.

It is very easy to overlook the tail end of these lists and assume that the most important gifts are listed at the beginning. However, it is vital to recognise that, in the case of 1 Corinthians 12, the two separate lists of gifts, one towards the beginning of the chapter and the other towards the end, wrap around Paul's teaching about the body of Christ, in which all are to be valued and the least given the greater honour. This suggests that rather than overlooking these apparently less important gifts, we should pay them the greater attention.

Two qualities in 1 Corinthians 12:28 have intrigued me for a long time. The first is, in Greek, *antilēmpseis*, and is often translated as 'help'. Thiselton argues, however, that in the plural, this is most likely to mean 'administrative support'. The word that follows it is *kubernēseis* and, although often translated as 'leadership', has, in plural, the implication of the ability to formulate strategy. Indeed the word is often used for the pilot of a boat who steers it to safety. I wanted to imagine a character who demonstrated these gifts in an exemplary fashion. Ultimately Stachys may, in the story, demonstrate both aspects.

For more on this see in particular Anthony C. Thiselton, *The First Epistle to the Corinthians* (Wm. B. Eerdmans, 2001, 1019–22).

PAUL'S SISTER

The only mention of Paul's family (other than references to his 'kin' in places like Romans 16:7 which most scholars take to mean that the people concerned were fellow Jews) is made in Acts 23:16, which tells the story, also told in my fictional letter from Paul's sister, of how Paul's nephew (unnamed in Acts) foiled an ambush and murder attempt on the life of Paul. It is one of those frustrating details mentioned by Luke, but not supported or expanded upon anywhere else.

PURIFICATION IN THE TEMPLE

The account given in Acts of Paul's visit to the temple for purification is, to say the least, a little confused. Luke's explanation for the purification has been questioned by some scholars. Acts states that there were four men under a vow – the best explanation of this was that they had taken the Nazirite vow, and that the purification process either signalled the end of their vow or that they had become defiled during it and needed purification in order to continue. In the case of Paul, his purification was not demanded by the Jews, but suggested by James as a token of good faith that he had not turned his back on Jewish life and practice. His uncleanliness (and subsequent need for purification) would have come from his lengthy time abroad, mixing with

Gentiles. The fact that Paul was prepared to undertake this extended period of purification is important, and suggests Luke wanted to show that Paul never turned his back on Judaism and the requirements of the law.

TROPHIMUS

Trophimus was one of eight friends who accompanied Paul to Jerusalem. The point of the Acts account in which he is mentioned (Acts 21:29) is that Trophimus was observed by Paul's enemies to be a companion of Paul, and that these enemies then assumed Paul had taken him into the temple (i.e. beyond the court of the Gentiles and into the court of the women). This would have contravened purity rules, and was enough of an excuse to whip up a crowd against Paul.

Trophimus is also mentioned in 1 Timothy 4:20 as a companion of Paul.

ANTIPATRIS

Antipatris was a city built by Herod the Great in honour of his father, Antipater, and was on the main road between Caesarea and Jerusalem.

Chapter 16

APPLAUSE

In Roman culture, applause was expressed in a variety of ways to show approval. While they did clap palms together as is often done today, they also snapped their fingers and thumbs together. In a small space, this is more likely to have been the kind of applause expressed.

DINING ROOMS

A Roman dining room was known as a *triclinium* (from the Greek *tri-* (three) and *klinē* (couch)). As the name suggests, three couches – each able to accommodate three people – would generally be found in a *triclinium*. The Romans adopted the Greek custom of reclining on these couches to eat while propped up on cushions, though not the custom of allowing only men to attend a feast; respectable Roman women were also invited to some feasts. There was a strict hierarchy to seating at feasts, with the location of each guest carefully chosen to indicate their value to the host. Sometimes more than nine people were invited to a feast, and the least important of those guests would be seated outside the dining room in the garden or in another room.

Chapter 17

WHERE THE PATRON SAT

When clients came to meet their patron, they would normally have been greeted by him or her in the atrium. An atrium would normally have a pool at its centre, and the patron would often sit on the far side of the pool, facing the *vestibulum*, or hall. The patron's seat could be portable or fixed depending on the house concerned.

For more on the patron–client relationship see notes for Chapter 2, page 248.

Chapter 18

No notes.

Chapter 19

TATA

In colloquial Latin, children called their fathers either papa or tata, and tata was, it seems, quite common in usage.

I am not ashamed of the Gospel

The grand opening of Paul's argument in his letter to the Romans is normally acknowledged to be 1:16–17: 'For I am not ashamed of the Gospel; it is the power of God for salvation to everyone who has faith, to the Jew first and also to the Greek.[17] For in it the righteousness of God is revealed through faith for faith.' The reference to shame – or lack of it – is significant. The Romans, like most ancient civilisations, lived in an honour/ shame culture. The challenge of Christianity was that it had at its heart, in the crucifixion of Jesus, an event of overwhelming shame. It is clear from 1 Corinthians 2:2 that Paul believed the heart of the 'Gospel' was 'Jesus Christ and him crucified'. In other words, the Gospel had shame at its heart. His statement that he was not ashamed of the Gospel, then, proclaims the powerful paradox of the Christian faith. That which is deemed most shameful is that which proclaims God's power in the world. That which is deemed most shameful is not something of which Paul is ashamed.

For more on this see Jewett, *Romans*, 136–8.

Chapter 20

The evil I do not want is what I do

The brief discussion between Prisca and Aquila about what Paul meant when he said: 'For I know that nothing good dwells within me, that is, in my flesh. I can will what is right, but I cannot do it.[19] For I do not do the good I want, but the evil I do not want is what I do' (Romans 7:18–19) is a discussion that rumbles on, unresolved, in New Testament scholarship, with people holding firmly to differing views on the subject. I have tried to represent some of these views in the discussion between Phoebe, Prisca, Aquila, and Peter.

For more on this discussion see Jewett, *Romans*, 462–66, and Wright, 'Romans', 564–68.

PETER'S STORY OF DISCIPLESHIP
It has been widely observed by Markan scholars that the depiction
of Peter within Mark's Gospel as someone who constantly got
things wrong – asked the wrong kinds of questions and tried to tell
Jesus that his calling as Messiah did not include dying – and who,
ultimately, denied Jesus, might corroborate the ancient tradition
that, in some way, Peter could be seen as the source of the tradi-
tions contained within the Gospel. It would certainly be unlikely
for the early church to have made up such an unflattering portrayal
of one of the earliest and greatest of all apostles. These emphases
in no way prove the theory (found in early writers such as Papias)
that the Gospel contains Peter's eyewitness testimony, but they do
raise the suggestion of a connection with Peter himself.

For a helpful discussion of the evidence see R. T. France, *The
Gospel of Mark: A Commentary on the Greek Text* (Wm. B.
Eerdmans, 2002, 35–41).

SEPPHORIS
Although never mentioned in the Bible, Sepphoris was a key
Roman-influenced city during the time of Jesus. Unlike the
majority of the rest of Galilee, its citizens, many of whom had
become wealthy under the Herodian family and the Romans,
remained loyal to Rome, and did not join the revolt against the
Romans during the Great Jewish war (AD 66–73).

Sepphoris' wealth and influence made it the major trading
city in Galilee, so fishermen like Peter and Andrew would have
had to sell their fish there (and be able to speak Greek well
enough to enable them to do so).

People often assume that the disciples were ignorant, labouring types with little education between them. The evidence
seems to suggest quite the opposite. Fishing was big business in
the first century, and fish were highly prized in Rome, so much
so that it was said that a fish would sell for far more than a cow.
We also know that the Zebedee family (i.e. that of James and

John) had hired hands, and that Simon Peter's house in Capernaum was much bigger than most other houses there. All of this suggests that Peter, Andrew, James, and John were highly successful businessmen who would probably have been fluent in Greek in order to maximise their sales.

For more on this see Jerome Murphy-O'Connor, 'Fishers of Fish, Fishers of Men' (*Bible Review* 15, no. 3, 1999, 22–27 and 48–49).

CAESAREA PHILIPPI

Caesarea Philippi was located around twenty-five miles north of Galilee, at the base of Mount Hermon, where there were springs that fed the River Jordan.

In this region, Jesus famously asked the disciples who they thought he was, and Peter equally famously said that he was the Christ (in Hebrew, Messiah – see Matthew 16:13–16; Mark 8:27–29). A similar conversation is recorded in Luke's Gospel (Luke 9:18–20) but not identified with Caesarea Philippi.

It is widely agreed that the two halves of the conversation – Peter's statement that Jesus was the Christ and his horror at the thought that Jesus might die – were connected, and that Peter's understanding of who the Messiah was meant that he expected Jesus to be a victorious military leader, not someone who suffered and died.

Chapter 21

GETHSEMANE AND DENIAL

For full accounts of what happened in the Garden of Gethsemane and at Peter's denial see Matthew 26:31–58 and 69–75; Mark 14:27–62 and 66–72; Luke 22:33–51 and 54–62; and John 18:1–12 and 15–27.

In all the different accounts, Peter denied Jesus in the court-yard, but only in Luke's Gospel was Jesus also in the courtyard while this happened. The dramatic power of Jesus looking at Peter after he denied him is so strong that I couldn't help but include that detail here.

JUDAS' DEATH

There are two different accounts of Judas' death in the New Testament. In Matthew's Gospel, Judas felt immediate remorse and attempted to return the thirty pieces of silver to the temple. When they refused, he went out and hung himself, presumably before Jesus had even died. In Acts, a different account is given. There Judas bought a field with the money he had received, and fell over in it, causing his bowels to gush out.

An interesting reflection on the person and character of Judas can be found in Peter Stanford's *Judas: The Troubling History of the Renegade Apostle* (Hodder & Stoughton, 2016).

THE JOHANNINE TRADITION

One of the important features of John's Gospel is that it contains stories about Jesus that are not found in the Synoptic Gospels. It is quite possible that while the Synoptic stories circulated widely in early Christianity, the Johannine stories were more isolated, kept within Johannine circles in the Ephesus region. This is a possibility I suggest in this story, proposing that Phoebe, in Corinth, had heard the main Synoptic accounts, but not John's versions.

CATCHING NO FISH

In Luke's Gospel (5:1–11) one of the first miracles Jesus performs is remarkably like the miracle that is recorded in John 21:1–22. In both, the disciples have been fishing all night with no success; in both, on Jesus' command they have one last try and catch vast numbers of fish. Although the first miracle is in Luke and not in John, and the last miracle is in John and not in Luke, it has caused some scholars to posit that John 21 and the miraculous catch of fish involves going back to the very start, and allows Peter to wipe the slate clean. Especially as the Johannine story ends with the command from Jesus to Peter to 'Follow me'.

Chapter 22

DO YOU LOVE ME?

One of the intriguing features of John's account in 21:1–22 of the conversation between Jesus and John is the fact that two words are used for love. The first two times Jesus asked Peter if he loved him using the verb *agapao* and Peter responded using the verb *phileo*. The third time Jesus changed verbs, using *phileo* to which Peter responded using the verb *phileo*. Scholars have spent a long time wondering about the change. The problem is that John does not use the two words very differently in the rest of the Gospel, and it is not very easy to be confident about the precise meaning of each verb. Some conclude that there is no significance in the change; others that there is a significance, and that Jesus was offering Peter a level of love that he couldn't quite accept. The problem lies in working out what the significance is. Given all the problems outlined above, and despite many people's love of the distinctions made between each verb, I have omitted any reference to them from Peter's account.

Chapter 23

CARE OF WIDOWS

It is clear from the New Testament both that sharing goods in common was held to be important by the earliest Christians, and that they interpreted what this meant differently from community to community, and circumstance to circumstance. There is no doubt that, in the early church, one way of expressing this was through caring for widows and orphans;

in other words for those who otherwise might have very little to live on.

1 Timothy 5:11–16 (which comes from the Pauline tradition, though there is debate among scholars about whether Paul himself wrote it) discusses what makes a real 'widow'. The argument there is that widows who have family members to care for them are not real widows, and shouldn't burden the church at large: only those entirely on their own should be supported by the wider church community. This reveals that caring for widows (and presumably also orphans) was common in the Pauline communities; so common, in fact, that abuses were beginning to be reported and needed limiting. I have taken this to be a fundamental part of Christian practice in Rome. At the heart of this practice was the need to support women who otherwise would have no income at all. Although women could, in certain circumstances, inherit wealth, it was far from a common practice. Those from poor families were particularly vulnerable after the death of a husband, especially if they had no other family to take them in. Women were not encouraged to work outside of the home, so those without a male protector of some kind would often face starvation.

A particularly helpful book on the variety of interpretations of 'sharing goods in common' among the early Christians is Fiona J. R. Gregson, *Everything in Common?: The Theology and Practice of the Sharing of Possessions in Community in the New Testament* (Pickwick Publications, 2017).

In addition to this, Acts 6:1–7 records the appointment of the first seven deacons. They were appointed, in this instance, to oversee the daily distribution of food to the widows, because widows from the Hellenists (i.e. Greek-speaking communities of Christians) felt that the Hebrews (i.e. Aramaic-speaking communities) were not giving them a fair share in the daily distribution. This account was understood for many years to indicate that the role of a deacon should be restricted to 'humble service'. The extensive work of J.N. Collins, however, has revealed that this is a misunderstanding of this text and others in the New Testament. Stephen and Philip, who were among the seven deacons selected, also proclaimed the Word. As a result, it is more likely that while deacons did oversee daily distribution of food to widows, this was not the sole extent of their 'service'. They were commissioned agents asked to undertake a range of tasks. The key element here, however, is that, as a deacon, it is probable that Phoebe would be accustomed to a role such as this.

For more on this see John N. Collins, *Diakonia: The Sources and Their Interpretation* (Oxford University Press, 1990), and Paula Gooder, 'Diakonia in the New Testament: A Dialogue with John N. Collins' (*Ecclesiology* 3, no. 1, 2006, 33–56).

BAPTISM

There is a considerable consensus among scholars that in the earliest church, baptism was by full immersion in running water. The Didache, a very early text that describes Christian life and practice dated by many to the late first century, says:

> And concerning baptism, baptise this way: Having first said all these things, baptise into the name of the Father, and of the Son, and of the Holy Spirit, in living water. But if you have no living water, baptise into other water; and if you cannot do so in cold water, do so in warm. But if you have neither, pour out water three times upon the head into the name of Father and Son and Holy Spirit. But before the baptism let the baptiser fast, and the baptised, and whoever else can; but you shall order the baptised to fast one or two days before.
>
> Didache 7

This would have meant that baptism in Rome probably took place in the Tiber, or one of its tributaries. Two other features of note can be found in the Didache – that those being baptised fasted for up to two days before the event, and that they were instructed in what the Didache called 'the two ways'. This instruction appears to be an early form of catechism.

For more on early Christian baptism see Andrew B. McGowan, *Ancient Christian Worship* (Baker Academic, 2016, 135–82).

Chapter 24

HONOUR AND SHAME IN ANCIENT ROME

Honour was crucial for Roman nobles. The task of a nobleman like Titus was, as his family had done for generations before him, to nurture the honour in which the family was held. Through offering the right kind of sacrifices, appearing in the right places at the right time, offering and receiving the most exquisite banquets, the edifice of honour was built and maintained. Rome was a world built on the foundations of honour and respect. The life of someone like Titus was focused on maintaining that honour at all costs, and avoiding anything that consciously or unconsciously might hint at shame.

Chapter 25

LITTERS

A litter (in Latin *lectia*) was a form of portable bed. They originated in the East, but by the time of the late republic and early imperial period they had become popular among the elite. They were to some extent a sign of status, and Plebeians were forbidden from travelling in a *lectia*.

BAPTISM OF WHOLE HOUSEHOLDS

One of the features of the New Testament that is hard for people in the twenty-first century to comprehend is the baptism of whole households. We live in a largely individualistic culture in which we consider that personal choices affect just the person making them. The first century was much more corporate in culture, recognising that actions and decisions affect all those around. As a result, baptism of a whole household would have been thought to be normal and natural, especially if the head of the household had decided a certain course of action. While this does not appear to be universal – for example the reference to 'those who belong to the family of Aristobulus' in Romans 16:10 implies that the household are Christians, but not Aristobulus – nevertheless, references in Acts to Lydia and her household (16:15) and the jailer in Philippi who was baptised with his whole household (16:33) suggest that this was common in the first century.

TOGAS IN ROME
Togas were a symbol of status in Rome. They could only be worn by male Roman citizens. Members of the Senate wore togas trimmed with purple. Togas were heavy and impractical garments and, by the time of the early empire, had begun to be worn only for formal occasions such as the law courts, the theatre, or the circus. Donning a toga, then, would indicate a formal visit.

THE CELEBRATION OF THE EMPEROR'S BIRTHDAY
The Roman calendar contained a wide number of festivals celebrating all sorts of national events, and among them were feasts to celebrate the emperor's accession and birthday. These celebrations varied from emperor to emperor, so it is not entirely clear what someone would be required to do at such a celebration. However, since, during the imperial period, the emperor was regarded as 'lord' of the world (even if this was not used as a formal title until the period of Diocletian), we can be confident that attendance at such a celebration would require this

declaration, as well as the eating of meat sacrificed in the temple.

It is also important to recognise that religious, political, and social events were not, as in the twenty-first century, separate; in the ancient world they were integrally combined. Religious allegiance had an impact both on social standing and on politics. It was simply expected that people would be present at religious ceremonies. Romans often had multiple religious allegiances, so attendance at a ceremony for the emperor did not in any way detract from their allegiance to other gods. These ceremonies were where people could declare their support for the emperor, where the 'best' families could mingle, and relationships could be forged or enhanced.

Christians struggled to join in with such events, because they couldn't declare the emperor to be lord, nor could they participate in the various sacrifices that took place. This meant, essentially, that they put themselves outside of social and political influence as well.

For more on the emperor as lord and the challenges that posed to Christians, see N.T. Wright, 'Paul and Caesar', 173–93.

HATERS OF HUMANITY

The Roman historian Tacitus, who wrote around AD 116, famously gave an account of Nero's attempt to blame the Christians for the great fire of Rome in AD 64, which began near the Circus and the Palatine Hill and spread rapidly, affecting all but four of Rome's fourteen districts. Although not all scholars are convinced that Tacitus' account accurately represents the events of AD 64 (some suggesting that he was influenced by the era of the emperor Domitian, which is closer to the time that he was writing) his description of Christians is very interesting. Although he claims that Christians were falsely blamed for the fire, he clearly regarded them with great suspicion.

But all human efforts, all the lavish gifts of the emperor, and the propitiations of the gods, did not banish the sinister belief that the conflagration was the result of an order. Consequently, to get rid of the report, Nero fastened the guilt and inflicted the most exquisite tortures on a class hated for their abominations, called Christians by the populace. Christus, from whom the name had its origin, suffered the extreme penalty during the reign of Tiberius at the hands of one of our procurators, Pontius Pilatus, and a most mischievous superstition, thus checked for the moment, again broke out not only in Judea, the first source of the evil, but even in Rome, where all things hideous and shameful from every part of the world find their centre and become popular. Accordingly, an arrest was first made of all who pleaded guilty; then, upon their information, an immense multitude was convicted, not so much of the crime of firing the city, as of hatred against mankind. Mockery of every sort was added to their deaths. Covered with the skins of beasts, they were torn by dogs and perished, or were nailed to crosses, or were doomed to the flames and burnt, to serve as a nightly illumination, when daylight had expired.

Tacitus, Annals, 15:44

The accusation that Christians were cannibals was much more common in the second century, but may have originated earlier.

For more on this see Andrew McGowan, 'Eating People: Accusations of Cannibalism Against Christians in the Second Century' (*Journal of Early Christian Studies* 2, 1994, 413–42).

CHRISTIANS AND THE USE OF THE NAME

There is extensive debate about when the name 'Christian' was first used and by whom. It is recorded in Acts 11:26 and 26:28, and 1 Peter 4:16. What is unclear, however, is whether it was developed as a self-designation by the followers of Christ, or as a derogatory term by their opponents. Either could be true. The term Herodianoi was used by Herod's followers to refer to themselves, but on the other hand, Augustianoi was used by others as a derogatory term to refer to the overzealous followers of Nero.

Whatever the origins of the term, its use in 1 Peter 4:16 as a self-designation ('Yet if any of you suffers as a Christian, do not consider it a disgrace') indicates that it had, by then, become used by Christians of themselves.

As a result, and especially because Paul does not use the word, I have attempted to use it as rarely as possible in the story, though, from time to time, it is the easiest word to describe all those in Rome who would have self-identified as followers of Christ.

THE MURDER OF AGRIPPINA

The account of the murder of Agrippina is told variously in Tacitus' Annals 14, and in Dio Cassius 61.12.1. Both authors regard the murder with shock, since in Roman culture the mother was 'the most sacred of icons' (Shotter, 74).

It is not easy to work out why Nero was so intent on murdering his own mother. The common explanation that he wanted to marry his mistress, Poppaea, seems unlikely, since even after Agrippina's death he remained married to Octavia for another three years. Some modern scholars point instead to their complex relationship, in which Agrippina domineered her son, causing him to feel frustrated and impotent.

For more on this see David Shotter, *Nero Caesar Augustus: Emperor of Rome* (Longman, 2008, 74–79).

Chapter 26

EUTYCHUS

The account of Eutychus' dramatic fall from a third-storey window can be found in Acts 20:7–12. The end of the story is odd, and scholars are divided about whether Paul healed the boy, or merely declared him to be alive. C.K. Barrett argues that the effect of the story is that Luke makes such miracles so commonplace that they require little to no comment. (See Barrett, *Acts*, 956.)

ATTITUDES TO WOMEN IN EARLY CHRISTIANITY
Some scholars argue that one of the issues around women's roles in early Christianity is that women would have been required to take a greater public role than would be normal in Roman society, and that, in a context where people were battling for Christianity to be seen as 'respectable', this brought the faith into disrepute. They argue that this is what lies behind Paul's arguments about women – that he was attempting to ensure that Christians were seen as being as respectable. I have tried to put this argument in the mouth of Patrobas in this chapter.

EATING MEAT OFFERED TO IDOLS
Paul's discussion of the 'weak' and the 'strong' in Romans 14 and 15 is a clever one that he turns on its head more than once. Romans 14:2 defines the 'strong' as those who eat anything (including meat offered to idols) and the 'weak' as those who eat only vegetables.

The issue is that hardly anyone in the community would have fitted into either category: Jewish Christians would not fit into the category of those who ate anything because of the purity laws around diet, and only a few of their Gentile counterparts would have felt at ease eating food offered to idols; conversely, only a few of those who didn't eat 'everything' would eat just vegetables. As a result, Paul set up a binary opposition into which almost no one fitted.

While we are left to believe that Paul himself was 'strong', he again subverts this in 15:2 by arguing that everyone must 'please our neighbour'. In other words, both the strong and the weak must act in the same way, so maybe the strong and the weak are not as easy to identify as he first led us to believe?

For more on this see Jewett, *Romans*, 831–85.

Chapter 27

WORKSHOPS IN THE VILLAS OF THE WEALTHY

The remains of the houses found in Pompeii indicate that villas had workshops or other kinds of shops at the front on the street. This meant that the public and family rooms of these large villas could be tucked away behind the busy street, and were accessed by a hallway. For a diagram of a Roman house see page 237.

Chapter 28

SHARDS OF POTTERY

There have been many shards of Roman pottery discovered that have writing on them. Archaeologists have concluded from this that the fragments of broken pots were hoarded to use for making lists and other such jottings in a world where parchment was extremely expensive.

ADOPTION AS HEIRS; ROMANS 8:15–17

As noted on page 272, Paul's language of adoption as sons/children of God has a particularly strong resonance in a Roman context, where adoption of adults, in order to ensure a legitimate heir, was commonplace. Many scholars also note that the Hebraic tradition of Israel being adopted by God must also have been in Paul's mind here.

It is, therefore, important to notice that Paul makes an explicit link between adoption and the fact that Christians are now heirs, as Christ is, of God's kingdom (though of course Paul uses the word 'kingdom' very rarely in his writing). Given this link, it is worth noting something that a number of modern

English translations fail to reflect. In 8:15, Paul uses the Greek word for sons (*huioi*), which in 8:16 he changes to the word for children (*tekna*) immediately before going on to mention inheritance. The obvious conclusion to draw from this is that he was signalling to the many female members of the community (some of whom he greets by name in Romans 16) that they too were heirs of God. Despite the varied inheritance laws that were in place in different parts of the empire and among different classes of people, the women were to understand that they also were included in the inheritance.

That was the good news. The bad news was that they received the same inheritance as Christ, an inheritance that included suffering as well as glory.

For more on this general theme see Trevor Burke, *The Message of Sonship* (IVP, 2011).

Chapter 29

PAUL'S JOURNEY TO ROME BY SHIP
One of the key issues of debate among New Testament scholars has been the historicity of Acts – or more accurately, the historical reliability of Acts. The problem is that it is very hard to marry historical details between Acts and Paul's letters. For example the Jerusalem council reported in Acts 15 is difficult to link with specific events Paul mentions in Galatians 2, and the miracle-working, confident orator that Paul is in Acts seems a far cry from the suffering, feeble speaker of Paul's letters. However, many modern scholars recognise that the differences between Acts and Paul's letters could well be as much about perspective, and the difference in worldview between Luke and Paul, as about inaccuracy.

For a very interesting exploration of this, see Charles H. Talbert, *Reading Luke-Acts in Its Mediterranean Milieu* (Brill, 2003, esp. 197–218).

Questions of historicity come to the fore in exploring Paul's sea voyage. Ironically the problem here is not with inaccuracy, but with the fact that the knowledge displayed and the technical terms used are too good. This caused scholars to wonder whether the account of the voyage has been taken from somewhere else and used, by Luke, to describe Paul's own journey. Some also question whether Luke would have been allowed to accompany the imprisoned Paul on his voyage to Rome.

For more on this see Darrell L. Bock, *Acts (Baker Exegetical Commentary on the New Testament)* (Baker Books, 2007, 726–48), and Craig S. Keener, *Acts: An Exegetical Commentary* (Baker Academic, 2015, Vol. 4, 24.1–28.31).

PUTEOLI

Acts 28:13 records that Paul's long sea voyage ended in Puteoli. Called Puzzuoli today, the city is on the coast near Naples. It was founded as a Roman colony in 194 BC, and had a Jewish population from as early as 4 BC. Puteoli is about 170 miles from Rome. It is mentioned in Josephus *Antiquities* 18:151, and Cicero *For Plancius* 26 [63] as a place where people paused on their way to or from Rome.

THE APPIAN FORUM AND THE THREE TAVERNS (ACTS 28:15)

The delegation of Christians from Rome who went out to meet Paul would have served an important function in the eyes of the Romans. Romans were generally hesitant about the rise of Eastern teachers, and would want confirmation that any teacher from the East was trustworthy and honoured. A delegation, such as went out to greet Paul, would have offered reassurance that this Eastern teacher was to be trusted by people from Rome itself.

The delegation had a long way to go. The Forum of Appius was about forty miles southeast of Rome, and the Three Taverns about thirty miles southeast. Both locations were ancient sites on the Appian Way. The Appian Way was one of the first and most important of the Roman roads that connected Rome to Brindisi in the south. It is named after the Roman Censor, Appius Claudius Caecus, who oversaw the building of the first section in 312 BC.

There has been a discussion about why Paul was met by two groups of Christians at different sites. Some argue that Jewish Christians went to one site, while Gentiles went to the other; others that different work schedules demanded two different trips. I have chosen to understand the two welcomes as an attempt to show maximum honour to Paul as he travelled to Rome.

For a full discussion see Keener, *Acts*, on 28:14–15.

THE ODD, BRIEF MENTION OF BELIEVERS IN ACTS 28:14–15, AND PAUL'S MEETING WITH THE JEWS

One of the odd features of Acts 28:14–15 is the extremely brief mention of the believers from Rome who then drop out of the narrative again entirely. The way that Acts tells the story implies that Paul had very little to do with the already established Christian community in Rome. If Luke is right in the telling of this, the reason is probably because Paul was so keen to focus his attention on those who had not yet heard the Good News of Jesus.

Chapter 30

JOHN MARK, AND HIS STORIES

The authorship of Mark's Gospel, like the authorship of all the Gospels, is a hotly debated subject. Issues under discussion include whether Mark – and then Matthew and Luke – used a common pre-written source called by scholars Q (after the German word for source, *Quelle*); whether the 'Mark' to whom the title ascribes the Gospel in some manuscripts (i.e. the Gospel according to Mark) is any of the Marks referred to elsewhere in the New Testament and where and when the Gospel was written.

Some of the earliest Church Fathers, from Papias onwards, connect the author of this Gospel with the John Mark mentioned first in Acts 12:12–17, who, according to this tradition, wrote down the words of Peter in Rome. The lack of evidence to support these early claims leads most scholars to argue that it is impossible to know the origins of Mark. I would agree, but in the absence of any better solutions have chosen to adopt the early tradition that John Mark began to write 'Mark's Gospel' in Rome around this period.

For the account of the conflict between Paul and Barnabas over John Mark see Acts 12:37–41.

For a more detailed discussion of the issues surrounding the authorship of Mark's Gospel, see R.T. France, *The Gospel of Mark: A Commentary on the Greek Text* (Wm. B. Eerdmans, 2002, 35–41).

RETRIBUTIVE VIOLENCE

Paul's teaching on retributive violence in Romans 12:17–21 was counter-cultural and costly. Scholars express huge uncertainty about whether Christians were as systematically persecuted as has been commonly assumed (for more on this, see page 301). What is certain, however, is that living in Rome was a brutal and dangerous experience. In a world before any form of policing, people were left to defend themselves against the violence all around them. Various Roman sources reveal that gang warfare was common in Rome, especially among 'associations' or groups who gathered together with a single cause. Justice – if it could be called that – was exclusively retributive. If one member of an association was attacked or robbed, then their fellow group members would go around to exact revenge on whomever had instigated the violence in the first place. As so often with retributive justice, this could lead to long and complex chains of violence. Paul's command to break these chains at their source exactly follows Jesus' teaching, but would have been a dangerous and costly practice. Without any form of defence, early Christians would have been very vulnerable.

For an excellent discussion of this see Oakes, *Reading Romans*, 123–26.

PERSECUTION OF THE EARLIEST CHRISTIANS

It is taken as read by many Christians that Christians have always been persecuted, from the stoning of Stephen (Acts 7) onwards, and that this persecution was deliberate and systematic, caused by claims about the person of Christ and who he was. However, many more recent scholars have begun to question this assumption. Evidence for extensive and systematic persecution of Christians is sporadic and limited, and some scholars argue that widespread systematic persecution of Christians was more mythical than real. An interesting example of such an argument can be found in Candida Moss, *The Myth of Persecution* (HarperCollins, 2013).

Many will feel that Moss' argument swings the pendulum too far in the opposite direction, but her viewpoint remains significant. What is helpful about it is that it prompts us to ask a more nuanced question about the cause of suffering experienced by early Christians. While a few may have been actively and deliberately 'persecuted' because of their faith, it is likely (as I have tried to show in this story) that other suffering came about as the consequence of the actions of Christians, i.e. the refusal to proclaim the emperor as lord, or the refusal to seek retributive justice. This kind of suffering was more indirect than direct persecution, and, in my view, helpfully disentangles questions of motivation in the suffering experienced by the early Christians.

Chapter 31

PRESENT YOUR BODIES

Romans 12:1–2 is, in my view, one of the most powerful passages, short though it may be, in which Paul lays out the implications for everyday living of all that God has done: Christians should present their bodies as a sacrifice – alive, holy and pleasing to God. This passage is normally translated in a slightly different way: 'present your bodies as a living sacrifice, holy and acceptable to God', with the first adjective before sacrifice, and the second two after it. However, the wording of the Greek and the fact that these three are all adjectives, it makes more sense to put them together after sacrifice, to give more depth to the nature of that sacrifice. When you do this, the radical nature of this passage becomes clear. The bodies we present to God will be alive, not dead, as in most sacrifices. These bodies, because God has made them, are holy and never impure, something very different from the purity codes of Leviticus, and, as a result, are automatically pleasing to God. The surrendering of our bodies (and who we really are) to God lies at the heart of being 'in Christ', and has a huge impact on how we live our lives afterwards in the service of God.

For more on this see Paula Gooder, *Body: Biblical Spirituality for the Whole Person* (SPCK Publishing, 2016, 104–06).

Peter Oakes, in his exploration of Romans, rightly points out how difficult it would have been for a woman who had had to sell her body to someone else to hear this verse. I have tried to reflect some of this in the story.

For more on this see Oakes, *Reading Romans*, 98–126.

Chapter 32

Tarshish

Many scholars consider Tarshish to be a mythical place that simply symbolised an exotic destination far away. Those who do try to locate it, however, place it in the Iberian Peninsula near Seville (though others identify it as Carthage).

The Great Fire of Rome

The Great Fire of Rome took place in AD 64. I have stretched customary timings just a little at the end of the book to have Phoebe leaving the city as the fire began. Those who think that Paul was released from prison and travelled to Spain suggest a date of AD 62 for this, so I was indulging in a small amount of artistic licence here.

The Great Fire caused as much controversy among ancient historians as it does among modern ones, as many ancient writers such as Cassius Dio, Suetonius, and Tacitus blamed Nero for setting the fire in the first place and then watching it burn. Tacitus then argued that he blamed the Christians for the fire, and persecuted them, torturing and killing large numbers of them in the most gruesome way. Tacitus was the only historian who linked Christian persecution with the aftermath of the fire, and this has led various historians to question the historicity of the account. For this reason, I decided to avoid setting any particular events around this time, as it is hard to know precisely what happened.

For more on this see Moss, *The Myth of Persecution*, 138–45, and Shotter, *Nero*, 139.

The end of Paul's imprisonment

One of the oddest features of the end of Acts is that it just ends, and no information is given as to whether Paul left prison or not. Scholars have inevitably spent a long time debating precisely what might have happened. The reason why it was left hanging in this way was probably because Luke wanted to avoid any implicit parallels between the life of Christ and the life of Paul. If Paul's death had been reported at the end of Acts, then there may have been a temptation to elevate Paul more than is reasonable. Leaving the ends loose avoids any possibility that his death could be compared to that of Jesus.

This leaves us with the question of what did happen to Paul at the end of Acts. The answer is that we really do not know. Paul may have been executed at the end of the two years; he may have been released and died in old age in Spain, or he may have been released, and then recaptured and martyred later. Christian tradition locates his bones beneath the Basilica of St Paul Outside the Walls in Rome. For more on the options, see Keener, *Acts*.

Luke ends his story with a question mark, and so must we. Whether Paul ever went to Spain or not I shall leave up to your imagination as you reflect on what might have happened next.

Select Bibliography

Adams, Edward, *The Earliest Christian Meeting Places* (T&T Clark, 2015).

Aldrete, Gregory S., *Daily Life in the Roman City: Rome, Pompeii and Ostia* (Greenwood Publishing Group, 2004).

Barrett, C.K., *Acts 15–28: 2* (T&T Clark International, 2004).

Belleville, Linda L., *Women Leaders and the Church: 3 Crucial Questions* (Revell, a division of Baker Publishing Group, 2000).

Betz, Hans Dieter, *Galatians* (Augsburg Fortress, 1979).

Bock, Darrell L., *Acts (Baker Exegetical Commentary on the New Testament)* (Baker Books, 2007).

Brown, Raymond, *Antioch & Rome* (Paulist Press International, U.S., 1983).

Burke, Trevor, *The Message of Sonship* (IVP, 2011).

Burtchaell, James Tunstead, *From Synagogue to Church: Public Services and Offices in the Earliest Christian Communities* (Cambridge University Press, 2008).

Capper, Brian, 'Order and Ministry in the Social Pattern of the New Testament Church', in C. Hall and Robert Hannaford, eds, *Order and Ministry* (Gracewing, 1996, 61–103).

Clarke, Andrew D., *Secular and Christian Leadership in Corinth: A Socio-Historical and Exegetical Study of 1 Corinthians 1–6* (Arbeiten Zur Geschichte Des Antiken Judentums Und Des Urchristentums 18.) (Brill, 1993).

Cohick, Lynn, *Women in the World of the Earliest Christians: Illuminating Ancient Ways of Life* (Baker Academic, 2009).

Collins, John N., *Diakonia: The Sources and Their Interpretation* (Oxford University Press, 1990).

Croft, Steven and Paula Gooder, eds, *Women and Men in Scripture and the Church: A Guide to the Key Issues* (Canterbury Press, 2013).

Dunn, James D.G., *Romans Volumes 38a and b* (Zondervan, 1988).

Epp, Eldon Jay, *Junia: The First Woman Apostle*, 1st edition (Augsburg Fortress, 2005).

Fitzmyer, J., *Romans* (Yale University Press, 2007).

France, R.T., *The Gospel of Mark: A Commentary on the Greek Text* (Wm. B. Eerdmans, 2002).

Friesen, S.J., 'Poverty in Pauline Studies: Beyond the So-Called New Consensus' (*Journal for the Study of the New Testament* 26, 2004, 323–61).

Furnish, Victor Paul, *II Corinthians* (Yale University Press, 1984).

Gooder, Paula, *Body: Biblical Spirituality for the Whole Person* (SPCK Publishing, 2016).

— 'Diakonia in the New Testament: A Dialogue with John N. Collins' (*Ecclesiology* 3, no. 1, 2006, 33–56).

Gorman, Michael J., *Inhabiting the Cruciform God: Kenosis, Justification, and Theosis in Paul's Narrative Soteriology* (Wm. B. Eerdmans, 2009).

Gregson, Fiona J.R., *Everything in Common?: The Theology and Practice of the Sharing of Possessions in Community in the New Testament* (Pickwick Publications, 2017).

Hermansen, Gustav, *Ostia: Aspects of Roman City Life* (University of Alberta, 1981).

Hock, Ronald F., *The Social Context of Paul's Ministry* (Fortress, 1980).

Holmberg, Bengt, *Paul and Power: The Structure of Authority in the Primitive Church as Reflected in the Pauline Epistles* (Wipf and Stock Publishers, 2004).

Jewett, Robert, 'Paul, Phoebe and the Spanish mission', in Howard Clark Kee and Jacob Neusner, eds, *The Social World of Formative Christianity and Judaism: Essays in Tribute to Howard Clark Kee* (Fortress Press, 1988, 144–64).

— *Romans: A Commentary* (Augsburg Fortress, 2006).

Keener, Craig S., *Acts: An Exegetical Commentary*, Har/Cdr edition, Vol. 4: 24.1–28.31. s.l. (Baker Academic, 2015).

— *Paul, Women, and Wives: Marriage and Women's Ministry in the Letters of Paul* (Baker Academic, 1992).

Knapp, Professor Robert C., *Invisible Romans: Prostitutes, Outlaws, Slaves, Gladiators, Ordinary Men and Women . . . the Romans That History Forgot* (Profile Books, 2013).

Lampe, Peter, *Christians at Rome in the First Two Centuries: From Paul to Valentinus* (Continuum, 2006).

Longenecker, Bruce W., *The Lost Letters of Pergamum: A Story from the New Testament World* (Baker Academic, 2016).

Martin, Dale B., *Slavery as Salvation: The Metaphor of Slavery in Pauline Christianity* (Yale University Press, 1990).

McGowan, Andrew B., *Ancient Christian Worship: Early Church Practices in Social, Historical, and Theological Perspective* (Baker Academic, 2016).

— 'Eating People: Accusations of Cannibalism Against Christians in the Second Century' (*Journal of Early Christian Studies* 2, 1994, 413–42).

Meeks, Wayne A., *The First Urban Christians: The Social World of the Apostle Paul* (Yale University Press, 1983).

Morley, Neville, 'The Transformation of Italy, 225–28 BC' (*The Journal of Roman Studies* 91, November 2001, 50–62).

Moss, Candida, *The Myth of Persecution* (HarperCollins, 2013).

Murphy-O'Connor, Jerome, 'Fishers of Fish, Fishers of Men' (*Bible Review* 15, no. 3, 1999, 22–27, 49).

— 'Prisca and Aquila – Traveling Tentmakers and Church Builders' (*Bible Review* 6, 1992, 40–51).

— *St. Paul's Corinth: Texts and Archaeology*, 3rd edition (Michael Glazier, 2002).

Neusner, Jacob, *Invitation to the Talmud* (HarperCollins, 1996).

— and Bruce D. Chilton, eds, *In Quest of the Historical Pharisees* (Baylor University Press, 2007).

Oakes, Peter, *Reading Romans in Pompeii: Paul's Letter at Ground Level* (SPCK Publishing, 2009).

Paul, Ian, *Women and Authority: The Key Biblical Texts* (Grove Books Limited, 2011).

Saldarini, Anthony J., and James C. VanderKam, *Pharisees, Scribes and Sadducees in Palestinian Society* (Wm. B. Eerdmans Publishing, 2001).

Sanders, E.P., *Paul and Palestinian Judaism* (SCM Press, 1977).

Shiell, William, *Reading Acts* (Brill, 2004).

Shotter, David, *Nero Caesar Augustus: Emperor of Rome* (Longman, 2008).

Stanford, Peter, *Judas: The Troubling History of the Renegade Apostle* (Hodder & Stoughton, 2016).

Stark, Rodney, *The Rise of Christianity* (HarperCollins, 1997).

Talbert, Charles H., *Reading Luke-Acts in Its Mediterranean Milieu* (Brill, 2003).

Theissen, Gerd, *The Shadow of the Galilean* (SCM Press, 2010).

Thiselton, Anthony C., *The First Epistle to the Corinthians* (Wm. B. Eerdmans, 2001).

Toner, Jerry, *How to Manage Your Slaves by Marcus Sidonius Falx* (Profile Books Ltd, 2015).

Wakefield, Gordon S., *An Outline of Christian Worship* (T&T Clark Ltd, 1998).

Wenham, David, *Paul: Follower of Jesus or Founder of Christianity?* (Wm. B. Eerdmans, 1995).

White, John Lee, *Light from Ancient Letters* (Fortress Press, 1986).

Wright, N.T., 'Paul and Caesar: A New Reading of Romans', in C. Bartholemew, ed., *A Royal Priesthood: The Use of the Bible Ethically and Politically* (Paternoster Press, 2002, 173–93).

— 'Romans', in Robert W. Wall, J. Paul Sampley, N.T. Wright, eds, *The New Interpreter's Bible: A Commentary in Twelve Volumes, Vol. 10: Acts, Romans, 1 Corinthians* (Abingdon Press, 2002).

Yinger, Kent L., *The New Perspective on Paul: An Introduction* (Cascade Books, 2010).

HODDER &
STOUGHTON

Hodder & Stoughton is the UK's
leading Christian publisher,
with a wide range of books from
the bestselling authors in the UK
and around the world ranging from
Christian lifestyle and theology to
apologetics, testimony and fiction.
We also publish the world's
most popular Bible translation
in modern English, the New
International Version, renowned
for its accuracy and readability.

Hodderfaith.com   Hodderbibles.co.uk
@HodderFaith   /HodderFaith